XEL - 2

XEL - SERIES, Volume 2

HIFLUR RAHMAN

Published by HIFLUR RAHMAN, 2024.

This is a work of fiction. Similarities to real people, places, or events are entirely coincidental.

XEL - 2

First edition. November 8, 2024.

Copyright © 2024 HIFLUR RAHMAN.

ISBN: 979-8224629633

Written by HIFLUR RAHMAN.

XEL 2: The Forbidden Secret Of The Hidden Island
Written By HIFLUR RAHMAN

"I am incredibly grateful to my family and my amazing readers, who have stood by me throughout this journey. Their unwavering support has turned **Xel** into an unforgettable triumph in my life—one that I never imagined achieving when I first set out to write. To my readers, I owe a debt so deep that no gesture, no amount of money, and no act could ever truly repay it. Your belief in me and my work touches my heart in ways I can't fully describe. It's more than just appreciation; it's something profoundly emotional. Every time one of you picks up my book, it feels like a shared connection, a bond that goes beyond words.

When I first began writing **Xel**, I was filled with uncertainty. As a beginner, I doubted my abilities, unsure if I could weave a story that would resonate. But your encouragement slowly erased those doubts. Page by page, your faith in my work helped build my own confidence. Your feedback, your messages, your excitement—each has been a pillar of strength for me, and for that, I am eternally thankful.

Now, as I write this, I am overwhelmed with emotion as I present to you **Xel 2: The Forbidden Secret of the Hidden Island**, the sequel to my very first creation. It's a story that has grown alongside me, shaped by all of you who believed in the possibilities. This new chapter is not just the continuation of a world I've crafted—it's a testament to how far we've come together.

Thank you, each and every one of you. Without your support, this journey would not have been the same, and for that, I am forever grateful."

Note

Most of the locations described in this story are entirely fictitious while some are real locations. If any resemblance to real places occurs, it's simply a strange coincidence! The writer has no intention of relating this narrative to anyone. If anyone feels a connection to the story, it is purely coincidental or a misunderstanding.

Prologue

The fog clung thickly to Xel Island, obscuring its jagged cliffs and ancient trees, creating an aura of mystery and foreboding. Legends spoke of Xel as a place where time twisted and the fabric of reality thinned, a land where shadows moved with purpose and the air was thick with whispers of the past. It was a sanctuary for lost souls, where the cries of those who had ventured too far echoed in the wind.

Xel was no ordinary island; it was a living entity, capable of sensing the fears and desires of those who approached. It lay in wait, patient and hungry, drawing adventurers and thrill-seekers into its depths. The very ground was treacherous, shifting like quicksand, making it easy for the unprepared to lose their footing. Many who attempted to explore its heart found themselves disoriented, unable to retrace their steps as the landscape morphed before their eyes. Trees twisted into grotesque shapes, their gnarled branches reaching out like skeletal fingers, ready to ensnare the unwary.

The island's cruelty was infamous, manifesting in numerous ways. One common tale recounted the fate of a group of explorers who sought to unveil its secrets. As they ventured deeper into the forest, the sun vanished behind a thick blanket of clouds, plunging them into a twilight that felt suffocating. The ground beneath them began to thrum, and whispers carried through the trees, filling their minds with doubt and fear. One by one, they succumbed to panic, running in different directions, only to be swallowed by the fog, their cries echoing in the silence. Not a single one returned.

Those who escaped spoke of the chilling sensation of being watched, the feeling of unseen eyes tracking their every move. Some claimed they saw ghostly figures flitting through the trees, shadows of those who had been claimed by the island. The cries of the lost mingled with the rustle of leaves, a haunting symphony that disoriented the living and left them questioning their sanity. Others reported strange visions, terrifying glimpses into the island's dark past—glimpses of rituals performed under the light of a blood-red moon, where the ground was soaked with the lifeblood of sacrifices.

Another chilling example of Xel's cruelty involved a shipwreck survivor who washed ashore, battered and desperate. As he crawled onto the beach, he felt a strange pull, an urge to explore. Ignoring the warnings etched in the faces of the wind-tossed waves, he plunged into the heart of the island. Days later, when rescuers arrived, they found only his footprints leading into the jungle, the trail vanishing without a trace. His screams, they said, were the last sounds to echo back to the shore, swallowed whole by the island's insatiable hunger.

Xel fed on the hopes of those who dared approach, turning dreams into nightmares. The island's lore was rich with tales of lost treasure, hidden knowledge, and ancient power, but each prize came with a heavy price. Many were drawn by promises of discovery, only to find themselves ensnared in a web of madness, their minds unraveling under the weight of what they had witnessed.

One of the most notorious stories involved a wealthy treasure hunter named Elijah, who believed he could outsmart the island. Armed with maps and legends, he set sail with a crew eager for riches. As they approached the shore, the water turned ominously calm, a stillness that enveloped them like a thick fog. Elijah dismissed the unease that crept through his crew, confident in his abilities and their combined knowledge. But the island had other plans.

Upon landing, they set out to explore, but the path shifted beneath their feet, transforming the forest into a labyrinth of despair. Elijah, determined to prove his superiority, pressed deeper into the heart of the island, convinced that treasure awaited him just beyond the next thicket. Days turned into weeks as crew members vanished one by one, their screams swallowed by the oppressive silence of the jungle. Elijah's bravado faded, replaced by a gnawing dread. He became increasingly paranoid, convinced that the island was alive and watching, waiting for him to make a fatal mistake.

His final days were a descent into madness. Elijah found himself alone, lost in a nightmare of his own making, hearing whispers that seemed to echo from the very trees. "Leave this place," they urged, "or join the others." But he could not turn back. The lure of the treasure, the promise of fame and fortune, blinded him to the danger. He had become a prisoner of his own ambition, ensnared in the island's cruel embrace.

The last sighting of Elijah was a figure staggering out of the mist, eyes wild and unrecognizable. He was found at the edge of the forest, muttering incoherently about the island's heart and the dark forces that dwelled within. "It knows your name," he hissed, his voice a frantic whisper. "It will come for you." He was dragged away, a broken man, never to speak of what he had seen again. Those who encountered him spoke of his haunted gaze, of the terror that clung to him like a shroud.

The island's influence spread beyond its shores, infecting the minds of those who heard the stories. Xel became a name whispered in fear, a place where hope perished and that those who once sought to uncover its secrets now whispered warnings instead. Yet, despite its dark reputation, Xel still beckoned to the curious, the adventurous, and the foolish, those who believed they could conquer the island where so many had failed.

As the years passed, Xel Island became a cautionary tale, a haunting legend that warned of the dangers lurking in the unknown. Yet still, the allure remained. The fog rolled in, and the whispers grew louder, inviting the next wave of adventurers to test their fates against the island's dark embrace, unaware of the fate that awaited them within its depths. Each heartbeat of the island echoed with the promise of discovery, a reminder that Xel was always watching, always waiting for its next victims to enter its cruel domain.

The island's legend only grew with time, entwining itself into the very fabric of the world beyond its shores. As new tales emerged, the lines between truth and fiction blurred, creating a tapestry of fear that held the attention of scholars, treasure hunters, and thrill-seekers alike. Xel had become an obsession, a destination shrouded in enigma, forever a beacon for those who craved adventure but were blissfully unaware of the perils that lay ahead.

Whispers of ancient artifacts and lost civilizations drew many to Xel, promising riches and knowledge, while the island's innate cruelty lay in wait, ready to ensnare the next unwary soul. And as long as the fog rolled in from the sea and the shadows danced beneath the trees, Xel Island would continue to weave its dark tapestry, forever drawing in the curious, the ambitious, and the foolish who dared to seek the truth within its depths.

The stage was set, and the island was hungry. It was only a matter of time before its call would once again resonate, and the cycle of intrigue and despair would begin anew.

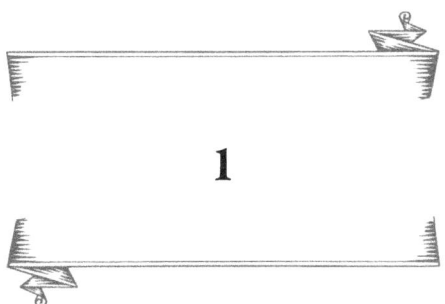

1

The Beginning Of The End

One man relentlessly dominated the headlines, capturing the world's attention, while **Xel** quietly carved out its own dark legacy in the background. Reports of **Xel** surfaced like clockwork, not with fanfare, but with a chilling regularity—every week brought grim news. Without fail, another brave sailor or an overly curious soul met their tragic end, their deaths a solemn reminder of the island's unforgiving mysteries. The once distant whispers about Xel had now grown into a foreboding legend, where the cost of curiosity was fatal, and each new casualty only deepened the island's ominous reputation.

The man who dominated the headlines was Dr. Adrian Locke. He was no stranger to the unknown. As one of the world's leading archaeologists, he had spent his career uncovering forgotten histories, lost civilizations, and the ancient artifacts left behind. His name had become synonymous with discovery, his reputation built on a sharp intellect and an unyielding curiosity. But beneath the professional accolades and scholarly pursuits, there was a restlessness in Adrian, a need to seek out what others could not explain.

Dr. Adrian Locke had always thrived on danger. As one of the world's foremost archaeologists, his name had become synonymous with uncovering the truths hidden in humanity's ancient past. But it wasn't just his academic brilliance that set him apart — it was his willingness to go where no one else dared. From remote deserts to forbidden tombs, Adrian Locke had ventured into the world's most perilous places, driven by a thirst for knowledge that bordered on obsession.

Xel Island had been a whisper on the lips of many in his field for years, a place that intrigued and terrified in equal measure. Legends of the island's strange occurrences, shifting landscapes, and haunting disappearances had swirled through the academic community, but no one dared go near. Yet for Adrian, it was more than just a story; it was a puzzle, an enigma that called to him like no other discovery had. It was the ultimate mystery, one that had eluded even the most determined explorers and scholars before him.

Evelyn first heard of Xel in her early years as a researcher, a mere footnote in a manuscript about ancient maritime routes. But the stories clung to him like a shadow. Over the years, as he uncovered relics from long-dead empires and solved the mysteries of forgotten peoples, the island lingered in the back of her mind, its secrets beckoning her.

Xel Island was not his first encounter with danger, nor was it the first time he'd faced something shrouded in myth. Years earlier, Adrian had ventured into deserts and jungles, seeking lost cities and relics of ancient civilizations, always driven by his obsession with the unknown. The locals called it the "City of Ghosts" and warned him to turn back, but Adrian had ignored their pleas. What he found buried beneath the dunes wasn't a city of gold or treasure but a desolate ruin filled with cryptic carvings and eerie sculptures — relics of a long-forgotten civilization obsessed with death and the afterlife. They had unearthed mummified remains that bore scars of strange rituals, leaving Adrian more questions than answers. But it was his work, and he was relentless.

Another of his expeditions had taken him deep into the Amazon rainforest, where he sought the remnants of a lost tribe that had vanished over a thousand years ago. The journey was fraught with disease, venomous creatures, and the jungle itself seemed to conspire against him. More than once, the oppressive heat and the relentless insects had nearly driven him to abandon the search. But Dr. Locke was not one to retreat. After months of digging, he had discovered a network of underground caves, their walls painted with scenes of gods and monsters battling for dominion over the earth. The artwork was unlike anything Adrian had ever seen, suggesting a complex belief system tied to the stars and celestial events. It was a breakthrough that propelled him further into the upper echelons of his field, solidifying his reputation as an explorer willing to risk everything for the truth.

However, despite these successes, there was something about Xel that unsettled him. His previous discoveries, while dangerous, had always been grounded in some form of logic or science, even if steeped in mystery. Xel Island, however, was different. It was not just another ruin hidden by time but an anomaly — a place where reality itself seemed to bend. There were stories of explorers lost to madness, of time behaving erratically, of landscapes shifting as if alive. And yet, for all its dangers, Xel fascinated him. It was the kind of mystery that had driven him for years.

As he studied the ancient texts and the scattered records of those who had tried and failed to explore Xel, Adrian felt that familiar pull — the thrill of uncovering the unknown. What lay beneath the island's fog, beneath its twisted history, was what he lived for. The more he learned, the more convinced he became that Xel held secrets older than any civilization he had ever encountered. His research led him to believe that the island might contain evidence of a lost culture, one that predated even the most ancient of known human societies. The symbols he had seen in old sketches and rare documents hinted at knowledge long forgotten, perhaps something that could change the very understanding of human history.

His curiosity burned brighter than his fear. The warning signs that had scared off other researchers were, to him, the ultimate challenge. Xel was an enigma, a riddle that had eluded scholars and treasure hunters for centuries. For Adrian, it represented the culmination of a lifetime of seeking the unknown.

Yet there was more to it than the thrill of discovery. Deep down, Adrian knew that this expedition could very well be his last. His body, hardened by years of grueling expeditions, was beginning to wear down. He had pushed himself to the edge more times than he could count, and each time he returned a little more weathered, a little more worn. The nightmares had begun a few years back, a reminder of the things he had seen — and done — in pursuit of knowledge. Sometimes it was the faces of those he couldn't save, other times the specters of the ancient ruins themselves.

But Xel — Xel was different. It was the mystery that could define his career, his final triumph. He needed it. Or perhaps, he needed the closure that it promised. The island, with all its dangers and dark allure, called to him in ways no other place had. It was the place where his life's work would either come to a glorious conclusion or be swallowed whole, just as it had swallowed so many before him.

Dr. Adrian Locke had always known that his pursuit of the past would come at a cost, but as he prepared for the journey to Xel Island, he wondered if this time, the price might be too high.

Now, with more than a decade of fieldwork behind her and a lifetime of navigating dangerous terrains, Evelyn was ready. She had prepared herself for years, studying every scrap of information she could find about the island and its dark reputation. Unlike those who had sought Xel for fortune or fame, she was driven by something deeper: the need to understand.

His research had led him to uncover disturbing connections between Xel Island and ancient civilizations known for their mastery of arcane knowledge. The symbols etched into rocks near the island's shore bore striking similarities to those found in long-abandoned temples she had excavated halfway across the world. Those discoveries hinted at something far older and far more dangerous than anyone had ever imagined. To Adrian, Xel was not just an island; it was a gateway to a forgotten past, one that might hold the key to understanding humanity's oldest mysteries.

But there was something else—something more personal. His work had always been about connecting the dots, piecing together the remnants of history into a narrative. Xel represented the final piece, the puzzle he had been chasing his entire career. It was, in a way, the culmination of everything he had ever studied, everything he had ever pursued.

Several years ago, during the fateful interview where Georgia met her tragic end, Adrian found himself in the role of a reporter, deeply invested in uncovering the truth behind the island's sinister reputation. With a mixture of determination and curiosity, he posed a pivotal question: "Are you suggesting that the island is responsible for these deaths?" His voice resonated with the weight of his ambition, reflecting his desire to unravel the enigma surrounding Xel. Yet, despite his earnest efforts, Adrian left that day with nothing but frustration; his expectations had plummeted into disappointment.

However, the fire of his ambition to solve the Xel mystery never truly extinguished. It simmered beneath the surface, a persistent whisper in the back of his mind. Unfortunately, his focus was divided. He was engulfed in other pressing duties and burdened by the grief of losing his father, which weighed heavily on his heart. The complexities of his personal life distracted him, pulling him away from the pursuit of the truth he so desperately craved. But deep down, he knew that one day, he would return to the island, driven not only by curiosity but by a profound need to understand the shadows that loomed over Xel.

Dr. Adrian Locke stood in his modest study, surrounded by towering shelves filled with books and artifacts collected over years of exploration. Dust motes danced in the shafts of late afternoon sunlight filtering through the window, illuminating the cluttered desk where maps lay scattered alongside a half-empty cup of coffee. Each book, each relic, told a story of adventure, discovery, and sometimes tragedy. Yet even as he prepared for the next expedition to Xel Island, his mind was heavy with memories of another journey — one that had shaped his path more than any other.

He remembered his father, also a renowned archaeologist, a man of unwavering resolve and a heart full of dreams. From a young age, Adrian had admired his father's tenacity, the way he would lose himself in research, often forgetting the world around him. As a boy, Adrian had followed his father on countless expeditions, trailing in his footsteps like a shadow, filled with awe at the wonders they uncovered together. It was during those formative years that the seeds of curiosity and exploration had been sown deep within him.

His father's passion was infectious. Adrian had watched in fascination as he uncovered the remnants of ancient civilizations, breathing life into the stories of those who had come before. He recalled the time they had unearthed a burial site in the Andes, where they had found mummies wrapped in layers of intricate textiles, their features preserved by the dry air. Adrian had marveled at the artifacts they had discovered, but more importantly, he had learned the value of history — the significance of understanding the past in order to inform the future.

But with each triumph came the shadows of danger. His father had a habit of pushing boundaries, often disregarding the warnings of others in pursuit of knowledge. Adrian had watched in dismay as his father took risks, his adventurous spirit leading him to remote locations, far from the safety of civilization. It was a trait that Adrian had inherited, but with a more tempered approach — a conscious effort to learn from the mistakes of his father.

The last expedition, however, had been different. Adrian could still remember the day his father had set out on that ill-fated journey, the excitement radiating from him as he spoke of ancient ruins deep in the jungle of the Amazon. It had been a project that ignited his father's passion, a chance to uncover the lost city of gold rumored to lie hidden beneath the foliage. Despite the dangers of the region — hostile tribes, venomous creatures, and treacherous terrain — his father had been resolute, believing that the discovery would cement his legacy.

Adrian had wanted to join him, to experience the thrill of the unknown firsthand. But his father had insisted he stay behind, claiming the expedition was too dangerous. "You have your own path to forge, Adrian," he had said, his voice steady yet tinged with urgency. "There will always be more opportunities, more adventures. Focus on your studies for now."

Those words had haunted Adrian since that fateful day. He had watched as his father prepared for the journey, filled with anticipation and determination. Yet as the weeks turned into months with no word, the excitement that had once filled the air was replaced with a growing dread. The news finally arrived, a bitter blow that shattered the remnants of his childhood — his father's team had gone missing in the jungle, presumed lost to the merciless grip of the Amazon.

Adrian remembered the moment the news had been delivered, the way time had seemed to slow as he processed the information.

The shock and disbelief morphed into an all-consuming grief, a sorrow that became a part of him. He had lost not just his father but the guiding light of his ambitions. The memories of their shared expeditions, the laughter and the lessons, became a heavy burden he carried, a reminder of the man who had inspired him to pursue the very life he now lived.

In the aftermath, Adrian threw himself into his work, desperate to honor his father's legacy by uncovering the mysteries of the past. He immersed himself in studies, pouring over ancient texts and artifacts, hoping to find answers that would never come. Each new discovery was a bittersweet reminder of the man who had taught him everything, a way to keep his memory alive.

But despite his best efforts, a void remained. Adrian often found himself standing at the edge of the abyss, questioning whether the pursuit of knowledge was worth the cost. He had witnessed the toll it took on those who ventured too far into the unknown. His father's fate had been a cautionary tale, yet it had not deterred him from his path. If anything, it had ignited a fire within him, a determination to uncover the truth no matter the risks.

Now, as he stood in his study, he felt the weight of that legacy pressing down on him. The walls seemed to close in, filled with echoes of the past — the laughter, the excitement, the lessons learned. He thought of his father's final mission, of the dreams that had been left unfulfilled, and the sense of responsibility that came with carrying his legacy forward. It was a burden he bore willingly, yet the pressure was immense.

Adrian picked up a faded photograph from his desk, a snapshot of him and his father standing in front of the ruins they had discovered in the Andes. They were both grinning, the thrill of discovery captured in that single moment. His father's eyes sparkled with the light of adventure, a reflection of the passion that had fueled his life. In that instant, Adrian felt a rush of emotions —

pride, love, and a deep-seated longing for the guidance he had lost. He traced the outline of his father's face with his finger, as if trying to bridge the gap between the past and the present.

He set the photograph down and turned to the window, watching as the sun dipped below the horizon, casting a warm glow over the city. The world outside was alive, bustling with energy, yet he felt isolated in his thoughts. As the colors shifted from gold to indigo, he could almost hear his father's voice urging him to pursue his dreams, to continue the legacy of exploration and discovery. "There is always more to learn, more to uncover," he had often said. "Never stop seeking the truth, Adrian."

The words echoed in his mind, igniting a spark of resolve within him. Adrian knew that to honor his father's memory, he needed to embrace the very essence of what made him an explorer. It was not enough to bury himself in research; he had to be willing to take risks, to step into the unknown. He would go to Xel Island, not just to satisfy his own curiosity but to uncover the mysteries that had eluded those before him. It was a chance to reclaim a part of himself, to confront the shadows of the past and forge a path forward.

Adrian straightened, a newfound determination coursing through him. He began to gather the materials he needed for his upcoming expedition. Maps of Xel Island lay sprawled across the desk, their edges worn from use. He had studied them meticulously, tracing the rumored paths and potential sites of interest. His heart raced as he considered the possibilities — what might he uncover? What secrets awaited him on that enigmatic island?

Yet even as excitement surged, a voice of caution echoed in the back of his mind. He couldn't ignore the warnings that surrounded Xel. The tales of those who had ventured there and never returned haunted him. He recalled the words of colleagues who had dismissed the island as a cursed place, too dangerous for any scholar to approach. But he felt a deeper connection to Xel, a calling that resonated with the very core of his being.

Adrian took a deep breath, letting the air fill his lungs as he steeled himself for the challenges ahead. He would not be driven by fear or by the legacy of loss. Instead, he would channel his father's spirit, embracing the adventurous heart that had defined his life. It was time to reclaim his own narrative, to weave his story into the fabric of exploration and discovery.

As he continued to prepare for the journey, his mind raced with possibilities. He thought of the countless artifacts waiting to be uncovered, the ancient knowledge that might lie hidden beneath the island's surface. Xel was a puzzle, and he was determined to solve it. The prospect of revealing the island's secrets filled him with anticipation, the thrill of discovery overshadowing the shadows of doubt.

In that moment, Dr. Adrian Locke resolved to honor not only his father's legacy but to create his own. The world was vast and filled with unknowns, and he would face them head-on. With each passing day, the adventure beckoned, and he would not shy away from its call. Xel Island awaited, and he was ready to embrace whatever mysteries lay ahead, armed with the knowledge that his father's spirit would always be with him — guiding him, challenging him, and inspiring him to continue the journey into the unknown.

As night fell, he glanced once more at the photograph, a reminder of the bond they had shared. He whispered a silent promise to his father, one forged in love and determination. "I will find the truth," he vowed, his voice steady and resolute. "I will honor your legacy."

With that, he set to work, fueled by the anticipation of adventure and the unbreakable bond of family. The weight of the past would not deter him; instead, it would propel him forward into the heart of Xel Island, where the past and future awaited to converge.

While Dr. Adrian Locke prepared for his expedition to Xel Island, a different kind of journey was unfolding elsewhere in the city. Alex Reid sat on a worn leather couch in his modest apartment, flipping through a stack of old photographs. The room was cluttered but cozy, adorned with relics of family memories and a few hastily taken pictures from his travels. The walls bore witness to both laughter and sorrow, each frame capturing moments of joy interspersed with the bittersweet pangs of loss.

Alex was the cousin of Marcus Bennet, a connection that held a deep significance for him. Growing up, the two had shared a bond that transcended mere familial ties. They were like brothers, navigating the trials of adolescence together. But while Marcus had carved his path in the world of law enforcement, dedicating himself to justice and protecting the innocent, Alex found solace in the world of archaeology. His fascination with history had always set him apart, a divergence that fueled a sense of identity that was uniquely his own.

He remembered summers spent at their grandparents' home, where Marcus would tease him about his obsession with ancient civilizations. Alex had been the quiet, introspective one, often lost in books while Marcus embraced the outdoors. Yet those books were more than just stories; they were gateways to worlds long forgotten. With each turn of the page, Alex ventured into realms of adventure and intrigue, uncovering the truths of those who had come before him. He had been captivated by the intricacies of cultures, the mysteries of their beliefs, and the artifacts that spoke of their lives.

Unlike Adrian, who was fiercely ambitious and often reckless in pursuit of knowledge, Alex approached his studies with a sense of reverence. He was meticulous, an explorer at heart but grounded in a philosophy that prioritized understanding over discovery. For him, archaeology was not just about unearthing treasures but about connecting with the human experience — understanding what it meant to be alive in different times and places.

In the weeks following Marcus's tragic death, the atmosphere around Alex had become heavy with grief and fear. Marcus had been a source of strength for him, a guiding light in his life. The loss felt insurmountable, leaving Alex to grapple with the reality of life without his cousin. Every corner of his home bore the weight of their shared memories, and every silence echoed with reminders of the laughter that once filled the air.

Alex found himself haunted by the circumstances surrounding Marcus's death. It was not just the loss that gripped him; it was the shadow of Xel Island, the place where his cousin had met his tragic end. The news reports had been relentless, detailing the expedition gone awry, the disappearances, the whispers of something dark lurking within the island's depths. The fear that had gripped the community began to seep into Alex's mind, filling him with dread and uncertainty.

He had watched as the island's reputation shifted from an alluring mystery to a harbinger of doom. The stories circulated like wildfire, tales of explorers who vanished without a trace, consumed by the island's insatiable hunger. Those who ventured there came back changed, their eyes haunted by the darkness they had encountered. For Alex, the thought of Xel was suffocating, an ever-present reminder of his cousin's fate and the unknown horrors that lay hidden within the mist.

On particularly sleepless nights, when the shadows grew long and the world outside fell silent, Alex would find himself spiraling into thoughts of Marcus. Memories of their childhood adventures would flood his mind, filling him with warmth and sorrow. He could almost hear Marcus's laughter, the way it echoed through the halls of their grandparents' home, a sound that had once been a source of comfort now turned into a haunting melody. The grief felt like a living thing, coiling around his heart, suffocating him with each passing day.

During the day, Alex tried to maintain a semblance of normalcy. He would take walks in the nearby park, seeking solace in nature, hoping the fresh air would clear his mind. But even in the tranquility of the park, he felt the weight of fear. The whispers about Xel Island echoed in his ears, cautionary tales shared among friends and family. "No one returns the same," they would say. "Those who go there often don't come back at all." Each word sent chills down his spine, a reminder of the fragility of life and the dangers that lurked beyond the known.

His friends tried to coax him out, suggesting outings, movie nights, anything to distract him from the spiral of despair. But Alex felt a growing detachment, as if he were watching his life unfold from a distance. Their laughter felt foreign, a world he could no longer access. He often declined invitations, retreating to the safety of his apartment, where he could drown out the noise with the comfort of books and the distant sound of the city outside.

In the evenings, he would find himself scrolling through articles about Marcus's last mission, piecing together the fragments of information that emerged after the tragedy. He craved answers, desperate to understand what had happened, but every article left him feeling more lost than before. The details were often vague, hints of something sinister lurking just out of sight. He wondered if Marcus had sensed the danger, if he had fought against the island's allure, or if he had been drawn in like so many others before him.

His phone buzzed one night, jolting him from his reverie. It was Sarah, a close friend from university. "Hey, Alex! Just checking in on you. We all miss you!" Her words were warm and filled with genuine concern, yet they also reminded him of the distance he had created. "We're going out this weekend. You should come!"

"I don't know, Sarah. I'm not really in the mood," he replied, the heaviness in his voice evident even through the screen.

"Come on! You can't hide away forever. You need to be around people, and we all want to see you," she encouraged, her enthusiasm palpable. "You're not alone in this. We're all here for you."

He hesitated, the invitation hanging in the air. A part of him wanted to reach out, to reconnect with the world outside his walls, but the fear held him back. The thought of facing questions about Marcus, the unspoken grief that would surely surface, filled him with dread. "I'll think about it," he finally replied, knowing he wouldn't go.

Days blurred into weeks, and the shadows in Alex's mind grew darker. As he sat alone in his apartment, the weight of grief felt like a tangible force, pressing down on him, making it difficult to breathe. He often found himself staring out the window, watching the world pass by while feeling utterly disconnected from it. The fear of Xel Island seeped into his thoughts, intertwining with the grief for Marcus, creating a suffocating fog that obscured any hope for the future.

One particularly stormy night, the rain pounded against the window, a relentless drumming that mirrored his turmoil. The thunder rumbled ominously, shaking the walls and sending shivers down his spine. He pulled the blanket tightly around himself, seeking warmth against the chill that seemed to seep into his bones. With every flash of lightning, memories of Marcus flickered through his mind, each one a reminder of what had been lost.

In a moment of weakness, he reached for his phone, scrolling through old messages from Marcus. There were pictures of them at the beach, smiles wide and carefree, the laughter frozen in time. There were plans for future adventures, dreams of exploring ancient ruins together, a future that would never come to pass. Tears pricked at the corners of his eyes as he felt the crushing weight of absence pressing down on him. "Why did you have to go?" he whispered into the darkness, the silence his only reply.

That night, as the storm raged on, Alex made a decision. He would confront his fears, not by seeking out Xel Island or the dangers that lurked within its depths, but by honoring Marcus in his own way. He would delve into their shared memories, allowing himself to feel the grief but also the love that had defined their relationship.

The following day, with the storm having cleared, he gathered his belongings and made his way to the park where they had spent countless hours. The sun shone brightly, illuminating the path ahead, as he walked with purpose. Each step felt lighter, as though he were shedding the weight of sorrow that had clung to him for so long.

Once at the park, he settled onto a bench, allowing the warmth of the sun to envelop him. He closed his eyes and took a deep breath, letting the fresh air fill his lungs. In that moment, he felt a connection to Marcus, the bond they shared transcending even death. "I will carry you with me, always," he murmured, feeling the presence of his cousin beside him.

As he sat in quiet reflection, Alex realized that he had the power to shape his own narrative. He could honor Marcus's memory not by retreating into fear but by embracing the adventurous spirit that had defined their relationship. He would continue to explore the world of archaeology, allowing it to be a testament to the bond they had shared, a way to keep Marcus alive in his heart.

In that moment of clarity, Alex felt the chains of grief begin to loosen. The fear surrounding Xel Island would always be there, but he wouldn't allow it to dictate his life. Instead, he would channel that energy into his work, using it as fuel to forge his own path — one filled with discovery, connection, and the unbreakable bond of family.

With a renewed sense of purpose, Alex stood from the bench and walked back toward home, ready to embrace whatever lay ahead. The world was vast and filled with unknowns, and he was ready to face them head-on, carrying Marcus's spirit with him on this journey through life.

As Alex walked home from the park, the warmth of the sun on his face felt like a balm for his spirit. Each step resonated with newfound determination, a conscious decision to honor Marcus's memory through action rather than despair. The fear that had once gripped him was beginning to ebb away, replaced by a sense of clarity and purpose that he hadn't felt in a long time.

The familiar streets of his neighborhood unfolded around him, each corner sparking memories of childhood. He passed the café where he and Marcus had spent countless afternoons discussing everything from their favorite books to their dreams for the future. The scent of fresh coffee wafted through the air, and he found himself momentarily lost in nostalgia.

"Let's meet here every week, just like this!" Marcus had suggested, his enthusiasm infectious. "We can talk about our adventures and plan new ones. Just you wait; we'll explore the world together!"

The memory tugged at Alex's heart, a bittersweet reminder of the dreams that had been cut short. But instead of retreating into sadness, he felt a surge of gratitude for those moments. They were a part of him, woven into the fabric of his identity.

As he stepped into the café, a sense of familiarity enveloped him. The barista, an older gentleman with a friendly smile, greeted him warmly. "Back for your usual?" he asked, preparing the order without missing a beat.

Alex nodded, settling into a corner table by the window. He took a moment to observe the bustling café, the laughter and conversations filling the air like music. He felt a connection to the life surrounding him, a reminder that he was still a part of the world despite the shadows that had threatened to engulf him.

As he sipped his coffee, the warmth spreading through him, Alex reflected on his journey thus far. He had spent so much time fixating on the fear that surrounded Xel Island and the loss of Marcus that he had neglected to embrace the present. The very act of stepping into the café, of allowing himself to be a part of life, felt like a small victory.

Days turned into weeks, and Alex began to rebuild his life piece by piece. He started attending lectures at the university, immersing himself in discussions about archaeology and history. He was surrounded by passionate individuals who shared his interests, and the camaraderie that formed among them became a source of inspiration.

One evening, after a particularly engaging lecture about ancient cultures, Alex lingered to chat with his classmates. The conversation flowed effortlessly, ideas bouncing back and forth like a lively game. He found himself sharing thoughts he had kept bottled up for too long, discussing the intricacies of past civilizations and the lessons they offered.

"It's fascinating how we can learn so much about ourselves by studying those who came before us," Alex said, his enthusiasm evident. "Every artifact tells a story, a piece of humanity that connects us all."

His classmates nodded, their faces lighting up with interest. Alex felt a rush of confidence as he spoke, realizing that he had valuable insights to offer. He was no longer just a quiet observer; he was an active participant in this world of discovery.

As he continued to engage with his peers, Alex formed deeper connections. He became close with Mia, a fellow student with a fiery passion for archaeology. Their late-night study sessions evolved into discussions about their aspirations, fears, and the adventures they dreamed of embarking on together.

Mia had always been the brightest in her class, standing out with her sharp mind and relentless drive. Her brilliance was evident from a young age. Even as a child, she displayed an insatiable curiosity and a natural talent for learning. While other kids played in the streets, Mia sat with her nose buried in borrowed textbooks, devouring every bit of knowledge she could find. Her family, however, was far from well-off. Growing up in a modest home where every penny mattered, Mia learned early on that if she wanted something, she'd have to work for it herself.

Her parents, though loving, couldn't offer much in the way of financial support. Her father worked long, grueling hours at a local factory, and her mother picked up odd jobs to help make ends meet. Despite their best efforts, money was always tight, and luxuries like private tutoring or extra materials were out of the question. Mia knew they wanted to help, but the weight of their own struggles was too heavy.

Determined to rise above her circumstances, Mia made a vow to herself: nothing would stop her from reaching her goals. While others had the luxury of tutors and resources, Mia became her own teacher. She would stay up late, poring over old textbooks and online resources, using whatever she could access. The library became her sanctuary, and the librarians—her only source of academic support—would often find her tucked away in a corner, scribbling notes with intensity.

Her dedication paid off. Year after year, Mia aced her exams, earning top marks and putting her at the forefront of her class. Her teachers took notice, often wondering how someone with so little could achieve so much. But Mia never bragged about her hard work. To her, it wasn't extraordinary—it was necessary.

Still, it wasn't without sacrifice. There were times she went without meals, choosing to spend what little money she had on textbooks or school supplies instead. She wore the same worn-out shoes year after year, quietly brushing aside comments from classmates who noticed. But none of that mattered to Mia. Every setback, every obstacle was just another challenge to overcome.

By the time she reached her final exams, Mia's name was known throughout the school. She had become a symbol of what pure determination could achieve. Her results were nothing short of extraordinary, and soon enough, universities began reaching out to her, offering scholarships—her golden ticket out of a life constrained by poverty.

Even then, Mia's focus never wavered. She knew her path wasn't about fame or recognition. It was about building a future for herself and her family, one that wasn't limited by financial hardship. Despite everything she had been through, Mia's heart remained full of hope, and her mind sharp as ever, ready to conquer whatever came next.

One evening, as they sat in the library poring over ancient texts, Mia turned to Alex, her eyes sparkling with excitement. "What if we organized a trip to a dig site this summer? It could be an incredible experience, and we'd learn so much!"

The idea resonated deeply with Alex. The thought of stepping into the field, of experiencing the thrill of discovery firsthand, sent a rush of adrenaline coursing through him. "That sounds amazing! I'd love to be a part of it," he replied, a grin spreading across his face.

In that moment, Alex felt a shift within himself. He had spent so long tethered to his grief, but now he was beginning to envision a future filled with possibility. The dreams he had shared with

Marcus began to take shape in a new light, a reminder that life could still be rich and fulfilling.

As summer approached, the trip became a reality. Alex, Mia, and a small group of fellow students organized the logistics, securing permissions and gathering supplies. The anticipation grew with each passing day, and Alex found himself brimming with excitement.

The night before their departure, Alex sat in his apartment, a mix of emotions swirling within him. He felt a pang of sadness as he thought of Marcus, wishing he could share this moment with him. But he also felt a sense of determination to carry his cousin's spirit with him on this journey. "I'll make you proud, Marcus," he whispered, a silent promise echoing in the quiet of his room.

When the day finally arrived, Alex stood among his peers, the air thick with anticipation. They loaded their gear into the van, laughter and chatter filling the space as they embarked on this new adventure together. Alex felt a sense of belonging, a camaraderie that reminded him of the bond he had shared with Marcus.

As they traveled, the landscape shifted, and Alex couldn't help but feel a sense of wonder. The fields gave way to rolling hills, the vibrant greens of nature enveloping them in a warm embrace. He felt alive, invigorated by the journey ahead, eager to uncover the stories hidden beneath the earth.

Upon reaching the dig site, a sense of purpose washed over him. The group set to work, brushing away layers of dirt and debris, uncovering artifacts that spoke of a bygone era. Alex reveled in the thrill of discovery, each find igniting a spark of joy within him.

As they unearthed pottery shards, ancient tools, and remnants of structures, Alex felt a connection to the past that transcended time. It was as though the stories of those who had come before him were intertwining with his own, creating a rich tapestry of history. He immersed himself in the work, feeling the weight of responsibility and excitement coalesce into something meaningful.

As the days passed, Alex began to feel more like himself. He laughed with his peers, shared stories around the campfire, and reveled in the joy of exploration. Each night, as they gathered to reflect on the day's discoveries, he felt a sense of purpose returning to his life.

But amidst the excitement, the memories of Marcus still lingered. Alex often found himself pausing in moments of silence, wishing he could share this experience with his cousin. Yet instead of retreating into sorrow, he embraced the memory, allowing it to fuel his determination.

One evening, as the sun dipped below the horizon, casting a golden hue over the landscape, Alex stood outside the campsite, taking in the beauty of the moment. He closed his eyes and inhaled deeply, the air rich with the scents of earth and adventure. In that moment, he felt Marcus's presence beside him, a reassuring warmth that reminded him he was never truly alone.

As he turned to join his friends, Alex realized that he was on a journey of self-discovery. The trip was more than just an archaeological expedition; it was a way for him to reclaim his identity, to forge his path while carrying the memories of those he loved.

He was ready to face whatever challenges lay ahead, eager to uncover the stories that would shape his understanding of the world. With each artifact unearthed and each connection made, Alex Reid was becoming more than just Marcus's cousin; he was becoming his own person, a passionate explorer in a world full of mysteries waiting to be discovered.

As the stars began to twinkle overhead, Alex knew that this journey was just the beginning. He felt a sense of hope blossoming within him, a realization that life could still hold wonder, joy, and adventure. The past would always be a part of him, but it wouldn't define him. He was ready to embrace the future, eager to see what awaited him on this path of discovery. He eventually returned home, seeking solace in the familiar comforts of his own space. Exhausted both mentally and physically, he craved a moment of peace, a brief escape from the relentless demands of his work and the weight of unanswered questions. Home was where he hoped to find that respite—a place to rest, recharge, and slip back into the rhythm of his normal life.

Yet, even as he tried to settle into the routine of his everyday existence, there was an undeniable restlessness gnawing at him. The comfort he sought was elusive, the quiet moments interrupted by the persistent echoes of the past. His mind wandered back to the mysteries he had left behind, the unanswered questions, and the lingering sense of unfinished business. Though his body was home, his thoughts were far from at ease.

His return to a so-called "normal life" was not as simple as he had hoped. The weight of his ambition and the haunting memories of what he had seen and heard clung to him like a shadow, making it difficult to truly relax. Despite his efforts to immerse himself in his daily routines, to pretend that nothing had changed, a deep part of him knew that his life could never return to the way it was before. Something had shifted within him, and no amount of rest could erase that.

After some hours, Alex Reid sat at the dining table, staring at the flickering candlelight, the gentle hum of the city beyond his apartment window blending into the background. He hadn't had dinner with his family in weeks. The empty chair across from him was a stark reminder of how disconnected he had become from the people who loved him most.

It wasn't that he didn't care; it was the weight of everything. The constant tug of memories, Marcus's death, the fear that lurked around every corner of his mind. His family had always been close-knit, bound by the love that had carried them through good times and bad. Yet, since Marcus's death, there had been a quiet distance growing between him and the rest of the Reids.

Alex picked up his phone, his thumb hovering over his mother's number. He hadn't spoken to her in days. She had called relentlessly after the funeral, offering comfort and support, but Alex always kept the conversations short, dodging her questions about how he was coping. He didn't know how to answer without feeling overwhelmed.

"Just call her," he muttered to himself, rubbing a hand through his hair. The guilt gnawed at him. His mother had always been the one to hold the family together, the anchor they all returned to. He missed her voice, the way she could make everything feel less chaotic.

Taking a deep breath, he pressed the call button.

"Alex, honey! It's been too long." Her voice was filled with warmth, and in an instant, Alex felt a wave of regret for not reaching out sooner.

"Hey, Mom. I know, I've been... I've been busy," he said, his voice quieter than he intended.

"I know you have, sweetheart. We've been worried about you, though. You've been so distant."

There was a pause, a heavy silence on the other end of the line. Alex closed his eyes, resting his forehead against his hand. He could feel the unspoken tension. Everyone in the family was grieving in their own way, but for Alex, it felt suffocating.

"I'm sorry, Mom," he said finally. "I just... It's hard. You know how much Marcus meant to me."

"I know," she replied gently. "He meant the world to all of us. But you don't have to go through this alone. We're your family. We need you just as much as you need us."

The words hit him hard, and Alex nodded, even though she couldn't see it. He knew she was right, but he still struggled to let his guard down. His father had always taught him to be strong, to face life head-on. Yet, the loss of Marcus had shaken that foundation. His father hadn't been the same since either, retreating into his own world of silence and brooding.

"When was the last time you saw Dad?" Alex asked, changing the subject abruptly.

"He's been working a lot," she said, her tone shifting slightly. "I think he's doing what he does best—burying himself in projects. You know how he is."

Alex did know. His father was the type who dealt with loss by keeping busy, throwing himself into work until the world around him was a blur. It was how he had dealt with the loss of his own parents, and now, Marcus's death had brought that cycle back. It was something Alex had inherited—this need to keep moving, to avoid sitting still long enough for the pain to catch up.

"I should come over," Alex said, making the decision without fully realizing it. "It's been too long since I've seen you guys."

His mother's voice brightened instantly. "Oh, honey, we'd love that. Come by this weekend. We'll have dinner, just like old times."

"Yeah, okay," he said, feeling the weight lift, if only slightly. "I'll be there."

They talked for a few more minutes, catching up on the smaller details of life—how his sister was doing at school, how the house was too quiet these days without the constant stream of family gatherings. It was the kind of conversation Alex had been avoiding, but now that it was happening, he realized how much he needed it.

After hanging up, Alex sat in the quiet apartment, thinking about his father. He hadn't spoken to him in weeks, and when he did, their conversations were brief, superficial. His father had always been the pillar of strength in the family, but Marcus's death had cracked that facade. There was a distance between them now, an invisible wall that neither of them knew how to break down.

The weekend came faster than Alex expected. When he arrived at his parents' house, the memories hit him like a tidal wave. Every corner of the place reminded him of the countless family dinners, holiday gatherings, and backyard barbecues with Marcus by his side. He could almost hear Marcus's laughter echoing through the hallways, and for a moment, it felt like he was walking into the past.

His mother greeted him with a warm embrace, her eyes filled with the kind of understanding only a mother could have. "It's so good to see you, Alex," she whispered, holding him a little longer than usual.

"I missed you too," Alex said, feeling the knot in his chest loosen just a little.

They moved to the living room, where his father sat in his usual chair, staring at the television, though it was clear he wasn't really watching. When Alex walked in, his father looked up, and for a moment, there was a flicker of something in his eyes—relief, maybe. But it was quickly replaced by the usual stoic expression.

"Hey, Dad," Alex said, trying to sound casual, but the weight of their shared silence was palpable.

"Alex," his father nodded, his voice gruff. "Good to see you."

They exchanged a few pleasantries, talking about work and the news, but it was clear neither of them knew how to address the elephant in the room—Marcus. His absence loomed large, and it wasn't until dinner that the tension finally broke.

His mother set the table, lighting candles and serving up a meal that reminded Alex of simpler times. They sat down together, the clink of silverware and plates the only sound for the first few minutes. But as they started to eat, his mother finally spoke.

"Marcus would have loved this," she said quietly, her voice trembling slightly. "This family dinner. He loved having us all together."

Alex felt his throat tighten, and he saw his father stiffen, the fork in his hand motionless. No one spoke for a moment, and then his father put the fork down, his eyes fixed on his plate.

"I miss him too," his father said, his voice barely above a whisper. "I miss him every day."

The vulnerability in his father's voice shook Alex. It was rare for his father to express emotion, but this moment of honesty broke through the wall that had been between them for so long.

"I know, Dad," Alex replied softly. "We all do."

They sat in silence, but it wasn't the heavy, suffocating silence of before. It was a shared grief, an acknowledgment that they were all feeling the same loss, even if they expressed it differently.

As the evening wore on, the conversation shifted to happier memories of Marcus—the time he'd convinced Alex to go hiking, only for them to get lost for hours; the way he'd always made everyone laugh at family gatherings; the way he loved life with such intensity. The laughter returned, though it was tinged with sadness, and for the first time in months, Alex felt like he was reconnecting with his family.

That night, as Alex lay in his old bedroom, staring at the familiar ceiling, he realized how much he had missed this—the connection, the support, the understanding that only family could provide. It didn't make the pain of losing Marcus go away, but it made it more bearable.

He knew the journey ahead wouldn't be easy, but for the first time since Marcus's death, Alex felt like he wasn't carrying the weight alone. His family was there, just as they always had been. And in that, he found a small measure of peace.

He jolted awake the next morning, heart racing as the bright sunlight streamed through the window, casting sharp shadows across the room. There was no time to waste. In a swift motion, he threw the covers aside and leaped out of bed, his feet meeting the cold floor with an electrifying chill that jolted him into action.

He darted to the bathroom, twisting the shower knob with urgency. Hot water poured down in a rush, enveloping him in steam as he scrubbed furiously, washing away the remnants of sleep. His mind buzzed with the day ahead, each thought a jolt of adrenaline propelling him forward. There was no luxury for reflection today—just the pulsating rhythm of his racing heart.

After a quick rinse, he dried off in record time, slipping into clothes that felt almost like a second skin. He barely paused to glance in the mirror, his focus honed in on the kitchen. With every step, the stillness of the house felt like a prelude to a storm, anticipation crackling in the air.

He burst into the kitchen, the smell of coffee filled the kitchen as Alex sat at the breakfast table, his fingers tapping nervously against the ceramic mug. His mother moved about, humming softly as she buttered toast, the clink of plates and utensils a comforting sound. It felt oddly familiar, like stepping back in time, but there was a tension beneath it all—a tension Alex couldn't shake.

His father, sitting across from him, was silently scanning the morning newspaper. The man had always been one for routine, for structure, especially now with Marcus gone. It was a way to keep the chaos at bay, but Alex could sense it—his father's discomfort, his uncertainty. They were both playing their parts, but they knew something had to break.

"So, how's work going?" his mother asked, breaking the silence as she slid a plate of toast in front of him.

"Busy, as usual," Alex replied, taking a bite even though he had little appetite. "Just trying to keep up with the research."

His mother nodded, but he could see the worry in her eyes. "You're looking tired. I know you're keeping yourself occupied, but you need to rest, Alex. You've been pushing yourself too hard since... since Marcus."

The name hung in the air, heavier than the conversation. His father's eyes lifted from the newspaper, glancing at Alex for a brief moment before returning to the page. They all felt it, the unspoken weight of Marcus's absence pressing down on them.

"I'm fine," Alex lied, his voice too calm. "It's just how I deal with things."

"You don't have to do it alone," she said softly. "We're here, you know. You don't need to keep shutting us out."

Alex shifted in his seat, his chest tightening. His mother's concern wasn't new, but today it hit differently. "I'm not shutting you out. I just... I don't know how to deal with all of this." His voice cracked, betraying the frustration and exhaustion simmering inside him.

His father let out a quiet sigh, folding the newspaper with precision before setting it aside. "You think we don't feel the same, Alex?" he said, his tone measured but carrying an edge. "You think we haven't been trying to deal with it too?"

Alex blinked, surprised by his father's words. They had barely spoken about Marcus since the funeral, and now, suddenly, the dam was cracking.

"I don't know, Dad," Alex replied, his hands gripping the edge of the table. "You don't talk about it. You never do. How am I supposed to know what you're feeling when you just hide behind that paper or your work?"

His father's gaze hardened, his jaw tightening. "You think hiding is what I'm doing? I've been trying to hold this family together. Trying to keep going."

"By pretending nothing happened?" Alex snapped, the frustration spilling out. "By acting like Marcus's death is just something we need to move on from?"

His father's eyes flashed, but before he could respond, his mother stepped in, her voice firm but gentle. "Enough. Both of you."

The room fell silent, the tension palpable. She looked between them, her gaze softening as she placed a hand on Alex's shoulder. "We're all hurting. We've all lost Marcus. But this fighting, this distance—it's not helping anyone."

Alex swallowed, the anger inside him suddenly deflating. He glanced at his father, whose face had softened slightly, though the tension in his frame remained.

"I'm not saying we have to move on," his father finally said, his voice low. "I'm just saying we need to find a way through it. Together."

The vulnerability in his father's voice was new, raw. Alex had never seen him like this. The man who had always been so strong, so composed, was now just as lost as he was.

"I don't know how to do that," Alex admitted, his voice quieter now. "I feel like I'm failing... you, Mom, Marcus. Everyone."

His mother's hand tightened on his shoulder. "You're not failing, Alex. You're just grieving. And we're all grieving in our own ways."

His father nodded slowly, the sternness in his features softening. "We don't have all the answers, son. But we need to stop pretending we do."

The honesty in his father's voice hit Alex like a punch. He had always seen his father as unshakable, the rock of the family. But now, for the first time, he realized that they were both stumbling through this darkness together.

For the first time in months, Alex felt something shift. The anger that had been bubbling inside him was still there, but it was joined by something else—understanding. His father wasn't hiding; he was just struggling to keep going, just like Alex. They were both floundering in the same storm, both trying to stay afloat.

"I miss him," Alex said quietly, his voice trembling. "I miss him so much, and I don't know what to do with that."

His father leaned back in his chair, exhaling a breath he seemed to have been holding for months. "I miss him too. Every day. But we have to keep living, Alex. Not for us, but for him."

There was a moment of silence as Alex let the words sink in. He hadn't thought of it that way before—living for Marcus, carrying on in a way that honored his memory instead of being consumed by it.

"I don't know if I can do that," Alex said after a long pause, his voice thick with emotion.

"You don't have to figure it all out right now," his mother said, her voice gentle. "But you're not alone in this. We'll get through it. All of us."

Alex looked at his father again, and this time there was a flicker of understanding between them. They weren't on opposite sides; they were standing on the same ground, grappling with the same loss.

"I'll try," Alex whispered, feeling the weight on his chest loosen slightly. "I'll try."

His father nodded, a quiet acknowledgment that said more than words could. It wasn't a solution, but it was a start.

As the breakfast continued, the conversation lightened. His mother spoke about everyday things—family updates, her gardening project, the upcoming holidays. Alex found himself listening, really listening, for the first time in a while. The ache of Marcus's absence was still there, but it was no longer the all-consuming force it had been.

By the time Alex left his parents' house later that afternoon, something had changed. The tension between him and his father was still there, but it was no longer an unspoken wall. They had started talking—really talking—and that was more than Alex had hoped for.

He drove home in silence, the city streets flashing by in a blur. As he pulled up to his apartment, he sat for a moment in the car, staring at the familiar building. The grief was still there, sitting heavy in his chest, but for the first time in months, it felt like something he could carry, not something that would bury him.

Alex stepped out of the car and walked toward his building, his mind still on his family. They were fractured, yes, but they were still a family. They had weathered storms before, and this one, though darker than the rest, was no different. They would find their way, together.

As he reached his door, Alex glanced at his phone, a new message lighting up the screen. It was from his father.

"I'm proud of you, son. We'll get through this. I promise."

Alex stared at the words, feeling a lump form in his throat. He wasn't sure when his father had last said he was proud of him, and the words now carried more weight than he could express.

He slipped the phone back into his pocket and stepped into his apartment. The silence of the room greeted him, but this time, it didn't feel as heavy.

For the first time in a long while, Alex felt like he wasn't completely alone.

2

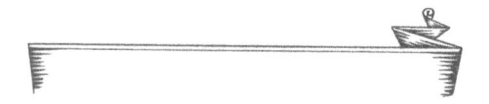

Unveiling Of The Remaining

Far from Alex Reid's family struggles, in the heart of a sprawling city dominated by skyscrapers and innovation, Emma Clarke sat in her sleek, minimalist office. She wasn't one for clutter; everything had its place—except for her mind, which constantly buzzed with ideas, calculations, and strategies. In her world of tech and algorithms, she was a master—unrivaled, respected, and occasionally feared for her ability to break down problems with laser-like precision.

Emma had built her career from the ground up. A true prodigy, she had been coding before she could drive and hacking her way into tech conferences by the time she was 16. By 25, she had her own tech startup that soared in success, and now, a few years later, she was in demand by the biggest names in the industry. Her latest breakthrough—an AI-driven predictive analytics program—had revolutionized how data was processed and understood. She wasn't just ahead of the curve; she was the curve.

But despite her fame, fortune, and genius, there was something gnawing at her. Emma, always the problem solver, was now up against something she couldn't quite debug: a deep, unshakable sense of isolation.

Her personal life was almost non-existent, with most of her interactions confined to the glowing screens of her computers. Friends and family had drifted away over the years, not because of ill will, but because Emma had always been too busy for them, too focused on her work. Now, at 30, she felt the emptiness of a life driven solely by innovation and achievement.

The loud **ping** of an alert snapped her back to reality. Her monitors, all seven of them, blinked to life with notifications, news updates, and system diagnostics. She exhaled, long and slow, rubbing her eyes. Sleep had been elusive lately, but she thrived under pressure. Some of her best ideas came at 2 a.m. when the rest of the world was asleep.

"Emma," came a voice from the doorway. It was Ben, her second-in-command at the company, holding a tablet and looking concerned. "You're needed in the lab. We've hit a snag with the new prototype."

Ben's life was a relentless push against the currents of fate. Born into a middle-class family, where his father worked long hours in a small, run-down barber shop, Ben learned the value of hard work at an early age. The shop smelled of talcum powder and aftershave, its walls adorned with old posters of hairstyles long out of fashion. For as long as Ben could remember, his father's calloused hands had been their lifeline.

His father was the kind of man who never complained, but Ben could see the toll life was taking on him. Every evening, the sound of the cash register closing seemed louder than it should have been—a reminder that some days were better than others, but none were ever easy.

By the time Ben was in high school, he was already working part-time at the shop, sweeping hair and cleaning up after customers. While other kids talked about weekend plans, Ben was saving every penny he made, knowing that college wasn't a guarantee. His father always told him, "Don't let this life be yours. Go make something of yourself." Those words echoed in his mind every time he wiped down the barber chairs, the worn leather beneath his fingers reminding him of the life he didn't want.

Despite his father's constant work, money was always tight. Ben's mother had passed away when he was young, leaving his father to juggle both parenting and keeping the shop afloat. The pressure weighed on Ben, too—he knew he had to succeed, not just for himself, but for the future his father never had.

In his final year of high school, a chance encounter changed Ben's life. The town's only tech store was down the street from his father's shop, and on quiet afternoons, Ben would slip in to watch the employees tinker with computers. One day, the store owner—an aging, gruff man with a passion for electronics—noticed Ben's fascination. "You want to learn?" he asked. Ben nodded, and that was the beginning of his double life.

Between school, shifts at the barber shop, and the tech store, Ben barely had time to breathe, but it didn't matter. Every moment spent learning about software, hardware, and the endless possibilities of technology felt like an escape, a glimpse of the life he wanted. The tech world was fast-paced, innovative, and full of potential—everything his life in the barber shop wasn't.

His dedication paid off. By graduation, Ben had built his first computer from scratch. He knew then that he had to leave his hometown, not just for his future, but for his father's sake too. With no scholarships in sight and little savings, he took out student loans and left for university, a decision that both terrified and excited him. It was his leap of faith.

University was a battlefield. Ben juggled coursework in computer science with part-time jobs—tech support, late-night coding gigs, anything to keep himself afloat. He was always one step away from burnout, but failure wasn't an option. His father's graying hair and tired eyes were a constant reminder of why he had to succeed.

It wasn't just about ambition—it was survival.

While his classmates came from wealthier families, with the luxury of focusing solely on their studies, Ben had to scrap for every opportunity. His work ethic didn't go unnoticed, though. One of his professors, impressed by his grit and raw talent, connected him with a start-up looking for a junior developer. The pay was barely enough to cover rent, but Ben took the job without hesitation.

That start-up was where Ben honed his skills, working 16-hour days and nights filled with debugging and programming. It was also where he learned the brutal truths about the tech industry. He saw companies rise and fall, projects get scrapped after months of work, and developers burn out faster than they could be replaced. But Ben thrived in the chaos. The tech world was cutthroat, but Ben had been fighting for his future long before he ever touched a keyboard.

By the time Ben met Emma Clarke, he had already carved out a reputation as a brilliant, if slightly reckless, coder. Emma saw something in him that no one else had—the same relentless drive that pushed her forward. She hired him as her second-in-command, and Ben quickly proved he was more than just a tech wizard. He had the strategic mind and determination to see projects through, no matter the cost.

Working with Emma was like sprinting in a marathon. She demanded excellence, and Ben delivered. He wasn't just following orders; he was shaping the future of technology alongside her. But as their projects grew more ambitious, so did Ben's desire for recognition.

No longer had content to be the kid sweeping hair in his father's shop, Ben wanted more. He wanted to prove that a boy from a middle-class background, who'd once worked every weekend cleaning up after customers, could become someone of importance in the tech world.

Yet, beneath Ben's rising success, there was always the shadow of his past. His father still ran the barber shop, too old to retire, but too proud to ask for help. Ben sent money home when he could, but it never felt like enough. As ClarkeTech grew, Ben felt pulled in two directions: his loyalty to Emma, and his growing ambition to step out of her shadow and create something of his own.

Tension began to mount. Emma, always the perfectionist, didn't take kindly to the idea of Ben splitting his focus. But Ben's ambition was like a fire—once lit, it couldn't be extinguished. He started working on side projects, slowly distancing himself from the company, even though it meant risking the trust he'd built with Emma.

When a rival tech firm approached Ben with an offer to lead his own division, the temptation was too great to ignore. This was everything he had worked for—a chance to step out from behind Emma's shadow, to finally prove to himself and his father that he had made it. But it also meant betraying the person who had given him the opportunity to rise in the first place.

The decision weighed heavily on him. Could he walk away from Emma and ClarkeTech, knowing that the only way forward was to leave behind everything they'd built together? Or should he stay loyal, even if it meant sacrificing his own ambitions?

In the end, Ben made the hardest choice of his life. He turned down the rival firm's offer, choosing instead to confront Emma directly about his ambitions. He didn't want to leave ClarkeTech, but he also didn't want to remain in her shadow forever. The confrontation was intense, filled with anger, respect, and a mutual understanding of their shared drive.

Emma, to Ben's surprise, respected his decision. Instead of firing him, she offered him more responsibility—a role that would allow him to lead projects on his own terms, while still working within ClarkeTech. It wasn't the clean break he had imagined, but it was a compromise that let him keep his loyalty while pursuing his ambition.

Ben's journey from a barber's son to a key player in the tech world was far from over. He knew there would be more challenges ahead, but he was ready. He had fought for every inch of his success, and he would continue to fight, not just for himself, but for the future he had promised his father.

Back in the story, Emma stood up, straightening her blazer, her mind already spinning into problem-solving mode. The prototype was a new type of wearable device—something so advanced that it could integrate seamlessly with neural activity, essentially allowing humans to control systems with their thoughts. It was cutting-edge, dangerous even, but that's what excited her the most.

"Lead the way," she said, her voice calm but sharp. She was already working through potential issues before she even reached the lab.

The walk to the lab was short, but in her mind, it felt like an eternity. Her company, ClarkeTech, had grown into a juggernaut in the tech world, and every project carried immense pressure. Investors wanted results, competitors wanted to outpace her, and Emma wanted to break new ground, constantly pushing the limits of what technology could do.

They entered the lab, a sprawling, futuristic space filled with gleaming servers, machinery, and sleek workstations. Engineers hovered around the malfunctioning prototype like concerned doctors around a sick patient. Emma approached the table where the device rested, its metallic surface reflecting the harsh lab lights.

"What's the problem?" she asked, already inspecting the device with her sharp eyes.

Ben handed her the tablet, showing the error logs. "We've been getting inconsistent neural feedback. The device is receiving signals, but it's not processing them correctly. It's like the brain is sending data, but the machine can't translate it fast enough."

Emma frowned. This wasn't just a minor glitch; it was a fundamental flaw. Neural feedback was the heart of the device, and without it, the entire project was at risk of failing.

"Run the diagnostics again," she ordered, tapping on the tablet and quickly navigating through the system. Her fingers flew across the screen as she pulled up the code, scanning for anything that might be off. "We're missing something, some variable that we haven't accounted for."

Ben nodded, running the diagnostic program as Emma dug deeper into the issue. The lab was silent except for the quiet hum of machines and the clicking of keyboards. Emma's brain was working overtime, and within minutes, she found it—a tiny error in the algorithm. It wasn't obvious, but to Emma's mind, it was glaring.

"There," she pointed at the screen. "We're overloading the system with too much data at once. The device can't handle the neural influx because we didn't optimize the compression rates. If we adjust that, it should stabilize the feedback loop."

Ben blinked, impressed. "That's... incredibly simple, but I don't know how we missed it."

Emma smirked slightly. "The simplest problems often have the most complex solutions, Ben."

Within the hour, the fix was implemented, and the device began responding smoothly. The relief in the room was palpable, but Emma didn't let it show. She had high expectations, not just for her team, but for herself.

"Good work, everyone," she said, stepping back from the table. "But we're not done yet. I want to stress-test this for the next 48 hours. If there's even a hint of instability, I want to know."

The team nodded, quickly getting to work on the next phase of testing. Emma watched them for a moment before turning on her heel and heading back to her office.

As she walked, her thoughts drifted once again to her personal life—or lack thereof. She hadn't seen her parents in over a year, and even then, it had been a brief visit. They lived in a quiet suburb, far removed from the hustle of the tech world, and though they were proud of her achievements, they always seemed concerned about the pace of her life.

"We worry about you, Emma," her mother had said during their last visit. "You're always so busy, so consumed with work. Don't you ever think about slowing down?"

Emma had brushed it off at the time, too focused on the latest project to really listen. But now, as she entered the quiet solitude of her office, the words echoed in her mind. Did she ever think about slowing down? The truth was, she didn't know how. Her life had always been about moving forward, breaking boundaries, and solving problems. To stop would feel like failure.

She sat at her desk, staring out the floor-to-ceiling windows that overlooked the city. The skyline was beautiful at night, with the glow of a million lights reflecting off the glass. It was a view that reminded her of how far she'd come, but also of the distance between her and everyone else.

Her phone buzzed, breaking her thoughts. It was a text from her brother, James.

"Hey, Em. Long time no talk. Thought I'd check in and see how you're doing. Mom and Dad miss you."

She stared at the message, her fingers hovering over the screen. James was always the one to reach out, the one who kept the family together. She envied his ability to balance work and life, to make time for the people he cared about. In many ways, he was everything she wasn't—grounded, connected, present.

"I'm good," she typed back, though the words felt hollow. "Just busy with work. How's everyone?"

"We're good. Dad's got a new project in the garden, and Mom's been asking when you'll come visit. Maybe you should take a break soon, yeah? They'd love to see you."

Emma exhaled, the guilt creeping in. She hadn't been home in so long. The idea of taking a break, though, felt impossible. There was always something that needed her attention, always another problem to solve.

"Maybe soon," she replied, though she knew she was lying to herself.

James responded with a thumbs-up emoji, and the conversation ended. Emma set the phone down, feeling the familiar pang of isolation settle in. She glanced at the clock—it was nearly 10 p.m. Another late night, another reminder that her life was dictated by the glow of her screens and the hum of technology.

But for the first time in a long while, Emma wondered what it would be like to slow down, to reconnect with the family she had all but abandoned. Her parents weren't getting any younger, and James was right—her absence was felt, even if they didn't say it outright.

Still, she couldn't shake the feeling that her work was all she had. It was the only thing that made sense, the only thing that kept her grounded in a world that felt increasingly distant.

She turned back to her monitors, her fingers hovering over the keyboard. There was always more work to do, more problems to solve. But tonight, as she stared at the code in front of her, the urgency wasn't there. For once, the excitement of solving another challenge didn't spark that familiar rush of adrenaline.

Emma leaned back in her chair, her mind wandering. Maybe it was time to re-evaluate. Maybe James was right. She couldn't keep running at this pace forever. But where did that leave her? What was she without her work? The questions gnawed at her, but she had no answers.

In the end, all she could do was stare out the window, watching the city lights flicker like stars, feeling more alone than ever in the world she had built.

As the city thrummed with life outside, Emma sat in her office, her thoughts swirling in a chaotic dance between her professional ambitions and her personal life. The rhythmic tapping of her fingers on the keyboard felt like a heartbeat, but tonight it lacked the fervor that usually drove her. She pushed away from the desk, rising to pace the length of her office.

The glow of the city lights illuminated her surroundings, casting long shadows that seemed to mock her restlessness. Her mind kept returning to her brother's text and the guilt that came with it. Emma could see her mother's face, could hear her voice filled with love and concern. "You're always so busy, Emma. When will you come home?"

Home. The word sent a pang of longing through her. She hadn't realized how much she missed her family, the warmth of their gatherings, the familiarity of their banter. But the work—it was her escape, her passion.

A soft beep interrupted her thoughts. It was an email alert from her team. With a deep breath, she glanced at the subject line: **"Urgent: Xel Island Incident."** Curiosity piqued, she opened the email and began to read. It was an update about a recent expedition to Xel Island, a place that had become synonymous with mystery and tragedy in the wake of Marcus Bennet's death. The report detailed the latest search efforts and the growing unease in the archaeological community.

Emma's heart raced as she scrolled through the email, recalling the stories she had heard about Xel Island—explorers who vanished without a trace, the dark allure of the place that had drawn so many into its depths. The email included a link to a news article, and without thinking, she clicked on it.

The screen filled with images of the island, its lush greenery juxtaposed against ominous headlines: **"Xel Island: The Enigma That Swallows Lives."** Emma's stomach knotted as she read through the details, her mind flashing to Marcus. She had never met him, but she had heard about his ambitious pursuits from her brother, stories that had painted him as a brave explorer—one who had paid the ultimate price for his curiosity and his bravery.

As the article detailed the recent tragic loss of another team member on Xel Island, Emma felt a chill run down her spine. It was the same cycle of fascination and fear, a dance that had claimed so many lives. The report mentioned a growing call for investigations into the island's mysteries, with some suggesting that the strange occurrences were not just random chance but something more sinister.

"Maybe someone needs to do something about it," Emma muttered to herself, half-joking. But the thought lingered in her mind, a seed of an idea that began to take root.

She thought back to the countless late nights she had spent coding and debugging, the thrill of solving complex problems that seemed impossible at first glance. Could she apply that same tenacity to understanding Xel Island? She was no archaeologist, but she was a tech genius. Perhaps she could find a way to analyze the data from the expeditions or even create a program to predict the outcomes based on past events.

But as soon as the idea surfaced, she pushed it away. This was beyond her—too risky, too personal. "What am I thinking?" she chastised herself, shaking her head. "I don't have time for that. I can't get involved in this."

Yet the thought nagged at her. The urgency of solving problems was ingrained in her, and the challenge of Xel Island was enticing.

But the risks were substantial, and deep down, she knew she had enough on her plate. The weight of her work was already heavy, and the idea of stepping into a new realm of danger felt reckless.

With a sigh, Emma returned to her desk, forcing herself to focus on the tasks at hand. But the news of Xel Island lingered in the back of her mind, intertwining with her emotions like a shadow that refused to fade. She pulled up her project on predictive analytics, trying to drown out the distraction, but the more she worked, the more her thoughts drifted back to the island.

As the hours passed, she found herself reading more articles, watching videos of the island, and diving deep into the history. The stories of loss and mystery surrounded her, capturing her imagination and fueling a burning desire to understand what lay beneath the surface.

Suddenly, the office door swung open, and Ben walked in, his expression a mix of concern and excitement. "Emma! You won't believe what just happened!"

"Let me guess," she said, rolling her eyes playfully, though her heart raced. "You found a way to make coffee faster?"

He grinned, shaking his head. "Close! We just received a call from one of the investors. They want to push our project ahead, but they want a demonstration of our predictive analytics by next week. They're offering to back us for an even larger deal if we can deliver!"

Emma felt a rush of adrenaline. "That's amazing!" She pushed the idea of Xel Island to the back of her mind, focusing on the task ahead. "We need to start prepping our data models and finalize the demo. Let's pull the team together."

Ben nodded, the excitement palpable in the air. "I already called a meeting. We'll need to brainstorm and make sure everything is ready to wow them. This could be huge for us!"

As they dived into preparations, the focus on their work helped Emma shake off the lingering thoughts about Xel Island. She felt invigorated by the challenge ahead, the weight of the news forgotten as she engaged with her team. They bounced ideas off each other, energy flowing as they brainstormed the best ways to showcase their capabilities.

But in quiet moments, when she found herself alone at her desk, the shadow of Xel Island crept back in. The stories haunted her; the lost lives felt personal, intertwining with the grief she had felt for her family. It became a constant push and pull in her mind—her dedication to her work battling against the call of something greater, something that felt unfinished.

The next few days were a whirlwind of activity. Emma threw herself into the project, the adrenaline of the upcoming presentation fueling her creativity. But even as she worked, the news of Xel lingered in the back of her mind, like a haunting melody she couldn't escape.

Then one evening, after a long day of meetings and demos, Emma returned home, feeling both exhausted and exhilarated. She poured herself a glass of water, leaning against the counter as she took a moment to breathe. The apartment felt quiet, almost too still, as though the world outside was holding its breath.

That's when her phone buzzed with a notification. It was a news alert about Xel Island. Curiosity piqued, she tapped the notification and opened the article.

"New Evidence Emerges in the Xel Island Mystery."

Emma's heart raced as she read through the details. The article discussed recent expeditions, new teams being assembled, and the ongoing search for answers surrounding the island's dark reputation. The urgency in the words struck a chord deep within her.

With every line she read, her mind whirred with possibilities. This was a puzzle, one that needed solving. The thought of uncovering the truth behind Xel ignited a spark of excitement she hadn't felt in ages.

But just as quickly, doubt crept in. "What are you doing, Emma?" she whispered to herself. "You can't get involved in this." The last thing she needed was to step into a world fraught with danger, especially after everything she had worked for.

Still, the idea lingered. There had to be a way to contribute without putting herself at risk. Perhaps she could use her tech skills to analyze data from the island's expeditions or offer support to the teams in a less direct way.

As the night wore on, she found herself pacing her apartment, the adrenaline surging through her veins. "This could be a breakthrough," she thought, envisioning the impact she could have. But the thought of leaving her comfort zone, of stepping into a world riddled with danger and tragedy, held her back.

"Maybe just one analysis," she said to herself, allowing the thought to settle in her mind. "I can help from a distance. It doesn't mean I have to go there."

Emma grabbed her laptop, opening multiple tabs as she began to compile data from recent expeditions to Xel Island. She researched everything—past reports, articles, expedition logs, and personal accounts. Hours slipped away as she delved into the information, piecing together patterns and anomalies that caught her eye.

The deeper she went, the more it became clear that the island was not just a place of danger; it was a complex puzzle with a history that begged to be uncovered. The patterns emerged, connections she could analyze. Emma felt herself getting lost in the data, her analytical mind kicking into high gear.

"Just a little more," she muttered, leaning closer to the screen, her heart racing at the thrill of discovery. "I can do this."

The clock struck midnight, and exhaustion threatened to overtake her, but Emma pushed through, driven by the allure of the unknown. She scribbled notes in a notepad, frantically jotting down her ideas, connecting dots that seemed invisible to others.

But just as she felt herself reaching a breakthrough, her phone buzzed again. This time, it was a message from her brother, James.

"Hey, Em. Mom's worried. Can we set up a family dinner soon? She wants to see you."

Emma stared at the screen, feeling the familiar pang of guilt. Her family had always been her anchor, yet she had drifted so far away.

Emma stared at her brother's message, her heart heavy with conflicting emotions. She wanted to respond with enthusiasm, to agree to a family dinner and reconnect with the warmth of her family. But the weight of the work she was doing, the tantalizing mystery of Xel Island, loomed large in her mind.

"Sure, let's do it," she finally typed back, the words feeling like a concession. **"I'll be there."**

As she hit send, a wave of guilt washed over her. She was putting her family on the back burner again, just when they needed her the most. But in her heart, she couldn't ignore the urge to dive deeper into the analysis she had begun. The stories surrounding Xel Island felt personal, pulling at her in ways she didn't yet understand.

That night, she barely slept. The data swirled in her mind, the patterns and anomalies whispering secrets that were just out of reach. She kept imagining the faces of the explorers who had vanished, the families left behind grappling with loss. The idea of helping them, of finding answers, became an obsession.

The following day, Emma arrived at the office, fueled by a restless energy. The usual buzz of her team greeted her, but today she felt different, as though she was on the cusp of something monumental. She needed to focus, to channel her thoughts into action. She gathered her team for a quick meeting.

"Listen up, everyone," she said, her voice sharp and commanding. "We've got to pivot our focus for a moment. I want us to pull all the data related to Xel Island from our systems. I believe there's something there that we need to investigate."

The team exchanged glances, some raising eyebrows in surprise. "Xel Island?" Ben asked, hesitating. "Isn't that the place with all the bad press? The disappearances?"

"Exactly," Emma replied, her eyes gleaming with determination. "And that's precisely why we need to dig into it. I think there's more to the story, and we can use our technology to analyze the data in ways others haven't."

One of her engineers, a young woman named Sarah, nodded eagerly. "I can start pulling together reports and expedition logs. We might find correlations we can visualize."

SARAH DONOVAN HAD ALWAYS been a dreamer. Growing up in a small town, she was captivated by the wonders of technology, often dismantling household gadgets just to see how they worked. Her father, a mechanic with a knack for fixing anything, encouraged her curiosity, turning their garage into a makeshift workshop. Together, they built everything from simple robots to intricate circuits, and it was during those late-night tinkering sessions that Sarah's passion for engineering was ignited.

But life wasn't easy. Sarah's family struggled financially after her father's mechanic shop went under. He worked multiple jobs to keep food on the table, and Sarah watched as he poured his heart into every task, never giving up despite the setbacks. Inspired by his resilience, Sarah promised herself she would rise above their circumstances. She poured herself into her studies, winning a scholarship to a prestigious university where she excelled in mechanical engineering.

At university, Sarah faced a different kind of challenge. Surrounded by peers from privileged backgrounds, she felt the weight of her humble beginnings. Imposter syndrome gnawed at her, but she refused to back down. She pushed herself to excel, often studying late into the night while holding down a part-time job to support her family.

One day, during a campus hackathon, she had a breakthrough: she developed a prototype for a low-cost, energy-efficient water filtration system that could be deployed in developing countries. This project won her acclaim, catching the eye of Emma Clarke, who was seeking fresh talent for her cutting-edge tech company, ClarkeTech.

When Emma hired Sarah, it was a turning point. Sarah was thrilled to work alongside brilliant minds, but she quickly realized the pressure to perform was immense. She poured herself into her work, often staying late at the lab, determined to prove herself. Yet, the demands began to take a toll on her mental health.

One evening, as Sarah was debugging a crucial component for a project, she received a call from her father. He was in the hospital after a car accident. Panic set in as she raced to his side. He lay there, frail but smiling, urging her to focus on her dreams. "You're doing great things, Sarah. Don't let anything hold you back," he said, his voice steady despite the circumstances.

That moment became a catalyst for change. Sarah returned to work with a renewed sense of purpose. She realized that her father's sacrifices fueled her ambitions, and she wasn't just working for herself but for him as well. She channeled her energy into her projects, collaborating closely with Emma and the team, offering fresh ideas that melded creativity with technical expertise.

Her ingenuity shone through as she led the team in creating a breakthrough wearable device that could monitor neural activity. Sarah's confidence grew as she stepped into leadership roles, guiding younger engineers and sharing her knowledge. She became a voice of innovation within ClarkeTech, known for her fierce determination and collaborative spirit.

As the deadline for their next major project loomed, Sarah faced a critical moment. During a team meeting, Emma voiced concerns about potential failures in the technology. Sarah stood up, fueled by her passion and newfound confidence. "We can't be afraid to push boundaries," she asserted. "Failure is part of the journey. Let's refine, iterate, and innovate!"

Her words inspired the team, igniting a fire within them. They rallied together, determined to create something extraordinary. With Sarah leading the charge, the team worked around the clock, fueled by their collective energy and shared vision.

When the project launched successfully, Sarah stood alongside Emma, her heart swelling with pride. She had not only proven her worth but had also become a vital force in the company. At that moment, she realized that her journey was just beginning. She was no longer the girl tinkering in a garage; she was a trailblazer, ready to conquer the world of technology.

BACK IN THE STORY, "Great," Emma said, her heart racing at the thought of collaboration. "I want everyone involved. This isn't just about finding the truth; it's about understanding the human element behind it—the families, the victims. We need to honor their stories."

The team rallied around her, energized by the mission. They divided tasks, gathering information, reports, and historical data. Emma felt the weight of excitement course through her. For the first time in a while, she wasn't just chasing deadlines; she was pursuing a cause that mattered.

As the hours passed, Emma became immersed in the work, her fingers dancing across the keyboard as she formulated algorithms to analyze patterns of disappearance related to the island. Her thoughts continually flicked to her family and their past interactions, especially as she worked on this new project. The memories of her childhood flooded back—the holidays filled with laughter, her father's storytelling, and her mother's warm embrace.

But there were shadows lurking in those memories too, moments where she had prioritized her work over her family. Emma couldn't shake the feeling of guilt for how she had distanced herself from them, particularly since Marcus's death. She had buried herself in her career, and now that seemed to leave a void that the urgency of Xel Island couldn't fill.

"Emma?" Ben's voice broke through her reverie. "We need you to take a look at this."

She turned, seeing Ben and Sarah gathered around a large monitor, eyes wide with excitement. The screen displayed a map, color-coded pins indicating the locations of reported incidents surrounding Xel Island. As she approached, she felt a flutter of adrenaline.

"We've pulled together the data from the last five years," Ben explained, his enthusiasm contagious. "These pins represent expeditions that had major incidents, including disappearances. Look at the clustering."

Emma leaned closer, examining the map. The pins formed a disturbing pattern, concentrated around specific points on the island. "This is more than coincidence," she murmured. "We need to overlay this with environmental data. What are the conditions like at those times?"

Sarah nodded, her fingers flying across the keyboard. "I'll pull up the weather patterns and geological reports from those dates. Maybe we can find some correlations."

As they worked, Emma felt the excitement build within her, a sense of purpose igniting. Each new piece of information brought them closer to something profound, and for the first time in ages, she felt a true connection to the work. It wasn't just data; it was lives—stories waiting to be told.

After hours of data analysis, the team found unexpected correlations. Several incidents clustered around certain environmental anomalies—unusual weather patterns and seismic activity. It was a breakthrough, and as Emma shared the findings with her team, the atmosphere in the room crackled with energy.

"This could explain why these disappearances are occurring," Emma said, her voice filled with excitement. "If we can prove that these factors influence the incidents, we can alert future expeditions and possibly save lives."

Just then, her phone buzzed again, this time again message from James. He just had sent this as a reminder "**Dinner at our place tomorrow night? Mom wants to cook your favorite. Please say you'll come.**"

James Clarke was always the calm in the storm, the one who never seemed to waver, even when the world was falling apart. As the elder brother to Emma, James had learned early on how to be the protector, a role he accepted without complaint. While Emma was the prodigy—coding by the age of 12, winning science fairs, and dazzling their parents—James was the one who held everything together behind the scenes.

Growing up, their parents doted on Emma's brilliance, often leaving James in the background. It wasn't out of neglect, but

Emma's spark was hard to ignore, and even harder to compete with. But James never cared about that. He was proud of his little sister and silently took it upon himself to watch over her, knowing that her intense drive would one day lead to something spectacular—or to burnout.

As Emma soared through school, building her reputation in tech, James took a different path. He was practical, drawn to engineering—not the coding side like Emma, but the mechanical. While Emma immersed herself in algorithms, James found solace in the tangible, in building things with his hands. He thrived in the calm of precision, quietly excelling in his field while never seeking the spotlight.

Despite their differences, the bond between the siblings was unbreakable. When their parents grew concerned about Emma's obsessive work habits, it was James who stepped in, offering his quiet counsel to Emma, reminding her to slow down, to breathe. He was the steady force in her life, the one who balanced her frantic pace with calm wisdom.

But life wasn't always smooth. In his late twenties, James faced his own crisis. After taking a job at a high-pressure engineering firm, he found himself in a leadership position he hadn't wanted. The responsibility was immense, and James, used to being the dependable one, suddenly found the weight unbearable. His work hours stretched into the night, his health began to falter, and the quiet stability he'd always prided himself on began to crack. For the first time, he understood the kind of pressure Emma lived with daily.

It was then that he realized something important: even the strongest need to step back sometimes.

After suffering through months of stress, James made a bold decision—he left his high-paying job and moved into freelance consulting, a move that baffled his peers but brought him peace.

He reconnected with his love for building, starting small projects that allowed him the freedom to work on his terms. More importantly, it gave him time for family—a luxury Emma no longer had.

Now in his early thirties, James watches Emma with concern. He's the one who still texts her to check in, knowing she won't respond right away, but hoping she'll remember to take a break. He can't protect her from the demands of her world, but he can be there, the quiet reminder that life doesn't have to be a race. Their conversations, though rare, are filled with his understated wisdom, urging her to find balance before the weight of her ambition crushes her.

James might not have Emma's genius, but he has something just as valuable—perspective. He knows the cost of burning too brightly and is determined not to let his sister fall into the same trap. Even if she doesn't always listen, James will always be there, the silent anchor, holding her steady when the storm hits.

Back in the story, Emma hesitated, glancing at the map on the screen, the urgency of the project tugging at her. But as she looked at the data, she thought of her family. "I need to make this right," she murmured.

"**I'll be there**," she typed back.

As the workday came to a close, Emma gathered her belongings, the weight of the day's discoveries still buzzing in her mind. She felt a renewed sense of connection not only to her team but to the people who loved her. She could make a difference, but she couldn't do it alone.

That night, as she prepared for her family dinner, the anticipation grew within her. Emma chose her outfit carefully, opting for something comfortable yet presentable. She glanced in the mirror, searching for a spark of confidence. It felt foreign after so long being immersed in work.

Arriving at her parents' home, Emma was greeted by the familiar warmth of their kitchen, the air rich with the scent of spices and the sound of her mother humming a tune. "Emma! You're here!" her mother exclaimed, enveloping her in a hug that felt like a healing balm.

"I'm so glad to see you, Mom," Emma replied, the warmth of the embrace filling her with nostalgia.

"Your father's been looking forward to this," her mother said, pulling back to smile at her. "He's been cooking all day, trying out a new recipe."

Emma chuckled, imagining her father in the kitchen, a place he rarely occupied unless it was a special occasion. "I can't wait to taste it," she said, stepping into the cozy living room, where family photos adorned the walls. Each frame told a story of love, joy, and shared experiences that tugged at her heart.

"Hey, sis!" James called from the couch, grinning as he set down his game controller. "Finally decided to show up?"

"Someone has to keep you in line," she shot back, unable to suppress a smile. The banter felt good, like slipping into a well-worn pair of shoes.

As they settled around the dinner table, Emma felt the tension from her earlier meetings fade away. Her parents engaged in light conversation, sharing stories about James's recent antics and her father's gardening projects. But as the evening progressed, the conversation naturally turned to Harry.

Harry Clarke had always been larger than life. He was the kind of person who could walk into a room and instantly command attention—not because he sought it, but because his energy was infectious. Where Emma was methodical and driven by intellect, Harry thrived on adventure. He was daring, always pushing boundaries, and living life with an intensity that sometimes left those around him worried. But Harry never seemed concerned with the risks. To him, life was meant to be lived on the edge, with no regrets.

He was Emma's older brother, the one who had been her protector, her confidant, and in many ways, her opposite. Where she delved into tech and problem-solving, Harry sought out thrill-seeking adventures—hiking in uncharted terrains, skydiving, and racing cars. It was this thirst for adrenaline that eventually led to the accident that claimed his life.

Emma could remember the day of the accident with painful clarity. Harry had just turned 20, full of plans for the future. He had talked about taking a gap year to travel the world, to see places that others only dreamed of. He was always moving, always chasing something. On that fateful afternoon, he and a few friends had decided to take their cars out for a joyride on the winding mountain roads outside the city—roads known for their beauty but also their danger.

"Come on, Em, live a little!" Harry had teased her that morning, playfully ruffling her hair. "One of these days, you're going to have to stop living life through a computer screen and experience it for real."

She had rolled her eyes, as she always did when Harry was in one of his daredevil moods. "Maybe some of us prefer not to end up in a hospital," she had shot back, half-joking, though the nagging worry about his stunts always lingered in the back of her mind.

He had laughed, that big, carefree laugh that seemed to shake the room. "I'll be fine. I always am."

But that afternoon, things didn't go as planned. As Harry and his friends sped down the sharp curves of the mountain road, one wrong move—a momentary loss of control—sent his car careening off the edge. The sound of screeching tires and the crash as his vehicle tumbled down the rocky slope was something Emma couldn't erase from her mind.

The call came hours later. Emma had been working, deep into a new coding project, when her phone rang. The voice on the other end was distant, almost as if she were hearing it from underwater. "There's been an accident. It's Harry… He didn't make it."

Her world had shattered in an instant.

The days following the accident were a blur of disbelief, shock, and unbearable grief. The family's home, once filled with Harry's laughter and boundless energy, was eerily quiet. Emma remembered the way her mother had sobbed uncontrollably, her father's face ashen, like a man whose spirit had been ripped away. Emma herself had retreated into silence, numb to the world around her. She had always been the rational one, the one who found comfort in solving problems, but there was no solution for this. There was no way to bring Harry back.

The funeral was a haze—people offering condolences, their voices muffled by the overwhelming weight of loss. Emma had stood by Harry's casket, staring at the stillness of his face, unable to comprehend that someone who had been so full of life was now gone. Her older brother, the one who had always teased her, pushed her to be more adventurous, and stood by her side through everything, was gone. Just like that.

The void Harry left in their family was immense. Emma's parents struggled to cope, their grief manifesting in different ways—her mother became more withdrawn, while her father buried himself in work, trying to distract himself from the pain. Emma, in typical fashion, threw herself into her studies and work, using technology and her career as a way to escape the overwhelming sense of loss. It was easier to focus on algorithms and codes than to confront the emptiness left by Harry's death.

But no matter how much time passed, the memory of that day haunted her. She could still hear his voice in her head, see his face so clearly, and feel the aching absence of him in every family gathering. Every time she achieved something in her career, she thought of how Harry would have been the first to congratulate her, to tell her to go even further. She missed his wild spirit, the way he lived life so fearlessly, even if that very fearlessness had led to his death.

The accident became a turning point in Emma's life. She had always been driven, but after Harry's death, her focus sharpened even more. She had something to prove—not just to herself but to the world. If she couldn't live as fully as Harry had, she could at least create something that mattered. She could build, innovate, and leave a legacy that would honor the brother who had always pushed her to be more.

Yet, underneath that drive, there was always a lingering sadness—a part of her that wondered if she had missed something. If maybe, just maybe, she could have stopped Harry from going on that drive. If she could have convinced him to slow down, to not take that risk. But those were thoughts she kept buried, tucked away beneath layers of work and achievement.

As the years passed, Emma had learned to live with the grief. It wasn't as sharp as it had been in those early days, but it never truly went away. It was part of her now, woven into the fabric of who she was. The adventurous brother who had once been the center of their family's world was now a memory, one that she held onto tightly, even as she moved forward.

And every time she stood on the edge of something new, something exciting and terrifying, Emma could still hear Harry's voice in her head, urging her forward. "Live a little, Em. Don't be afraid."

"Do you remember that time he tried to convince us to go camping?" James began, his tone playful. "He was so sure we could handle it, and we ended up lost for hours!"

Their laughter filled the room, and for a moment, the absence of Harry felt less heavy. They shared stories, each one a reminder of the bond they had, of the joy Harry had brought to their lives. Emma felt a warmth spreading through her, the connection with her family slowly rebuilding itself.

"I still can't believe he wanted to take us hiking in the middle of nowhere," Emma said, wiping away tears of laughter. "He thought he could navigate by the stars."

"Classic Harry," James said, shaking his head with a smile. "I miss him."

The atmosphere shifted slightly, the laughter fading into a reflective silence. Emma looked at her mother, whose eyes shimmered with unshed tears. "We all miss him," she said softly. "But he wouldn't want us to stay sad. He would want us to keep living, to create new memories together."

"Exactly," her father chimed in, his voice steady but tinged with emotion. "We need to honor his memory by cherishing the time we have now."

Emma felt a swell of gratitude toward her family, the bond growing stronger in the shared vulnerability. They were all in this together, navigating the aftermath of loss, but also celebrating the life that had been lived.

As the dinner wound down, her mother insisted on bringing out dessert—homemade chocolate cake, Harry's favorite. The smell wafted through the air, and Emma felt a twinge of warmth, remembering Harry's infectious enthusiasm whenever cake was served.

"Let's make a toast," her father said, raising his glass. "To family. To love. And to Harry, who will always be with us in spirit."

They clinked their glasses together, the simple act resonating with meaning. Emma felt tears prick her eyes, but this time, they were tears of hope. She knew Harry was gone, but his spirit might be with them.

They clinked their glasses together, and for the first time in a long while, Emma felt a sense of peace. The memories of Harry were no longer overwhelming waves of sadness but gentle reminders of the love they had shared as a family. The grief was still there, of course, but it had softened, giving way to the warmth of their togetherness. For the first time in a long while, Emma felt that Harry's presence still lingered with them, not as a shadow, but as a light.

As the night drew on, the family moved to the living room, settling into the familiar comfort of their old routines. James, always eager to entertain, pulled out a deck of cards and began shuffling them, grinning mischievously.

"Come on, Em," James teased, "You're always so analytical—let's see if that mind of yours can handle a game of luck for once."

Emma laughed, a genuine sound that surprised even her. "Luck? I think we both know I can outthink you in any game, James."

"Oh, we'll see about that," he shot back, already dealing the cards with a flourish.

Their mother and father joined in, and soon the room was filled with playful banter, light-hearted accusations of cheating, and the kind of laughter that Emma had missed more than she realized. The card game was simple, but it brought them all together, their bond feeling stronger and more resilient with each passing moment.

As the hours slipped away, and the card game finally wound down, Emma found herself sitting in the quiet living room, her family surrounding her, but her mind elsewhere. She gazed at the framed photos on the walls—snapshots of their lives, Harry's smile in almost every one of them. It was bittersweet, but tonight, for the first time, the pain felt bearable.

"Em?" her mother's voice gently interrupted her thoughts. "You okay?"

Emma nodded, blinking away the tears that threatened to spill over. "Yeah. I'm... I'm good," she said, her voice soft but steady. "I was just thinking about how much I miss him. But also about how lucky we were to have him, even if it wasn't for long."

Her mother reached over, giving Emma's hand a gentle squeeze. "We were lucky, weren't we? And we still have each other."

Her father, usually quiet and stoic in these moments, added, "We've been through a lot, but we've always found a way to keep going. And that's what Harry would've wanted. For us to keep going."

Emma nodded, feeling the truth of her father's words. "I think you're right. I've been so focused on work, on pushing everything away... but I'm realizing now that it's okay to stop and let myself feel. To just be here with all of you."

James, who had been unusually quiet during the exchange, leaned back in his chair and sighed. "You know, Harry always said you were the smartest one in the family, but I think he also knew you carried a lot on your shoulders, Em. I think he'd be proud of you for realizing this."

Emma smiled, the weight on her chest lifting even more. "Thanks, James. That means a lot."

The night wrapped up in warmth and quiet conversation, and as Emma hugged her family goodbye, she felt a sense of clarity she hadn't felt in years. She realized she needed them, just as much as they needed her. As much as she prided herself on independence and success, her family was her anchor, and reconnecting with them felt like coming home.

When she finally returned to her apartment, the glow of the city lights through her window didn't feel as isolating as it had before. She dropped her bag by the door and wandered into the kitchen, still replaying the night in her mind. The smell of her mother's chocolate cake lingered on her clothes, a small but comforting reminder of home.

Emma sat at the kitchen counter, her laptop open in front of her. She had left the screen paused on the data from Xel Island—the project that had consumed her for days. The charts and maps glared back at her, beckoning for her to dive back in.

But tonight, something was different. She no longer felt the same urgency, the need to immerse herself in work to escape everything else. She was still intrigued by the mystery of Xel Island, of course—her mind never stopped searching for answers—but the pull wasn't as frantic.

She took a deep breath, her fingers hovering over the keyboard. For so long, she had buried herself in work to avoid dealing with her emotions, but now she realized that she didn't have to run from either.

Just then, her phone buzzed again, this time with a message from James.

"Hey, sis. Just wanted to say, tonight was really nice. I miss Harry too, but I'm glad we have each other. Love you."

Emma smiled, her heart swelling with love for her brother and family.

"Love you too, James," she typed back, the simplicity of the message filled with more emotion than she could express in words.

She looked at her laptop again, her mind still swirling with thoughts about the project, about Xel Island, about the risks and the unknowns that came with it. But now, instead of rushing headfirst into it, she felt grounded. She didn't have to solve everything tonight.

With a small, satisfied sigh, Emma closed the laptop and stood up. For the first time in a long time, she felt like she could step away from work without guilt. She turned off the kitchen light and made her way to bed, feeling at peace with both her past and her future.

The next morning, Emma woke up with a clarity she hadn't felt in years. She had taken a step toward healing with her family, but she knew there was still work to do—both with them and within herself. She also knew that she wasn't done with Xel Island, not by a long shot.

Sitting at her kitchen table with her cup of coffee, she glanced at her laptop again, wondering what to do next. There were unanswered questions, patterns she still hadn't deciphered. The island was a mystery she couldn't walk away from completely, but she now knew that it didn't have to consume her.

As she sipped her coffee, a thought crossed her mind. Maybe, just maybe, she could help uncover the truth about Xel Island without losing herself in the process. She could use her skills, her brilliance, but balance it with what mattered most—her family, her mental health, her life outside of work.

She grabbed her phone and sent a quick message to the research team she had been collaborating with.

"Hey all, let's schedule a meeting to go over the latest findings. I've got some ideas that could take this project to the next level."

Setting the phone down, Emma felt a surge of excitement at the thought of diving back into the work—but this time, it felt different. She wasn't escaping anymore. She was in control.

The meeting was scheduled for later that week, and Emma threw herself into preparation. She combed through every detail of her data, fine-tuning her analysis and making sure everything was airtight. The mystery of Xel Island still fascinated her, but now, she approached it with a calm determination rather than a frantic need to solve it all at once.

The day of the meeting arrived, and as she presented her findings to the research team, Emma felt a surge of pride. Her work was sharp, focused, and innovative—everything she prided herself on. But more than that, she felt a balance she hadn't felt before. She was contributing to something meaningful, but she wasn't losing herself in the process.

After the meeting, as she packed up her laptop and prepared to leave, her phone buzzed again. This time, it was a message from her father.

"**Proud of you, Emma. Looking forward to having you over again soon. Love you.**"

Emma smiled, the words filling her with warmth. She had spent so much time chasing success, but now, she realized that the greatest success she could have was the love and support of her family.

She typed a quick response. "**Love you too, Dad. I'll be over soon.**"

As she walked out of the office that day, Emma felt lighter, more centered. The mystery of Xel Island was still out there, waiting to be uncovered, but now she knew she could approach it without losing herself. She could find balance between the drive to solve the unsolvable and the need to stay connected to the people who mattered most.

And with that realization, Emma Clarke knew she was ready for whatever came next—whether it was uncovering the secrets of a mysterious island or simply making time for dinner with her family.

While she was busy, another story had unfolded in another place of the world. The life of George Matts who was recalling his memories from his past adventures. As he sat in a lone corner of his room, he had his mind waving his past memories and it all started here.

As George Matts sat at the edge of the dock on Bermus Island, the golden rays of the sun cast long shadows across the tranquil waters. He leaned against the railing, soaking in the familiar scent of salt and earth. This was where he felt most alive—on the cusp of adventure, staring into the unknown.

George had always been an explorer at heart. From a young age, he was captivated by tales of lost civilizations and uncharted territories, and he dedicated his life to uncovering the secrets of the world. However, Bermus Island had become a personal obsession. Its legends, entwined with whispers of ancient cultures and mysterious occurrences, had drawn him back time and again.

Despite his adventurous spirit, George grappled with a growing sense of loneliness. While he had traveled the globe—trekking through dense jungles and scaling rocky mountains—he often found himself alone. Friends had come and gone, and each attempt to gather a group for an expedition ended in disappointment. Most people, he realized, were too fearful to face the dangers associated with places like Bermus Island.

"George, you're crazy for wanting to go back there," his friend Mike had said the last time they spoke. "People are disappearing. Just let it go."

But George couldn't let it go. He felt a connection to the island, a calling he couldn't ignore. "You don't understand," he had replied, his voice filled with urgency. "There are secrets here waiting to be uncovered. This place could teach us so much about our past."

As he stood on the dock that day, the warmth of the sun on his back, George took a deep breath, determined to face the island's mysteries once again. He grabbed his gear—filled with essential supplies like maps, a compass, and notebooks—and set off toward the heart of Bermus.

The path wound through the dense foliage, each step familiar yet exhilarating. The vibrant greens of the jungle enveloped him, and the sounds of nature filled the air. Birds chirped, insects buzzed, and somewhere in the distance, a waterfall cascaded, its soothing sound a reminder of the island's untamed beauty.

George reveled in the solitude, feeling the weight of the world lift off his shoulders. He often preferred the company of nature over people, but today felt different. He longed for companionship, someone to share in the excitement of discovery. As he trekked deeper into the island, he couldn't shake the feeling that it was time for a change.

Just then, he heard a rustling in the bushes. George turned, ready to greet a fellow adventurer or perhaps an animal. To his surprise, a young woman emerged, her eyes wide with curiosity.

"Whoa! You scared me!" she exclaimed, brushing her dark hair back from her face. "I didn't think anyone else would be here!"

George blinked, momentarily taken aback. "You're here to explore?"

"Yeah, I heard about the island and wanted to see it for myself," she said, stepping closer. "I'm Ria, by the way."

"George," he replied, feeling a rush of excitement at meeting someone who shared his passion for exploration. "I come here often. It's one of the most fascinating places I've ever been."

Ria's eyes lit up. "Really? I've been reading about the history of Bermus Island, the cultures that existed here. There's so much mystery! I've always wanted to see it up close."

As they began to explore the ruins together, George felt a renewed sense of purpose. Ria was spirited, intelligent, and filled with an energy that mirrored his own. They walked through the ancient structures, discussing their thoughts on what the remnants might have been used for, sharing theories about the lives of the people who had once inhabited the island.

"Do you think we'll find anything cool?" Ria asked, her eyes sparkling with enthusiasm.

"I hope so," George replied, excitement bubbling within him. "This place is full of surprises. Each step could lead us to something incredible."

As they delved deeper into the island's mysteries, George felt a sense of camaraderie he hadn't experienced in years. Emma's enthusiasm fueled his own, and the two of them quickly fell into a rhythm. They climbed over fallen stones, ducked under low-hanging branches, and shared their discoveries, laughter echoing through the jungle.

"Do you think we'll find artifacts?" Ria asked, her eyes wide.

"Maybe," George replied, his mind racing with possibilities. "This island has so much history. There's bound to be something worth uncovering."

After hours of exploring, they paused on a ledge overlooking the breathtaking coastline of Bermus Island. The sun began to set, casting vibrant hues of orange and pink across the sky. Ria leaned back against a rock, her gaze fixed on the horizon. "This is incredible," she said, a hint of awe in her voice.

"It really is," George replied, taking a moment to appreciate the beauty before them. "I can't believe I finally found someone who understands why I love this so much."

Ria turned to him, her expression earnest. "I think it's amazing what you do. Most people shy away from adventure, but you embrace it. That's inspiring."

George felt a warmth spread through him, a mix of pride and gratitude. "Thank you. I've always felt like I was meant to be out here, exploring, uncovering the unknown. It's who I am."

As they sat in companionable silence, the connection between them deepened. Ria was more than just a companion; she was someone who challenged him to rethink his approach to exploration, to consider the stories behind the places he visited. For the first time in a long while, George felt like he wasn't alone in his journey.

"Do you think you'll come back?" Ria asked, breaking the silence.

"Absolutely," he replied without hesitation. "This island has so many secrets. I could spend a lifetime uncovering them."

"Maybe I'll join you," she said, a playful grin crossing her face. "I could use some adventure in my life."

George chuckled, imagining the two of them diving into the heart of Bermus together. "That would be great. The more, the merrier, right?"

As the sun dipped lower, painting the sky with brilliant colours, they talked about their aspirations and dreams. Emma shared her love for history and how she had always wanted to work on archaeological digs, while George recounted tales of his adventures around the world.

"I've explored places that most people only read about in books," he said, a glimmer of excitement in his eyes. "But nothing compares to the thrill of being right here, right now, with someone who understands the magic of exploration."

"Why do you think you always ended up alone?" Ria asked, her tone thoughtful.

George paused, considering her question. "I think it's because I've always been so focused on the journey that I forgot to bring people along with me. I've chased the thrill and left my friends behind."

Ria nodded, her expression understanding. "I get that. Sometimes we lose ourselves in our passions, forgetting that life is more enjoyable when shared."

Their conversation flowed easily, like a stream meandering through a forest. It was refreshing to share thoughts with someone who genuinely understood the call of adventure. But as they talked, George couldn't help but think about his past experiences.

"Once, I took a group of friends on a hike," he recalled. "We thought we could handle it, but things went wrong. We lost our way, and it turned into a nightmare. I felt responsible, and ever since then, I've preferred to explore alone."

Ria frowned, sensing the weight of his story. "You shouldn't carry that burden alone. It's part of the adventure, and sometimes things just happen. It doesn't mean you should stop exploring or connecting with others."

"I know that now," he admitted, meeting her gaze. "But it's hard. I've built this wall around me, and I guess it's easier to stay behind it than to risk getting hurt again."

"Life is full of risks," Ria said gently. "But it's also full of rewards. You've seen that today. You're already breaking down those walls by letting me join you."

George felt a spark of hope ignite within him. Maybe this was a new beginning. The idea of sharing future adventures with Ria filled him with excitement. The camaraderie he had longed for was finally here, but could he truly open himself up to it?

The sky turned dark as the stars began to twinkle above them, and the sounds of the jungle came alive. They sat in silence for a while, watching the night unfold, each lost in their thoughts.

Eventually, George broke the silence. "What do you think lies beyond this island? What secrets are waiting for us?"

Ria smiled, a glint of mischief in her eyes. "That's the beauty of exploration, isn't it? The unknown holds endless possibilities. Who knows what we'll find?"

"Let's make a pact," George said, his excitement bubbling over. "No more solo expeditions. From now on, we explore together."

"I like that idea," Ria replied, her smile widening. "Partners in adventure."

They both chuckled, the weight of their pasts lifting just a little. As they continued to talk and share their dreams under the stars, George felt a shift within him. The darkness that had once surrounded his heart began to recede, replaced by the warmth of companionship and hope.

After hours of exploration, they reluctantly decided to head back. The path through the jungle was familiar to George, but as they walked side by side, he felt like he was navigating a new terrain—one filled with potential and connection.

"Next time, we should bring more supplies," Ria suggested, glancing over at him with excitement. "And maybe even a tent! I'd love to camp out here."

"Camping?" George raised an eyebrow playfully. "I'm not sure if you're ready for that level of adventure."

"Please!" she shot back, a mock-indignant expression on her face. "I can handle it. Bring it on!"

As they reached the dock and the cool breeze brushed against them, George smiled, feeling a sense of belonging he had long missed. He had ventured into the heart of Bermus Island seeking secrets, but he had found something far more valuable—a partner in exploration, a friend who understood the thrill of adventure.

As they prepared to leave, George turned to Emma, his heart full of gratitude. "Thank you for today. It was more than I could have hoped for."

"No, thank you," Emma replied, her smile warm. "This was exactly what I needed."

With a newfound sense of purpose and a commitment to explore the mysteries of Bermus Island together, George realized he wasn't just embarking on a new adventure; he was opening the door to a friendship that could change everything. The journey ahead promised not just discoveries of the island's secrets but also the potential for deeper connections that he had been yearning for.

As the sun set behind them, the promise of tomorrow shimmered like the stars above, illuminating the path to adventure—and companionship—that lay ahead.

Those were lovely memories of the works of George and his friend exploring the great Bermus Island which too had a legacy that Xel held, but a bit weaker.

George Matts was lost in thought, the warm glow of the setting sun casting a golden hue across the walls of his room. Memories of his adventures on Bermus Island danced through his mind, mingling with the fleeting recollections of his solo journeys, the thrill of exploration tinged with an ever-present sense of longing for companionship. He was reminded of the thrill he had felt during his first explorations, but those memories were abruptly cut short when the door creaked open.

Ria stepped into the room, her presence filling the space with a warmth that contrasted the fading light. Her bright smile was like a beacon, instantly drawing George out of his reverie. She had become his wife after they had openly admitted their love for each other.

Ria George and George Matts both shared an insatiable passion for exploration, driving them to the farthest corners of the earth in search of adventure and discovery. Their mutual love for the unknown created a unique bond between them, yet their paths diverged significantly in one crucial aspect: their interpersonal relationships.

While George was a magnetic presence, effortlessly gathering a diverse circle of friends wherever he went, Ria found herself on a different trajectory. She had always been somewhat of an outsider, her intense dedication to exploration often alienating her from her peers. Many admired her adventurous spirit but hesitated to approach her, perceiving her as a lone wolf too engrossed in her pursuits to engage in casual friendships.

Despite her considerable wealth—accumulated from a family that had long enjoyed a prosperous lifestyle— Ria did not flaunt her affluence. In fact, she often downplayed it, believing that genuine connections mattered far more than material possessions. While George reveled in the camaraderie of shared adventures, Emma longed for similar bonds but found them elusive. Her unwavering commitment to her passion for exploring overshadowed her social life, leaving her with only a handful of close friends.

As George thrived in social settings, surrounded by laughter and camaraderie, Emma often felt like a spectator at her own life. She admired the friendships he cultivated, secretly wishing for the same kind of warmth and connection. However, her relentless pursuit of exploration often required sacrifices. She would spend countless hours studying maps, planning expeditions, and diving into research about the places she yearned to visit, leaving little room for casual conversations or social gatherings.

This stark contrast between them became a source of contemplation for Emma. She realized that while her wealth and passion could open doors to thrilling adventures, they came at the cost of meaningful relationships. Yet, the more she delved into the world of exploration, the more she understood that her true treasure lay not in riches but in the experiences she accumulated and the few friends who genuinely understood her spirit.

As they continued their journeys, George's laughter echoed in the air around him, while Ria often wandered the trails, lost in thought, dreaming of the friendships she desired yet struggled to forge. Her heart yearned for companionship, a kindred spirit who could share in the beauty of the world she so passionately sought, yet her commitment to her calling remained unwavering, even if it meant navigating her adventures alone.

Back in the story, "Hey there, explorer," she said, her tone playful as she leaned against the doorframe, arms crossed. "Lost in thought again, I see."

"Guilty as charged," George replied, grinning as he shifted his focus to her. Emma had always had a way of grounding him, pulling him back from the edge of his wandering mind. "Just reminiscing about Bermus and the time I spent there. You know, the thrill of adventure and all that."

Ria rolled her eyes affectionately. "You mean the thrill of nearly getting yourself lost? I remember you coming home with those wild stories of chasing after legends while I was trying to keep our home from falling apart." She stepped further into the room, her laughter filling the air, a sound that was music to George's ears.

"It's all part of the adventure!" he protested, his voice light. "Besides, you know I'd never truly get lost. I have a knack for navigation."

"Sure, if you're navigating by the stars," she teased, plopping down onto the edge of the bed. Her expression softened, and her eyes sparkled with mischief. "But in all seriousness, I worry about you. The last expedition you went on was pretty risky."

George moved to sit beside her, the weight of her concern heavy in the air. "I know. That's why I'm trying to find a balance. I don't want to put us in danger, and that's why I'm thinking of taking fewer solo trips. I want you with me. It's better to explore together."

Ria's gaze softened further as she met his eyes. "You know I love that idea. But you also need to remember that I'm not just a support system. I want to be out there with you, living the adventure, not just hearing about it when you get back."

Her passion ignited something deep within George, fueling his desire to share every moment of exploration with her. "I wouldn't have it any other way," he said earnestly, reaching for her hand.

"Every journey feels incomplete without you by my side. It's better to face the risks together than to live apart and worry."

The silence that enveloped them was charged with understanding, a mutual respect for the thrill and the dangers that came with their shared love for adventure. George reflected on how they had navigated the challenges of their relationship—how they had built a life together rooted in love and trust, while also respecting the wildness that lay within both of them.

"I know we can't avoid danger altogether," Ria said, breaking the silence as she leaned closer. "But we can be smart about it. We can work together, plan better, and prepare ourselves for whatever comes next."

"Exactly!" George replied, excitement bubbling up. "If we explore Bermus together, we can gather data, share the burden, and still enjoy every moment. It's about balancing the risks and rewards."

"Then let's do it," Ria said, determination shining in her eyes. "Let's plan our next trip together. I've been itching for some real adventure, and I want to experience it with you."

George felt a sense of exhilaration wash over him as he imagined the two of them trekking through the dense jungle, uncovering hidden ruins, and sharing in the thrill of discovery.

"What if we document everything?" George suggested, his eyes lighting up. "We could create a travel log, record our findings, and maybe even start a blog about our adventures. It could inspire others to explore too."

Ria's face broke into a wide smile. "I love that idea! We could share our stories, photos, and insights. And who knows? It might even help connect us with other explorers who feel the same pull."

"Exactly!" George exclaimed, feeling the excitement bubbling over. "We could build a community around exploration—people who understand the thrill and the risks, who are eager to share their stories and learn from each other."

As they bounced ideas off one another, George felt a profound sense of gratitude for Emma. She was his partner in every sense, someone who not only shared his love for adventure but also challenged him to think beyond the immediate thrill. Together, they could take on the world, face whatever dangers lay ahead, and turn every moment into an opportunity for growth.

But just as the conversation began to flow more freely, George felt a sudden wave of nostalgia wash over him. "You know," he began, his tone turning more serious, "when I think about Bermus Island, I can't help but remember why I started exploring in the first place. It was all about the thrill of discovery, the passion for uncovering hidden truths."

Ria nodded, sensing the shift in his mood. "And you've always been drawn to those hidden truths. That's what makes you who you are, George. But you don't have to face that journey alone anymore. We're in this together."

Her words echoed in his mind, and George felt the weight of his past adventures settle on his shoulders. He had spent so much time chasing after mysteries alone, feeling the loneliness of the journey even as he reveled in the thrill. But now, with Emma by his side, that weight felt lighter.

"Do you think we'll uncover something significant on this next trip?" George asked, looking into Emma's eyes.

"Absolutely," she replied confidently. "But it's not just about what we find. It's about the experience, the stories we create, and the memories we'll share. That's the true treasure of exploration."

As they continued to plan, George felt a renewed sense of hope and excitement. Together, they had faced the dangers of Bermus Island, uncovered its secrets, and created a tapestry of adventures that had intertwine their lives forever.

Just then, Ria glanced at the clock, her expression shifting from excitement to mild concern. "Oh! I didn't realize how late it was. We should probably head out soon. I have that presentation tomorrow, remember?"

George chuckled, the reality of their busy lives settling in. "Right! Your big moment. You've got this."

"I hope so!" she said, a hint of nervousness creeping into her voice. "I've been working so hard on it, but the pressure is intense."

"You'll be amazing," George reassured her, wrapping an arm around her shoulders. "Just remember, you're not alone. I'll be cheering you on from the front row."

As they prepared to leave, George felt a renewed sense of gratitude for the journey ahead—both in their lives together and the adventures that awaited them. With Ria at his side, the future felt bright and filled with possibilities.

The next day, as they stepped outside, the evening air was cool against their skin, a refreshing reminder that the world was still full of wonder and mystery waiting to be explored. They walked hand in hand, showcasing their bond and their mutual understanding to the outsiders, who may be peeping at them.

3

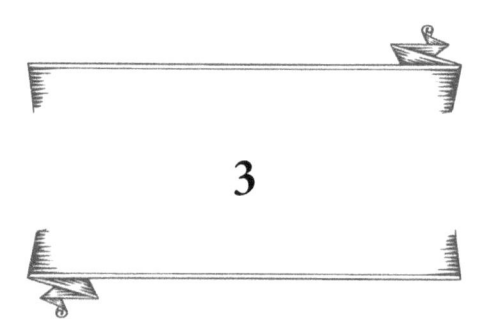

The Rising Stakes

Back to Dr. Adrian Locke in his office, Dr. Adrian Locke rubbed his temples as he stared at the dimly lit screen of his laptop, frustration growing with each passing minute. Xel Island had been the focus of his research for months—an obsession that gnawed at him, refusing to be silenced. The mystery of the island haunted his thoughts day and night. Its strange history, the disappearances, and the unexplainable phenomena—it was a puzzle no one had been able to solve.

His father had been one of the many explorers who had ventured to high risks, never to return. That loss was personal, the driving force behind Adrian's obsession with uncovering the truth. He'd spent years trying to piece together what had happened, but the more he dug, the more questions arose.

Now, alone in his study, he felt the weight of it all pressing down on him. "I can't do this alone," he muttered, pacing the room. His father had tried, and it had cost him his life. Adrian wouldn't make the same mistake.

He stopped by the window, staring out into the dark, silent street. The idea had been festering in his mind for days, but he kept pushing it aside. He didn't like the thought of working with strangers, but he needed a team. A strong one. People who weren't afraid of danger, who had the skills to navigate the unknown.

Turning back to the laptop, Adrian finally made his decision. He sat down, opened a new tab, and began typing.

"Explorers, adventurers, and scientists wanted for a high-risk, high-reward expedition to Xel Island. Seeking individuals with experience in archaeology, survival, and unexplained phenomena. Inquire within for details. Serious inquiries only."

He stared at the words for a moment, wondering if anyone would take the bait. Xel Island was notorious for its dangers; anyone who knew anything about it would be hesitant. But he hoped the promise of uncovering something extraordinary would draw the right people in.

With a click, the ad was live. Now, all he could do was wait.

The next few days were filled with anticipation. Adrian tried to distract himself by diving back into his research, poring over old maps and journals his father had left behind. But his mind kept drifting back to the ad. Would anyone respond? Would they be qualified? Could he even trust them?

On the fourth day, as he sipped his morning coffee and scrolled through his emails, a notification popped up. **"Reply to Xel Island Expedition Inquiry."**

Adrian's heart skipped a beat. He clicked it open.

"My name is Georgia Matthews. I've been following the mysteries of Xel Island for years. I'm an experienced survivalist and former military officer. I can handle myself in dangerous situations, and I believe I could be of help to your expedition. I've been wanting to explore Xel for a long time, and your ad seemed like the perfect opportunity. Let's talk."

Adrian leaned back, intrigued. Georgia sounded promising, but one person wasn't enough. He needed more.

By the end of the week, the responses had started to come in steadily. Some were clearly thrill-seekers looking for a quick adrenaline rush, but none stood out.

Adrian reviewed the profiles and qualifications of each candidate carefully. He needed a mix of skills—people who could handle the dangers of the island, but also those who could help uncover its secrets. By the end of the week, he had only one eager member, who he hasn't yet interviewed.

The next step was meeting them.

The café Adrian chose for the meeting was quiet, tucked away in a corner of the city where few people would overhear their conversation. He arrived early, as always, scanning the room for a private booth. His mind was racing, running through every scenario—what if the team didn't get along? What if they weren't prepared for the reality of Xel Island?

He was still deep in thought when Georgia Matthews walked in. She was tall, with a confident stride and an air of authority about her. Her dark hair was pulled back in a ponytail, and her eyes scanned the room before locking onto him.

"Adrian Locke?" she asked, extending a hand.

He nodded, standing to shake her hand. Her grip was firm, and he could feel the strength behind it. "Georgia. Thanks for coming."

They sat down, and she wasted no time. "So, you're looking for a team to go to Xel Island. I've been following that place for years. I've seen what happens to the people who go there, and I'm not afraid of it. But I need to know—what are you hoping to find?"

Adrian appreciated her directness. "I'm looking for answers. My father was one of the explorers who disappeared on Xel Island, and I need to know what happened. But more than that—I think there's something on that island that no one has discovered yet. Something big."

Georgia nodded, her expression serious. "I can respect that. I've been in dangerous situations before. If there's something on that island, I'll help you find it."

Before they could continue, another figure walked in—Alex Reid. He was younger than Adrian had expected, with an eagerness in his eyes that reminded him of his younger self. He spotted them and approached with a warm smile.

"Adrian? Georgia?" Alex asked, shaking both their hands. "I can't believe I'm finally meeting people who are as fascinated by Xel Island as I am."

"Let's hope that fascination doesn't get us killed," Georgia muttered.

Alex laughed nervously, but there was an undeniable passion in his eyes. "I've been studying Xel Island for years. The civilizations, the artifacts—it's a treasure trove of history. If we can crack its secrets, it could change everything we know."

Adrian smiled, feeling a surge of excitement. "That's exactly what I'm hoping for."

As they sat and talked, the energy at the table shifted. Each of them shared their thoughts, their fears, and their hopes for the expedition. Adrian could already tell that Georgia's no-nonsense approach would balance Alex's enthusiasm. Then he soon appointed her as one of the crew members in his team.

Adrian Locke had been excited when he first selected Georgia Mathews as the inaugural member of his crew. He'd heard whispers of her remarkable skills in survival and exploration, her tenacity in the wild, and her ability to navigate some of the most hostile terrains on earth. To him, she seemed like the perfect fit—a strong, independent woman who shared his passion for discovery.

When Adrian sent her the invitation to join the expedition, her response was swift. "Count me in," she'd said confidently over the phone. There was a thrill in her voice, an eagerness that matched

Adrian's own. He imagined this expedition would be the beginning of something incredible. With Georgia onboard, success seemed inevitable.

After Georgia had boarded, Adrian added two final members to the team: Mia, who had been a reliable presence from the start, and John Thompson, a newcomer who intrigued Adrian from the moment they met. John was young but carried himself with the quiet confidence of someone who had seen the world. His background was impressive—military training combined with degrees in engineering and technology made him a valuable asset. But there was more to him than just his résumé.

From the moment John arrived, he radiated an energy that was hard to ignore. He wasn't loud or boisterous like some might expect from someone with his military experience. Instead, he was calm, observant, and meticulous in everything he did. His sharp eyes took in every detail, analyzing the terrain, their gear, and even the interpersonal dynamics within the crew.

Adrian was immediately struck by John's professionalism. "You're not just here for the adventure, are you?" Adrian had asked when they first met.

John had smiled slightly, his expression unreadable. "Adventure's part of it, sure. But I'm here to solve problems. That's what I'm good at."

And solve problems he did. When the crew's equipment malfunctioned during a routine test, it was John who stepped up without hesitation. His engineering skills came to the forefront, diagnosing the issue with precision and efficiency. Within an hour, what could've been a major setback had been fixed. Adrian was impressed.

"Where'd you learn that?" Adrian asked, genuinely curious.

"Military," John replied, but there was something in his tone—a slight distance that hinted at more to the story. He never elaborated, and Adrian didn't push.

As the days passed, it became clear that John's military training wasn't just about physical endurance or technical know-how. He had a strategic mind, always thinking several steps ahead. Whether it was mapping out potential escape routes in case of emergencies or suggesting alternative approaches to their exploration plans, John's input was invaluable. He wasn't just following orders—he was shaping the mission.

But despite his competence, John remained somewhat of an enigma to the rest of the crew. He rarely spoke about his past, offering only vague details when asked. "What about your family?" Mia had once inquired during a late-night conversation around the campfire.

John had shrugged, his face shadowed by the flickering flames. "Not much to tell. I've been on my own for a while now." His tone made it clear that was all he was willing to share, and the conversation shifted away from personal matters.

Adrian, however, sensed that John's past weighed heavily on him. There was a certain edge to John, a guardedness that only surfaced in brief flashes. It was in the way he tensed whenever discussions drifted toward personal loss or trauma. It wasn't long before Adrian realized that John was running toward adventures and was full of eager.

One evening, while they were going over logistics, Georgia's demeanor began to shift. Her smile, once sharp with confidence, now seemed colder, and her words carried an edge that unsettled him. "You know, Adrian," she began, her tone almost teasing but with a cruel undercurrent, "this whole expedition? I could do it alone. I don't really need you or the rest of the crew."

Adrian raised an eyebrow, surprised by the sudden arrogance in her voice. He let out a nervous laugh, hoping to diffuse the tension. "Teamwork's the name of the game, Georgia. No one's doing this solo."

Her eyes narrowed slightly, her smirk growing more sinister. "We'll see."

That night, Adrian found himself tossing and turning. Something about Georgia's comment stuck with him, like a warning bell in his head. He didn't like the idea of having a potential loose cannon on the team. Still, he convinced himself that one offhand comment didn't necessarily reflect her true character.

But things escalated quickly. During a meeting with the rest of the crew, Adrian noticed how Georgia subtly undermined their plans. She would interject with passive-aggressive remarks, make snide comments about their skills, and laugh at their ideas as if they were beneath her. And the cruelty? It was creeping into her every interaction. Her words cut deeper with each passing day.

At one point, John Thompson, another crew member, suggested altering their route to avoid a dangerous section of the jungle. Georgia shot him a glare. "If you're too scared to do this properly, maybe you should stay behind," she snapped, her voice laced with disdain.

The room fell silent. Adrian could feel the tension thickening, and he knew he had to step in. "That's enough, Georgia," he said firmly. "We're a team. Everyone's input matters."

She simply shrugged, unbothered by his reprimand. "Fine. But don't come crying to me when things go south."

As the days dragged on, Georgia's behavior grew worse. She sabotaged small tasks, causing delays and frustration among the crew. She seemed to thrive on creating chaos, enjoying the discomfort she spread. Adrian tried to confront her several times, but she always brushed him off with a dismissive wave or an icy smile, making him question whether he was imagining things.

One night, he overheard her talking to another crew member, Mia. "You know, you're only here because Adrian's too soft to cut you. If it were up to me, you'd be gone in a heartbeat," Georgia hissed, her voice dripping with malice.

Mia looked shaken, her eyes darting toward Adrian as if begging for intervention. He had heard enough. The crew couldn't survive Georgia's toxic presence. Adrian needed to act, and fast. The next morning, he called Georgia aside, his heart pounding in his chest. "We need to talk," he began, keeping his voice calm but firm.

She crossed her arms and leaned against a tree, clearly uninterested. "About what?"

"Your behavior. It's disruptive, and it's affecting the team."

Georgia rolled her eyes. "Oh, please. If anyone here's a problem, it's you. You're too weak to lead this expedition. Honestly, Adrian, I thought you were more competent."

Adrian felt a surge of anger rising inside him. He had worked tirelessly to build this team, to plan every detail of this expedition, and here she was tearing it apart. "This isn't about me, Georgia. This is about you crossing lines, belittling the crew, and thinking you're above everyone. If you can't work with the team, then you can't be part of it."

For a brief moment, he thought he saw a flicker of vulnerability in her eyes, but it vanished as quickly as it appeared. She stepped closer to him, her voice low and threatening. "You're making a mistake, Adrian. Without me, this expedition will fail."

"I'll take my chances," Adrian said, his voice resolute. He could no longer ignore the destructive presence Georgia had become. The expedition was too important, and the crew deserved better than to work in a toxic environment.

"Fine," she said coldly. "But don't think you'll get far without me."

Georgia stormed off, and Adrian watched her go, feeling a weight lift from his shoulders. The crew had witnessed the exchange, and there was a palpable sense of relief among them. It was clear that Georgia's departure was necessary, even if it stung to lose someone with her skills.

Adrian took a deep breath, resolving to move forward with the team he had left. They may have lost Georgia's expertise, but they gained something far more valuable—unity.

As the days went on, Adrian couldn't shake the feeling of relief mixed with regret. He had been so eager, so blinded by Georgia's reputation, that he hadn't seen her true nature. But now, with her gone, the crew worked better together, and for the first time since the expedition began, they felt like a team.

"I won't make that mistake again," Adrian muttered to himself, pushing forward with renewed determination. Georgia had taught him a hard lesson about leadership and trust, one he wouldn't soon forget. Now, he had a work to do. He had to find new crew members to fill the shoes of Georgia Mathews, so he reposted the same thing which he posted earlier. This time, he thought to be very careful to not take any bad decisions as he was the leader.

Back to Emma Clarke, who had always been driven, a woman of relentless focus and boundless curiosity. She was busy with her work and her research about Xel.

Her days were spent in front of multiple screens in her sleek, modern apartment. The walls were lined with framed accolades—certificates of recognition from tech companies, awards from universities, and even a few photographs of Emma at high-profile tech conferences. Yet, despite her professional achievements, Emma had a lingering feeling that something was missing. It wasn't just the prestige or money that drove her anymore; it was the need for a challenge that went beyond the virtual world.

Lately, she had become fixated on something new. Xel Island. It had started innocently enough—Emma had once stumbled across a vague mention of the island in a forgotten corner of the internet. The stories surrounding it were the stuff of legends: mysterious disappearances, strange phenomena, and whispers of an ancient civilization that had once inhabited the island before vanishing without a trace. But despite her efforts to uncover more, solid information about Xel was surprisingly sparse. It was almost as if someone—or something—was deliberately keeping the truth hidden.

Minutes turned into hours while, Emma had devoted countless hours to researching the island. She combed through academic papers, old news articles, and obscure message boards, yet every avenue led to a dead end. It was as if the island didn't want to be found, as if it were hiding just beyond the reach of modern understanding.

One afternoon, Emma found herself at her desk, her fingers flying across the keyboard as she ran yet another search. A collection of old expedition logs flashed across her screen, but most of them were incomplete, with key pieces of information either missing or heavily redacted. She leaned back in her chair, frustration gnawing at her.

"Come on, there has to be something," she muttered to herself, her mind racing.

Her phone buzzed, interrupting her thoughts. It was a message from her mother. "**Dinner at our place tonight? Your father and I miss you. Come spend some time with us. We soon started feeling alone without you even though your brother was with us. You are special for us.**"

Emma sighed, running a hand through her hair. It had been a while since she had seen her parents. Between her work and her obsessive search for information about Xel, she had all but cut herself off from the people she cared about. She glanced at the clock—it was already late afternoon. Maybe she needed a break. After all, her searches for clues had led her nowhere so far.

She texted back quickly. "**I'll be there around 7. Can't wait to see you guys.**"

Later that evening, Emma pulled into the driveway of her childhood home. The house was a cozy, two-story suburban dream, nestled in a quiet neighborhood where the trees seemed to have stood forever. Emma felt a wave of nostalgia wash over her as she walked up the steps to the front door.

Her mother greeted her with a warm hug as soon as she stepped inside. "It's so good to see you, Emma. We've missed you, eventhough we had met recently."

"I've missed you too," Emma replied, offering a genuine smile as she stepped into the familiar comfort of her home.

Her father appeared from the kitchen, a spatula in hand. "Hey, kiddo! You're just in time—dinner's almost ready. I hope you're hungry."

Emma laughed, feeling the tension from the last few weeks melt away. "Starving, actually. What's on the menu?"

"Your favorite," her father replied with a grin. "Spaghetti and meatballs. Thought we'd go classic tonight."

As they gathered around the dining table, Emma couldn't help but feel a sense of peace settle over her. The conversation flowed easily, with her parents catching her up on family news, their latest hobbies, and some of the neighborhood gossip. It was a world far removed from the intensity of her work, and for the first time in what felt like months, Emma allowed herself to relax.

Her mother watched her carefully, though, a slight frown creasing her brow. "You look tired, honey. Have you been working too hard again?"

Emma shrugged, not wanting to burden them with the details of her fruitless search for information. "It's just the usual. A few big projects on the horizon, but nothing I can't handle."

Her father chimed in with a chuckle. "She says that every time. You've always been a workaholic, Emma."

"Yeah, well," Emma grinned. "Comes with the territory."

Her mother reached across the table, placing a gentle hand on hers. "Just make sure you're taking care of yourself. You can't keep burning the candle at both ends."

Emma nodded, appreciating the concern but brushing it off. "I will, Mom. Don't worry."

But even as she said it, she knew that her obsession with Xel Island was consuming more of her time than she wanted to admit. The mystery gnawed at her, making it difficult to focus on anything else. She felt like she was on the verge of something, but every time she got close, the trail went cold.

After dinner, they moved to the living room, where her father pulled out a photo album. "I thought we could go through some old pictures, take a trip down memory lane," he said, flipping open the worn leather cover.

Emma leaned in as her father began to turn the pages, revealing photos from her childhood—family vacations, birthdays, holidays. She smiled as she saw pictures of herself as a young girl, always curious, always trying to figure things out. There was a shot of her at the beach, her face lit up with excitement as she tinkered with a makeshift sandcastle contraption she had built.

"You've always been a problem solver," her father remarked, noticing where her eyes had landed. "Even back then, you were never satisfied until you figured out how things worked."

Emma chuckled softly. "I guess some things never change."

They spent the rest of the evening reminiscing, laughter filling the room as they shared stories and memories. But as the night wore on, Emma's thoughts began to drift back to Xel Island. It was as if the island had planted itself in her mind, refusing to let go.

By the time Emma left her parents' house and drove home, the quiet of the night seemed to amplify her frustration. She still hadn't found any concrete leads, and the longer she searched, the more it felt like the island was deliberately eluding her.

The next day, Emma was back at her desk, the glow of her laptop illuminating the darkened room. She had been at it for hours again, scouring the web for any new information, but the results were the same—empty leads and fragmented data. She leaned back in her chair, rubbing her eyes in frustration.

"Maybe I'm just chasing a ghost," she muttered, staring at the blinking cursor on her screen.

She was about to close her laptop and call it a night when something caught her eye. A new post had appeared on one of the obscure forums she frequented. It was buried deep in the thread, almost as if it had been intentionally hidden. The subject line was simple but immediately grabbed her attention: **"Xel Island Expedition—Team Wanted."**

Emma's heart skipped a beat. She clicked on the post, her pulse quickening as she read the brief message:

"Seeking individuals for a high-risk expedition to Xel Island. Must have experience in survival, exploration, and advanced technology. Looking for those with a passion for discovery and the willingness to face the unknown. Contact if interested."

The post was signed by someone named Adrian Locke.

Emma's mind raced as she stared at the message. This was it—the opportunity she had been waiting for. Someone else was planning to go to Xel Island, and they were looking for people with her exact skill set. Without hesitation, Emma clicked on the reply button and began typing.

"**My name is Emma Clarke. I'm a technology expert with years of experience in data analysis, drone technology, and mapping systems. I've been following the mysteries of Xel Island for some time, and I believe I can contribute to your expedition. Let's talk.**"

She hit send before she could second-guess herself.

Leaning back in her chair, Emma felt a surge of excitement. For the first time in weeks, she had a sense of direction. She didn't know much about Adrian Locke or his plans for Xel Island, but she had a feeling that this was exactly what she needed—a chance to be part of something bigger, to finally unravel the mystery that had been eluding her.

As she sat there, waiting for a reply, Emma allowed herself to dream of what they might find on Xel Island. The secrets, the dangers, the discoveries—it was all within reach now. And this time, she wouldn't be chasing shadows alone.

The next chapter of her life was about to begin.

Back to George in his area, he had sat in the sun-dappled living room of the house he shared with his wife, Ria. Stacks of notebooks, cameras, and scattered papers covered the table, remnants of their recent adventures. George flipped through one of their travel logs, grinning as he came across photos of their last trip—an impromptu hike in a rainforest that had nearly ended with them stranded due to a landslide.

Ria was seated across from him, typing away on her laptop, her brows furrowed in concentration as she organized the day's work. Their life, filled with exploration and discovery, had settled into a kind of rhythm that George both loved and occasionally found a little too predictable. They had always shared a passion for adventure, documenting their experiences on a blog that had gained a modest following. But lately, George could sense an itch beneath the surface—something that made him long for a challenge, a journey beyond the ordinary.

"I still can't believe we made it out of that jungle in one piece," George mused, breaking the comfortable silence.

Ria glanced up, a smile tugging at her lips. "You were the one who wanted to keep going, even when the path was completely washed out."

He chuckled. "Well, you didn't exactly object. If anything, I think you were egging me on."

Ria's smile turned into a soft laugh. "You know me. I can't resist the thrill of the unknown."

"That's why we work so well together." George leaned back, tossing the notebook aside and staring up at the ceiling. "But don't you ever feel like we're missing something? Like we're only scratching the surface of what's out there?"

Ria studied him for a moment, her expression thoughtful. She saved her work and closed the laptop, leaning back into her chair. "I know what you mean. It's been a while since we've really pushed ourselves. Our trips have become... comfortable."

"Exactly," George said, sitting up straighter. "I want more. I want that sense of real discovery again—something that makes us feel alive, you know?"

Ria nodded slowly. "I do. But where would we even start? We've been to so many places already."

As if the universe had decided to answer his question, George's phone buzzed with a notification. He picked it up absentmindedly, expecting it to be some irrelevant message, but his eyes widened as he read the screen.

"What is it?" Ria asked, noticing his sudden stillness.

"Take a look at this," George said, passing the phone to her. The screen displayed an online post—"**Xel Island Expedition—Team Wanted**"—along with a brief description: "**Seeking explorers, adventurers, and researchers for a high-risk expedition to Xel Island. Must be prepared for the unknown. Contact if interested.**"

Ria's eyebrows shot up as she read the post. "Xel Island? Isn't that the place everyone avoids because of all the disappearances?"

"Yep, that's the one," George replied, excitement bubbling up in his chest. "But think about it, Ria. This is exactly what we've been looking for. It's not just another hike or a mountain climb. It's real, raw exploration. We could be part of something that no one else has dared to finish."

Ria remained quiet for a moment, her gaze fixed on the phone screen. The mention of Xel Island brought with it a certain level of danger, and they both knew it. The island's history was riddled with stories of failed expeditions, strange occurrences, and unsolved mysteries. But at the same time, there was an undeniable allure—a chance to uncover something truly groundbreaking.

Finally, she looked up, meeting George's gaze. "You really want to do this?"

George nodded, his eyes gleaming with excitement. "I do. We've always talked about pushing ourselves further, about finding something that goes beyond the ordinary. This could be it. Besides, I can't think of anyone I'd rather face the unknown with than you."

Ria sighed, a mixture of nervousness and excitement flashing across her face. "Well, it does sound like the kind of adventure we've been craving. But we need to be smart about it, George. Xel Island isn't some easy trip. It's dangerous, and we need to be prepared for anything."

"Agreed," George said quickly. "We'll do our homework. Make sure we have the right gear, the right plan, and stay sharp. But this is the kind of thing we live for."

Ria smiled, and George could see the excitement starting to creep into her eyes as well. "Alright, then. Let's do it."

Without another word, George grabbed his laptop and typed out a quick response to the post:

"My name is George Matts, and my wife, Ria, and I are experienced explorers with years of survival and adventure behind us. We've documented countless trips through jungles, mountains, and uncharted territories. We'd love to be part of your team to Xel Island. Let's talk."

He hit send, then looked up at Ria with a grin. "It's done. Now we just wait."

The next few days passed in a blur of anticipation. George and Ria threw themselves into preparing for the potential expedition, researching everything they could about Xel Island. What little information they found was cryptic at best—vague accounts of strange occurrences, explorers who had gone missing, and mysterious symbols found in the ruins scattered across the island. There was no clear map, no definitive guide. Every piece of information felt like a puzzle waiting to be solved.

At the same time, they continued documenting their daily lives for their blog. It had become a kind of routine for them—posting photos of their adventures, writing about the challenges they faced, and offering tips to their growing audience of fellow explorers. But even as they went through the motions of updating the blog, George could sense that their focus had shifted. Their thoughts were consumed by the possibility of what lay ahead.

One evening, as they sat in their small home office, going over their latest blog post, George glanced over at Ria. "You think we're ready for this?"

Ria didn't look up from the laptop, her fingers still tapping away at the keyboard. "We've faced worse, haven't we? I mean, remember that time we almost got lost in the Sahara? Or the time we thought we'd never make it off that mountain in Alaska?"

George chuckled. "True. But this feels different. Xel Island is... I don't know. It feels like it's hiding something."

Ria finally looked up, her expression thoughtful. "That's exactly why we need to go. It's the unknown that makes it exciting. We've always wanted to find something truly unique, something that hasn't been touched by the world yet. Maybe this is it."

George nodded, feeling a wave of determination wash over him. "Yeah. You're right."

As they continued working, George's laptop chimed, signaling a new email. His heart skipped a beat as he saw the subject line: **"Xel Island Expedition Inquiry Response."**

He opened the email, and his eyes scanned the message quickly:

"George and Ria, thank you for your interest in the Xel Island expedition. I've reviewed your background and experience, and I believe you would be a valuable addition to the team. Let's set up a time to discuss the details further. Looking forward to hearing from you. We expect you to arrive by 0900 hours at the coordinates provided. – Adrian Locke"

George read the email aloud to Ria, and as he finished, she broke into a wide grin. "Looks like we're in."

Ria, sitting across the table, leaned back in her chair and let out a breath she didn't know she'd been holding. "Looks like we're in."

George smirked, though the weight of the situation hadn't fully hit him yet. "Yeah, we're in. But that's only step one. You know Adrian Locke is no easy man to impress."

Ria's grin widened. "I know. But if anyone can pull this off, it's us."

The two exchanged a look, the adrenaline already kicking in. They had dreamed of this—an opportunity to join a team heading to Xel Island. The place was shrouded in mystery, whispered about in both academic circles and among thrill-seekers like them. But George knew this was no vacation. Xel Island was deadly, and they were about to meet the man who had made a career out of surviving the impossible: Dr. Adrian Locke.

Later that week,

George and Ria stood at the foot of the location coordinates Adrian had sent them. The area was remote, a small, inconspicuous clearing far from any city. It was strange, arriving at a place so unremarkable, considering the magnitude of the task ahead. They hadn't expected grandeur, but this was more... isolated than they anticipated. It heightened the unease that had been building since they left.

"You think this is some kind of test?" Ria whispered, adjusting her backpack straps. "Maybe he wants to see if we freak out over the middle of nowhere?"

George chuckled, his hand resting on the worn leather journal tucked in his jacket. "Could be. Or maybe he's just testing our patience."

Before Ria could respond, the hum of an engine broke through the air, growing louder as a sleek, unmarked helicopter appeared on the horizon. They exchanged a glance. This was it.

The helicopter touched down gently, and as the blades slowed, the door slid open. Adrian Locke stepped out, his silhouette as sharp and imposing as the reputation that preceded him. Following closely behind was Mia, her face impassive but her eyes observant, analysing everything.

Adrian's gaze flickered between George and Ria as they approached. "George Matts and Ria Thompson?" His voice was low, commanding.

"That's us," George confirmed, extending a hand.

Adrian eyed the hand for a brief second before shaking it, his grip firm but brief. "We don't have much time. Emma Clarke is en route. We'll begin the interviews once she arrives."

Ria nodded, her usual confidence replaced with quiet anticipation. She had read about Adrian Locke—his meticulous nature, his ruthless efficiency. But meeting him in person was an entirely different experience. He was an enigma, every word calculated, every movement deliberate.

Minutes later, another figure emerged from the helicopter: Emma Clarke. She was as sharp and precise as the technology she created, her reputation for brilliance well-known. Adrian greeted her with a nod, and they all headed to a small tent set up in the clearing.

Inside, Mia wasted no time. "We'll start simple. We've reviewed your applications, but we need to understand what drives you. What do you hope to gain from this expedition?"

George spoke first. "Adventure, sure. But more than that—discovery. Xel Island is the last great mystery. I want to be part of something bigger than just the thrill of it. The history, the unknown—it's what I live for."

Adrian studied him for a moment before turning to Ria.

Ria, always the firebrand, grinned. "I've spent my life chasing storms—metaphorically and literally. This island? It's the biggest storm of all. I'm in for the ride, but also because I know I'm capable of surviving it."

Mia's eyebrows lifted slightly. "Survival is key. Xel isn't a place for glory seekers. You'll face more than physical dangers. We've lost good people—smart people."

Emma, who had been listening quietly, leaned forward. "And you, Emma Clarke. You're not exactly known for adventuring. What brings you here?"

Emma's eyes flickered with something unreadable. "Curiosity. Xel Island has a tech history that no one's touched. My skills are in figuring out systems, and I have a feeling the island has one of its own. I want to understand it."

Adrian exchanged a look with Mia before standing. "We'll reconvene. Give us a few hours."

The trio watched as Adrian and Mia stepped outside, leaving them in silence. George exhaled, finally able to release some tension. "That went better than I thought."

Emma shrugged, though her brow furrowed in thought. "I'm not sure what they're looking for exactly. He's a tough one to read."

Ria stretched, her confidence returning. "Doesn't matter. We know what we're capable of. All we have to do now is prove it."

Three hours later,

Adrian and Mia sat across from George, Ria, and Emma. The sun was beginning to set, casting long shadows across the clearing.

"We've talked it over," Adrian began, his gaze sharp as ever. "You three are in. But I need you to understand—this isn't a victory. The real work starts now."

Emma's lips quirked into the faintest smile. "I wouldn't have it any other way."

Mia crossed her arms, her expression serious. "You'll be briefed on the details soon, but Xel Island is like nothing you've ever faced. We'll need you at your best—mentally and physically."

George nodded, excitement bubbling beneath his composed exterior. "We're ready."

Adrian's stare lingered for a moment, as if assessing something unseen. "You better be. Xel doesn't give second chances."

Later that evening,

George and Ria sat together by the fire, their gear packed and ready for the journey ahead. Emma sat a few feet away, working on a tablet, her mind clearly elsewhere.

"You think we're really ready for this?" Ria asked, poking at the fire.

George smiled, but it didn't quite reach his eyes. "We'll have to be. Xel Island isn't forgiving."

They sat in silence for a while, the crackling of the fire the only sound between them. The weight of the journey ahead was beginning to sink in. They had gotten what they wanted—a chance to be part of something greater. But now that they were on the cusp of it, the reality was beginning to set in.

"You guys coming?" Emma's voice cut through their thoughts. She stood, motioning toward the tents. "Big day tomorrow." Dr. Adrian Locke had built tents for his three crew members, who had newly joined his crew.

George and Ria exchanged a glance before standing.

As George and Ria stood from the warmth of the fire, the weight of tomorrow's journey settled heavily between them. Emma had already retreated to her tent, the soft glow of her tablet casting shadows on the canvas, but George and Ria lingered. They didn't speak immediately, the crackle of the fire filling the silence as they exchanged an unspoken understanding.

Ria broke the quiet first, her voice low and reflective. "It's surreal, you know? All the stories, all the myths... we're actually going to see it. Xel Island. We're walking into a place that swallows people whole."

George nodded, poking absently at the embers. "Yeah. And I'm not sure if I'm more excited or terrified."

Ria let out a soft laugh, but it was more out of nerves than amusement. "Same. I keep telling myself we're ready. I mean, we've trained for this—adventure, survival. But this... this feels different. Like... like we're walking into the unknown."

George didn't answer right away, his mind swirling with thoughts. He stared into the flames, the orange glow reflecting in his eyes. "You're right. We're not just climbing a mountain or trekking through a jungle. There's something else about that island... like it's alive. And it doesn't want us there."

Ria's grin faded slightly, her usual bravado giving way to a more honest expression. "You really think it's that bad?"

George shrugged, his gaze distant. "I don't know. But I can't shake the feeling that we're... intruding. Like we're trespassing on something ancient, something that doesn't want to be disturbed."

Ria tilted her head, studying him. "You're not usually the superstitious type. What's got you spooked?"

George hesitated, choosing his words carefully. "It's not about superstition. It's just... I've been on expeditions before, dangerous ones, but this... feels different. Like the stakes are higher. And not just for us—there's more riding on this than we know."

Ria was quiet for a moment, letting his words sink in. Then she offered him a small, lopsided smile. "You're right. But that's why we're here, isn't it? We've spent our whole lives looking for something bigger. And now we've found it."

George finally looked at her, his own smile creeping back. "Yeah. I guess that's true."

They lapsed into silence again, but it wasn't uncomfortable. It was the kind of silence that came with understanding—of the situation, of each other, of the enormity of what they were about to face.

After a few minutes, Ria stretched, her joints cracking in the quiet night. "I should probably get some sleep. Big day tomorrow and all that."

George smirked, watching as she stood. "You mean you're actually going to sleep? I thought you thrived on sleepless nights before a big adventure."

Ria chuckled softly. "Normally, yeah. But this time... I think I'll need all the rest I can get. Something tells me tomorrow's going to be a whole new level."

George nodded, standing as well. "Yeah. You're probably right."

As they turned toward their tents, Ria paused, glancing over her shoulder at George. "You're not going to bail on me, right?"

George raised an eyebrow, amused. "Bail? Me? C'mon, Ria. You know I'm in this as deep as you are."

Ria grinned, though it didn't reach her eyes. "Good. Just... don't let your gut feelings spook you too much. We've got this."

George chuckled, but there was a seriousness beneath his response. "Let's just make sure we come back in one piece."

Ria held his gaze for a moment longer before nodding. "Yeah. Let's do that."

They both paused their conversation and went into their tent. George laid on his cot, staring at the ceiling of the tent, he replayed their conversation in his mind. Ria was always the fearless one, the one who charged headfirst into the unknown. But tonight, even she seemed to sense the gravity of what was coming. They lay together, the warmth of their bodies slowly merging with the stillness of the night. Wrapped in each other's arms, a quiet intimacy settled between them, the kind that didn't need words to be understood. As their breathing synced, a gentle silence filled the room, charged with unspoken emotions.

Her head rested on his chest, and he could feel the soft rhythm of her heartbeat, steady and calming. The world outside faded into nothingness, leaving only the warmth of their embrace. Slowly, their gazes met, and in that shared moment, everything else disappeared—the doubts, the fears, the uncertainties of the day.

With a tenderness that made time seem to stop, he gently lifted her chin, their faces just inches apart. The soft glow of the moonlight filtered through the window, casting delicate shadows across their faces. Without a word, their lips found each other in a kiss—slow, deep, and filled with the kind of longing that only comes after waiting for what feels like a lifetime.

The kiss lingered, and with each passing second, the intensity deepened, as if they were pouring every unsaid feeling into that one perfect moment. It was more than just a kiss; it was a promise, an unspoken vow that they were safe, here, together.

As they pulled away, their foreheads rested gently against one another, eyes half-closed, both of them lost in the quiet afterglow. The weight of the day slowly ebbed away, replaced by a calm that only they could give each other. Without a word, they settled into the comfort of the night, their bodies entwined. And just before the veil of sleep fully claimed them, they shared one final, soft kiss—one that spoke of peace, contentment, and the simple joy of being close.

In the silence that followed, they drifted into sleep, wrapped in warmth and each other's presence. The world could wait. For now, they had all they needed in this moment.

George shifted restlessly, unable to quiet his thoughts. Xel Island was no ordinary adventure. It wasn't a place you could conquer with sheer willpower or survival skills. It was something else, something that seemed to breathe with its own dark energy.

George took a deep breath, forcing his mind to settle, while having a sleep. He couldn't let doubt creep in now. They had come too far, and worked too hard to turn back. And yet, despite his resolve, a small voice in the back of his mind whispered that this journey would change them all—whether they survived or not.

Tomorrow would bring the answers. But tonight, all George could do was rest and wait.

As George drifted into a restless sleep, Ria lay beside him, her breathing uneven despite the warmth of their embrace. The weight of the day lingered in her mind, but exhaustion finally claimed her, pulling her into a heavy slumber.

But it wasn't peaceful.

In the depths of her sleep, Ria found herself standing alone in a dense, suffocating fog. The air was thick with the damp scent of rotting leaves and the unsettling feeling that something was terribly wrong. Her heart pounded in her chest as she looked around, searching for any sign of George.

"George?" she called out, her voice echoing into the endless mist.

No response.

She began to walk, her steps hurried as panic clawed at her. The landscape around her shifted, the ground unstable, as if the island itself was alive beneath her feet. The trees twisted grotesquely, their branches like skeletal arms reaching toward her, casting long, menacing shadows that seemed to close in with every step she took.

Suddenly, she heard it—George's voice, faint and filled with pain.

"Ria... help."

Her breath hitched. She spun around, trying to locate him. "George? Where are you?!"

His voice came again, but this time it was closer, more desperate. "Ria... please."

She broke into a run, her pulse racing as the fog thickened. The oppressive air pressed down on her chest, making it harder to breathe. Her surroundings blurred as she sprinted forward, driven by the need to find him.

And then she saw him.

George stood just ahead, but something was wrong. He was pale, his eyes wide with fear, and his body was stiff, unnaturally still. Ria slowed her steps, dread creeping into her veins. She wanted to call out to him, but her voice caught in her throat.

As she approached, her eyes locked on something behind George—a dark figure, barely visible in the mist, its presence chilling. The shape was humanoid but distorted, its features shadowy and grotesque. A soft, malevolent whisper filled the air, barely audible but unmistakably sinister.

"George..."

Ria's voice trembled as she reached out toward him. "George, move!"

But it was too late.

The figure behind George shifted, its form growing more distinct—a ghostly apparition with hollow eyes, its face twisted in anguish. It moved swiftly, unnaturally, closing the distance between itself and George in an instant.

"NO!" Ria screamed, her voice breaking as she lunged forward, but her feet were rooted in place. She watched, helpless, as the ghostly figure wrapped its icy, spectral fingers around George's throat.

George's eyes widened, his mouth opening in a silent scream as the ghost squeezed tighter. His body convulsed, his face contorting in pain as the life drained from him. The ghost's hollow eyes locked onto Ria, its gaze filled with an otherworldly malice. It was feeding on George's life, draining him slowly, agonizingly.

Tears blurred Ria's vision as she struggled to move, her muscles refusing to respond. "Let him go!" she cried, her voice raw with desperation. "Please!"

But the ghost didn't stop. George's body went limp, his skin turning ashen. His once-bright eyes dimmed, and with one final, sickening twist, the ghost snapped his neck.

Ria's scream ripped through the night.

She bolted upright in her tent, drenched in sweat, her heart slamming against her ribs. Her hands shook uncontrollably as she pressed them to her mouth, stifling the sobs that threatened to escape. The nightmare clung to her, vivid and horrifying, the image of George's lifeless body burned into her mind.

Beside her, George stirred, his brow furrowing as he awoke to the sound of her ragged breathing.

"Ria? What's wrong?" His voice was thick with sleep, but the concern in his eyes was immediate as he sat up, reaching for her.

She shook her head, her breath still shallow as she tried to ground herself in reality. "It was just... a nightmare," she whispered, her voice trembling. "You... you were—"

"I'm right here," George murmured, pulling her close. His arms wrapped around her, his touch steady and warm. "I'm okay."

Ria buried her face against his chest, but the terror from the dream lingered, gnawing at her. The ghost had felt so real, so deliberate. It wasn't just a figment of her imagination. It was a warning—a dark premonition of what might come.

"I'm not going anywhere, Ria," George reassured her, his voice gentle as he stroked her hair. "We're going to get through this. Together."

But Ria couldn't shake the feeling that the island had already marked them, and that the nightmare was just the beginning.

After Ria had drifted back into an uneasy sleep, George lay awake, his arms still wrapped protectively around her. He could feel her body relaxing against him, the tremors from her nightmare gradually fading, but her fear lingered in the air like a thick fog. George told himself it was just a dream, a byproduct of their anxiety about the expedition to Xel Island. And yet, deep down, a part of him couldn't ignore the dread Ria's nightmare had stirred within him.

Eventually, George's own exhaustion pulled him under, and he fell into a heavy sleep. But his mind offered no respite from the unease.

IN HIS DREAM, GEORGE found himself standing in an unfamiliar city, the night around him thick with danger. The dim glow of streetlights barely penetrated the oppressive darkness, and the cold air was filled with the low hum of distant activity. He scanned the streets, his heart quickening as he realized Ria was nowhere to be seen.

"Ria?" he called, his voice bouncing off the walls of the narrow alleyway.

There was no answer.

George's pulse pounded in his ears as he pushed through the darkness, desperate to find her. Every shadow seemed to hide a threat, and every step felt like he was being pulled deeper into something sinister. The alleyways twisted and turned, unfamiliar and suffocating. He couldn't shake the sensation that he was being watched, that something dangerous lurked just out of sight.

Suddenly, he heard it—a sharp, terrified scream.

"Ria!"

George sprinted toward the sound, his breath coming in frantic gasps as the streets became narrower and darker. His feet pounded against the cracked pavement, his heart racing as the scream echoed again, more desperate this time. He turned a corner and stopped dead in his tracks.

There she was.

Ria knelt on the ground, her hands bound behind her back, a look of terror etched into her face. She was surrounded by a group of men, their faces obscured by the shadows, but the menace in their posture was unmistakable. The largest of them, a man with a hulking frame and cold, ruthless eyes, stood over her, a gleaming knife in his hand.

George's blood ran cold. He opened his mouth to shout, to warn them off, but his voice was trapped in his throat, paralyzed by fear. The gangster's hand gripped Ria's hair, yanking her head back as he brought the blade dangerously close to her throat.

"Ria!" George screamed, but it was like shouting into a void. His feet refused to move, the nightmare holding him in place as though the air had turned to concrete.

The gangster sneered, his voice low and filled with malice. "This is what happens when you cross the wrong people. Time to pay."

Ria struggled against her bindings, her eyes wild with fear as she locked onto George's. "George, help me!" she cried, her voice breaking with desperation. "Please!"

George fought against the invisible force holding him back, his entire body trembling with the effort. But no matter how hard he tried, he couldn't move. He was powerless, trapped in his own nightmare.

The gangster's laugh was cold and empty, and with a cruel flick of his wrist, he pressed the blade to Ria's throat. George's scream tore through the air as he watched in horror, unable to stop it.

The knife flashed in the dim light, and in one brutal motion, the gangster slashed Ria's throat.

Blood poured from the wound, crimson and violent, staining the ground beneath her. Ria's eyes widened in shock, her hands twitching in one last futile attempt to fight. She gasped for breath, her voice a wet, gurgling sound as she crumpled to the ground, the life draining from her.

George's heart shattered as he screamed her name, falling to his knees. Tears blurred his vision as he stared helplessly at Ria's lifeless body, the gangster's laughter echoing in his ears. The man stood over her, wiping the blade clean, his expression smug and indifferent. He had taken everything from George in a single, merciless act.

"No... no... no..." George whispered, his voice breaking as the weight of the nightmare crushed him. The darkness closed in, suffocating him, filling him with a cold, unrelenting despair.

Suddenly, the scene around him began to dissolve, the city melting away into nothingness. The gangster and his men disappeared, leaving only the haunting image of Ria's body lying in the street.

✕

GEORGE BOLTED UPRIGHT in the tent, his chest heaving as he gasped for air. His heart pounded so violently that it felt like it might burst from his chest. Sweat drenched his skin, his entire body trembling with the intensity of the nightmare.

Beside him, Ria stirred, waking to the sound of his labored breathing. She turned to him, her face still pale from her own nightmare. "George? What is it?"

George couldn't speak at first, the nightmare still clinging to him like a suffocating weight. He pressed a hand to his forehead, trying to shake the horrifying image of Ria's death from his mind.

"George?" Ria's voice was soft but urgent, her hand resting gently on his arm. "What happened?"

He turned to her, his eyes wide with fear, and for a moment, he couldn't even process that she was alive—that the nightmare wasn't real. When his mind finally caught up with reality, he pulled her into a tight embrace, holding her as if letting go would mean losing her for real.

Ria was startled by the intensity of his grip but returned the hug, concern flickering in her eyes. "What did you see?" she asked, her voice a soft whisper in the stillness of the tent.

George pulled back just enough to meet her gaze, his voice barely above a whisper. "You... you were killed. I couldn't stop it. This man, this... gangster, he—" His voice broke, and he looked away, unable to finish the sentence.

Ria's heart clenched as she realized the weight of his nightmare. She could see the fear in his eyes, the raw emotion that told her it had felt real—too real.

"Hey," she said softly, cupping his face in her hands. "I'm right here. It was just a dream."

George shook his head, his voice hoarse. "It felt like more than that. I was helpless. I couldn't save you."

Ria rested her forehead against his, her voice steady but filled with quiet reassurance. "You don't have to save me, George. We're going into this together. We'll face whatever comes our way—together."

George closed his eyes, breathing in her presence, trying to push the lingering terror away. "I don't know why we're both having these nightmares. It's like... like something's warning us."

"Maybe it is," Ria murmured, her fingers tracing soft circles on his arm. "Or maybe we're just scared out of our minds because we know what's waiting for us. But we can't let fear win, George. Not before we've even started."

He nodded slowly, the knot in his chest loosening, but the fear still lingered at the edges of his mind. He pulled Ria close again, holding her like an anchor in the darkness, refusing to let go.

"Promise me," he whispered, his voice thick with emotion. "Promise me we'll make it through this."

Ria pulled back just enough to look him in the eyes, her gaze steady and unwavering. "I promise. We'll make it out of this. You and me."

Their foreheads touched again, a quiet understanding passing between them. They had no idea what awaited them on Xel Island, but they knew one thing for sure—whatever it was, they would face it together.

As the night stretched on, George's grip on Ria never loosened, and despite the lingering fear in the air, they both managed to drift back into a fragile sleep, knowing that the real battle was only just beginning.

As George and Ria finally found a fragile sleep, the camp outside their tents remained eerily quiet, save for the soft rustling of the wind through the trees. Inside her own tent, Emma Clarke lay in a peaceful slumber, her breathing deep and steady. Unlike her companions, she had fallen asleep easily, her mind unfazed by the looming threat of Xel Island.

For Emma, the thrill of the unknown was something she could rationalize. Fear had little room in her mind, always compartmentalized, processed, and neatly tucked away. After all, she was used to solving problems. Life was a puzzle, and Xel was simply another equation waiting to be decoded. Tonight, though, something far more primal stirred in the shadows.

It began with a faint sound—barely perceptible, but there, on the edge of sleep. Emma's brow furrowed, her mind pulling her from the depths of her rest. At first, she thought it might be the wind or the forest shifting in its nocturnal rhythm. But as she listened more closely, a deep unease started to settle over her.

The noise was strange, irregular, like heavy footsteps but not quite human. They were far away at first, but growing louder, heavier, like something was approaching the camp. Emma's eyes fluttered open, her heart rate accelerating slightly as her senses sharpened.

She sat up, listening intently, the noise now unmistakable. It was a low, guttural sound—almost like a growl—followed by the unmistakable sound of branches snapping. Whatever it was, it was close. Too close.

Emma's throat tightened, her pulse quickening as she grabbed a flashlight, the cool metal of the device suddenly uncomfortable in her hands. Her mind raced through logical possibilities. It could be an animal, or maybe just the wind playing tricks on her ears. But instinct told her otherwise.

She quietly unzipped her tent, peeking out cautiously, her flashlight illuminating the space just beyond. The campfire had long since died down, leaving only embers glowing faintly in the center of the clearing. She panned the light slowly across the perimeter of the camp. Nothing. The trees swayed gently, their shadows stretching ominously across the ground, but no movement—no sign of whatever had made that terrifying sound.

Just as she was about to retreat into the relative safety of her tent, the noise came again, closer this time. A sharp, scraping sound followed by a low, unearthly groan, like something ancient and angry. Emma's breath caught in her throat, her grip tightening around the flashlight as she strained her eyes, scanning the darkness.

Nothing. Not a single thing in sight, yet the air felt thick with an unseen presence. She could feel it—something watching her, lurking just out of view, waiting. Her skin prickled with a sensation she hadn't felt in years. Fear.

Emma swallowed hard, forcing herself to focus. Fear was a distraction. An enemy she couldn't afford to entertain. Slowly, she backed into the tent, zipping it up with deliberate slowness. She sat there for several minutes, waiting, listening, her heart pounding in her chest. But the sounds stopped, as if the night had finally grown still again.

For a long time, she remained alert, every muscle tense, but as the minutes ticked by and no further noises came, her body began to relax, exhaustion creeping back in. Eventually, she convinced herself it had been nothing more than an animal passing by. With a sigh, she lay back down, pulling her blanket tight around her, her eyes still flickering toward the entrance of the tent.

It took some time, but eventually, her body succumbed to the fatigue of the day, and she slipped back into a restless sleep. But the moment she did, her mind plunged into a nightmare so vivid, it felt all too real.

IN HER DREAM, EMMA was back in the familiar setting of her childhood home—a place filled with memories, both good and bad. The walls were lined with photographs of her family, and the warm glow of the lamps cast soft shadows across the living room.

But there was something wrong. The house was too quiet, too still, as if it were holding its breath.

"Mom? Dad?" Emma called, her voice echoing unnaturally down the empty hallways.

She walked through the house, her footsteps eerily muted as she moved from room to room. Every corner she turned was empty, and the sense of dread grew heavier with each passing second. Something was horribly, terribly wrong.

Suddenly, the lights flickered, plunging the house into darkness. Emma's heart raced as the shadows deepened, twisting and contorting into grotesque shapes. She turned around, only to hear the sound of heavy, booted footsteps behind her.

She wasn't alone.

The footsteps grew louder, closer, until they stopped just behind her. Emma turned slowly, her breath catching in her throat.

Standing there, blocking the doorway, was a group of men—five of them, their faces obscured by black masks. Each one carried weapons—knives, bats, guns—and the malicious intent in their posture sent a jolt of fear through Emma's entire body.

"Where is everyone?" she demanded, trying to sound stronger than she felt. But her voice wavered, betraying her terror.

One of the men chuckled, his voice low and cruel. "You're too late, Emma. They're already dead."

Emma's heart dropped, her stomach twisting violently. "No... no, that's not possible."

The man stepped forward, and with a single, cruel motion, he flung something onto the floor. Emma's blood ran cold as she saw it—her father's watch, stained with blood.

"No!" she screamed, lunging forward, but the men surrounded her, their laughter cold and merciless. They moved toward her with terrifying purpose, their weapons glinting in the darkness.

Before she could even react, one of the men pulled out a gun and fired a single shot. The sound was deafening, and Emma screamed again, her body frozen in place as the world around her slowed to a crawl.

She turned, and there, sprawled on the floor, was her mother—lifeless, blood pooling beneath her. Her father lay beside her, his body broken and still. Emma's vision blurred with tears as the realization hit her like a freight train.

They were all dead.

The killers stood over her family, their eyes gleaming with sadistic pleasure, as if they had been waiting for this moment. Emma's knees buckled beneath her, the weight of the horror overwhelming her. She tried to scream, to fight, but her body wouldn't obey.

And then, one of the killers—a tall man with a scar running down his face—turned his attention to Emma. Slowly, deliberately, he raised his gun, pointing it directly at her.

"Now it's your turn," he said, his voice dripping with malice.

Emma's entire world narrowed to that single moment, the cold metal of the gun, the man's finger tightening on the trigger. She closed her eyes, bracing herself for the inevitable.

※

EMMA WOKE WITH A GASP, her body jerking violently as she sat up in her tent. Her breath came in ragged, shallow bursts, her heart hammering against her ribs. The vividness of the dream left her disoriented, her mind reeling from the brutal images.

For several long moments, she sat there in the darkness, her body trembling with the aftershock of the nightmare. She pressed her hands to her face, trying to steady herself, but the horror of what she had just witnessed clung to her like a dark shadow.

Her family... her entire family... gone.

Emma wiped her face, forcing herself to breathe slowly, to calm down. It was just a dream. Just a nightmare. But even as she repeated the words in her mind, she couldn't shake the feeling that something—someone—was watching her. Just like in the nightmare, the air around her felt oppressive, charged with an unseen malice.

She lay back down, her body rigid, and closed her eyes, though sleep seemed impossible now. The night stretched on endlessly, her mind replaying the horrific scene over and over. And deep down, a small voice whispered that this nightmare, like the ones George and Ria had faced, was more than just fear.

It was a warning. A dark premonition of the dangers that awaited them.

As the night deepened around the camp, Adrian Locke and Mia slept in their respective tents, each wrapped in the stillness of the forest. For most of the evening, Adrian had fallen into a deep, dreamless sleep—his usual state of calm that years of hardened experience had provided him. Mia, equally disciplined, had drifted off after hours of mentally preparing for the next day's mission.

But tonight was different.

4

The Echoes Of The Awakening Nightmare

In the dead of night, something stirred within both of them—a presence they couldn't ignore. Unbeknownst to each other, they both began to experience the same vivid nightmare, a haunting that felt all too real.

ADRIAN'S MIND PLUNGED him back into his past, to a time he had long buried. The setting was eerily familiar: a remote research site, deep in an uncharted territory, where he had often accompanied his father on archaeological missions. Adrian's father was alive, as real as he had ever been, his strong hands gently brushing dirt away from an artifact they had uncovered. The air was warm, the sun hanging low in the sky.

Adrian knelt beside him, feeling an odd sense of comfort and nostalgia. His father smiled at him, the kind of proud smile Adrian hadn't seen in years. For a moment, everything felt right—like time had reversed, and he was a boy again, eager to impress the man he looked up to more than anyone.

"You've done well, son," his father said softly, his voice carrying that calm authority Adrian had always admired.

But the warmth of the moment didn't last.

A sudden, unsettling shift in the air made Adrian's skin prickle. Shadows danced unnaturally at the edges of the site, and the once-familiar warmth turned cold. He stood up, instinctively reaching for something to defend them, though nothing seemed out of place. His father was still kneeling, focused on his work, as if unaware of the looming danger.

That's when they came.

Out of the shadows emerged a group of men—thieves by the looks of them. Rough, unshaven, and carrying weapons. Their eyes gleamed with greed as they approached, and Adrian's heart dropped. He recognized the look in their eyes—they were here to take everything.

"Stay back!" Adrian shouted, stepping between them and his father, but his voice felt small, muffled by the growing tension in the air.

The leader of the thieves—a towering figure with a scar running down his face—laughed darkly. "We're not here for you, kid. Hand over the artifact, and no one gets hurt."

Adrian's father, oblivious to the danger, finally looked up, his brow furrowed in confusion. "What's the meaning of this? We're here on a peaceful expedition—"

But before he could finish, one of the thieves pulled out a gun, and in one swift, brutal motion, fired.

The gunshot echoed through the air, and Adrian's father crumpled to the ground, blood pooling beneath him. Adrian's breath caught in his throat as he stared at the lifeless body of the man who had been his hero, the man who had taught him everything.

"NO!" Adrian screamed, charging toward the thieves with blind rage. His fists collided with the nearest one, but he was quickly overpowered. The thieves were faster, stronger, more ruthless than he anticipated. One of them struck him across the face, sending him sprawling to the ground.

Before Adrian could recover, the leader loomed over him, sneering. "You really thought you could stop us?"

Without warning, the leader plunged a knife into Adrian's chest, twisting it cruelly. Pain shot through his body, his vision blurring as the blood drained from his wound. Adrian gasped, his strength fading, as he collapsed beside his father's corpse.

As Adrian lay there, gasping for breath, he turned his head and saw Mia. She had been there, part of the team. She had tried to fight them off, but she, too, was now on the ground, her body riddled with wounds. Her face was twisted in agony, her breaths shallow and pained. She was barely hanging on.

The thieves stood over them, their weapons dripping with blood. One of them kicked Adrian's father's body, laughing cruelly. "Worthless old man."

Another one spat near Adrian's head. "Thought you could play the hero, huh? Look at you now."

They began to tease and mock the fallen, kicking their bodies as if they were nothing but discarded trash. One of them crouched down beside Mia, his hand trailing along her face, causing her to flinch in disgust and pain.

"Such a waste," he muttered, his voice dripping with malice. "You could've lived, sweetheart."

The leader of the group stepped forward, wiping the blood from his knife with a rag. "Leave them. Let them rot here, with their precious little treasures."

Adrian's vision blurred further as darkness closed in around him. The laughter of the thieves echoed in his mind, haunting and cruel, as his body went cold. His last thought, before everything faded, was of his father, lying dead beside him. He had failed. Failed to save him. Failed to stop the thieves. Failed to protect Mia.

ADRIAN AWOKE WITH A start, his body drenched in sweat. He sat up quickly, his breath ragged, his mind still trapped in the horrific nightmare. The vividness of it clung to him, the image of his father's body lying motionless beside him, the blood, the mocking laughter of the thieves—it all felt so real.

"Dammit..." Adrian muttered under his breath, running a shaky hand through his hair.

Adrian sat up, still gasping, trying to shake off the lingering horror of the nightmare. His heart was pounding as if he had truly been there, helpless and broken beside his father. But as he forced himself to breathe slowly, the weight of the dream wouldn't lift. The cold emptiness it left behind was suffocating.

Suddenly, a rustling came from outside his tent. Adrian tensed, his body still on edge, but then Mia's voice called out quietly, "Adrian?"

He unzipped his tent and stepped out, his muscles still tight with tension. Across from him, Mia stood, pale and visibly shaken. Her eyes were wide, and Adrian could see the terror still lingering in her expression. She looked like she'd just stepped out of the same nightmare.

"You too?" Adrian asked, his voice low, trying to suppress the tremor that threatened to surface.

Mia nodded, her lips pressed into a thin line. "It wasn't just a nightmare, Adrian. It felt... real."

Adrian swallowed hard, his mind racing. He knew what she meant. It had felt far too vivid, too personal. "What did you see?"

Mia hesitated for a moment, the words seeming to catch in her throat. "We were... on a mission, like the ones before. But then your father—he was there. Alive. He tried to stop them, but they... they killed him. And then you. I... I couldn't stop it. I was—" Her voice faltered, her composure slipping for the first time in as long as Adrian could remember.

Adrian's blood ran cold. It was the same nightmare. They had both witnessed the same twisted scene, down to the very last detail—the thieves, the brutal murders, the mocking voices. He had never heard of anything like this before, and the sheer impossibility of it chilled him to the bone.

"I saw it too," Adrian said quietly, his eyes dark with unresolved pain. "My father... I couldn't save him. And then... you were there, bleeding out."

Mia wrapped her arms around herself, her eyes darting to the surrounding darkness of the camp. "I don't understand what's happening. I've had bad dreams before, but this... Adrian, what if it wasn't just a dream? What if it's... a warning?"

Adrian clenched his fists, his mind whirling. He didn't want to believe it, but there was something about the nightmare that felt more like a message than just his subconscious fears. The presence of his father, the way the thieves had ruthlessly mocked them—it wasn't just his mind playing tricks on him. And for Mia to have experienced the same thing?

"Xel Island," he muttered, the name alone feeling cursed on his lips. "There's something about this place. Something it's trying to tell us."

Mia's eyes narrowed, her voice shaking. "But what? That we're going to die? That we're walking into our deaths?"

Adrian shook his head, but uncertainty gnawed at him. He wasn't a man easily frightened, but the nightmare had left him rattled in a way nothing else had before. "I don't know. But we're here for a reason. We've come too far to turn back."

Mia exhaled sharply, brushing a hand through her short hair. "Do you think the others—George, Ria, Emma—do you think they're... experiencing the same thing?"

Adrian frowned, considering the possibility. If he and Mia had been affected by the same nightmare, what were the chances that the rest of the team had been too? His gut told him they weren't alone in this.

"We'll check on them in the morning," Adrian replied, his tone resolute. "For now, we need to stay focused. Whatever that dream was, it can't shake us."

But even as the words left his mouth, Adrian knew they were hollow. The dream had already shaken him to his core. He could see the same fear etched into Mia's features. There was something deeply wrong with this place, something that went beyond the physical dangers they had anticipated.

Mia nodded, though her eyes were still clouded with doubt. "Alright. But Adrian... if these nightmares keep happening—if they get worse—"

"We'll deal with it," Adrian cut in, his voice firmer now. "We have to. There's no other choice."

Mia stared at him for a moment longer before giving a curt nod. "Okay. We'll deal with it."

The two of them stood in silence for a while, the only sound the faint rustle of the forest around them. Despite their resolve, an unspoken fear lingered between them, a shared understanding that something was shifting beneath the surface of their expedition.

Adrian looked up at the stars, the sky seemingly indifferent to the horrors they were about to face. His mind drifted back to the image of his father, crumpled and bleeding at his feet. It had been a long time since he had allowed himself to think about his death, to let that grief resurface. But now, in this dark and twisted place, it seemed like Xel Island itself was forcing him to confront the pain he had buried.

With a deep breath, Adrian turned back toward his tent. "Get some rest, Mia. Tomorrow... we'll figure this out."

Mia gave a weary smile. "Rest. Right."

She disappeared into her tent, leaving Adrian alone with his thoughts. He lingered for a moment longer, the weight of the night pressing heavily on him. Then, with a final glance into the darkness, he returned to his tent, knowing that sleep would bring no peace.

As he lay down, the vivid memory of the nightmare still fresh in his mind, Adrian couldn't help but wonder: was this island already breaking them? Was it already too late?

The camp remained quiet, the team each wrestling with their own demons in the silent hours before dawn. The island watched, unseen but ever-present, and as they drifted back into uneasy sleep, the whispers of the night lingered, a reminder that the true nightmare was yet to come.

As the night crept on, Adrian lay in his tent, sleep eluding him. The vivid nightmare of his father's death still gnawed at his mind, twisting his stomach with guilt and dread. He closed his eyes, trying to shut it all out, but the darkness was suffocating. The island felt alive around him, like it was breathing, waiting, preparing to strike again.

Eventually, exhaustion overtook him, and he drifted back into an uneasy sleep. But this time, the nightmare that gripped him was even more terrifying, more dangerous than before.

IN THE DREAM, ADRIAN found himself alone in a vast, open field. The sky above him was an unnatural, sickly gray, and the air smelled of decay. The field stretched endlessly in all directions, but despite the openness, Adrian felt trapped, as though the ground beneath him could swallow him whole at any moment.

He turned around, searching for something—anything—familiar, but there was nothing. No signs of his team, no landmarks, just an overwhelming sense of isolation.

His heart pounded in his chest, his instincts screaming at him that something was horribly wrong.

Suddenly, the earth beneath his feet trembled, a low rumble vibrating through the ground. Adrian's pulse quickened as he looked down, only to see the soil cracking open beneath him. From the cracks emerged thick, black smoke, swirling upward like ghostly tendrils reaching for the sky.

And then he heard it—a voice, faint at first, but growing louder with each passing second. It was a voice he hadn't heard in years.

"Adrian..."

He froze, his blood turning to ice. He knew that voice. It was his father's.

Slowly, he turned, his heart lodged in his throat. Standing there, just a few feet away, was his father, but he looked different this time. His once kind and strong face was twisted in agony, his body gaunt and frail, as if something had drained the life out of him. His eyes were wide, unblinking, filled with a deep, unnatural sadness.

"Dad?" Adrian's voice cracked as he took a hesitant step forward. "How—how are you here?"

But his father didn't respond. Instead, his face contorted in pain, and he raised his hands, pointing at Adrian with fingers that were bony and sharp, almost skeletal.

"Why didn't you save me, Adrian?" his father's voice rasped, full of accusation and sorrow. "You let me die."

Adrian's heart pounded in his chest as guilt flooded him. He took another step forward, his hands trembling. "I tried. I—there was nothing I could do."

But his father shook his head slowly, his face warping further into something grotesque, something inhuman. "You didn't try hard enough. You abandoned me."

The ground trembled again, the cracks widening beneath Adrian's feet. His father's figure began to distort, his body warping and stretching, growing taller and more monstrous with every passing second. His skin peeled away, revealing raw, blackened muscle underneath. His eyes—once familiar—became dark pits of shadow, hollow and terrifying.

"I'm not your father anymore, Adrian," the creature hissed, its voice now guttural, barely human. "You failed. Now you'll pay."

Without warning, the monstrous figure lunged at Adrian, its hands outstretched, claws reaching for him. Adrian stumbled backward, barely avoiding the swipe, his heart racing as adrenaline surged through his veins. He turned and ran, the ground crumbling beneath him with each step, the creature's grotesque form chasing him, its claws scraping the earth with a sickening screech.

But no matter how fast Adrian ran, the creature was always just behind him, relentless, its voice echoing in his mind. "You can't escape! You'll never escape!"

Adrian's lungs burned as he sprinted across the field, but there was no end in sight. The horizon stretched endlessly, and the creature was gaining on him. His legs felt heavy, as though the ground was trying to pull him down, trap him in place.

Suddenly, the landscape shifted. The ground beneath Adrian gave way entirely, and he fell—plummeting into a dark, endless abyss. The air rushed past him, the creature's distorted laughter echoing in his ears as he tumbled through the void. His body twisted and turned, weightless, disoriented, his heart hammering in his chest.

Then, with a violent jolt, Adrian hit the ground hard. The impact knocked the air from his lungs, pain searing through his body. He groaned, struggling to push himself up, but when he opened his eyes, the sight that greeted him made his blood run cold.

He was no longer in the field. He was back in the camp—but it wasn't the camp he knew.

Everything was wrong.

The tents were torn apart, shredded like paper. Blood stained the ground, dark and still. And the bodies of his team—George, Ria, Emma, and Mia—lay scattered across the clearing, their lifeless eyes staring up at the sky. Each of them bore horrific injuries, their bodies broken and mangled beyond recognition.

Adrian's breath hitched as he stumbled forward, his mind reeling. "No... no, this can't be real."

But as he moved closer to the bodies, the air around him grew colder, heavier. A shadow fell over the camp, and when Adrian turned, he saw them.

The thieves.

The same thieves from his earlier nightmare, but this time they were worse. Their faces were twisted, monstrous, their eyes glowing with an eerie red light. They stood over the bodies of his team, laughing, mocking, just as they had before.

One of the thieves kicked George's body, sneering. "Thought you could survive this island? Pathetic."

Another thief crouched beside Mia's lifeless form, his hand brushing against her bloodied cheek. "They didn't stand a chance."

Adrian's body trembled with rage, but his limbs were frozen, his feet glued to the ground. He wanted to scream, to attack, to stop them—but he couldn't move. He was powerless.

The leader of the thieves stepped forward, his scarred face twisted into a wicked grin. "You failed them, Adrian. Just like you failed your father. Now look at them."

The thief's words sliced through Adrian like a knife. His team—his friends—lay dead at his feet, and there was nothing he could do to stop it.

"You'll die here too," the leader sneered, his voice dripping with malice. "Just like them."

The shadow of the leader loomed over Adrian, suffocating him as the thief's hand shot out, gripping his throat. Adrian gasped, struggling to breathe as the pressure increased, the thief's hand tightening like a vice.

"You don't belong here," the leader hissed. "This island will devour you, just like it did them."

The darkness swallowed Adrian whole, his vision fading as the leader's grip closed around him, suffocating, crushing. And just as everything went black, the last thing he heard was the sound of cruel laughter echoing through the void.

※

ADRIAN SHOT UP IN HIS tent, drenched in sweat, his chest heaving as he gasped for air. His hands flew to his throat, the sensation of being strangled still painfully fresh. His heart pounded violently, the memory of the nightmare vivid and searing in his mind.

For a moment, he was paralyzed, unsure of what was real and what wasn't. The cold, suffocating dread of the dream still clung to him, choking him. But as his surroundings slowly came into focus, he realized he was back in his tent, alive.

His body trembled as he pressed a hand to his face, trying to steady his breathing. But no matter how much he told himself it was just a dream, the horror of it lingered, gnawing at him.

This wasn't just fear.

Something darker was at work here. Something far more dangerous than they had anticipated.

Adrian swallowed hard, his hands still shaking as he sat there in the dark. Whatever was happening on Xel Island, it wasn't just physical. It was something far more insidious—something that could destroy them from the inside out.

And he wasn't sure they could survive it.

Adrian Locke sat cross-legged on the cold, hard floor of his tent. The thick fabric barely kept out the biting wind that howled like a ravenous beast, rattling the pegs driven into the frozen ground. His hands trembled, not entirely from the cold, but from the gnawing feeling of dread that had settled in his gut. It had been building for hours now, a creeping sensation that something was not quite right. The forest was too quiet, the moon too high, casting long, jagged shadows across the clearing where his small, solitary tent sat.

He stared into the dim glow of his camping lantern, trying to focus on anything but the oppressive silence that seemed to close in on him from all sides. The fire outside had died hours ago, leaving him in the darkness with nothing but his own thoughts for company.

Suddenly, a noise cut through the silence like a knife. A rustling, faint at first, but unmistakable. Adrian's heart leaped into his throat. His spine stiffened. The sound wasn't distant—no, it was close. Too close. Right outside the tent.

Something's out there.

His breath caught in his chest as the realization hit him. He swallowed hard, trying to moisten his suddenly dry throat, but it felt like his heart was pounding in his mouth, his pulse erratic.

"What the hell... what the *hell* was that?"

His whisper barely broke the suffocating stillness. The rustling continued, the sound of something—or someone—moving just beyond the thin canvas walls of his shelter. His fingers twitched toward his knife, the cold steel lying uselessly beside him. He wanted to reach for it, to clutch it like a lifeline, but his hand hovered, paralyzed in fear.

Get it together. Come on! You're being paranoid. There's nothing out there. Nothing.

But then, the shadow appeared. Faint at first, just a dark, indistinct blur against the canvas. His heart stopped. The shape shifted, stretched, moving closer. His breath came in shallow, rapid gasps now, a wild panic bubbling up from somewhere deep inside him.

No, no, no... what is that?

He bit his lip hard enough to draw blood, hoping the sting would snap him out of his terror. But the shadow kept moving. It was deliberate now, slow and methodical, like it was *hunting*. His mind raced, trying to make sense of the figure, but the more he stared, the less human it seemed. The outline was wrong—too tall, too thin, limbs that moved unnaturally.

Adrian's hands balled into fists, his knuckles white with the strain. He could feel his heartbeat hammering in his ears, so loud he thought for sure whatever was outside could hear it too. Every instinct screamed at him to get up, to burst out of the tent, to confront whatever was lurking beyond the canvas walls—but his body refused to obey.

What if it's dangerous? What if it's waiting for you to come out?

His mind betrayed him, feeding him visions of monstrous shapes, unseen predators just beyond the veil of night. He clenched his eyes shut for a moment, willing the thoughts away, but when he opened them again, the shadow was gone.

For a second, hope flickered inside him.

Maybe it's gone. Maybe it was nothing at all.

But then, the scratching began.

A soft, deliberate scraping sound against the side of the tent. Slow, persistent, like fingernails dragging against fabric. The sound sent a jolt of electricity down his spine, every hair on the back of his neck standing on end. His stomach churned with nausea.

"Oh God... oh no."

He couldn't help the words from tumbling out, his voice a shaky whisper. He needed to do something—anything—but his body remained frozen, as if the fear had rooted him to the spot. His eyes darted to the zipper of the tent, his mind racing with the possibilities of what lay just beyond it.

Do I unzip it? Do I look? What if it's waiting for me?

Sweat slicked his palms despite the frigid air. He knew he should grab his knife, his flashlight, something—but his limbs wouldn't cooperate. His brain screamed at him to move, to do something, but the fear was too powerful, a heavy weight pressing down on his chest.

The scraping grew louder, more insistent. It moved from one side of the tent to the other, circling him like a predator sizing up its prey. His mouth was dry, his throat tight, but still, he couldn't make a sound.

Please... just go away.

The shadow reappeared, larger now, looming over the thin fabric of the tent. It was closer this time, the outline sharper, more defined. He could see the long, spindly limbs, the unnatural angle of the joints as they moved.

Adrian's breath hitched. He felt lightheaded, like the air was being sucked out of his lungs. He tried to steady himself, tried to push the terror down long enough to think clearly, but the scratching was relentless. It was inhuman, like claws dragging across the canvas, slow and deliberate.

It knows I'm in here. It knows.

A sudden, sharp sound—a twig snapping underfoot—made his heart leap into his throat. The shadow paused for a moment, as if listening, and then began to move again, this time with purpose. The scraping turned to tapping, like knuckles rapping against the fabric, growing louder and more frantic with each passing second.

Adrian's mind raced. He had to do something—he couldn't just sit there, waiting for whatever was out there to make the next move. He had to act.

But what if it's a person? What if it's just someone lost in the woods?

His rational mind tried to latch onto the idea, but deep down, he knew better. No human moved like that. No human cast a shadow that made his skin crawl with revulsion.

The tapping grew louder, more aggressive, as if whatever was out there was losing patience. Adrian could feel his heart pounding in his chest, a wild, uncontrollable rhythm that made his vision swim. He had to do something. He had to—

The zipper of the tent began to move.

Adrian's breath hitched in his throat, his entire body going rigid with terror. The metal teeth of the zipper began to part, slowly, agonizingly, as if whatever was outside was toying with him, savoring his fear. The cold night air rushed in through the widening gap, carrying with it the scent of damp earth and something else—something foul, like rotting meat.

No, no, no, no!

He wanted to scream, to shout, but the sound wouldn't come. His throat was tight, his mouth dry. All he could do was watch in horror as the zipper continued to slide down, inch by inch, exposing more of the darkness outside.

Move! You have to move!

But he couldn't. His body was locked in place, paralyzed by the sheer, overwhelming terror that gripped him. His mind raced, his thoughts a chaotic jumble of fear and panic, but his body refused to obey.

Then, the zipper stopped.

The silence that followed was deafening. Adrian held his breath, his heart pounding so hard he thought it might burst from his chest. The opening of the tent was now wide enough for something to slip inside, but nothing happened.

Is it gone? Did it leave?

He couldn't bring himself to look, couldn't bear to turn his head and see what might be lurking just outside the tent. Every instinct screamed at him to close the zipper, to seal himself back inside the flimsy shelter, but his hands remained frozen at his sides.

And then, slowly, something began to push its way through the opening.

It was small at first—a hand, or what looked like a hand. Thin, bony fingers curled around the edge of the tent, the skin pale and sickly, almost translucent in the faint moonlight. The fingers twitched, flexing as they gripped the fabric, and then another hand appeared, followed by a head.

Adrian's breath caught in his throat as he stared at the thing crawling into his tent. Its face was wrong—unnatural. The skin was stretched too tight over the bones, the eyes sunken deep into their sockets, black and hollow. It didn't blink, didn't breathe. Its mouth hung open, a gaping hole that oozed a dark, viscous liquid that dripped onto the floor of the tent with a sickening splatter.

Oh God... oh God, no.

He wanted to scream, wanted to run, but his body remained frozen, locked in place by the sheer, overwhelming terror that gripped him. The thing continued to crawl closer, its movements slow and deliberate, as if it had all the time in the world.

The smell hit him then—thick and pungent, like decay and death. His stomach lurched, bile rising in his throat, but he swallowed it down, his body too numb to do anything but tremble in silent horror.

The creature's eyes—or the empty pits where its eyes should have been—locked onto him, and for the first time, Adrian felt a surge of cold, primal fear. This thing wasn't human. It wasn't even close.

It reached for him, its fingers outstretched, the long, bony digits twitching as they neared his skin.

Move! For the love of God, MOVE...

Adrian's heart thudded so violently in his chest that he was sure it would explode. His breath came in ragged gasps, shallow and frantic as he watched the thin zipper of his tent slowly edge down. The shadowy figure outside was there—creeping, deliberate, its long fingers testing the canvas of the tent, pushing, probing like it was seeking a weakness.

Move! Do something!

His mind screamed at him to act, but his body was a prisoner of his fear. He could feel his pulse roaring in his ears, the sound of it louder than the frantic rasp of the zipper. His knuckles were white as his hands gripped the sleeping bag, holding it against him like a shield. He swallowed hard, trying to breathe, but it felt like there wasn't enough air in the world to fill his lungs.

Then, as suddenly as it had begun, the zipper stopped.

The hand—those twisted, spindly fingers—disappeared from sight. Silence. Only the soft rustling of wind through the trees and the distant sound of the forest filled the air. The thing, whatever it was, had stopped.

Is it gone?

For a moment, Adrian felt the crushing weight of terror lift slightly. He could still hear the faint rustle outside, the unmistakable shuffle of something moving, but it wasn't coming toward him anymore. The shadow shifted, moving away from the tent's entrance. His breath hitched, a small fragment of hope breaking through the oppressive fear.

He stayed perfectly still, his mind racing. *What was that?* His body was frozen, his muscles coiled so tightly that he thought he might snap at any moment. The moments dragged on like hours, each second stretching into an eternity.

The shadow was still there, moving. Not gone. *No. Not yet.*

Adrian felt the pressure inside his chest release, like a dam breaking under the weight of fear. He sucked in a breath, but the air tasted stale, his lungs still tight. The shadow outside shifted, slow, deliberate, as if it were considering its next move. His ears strained, catching every rustle of the trees, every crunch of leaves beneath its feet. *It's leaving... right?*

The weight of dread hung thick in the air. It was too quiet—unnaturally so. No birds, no insects. Just the sound of his own ragged breath and the faint shuffle of that thing outside. Adrian's body ached, cramped from sitting frozen for so long, but he still couldn't move. Not yet. *What if it's still there?*

His mind clawed at the possibilities. *What if it knows you're here? What if it's waiting?*

"Maybe it's gone..." He whispered it to himself, more a hope than a truth. His body, still humming with fear, didn't believe it.

A chill rolled down his spine, raising every hair on his arms. He forced himself to inch forward, his hand brushing against the cold metal of his flashlight, though his knuckles trembled with the thought of shining it outside. *What if I see something I don't want to?* His breath hitched, the flashlight heavy in his hands, the air stifling inside the tent.

Check. Just check. He needed to know. He couldn't stay trapped here forever.

Adrian crept closer to the zipper, his fingers gingerly grasping the edge. His heart pounded so hard it shook his entire body. Slowly, achingly slow, he pulled it open just a fraction—enough for his eyes to peer through.

God help me.

At first, he saw nothing but the still, dark trees swaying in the pale moonlight. His breath came quicker, shallow and uneven. The shadow... it was gone. The clearing around his tent was still. Quiet.

Maybe I was imagining it...

But then, movement. A slight shift in the distance. His eyes locked onto the source—a figure, hunched over by a large rock, moving slowly, methodically.

What the hell?

Adrian's heart stopped in his throat. The figure was human—or at least, it seemed human. They moved with a strange jerkiness, like their limbs weren't fully under control. Pale, gaunt, and dressed in tattered, oversized clothing that hung from a bony frame. Whoever—or whatever—it was, digging in the dirt, muttering to itself.

The moonlight caught its face, and Adrian's stomach twisted. The figure's face was gaunt and skeletal, their eyes hollow and wild, darting in frantic movements as they scratched at the ground like a starved animal. Their fingers—long, thin, almost claw-like—dug into the dirt with a sickening intensity.

What is wrong with it?

Adrian swallowed hard, his throat dry. His breath caught, and he instinctively pulled back from the opening, but not before the figure's head snapped up. Their eyes—huge, white, and feverish—locked onto his tent, staring directly at him. A twisted grin spread across their face, a grotesque mimicry of a smile, teeth yellowed and uneven. The sight sent a bolt of ice through his veins.

No... no, no, no...

The figure rose to its feet, stumbling slightly, their movements shaky. They clutched a small, rusted knife in one trembling hand. Adrian's eyes widened as they took a slow, deliberate step toward him, the knife catching the faint moonlight, its surface dull and stained.

He scrambled backward, his heart slamming into his ribs. "What... the hell... do I do?" His voice was barely a whisper, a broken plea to no one. His hands fumbled for the knife he had left beside him, his mind spinning in a whirlwind of panic.

It's just a thief. A weak, desperate thief.

But deep down, he knew something was wrong. The way they moved. The way their eyes gleamed, feverish, like they hadn't slept in days. Like they weren't entirely human anymore. The grin on their face was too wide, too forced. Their steps—staggered, uneven—didn't match the eerie calm of their expression. Something was **off**.

The figure lurched forward again, their body shaking violently as they raised the knife higher. "Found it... found it... can't leave without it..." Their voice was hoarse, strained, as if they had been screaming for hours. Adrian's hands shook, gripping his knife tighter.

"What the hell are you talking about?!" he whispered, his voice cracking. **What do you want from me?**

The figure stopped, his head tilting unnaturally to the side, like they were trying to listen to something that wasn't there. His lips moved, but the words were nothing but broken murmurs. Then, without warning, they started laughing—high-pitched, frantic laughter that sent a shiver crawling up Adrian's spine.

"I have to... have to take it... or else..." The figure took another step, his wide eyes unblinking, his grin widening further. "You have it... you have what I need..."

Adrian's mind raced. His pulse thundered in his ears, drowning out every other sound. He wanted to scream, to run, but he couldn't. His body was frozen, pinned down by a terror that gripped him tighter than a vice.

The figure was closer now. Too close. He could see the way their skin stretched over their bones, pale and bruised. Their breath came in ragged, shallow gasps, and their eyes were wild with a hunger he couldn't understand.

"I... I don't have anything!" Adrian's voice trembled, barely audible. He could feel the sweat trickling down the back of his neck, his entire body trembling uncontrollably.

But the figure didn't stop. His grin twisted into something darker, their breath hitching with each uneven step. "You do... you took it... and I need it back."

Adrian's blood ran cold. **What the hell is he talking about?** His mind scrambled for answers, but none came. He had nothing—nothing that could explain this madness. His knuckles were white as he gripped the knife tighter, his mind screaming at him to act, to move, to do anything but sit there frozen in terror.

The figure's hand twitched, the knife trembling in his grasp as he lifted it higher, the blade glinting under the pale moonlight. "Give it back..."

Adrian's breath caught in his throat, his vision swimming. **I can't... I can't just let this happen!**

In a desperate surge of adrenaline, he lunged forward, brandishing the knife in front of him. His voice came out in a raw, desperate shout. "Stay back! I don't have anything!"

For a split second, the figure froze, his eyes flicking to the blade in Adrian's hand. The grin faltered, just for a moment. But then it returned, wider than before, his laughter echoing through the night like a broken record.

"You don't understand... it's not yours..." His voice was low, almost a whisper. "It's never been yours..."

Adrian's pulse spiked. The figure took another step, his hand reaching out, fingers trembling. "It belongs to me..."

Him? Adrian's mind reeled. The words made no sense. He wanted to yell, to demand answers, but his voice was gone, strangled by the rising panic. The figure's eyes bore into his, wide and gleaming, their hand now just inches away.

Suddenly, he stopped, her body shuddering violently. Their grin faltered, the wild light in their eyes dimming. For a moment, they just stood there, shaking, their breath ragged and shallow.

Then, without a word, they turned and staggered away, their form disappearing into the trees, leaving Adrian alone in the silence.

He collapsed back into the tent, his entire body trembling. His breath came in gasps, his mind spinning in a haze of fear and confusion. The knife slipped from his hand, clattering to the ground as he struggled to process what had just happened.

His pulse was still pounding in his ears, the terror still clinging to him like a second skin. The thief—or whatever they had been—was gone. But the dread remained, thick and suffocating.

And in the stillness of the night, Adrian couldn't shake the feeling that something far worse was watching from the shadows.

Adrian staggered back into his tent, his heart still racing from the chilling encounter with the thief. The moonlight streamed through the thin fabric, casting eerie shadows that danced on the walls, but all he could see was that twisted grin, the wild eyes staring back at him. *What the hell was that?* He shivered, the memory of the thief clawing at his mind like a predator hungry for flesh.

This place is insane.

He clenched his fists, forcing himself to breathe slowly, to regain control. But the pounding of his heart was relentless, echoing in his ears like the thrumming of some primal drum. He had nearly forgotten his own surroundings when he heard it—Alex's voice cutting through the stillness of the night.

"Adrian! Adrian! Are you in there?"

He shot up, his breath hitching in his throat. "Alex!" he called out, scrambling to unzip the tent. The last thing he wanted was to face the thief again, but the relief of hearing a young man's voice made his heart race for a different reason now. *Maybe he'll know what to do.*

The zipper pulled down, and he stumbled outside, blinking against the sudden brightness of the moonlit clearing. There was Alex, standing a few feet away, panting and looking ruffled, but triumphant. He held a small, ragged figure in a headlock—none other than the very thief that had terrorized Adrian just moments ago.

"Look what I found!" Alex exclaimed, a mix of exhilaration and disbelief in his voice.

Adrian's breath caught as he took in the sight before him. The thief was still twitching, their limbs trembling as they squirmed against Alex's grip, clearly caught off-guard. The wildness in their eyes was still there, but now it was mingled with fear and desperation. Adrian was also confused, *Why did Alex come in themed of the night while Adrian had instructed him to come at tomorrow's day?* but it didn't matter right now for him, as he stood infront of the desperate thief.

"Get off me!" the thief rasped, struggling weakly against Alex's hold. "Let me go! I didn't mean any harm!"

"What the hell happened?" Adrian asked, his mind racing. "How did you catch him?"

Alex grinned, eyes gleaming. "I was out scouting the perimeter after I landed here, hours earlier than you had instructed me. I just thought it would be better to arrive earlier than postponing a work. Then I heard some rustling and saw the guy creeping around your stuff." He tightened his grip slightly, but not enough to hurt. "I didn't want to scare him off, so I waited for the right moment. Then I jumped him!"

Adrian couldn't help but laugh, relief flooding through him. "You actually tackled him?"

"Yeah!" Alex chuckled, the adrenaline still coursing through his veins. "It was a bit reckless, but he didn't see it coming. I just lunged forward and slammed into him, knocked him right into the dirt. Thought he might take off, but he just... flopped around like a fish!"

Adrian shook his head, half in disbelief, half in admiration. "And he's really not a monster?"

"Nope, just a scared thief," Alex said, glancing down at the thief, who was still trying to wriggle free. "I think he's just desperate. Maybe he saw our camp as an easy target, but now... well, it seems he's more scared than dangerous."

The thief, still caught in Alex's grip, looked up with wide, pleading eyes. "Please! I'm sorry! I didn't mean to frighten anyone!" They stuttered, their voice shaking. "I just needed to eat!"

Adrian frowned, his mind racing with conflicting thoughts. The thief looked even worse up close—eyes sunken, skin stretched tight over bones, clothes filthy and torn. He felt a pang of sympathy mixed with caution.

"What were you doing out here?" Adrian asked, his voice steady. "Did you think you could just break in and take something?"

"Please, just let me explain!" The thief's voice was almost a whimper, desperation creeping in. "I've been wandering these woods for days. I didn't mean to scare you. I... I thought you might have food, and I didn't want to hurt anyone. Just let me go, and I'll never come back!"

Adrian exchanged a glance with Alex. The wildness in the thief's eyes was unsettling, but there was also something raw and real. It was a look he recognized—the kind of look that came from being lost, hungry, and frightened.

"What's your name?" Adrian asked, feeling the weight of the moment settle around him.

"Wren," the thief said, their voice trembling as they tried to look up at him. "Please, I swear I won't cause any trouble. Just let me go. I promise I won't come back here!"

Adrian felt the remnants of fear mixing with a deep sense of compassion. He glanced back at Alex, who still held the thief firmly, but with a softer grip now.

"What do you think?" Alex asked, his brow furrowed with thought. "We can't just let him go, can we? What if he comes back?"

Adrian shook his head, feeling the conflict raging inside him. *But what if he's telling the truth?* "I don't know... maybe we can help him? He looks like he's barely hanging on."

"What? Are you kidding?" Alex's eyes widened in disbelief. "He just tried to rob us!"

"Yeah, but he's not a monster. He's just... desperate." Adrian stepped closer, still cautious, but feeling a strange urge to reach out. "We can't just toss him aside. We should at least hear him out."

Wren looked up, hope flickering in their eyes. "Please... I just need a little food. I won't steal again, I promise."

Adrian took a deep breath, glancing around the clearing. The night was still, the air thick with tension and unspoken words. "How about this? We'll let you go, but you have to promise to leave us alone. No more sneaking around. Just tell us where you've been, and we'll give you some food."

Wren nodded vigorously, relief flooding their features. "Thank you! Thank you so much! I promise—I won't come back! Just please, let me eat something."

"Alright," Adrian said, steeling himself. "But you have to promise not to lie to us. If we help you, you need to be honest."

"I swear!" Wren exclaimed, voice earnest. "I haven't eaten in days. I'll tell you everything. Just let me go."

Alex hesitated, still holding the thief tightly. "You sure about this, Adrian?"

"Yeah," Adrian said, his resolve hardening. "Let him go. We'll get him some food."

With a reluctant nod, Alex loosened his grip and released Wren, who stumbled backward, eyes wide with gratitude and surprise. The thief fell to the ground, breathless, looking like a shaken bird ready to take flight.

"Thank you! Thank you!" Wren stammered, hands raised in surrender. "I won't forget this!"

"Just stay where you are," Adrian warned, his voice steady. "We'll get you some food."

As Adrian turned, he felt the adrenaline still coursing through his veins, a mix of relief and lingering fear. He glanced back at Wren, who was now sitting on the ground, trembling but looking hopeful. "Just... don't run off, alright? We want to help, but we can't if you disappear."

Wren nodded fervently, their eyes wide. "I promise, I won't run away."

Adrian led the way back to his tent, Alex following close behind, still glancing over his shoulder at the thief. Inside, Adrian rummaged through their supplies, his heart racing with the unusual act of kindness. He found some granola bars and a few cans of beans, things that would provide a bit of nourishment without putting their camp in jeopardy.

"Here," he said, turning back to Wren, who watched with wide, hungry eyes. "This should help."

Wren's fingers trembled as they accepted the food, their face lighting up with a mix of disbelief and gratitude. "You're... really giving this to me? Thank you! Thank you so much!"

"Just eat it," Adrian said, feeling a surge of warmth mixed with caution. "But tell us how you ended up out here."

Wren nodded, tearing into the granola bar with desperate fingers. "I... I got lost in the woods," they stuttered between bites. "I thought I could find my way back, but I couldn't. It's been days. I was trying to find anything to eat. I didn't mean to scare you. I didn't mean to sneak around. I thought you were camping and had food. I was just so hungry."

Adrian watched, torn between pity and caution. "How did you end up lost? Did you come out here alone?"

"I was with a friend, but we got separated during a hike," Wren explained, their voice trembling. "I thought I could follow the trail, but everything looks the same. I ran out of food... then I just kept walking. I thought I would find help."

Alex leaned against a nearby tree, arms crossed, still eyeing Wren suspiciously. "And you thought stealing from us was the answer?"

"I was desperate! I swear! I didn't know what else to do!" Wren pleaded, their eyes wide and desperate. "I'm not a bad person. I just... I just made a mistake."

Adrian felt the conflict inside him simmering. "You could have just asked."

"I was afraid!" Wren said, voice rising with frustration. "I didn't think you'd want to help me! I thought you'd just chase me away or call the cops! People don't want to help anymore, you know?"

The words hung heavy in the air, and Adrian felt a pang of empathy, recognizing the truth in Wren's voice. The world was a harsh place, and desperation often drove people to do terrible things. He glanced at Alex, who seemed torn, watching Wren with a mixture of wariness and concern.

"What now?" Alex finally asked, breaking the silence.

Adrian sighed, feeling the weight of the decision pressing on his shoulders. "Let's give him some food and then figure out what to do. We can't just leave him out here."

Alex nodded slowly, still uncertain. "But what if he comes back? What if he tells others?"

"He won't," Adrian insisted. "He knows what he did was wrong. Besides, if we're careful, we can keep this quiet. We just need to help him get on his feet."

Wren looked up, eyes shining with a mixture of fear and gratitude. "I promise I won't come back. I just need a chance to get home. Please, I don't want trouble."

Adrian felt the knot in his stomach loosen a bit. "Alright, let's figure this out. We'll help you, but you have to promise us you'll be honest. No tricks."

"I promise!" Wren exclaimed, relief flooding their features. "I'll do whatever you say. I just want to get out of here."

Adrian nodded, feeling the weight of the decision settle. "Okay, let's get you some more food and find a way to get you back on your feet."

As they prepared to help Wren, Adrian felt a sense of resolve wash over him. *Sometimes, kindness was the hardest thing to give, especially in a world that seemed so dark.*

And as the moon shone down on their small gathering, he realized they were all just trying to survive, to find their way in a world that often felt lost.

The journey to help Wren had just begun, but in that moment, they were united by a shared struggle—an unexpected bond formed from desperation and the faint glimmer of hope.

Adrian watched as Alex retreated to his ready-made tent, its neat, organized structure standing out against the rugged terrain. The sky was blanketed in deep, inky blackness, and the only source of light now was the faint glow from the lantern inside Adrian's tent. The night had been exhausting, but there was still a lingering tension in the air, a kind of unresolved energy that crackled between them.

Adrian glanced at Wren, who was seated inside the tent, looking a little less haunted now but still weary, his eyes reflecting a mix of uncertainty and exhaustion. The strange thief who had once been an unsettling figure now seemed like a shell of that fearsome presence, replaced by someone raw and vulnerable.

Alex, with a casual nod and a yawn, zipped his tent shut. "I'll catch you both in the morning. Don't stay up too late, huh?" His voice was light, teasing, but Adrian could hear the weariness underneath. The day had been long, and Alex was clearly spent.

"Yeah, sure," Adrian replied, though his mind wasn't quite ready for sleep. His nerves were still on edge after everything that had happened.

Once Alex had disappeared behind his tent's walls, Adrian turned his attention fully to Wren. The dim glow of the lantern softened the sharp lines of Wren's face, casting flickering shadows that seemed to dance as the flame wavered.

"So," Adrian started, his voice quiet but firm, "I think it's time you told me everything. The full story. No half-truths, no dodging."

Wren swallowed, his hands clasping tightly in his lap as if holding himself together. The young man was a mixture of nerves and tension, and for a moment, he didn't respond. He just sat there, staring at the ground.

Adrian, sensing Wren's hesitation, leaned forward. "Listen, I'm not going to judge you. I just need to understand. You're safe here, but if you want to stick with us, you've got to trust me."

Wren looked up slowly, meeting Adrian's eyes. His voice came out low and shaky at first. "You really want to know? All of it?"

Adrian nodded, his expression unwavering. "All of it. No holding back."

Wren sighed, his shoulders sagging as if the weight of his past was pressing down on him. He stared at the lantern for a moment, watching the flame flicker. Then, after a long pause, he spoke.

"I wasn't always like this. You know... scared and desperate." He rubbed his hands together, trying to warm himself. "I was just like you guys once. Normal, excited about life, about the future. I had a good friend... his name was Ethan. We used to plan these trips, just like the one you're on right now."

Wren's voice softened, and Adrian could hear the pain creeping into his words. "We planned this hiking trip for months. We'd been talking about it forever. It was supposed to be an escape, a way to clear our heads and get away from everything for a while."

He glanced up, his eyes glassy as memories flooded back. "Ethan and I had this dream of going on this crazy adventure. We picked this spot—a hilly area that was supposed to have some great trails. We heard about the forests, about how beautiful it was, and it just felt... right. Like the kind of place where we could get lost in nature and find ourselves."

Adrian listened intently, leaning back slightly as Wren continued.

"We set out early in the morning, backpacks full of supplies, spirits high. We were laughing, joking, not a care in the world. The first day was perfect. The trails were easy to follow, the weather was great, and we were having the time of our lives." Wren paused, his voice hitching slightly. "But things changed fast."

Adrian frowned, his mind already racing ahead to where the story might be going. "What happened?"

Wren looked down at his hands, his knuckles turning white as he clenched his fingers. "We made a wrong turn. Somewhere along the way, we went off the trail. At first, we didn't even realize it. The forest looked the same, and we thought we'd just find our way back eventually. But we didn't. We kept walking, thinking we'd recognize something, but nothing was familiar."

Adrian could feel the fear building in Wren's voice as he spoke. "The further we went, the more lost we became. We tried to stay calm, but you could feel the panic creeping in. It started getting dark, and we hadn't seen anyone for hours. The trail markers were gone, and we had no idea where we were."

Wren's voice grew quieter, more distant. "That night, we decided to camp. Ethan said we'd figure it out in the morning, that we just needed to get some rest. But when I woke up... he was gone."

Adrian's heart skipped a beat. "Gone? Just like that?"

Wren nodded, his expression pained. "I don't know what happened. I don't know if he wandered off, if he went looking for help, or if something... else happened. But when I woke up, I was alone. His stuff was still there, but he was gone. No tracks, no sign of where he went."

The air in the tent felt heavy, like the weight of Wren's words was filling the space between them.

"I searched for him for days," Wren continued, his voice cracking slightly. "I called out, I looked everywhere, but there was no sign of him. Eventually, I ran out of food, out of energy. I was just... lost."

Adrian swallowed hard, trying to imagine the sheer terror Wren must have felt. "That's when you found us?"

Wren nodded again, his face tight with emotion. "I didn't know what else to do. I saw your camp, and I thought maybe you could help, but I was too afraid. I didn't want to come off as crazy or dangerous. So... I tried to take some food. It was stupid. I know that now."

Adrian sat in silence for a moment, letting Wren's story sink in. The fear, the desperation, it all made sense now. Wren wasn't just some petty thief; he was someone who had been pushed to the brink by fear and loss.

"I get it," Adrian said softly. "You were just trying to survive."

Wren looked up at him, eyes filled with a mix of gratitude and shame. "I didn't mean to scare you. I just... I didn't know what else to do."

Adrian nodded, his expression thoughtful. "It's okay. You're here now, and we're going to figure this out."

Wren's face softened, a flicker of hope in his eyes. "What happens now?"

Adrian hesitated for a moment, considering his next words carefully. Then, with a deep breath, he made his decision. "Well, here's the thing. We're here on an adventure of our own. We're trying to uncover some mysteries in this area. It's... complicated, but we could use someone like you. Someone who knows the terrain, who's been out here and understands how to navigate."

Wren blinked, clearly caught off guard. "You want me to help?"

"Yeah," Adrian said, his voice firm. "We're a small team, but having you with us could be a game-changer. You've been through a lot, and I think you could handle whatever's out there better than most people. Plus, it's a chance to do something more than just survive. It's a chance to find answers."

Wren looked stunned, his mouth opening and closing as if he wasn't sure what to say. "I... I don't know. I'm not sure if I'm ready for that."

Adrian leaned in, his gaze steady. "Listen, Wren. You survived out here for days on your own. You made it through something most people wouldn't have. That takes guts. You're stronger than you think, and right now, we could use someone like you."

Wren looked down, his mind clearly racing. After a long moment of silence, he finally nodded. "Okay. I'll do it. I'll join you."

Adrian smiled, feeling a sense of satisfaction. "Good. Welcome to the team."

Wren managed a small smile, though it was clear he was still processing everything. "Thanks. I won't let you down."

"I know you won't," Adrian said, standing up and stretching. "But for now, let's get some sleep. Tomorrow's going to be a long day."

Wren nodded, pulling the blanket closer around himself as he lay back down. "Yeah, sleep sounds good."

Wren's eyes fluttered shut as exhaustion finally overtook him. The warmth of Adrian's tent, the sound of the quiet forest outside, and the faint rhythm of his own heartbeat lulled him into a deep, dream-filled sleep.

And then, it began.

IN THE DREAM, WREN was no longer the ragged, desperate figure lost in the woods. Instead, he was strong, confident, standing tall alongside the others—his new crew. The scene around him was alive with vibrant colours and the hum of adventure. They were on a high ridge, overlooking a sprawling forest below, the horizon painted in shades of gold and orange from the setting sun. The air was crisp, filled with the scent of pine and damp earth, and a sense of excitement buzzed through the group like electricity.

Adrian stood beside him, a determined glint in his eyes. Alex was just behind them, already checking his gear, his ever-present smirk on his face. George, Ria, and Emma were ahead, mapping out the trail, their voices filled with enthusiasm as they discussed the next steps of their journey.

Wren felt a surge of energy pulse through him. They were a team now—a real team—and they were about to solve a mystery that had haunted the hills for generations.

"Alright, team," Adrian called out, his voice cutting through the cool evening air. "We've come this far. The last clue pointed to the caves just beyond that ridge. If we can make it before nightfall, we should be able to set up camp and start our investigation."

Wren grinned, his heart racing with anticipation. *We're doing it. We're actually doing it.*

Emma, always the practical one, glanced up from the map she was holding. "We'll need to move fast, though. That ridge is steep, and I don't want us caught in the dark without a plan."

George, ever the optimist, shrugged. "Come on, it's not that bad. We've handled worse. Remember that storm last week? This'll be a breeze compared to that."

"Yeah, well, this isn't just about getting over a ridge," Ria chimed in, her eyes narrowing as she peered into the distance. "Something's out there. We all feel it. The closer we get to the caves, the more... off things seem."

Wren exchanged a glance with Adrian, feeling a flicker of unease. *She's right. Something's different here.*

But the thrill of the mystery kept his spirits high. "Whatever's out there, we're ready for it," Wren said, surprising even himself with the confidence in his voice. "We've come too far to turn back now."

Adrian clapped him on the shoulder, a grin spreading across his face. "That's the spirit. We've got this."

Together, they pressed forward, moving swiftly along the narrow trail that wound up the rocky ridge. The sun dipped lower, casting long shadows over the landscape, but the team's energy never faltered. Wren could feel the anticipation building with each step, like they were on the verge of discovering something monumental.

The ridge was steep, just as Emma had warned, but they climbed it with ease, their movements fluid and coordinated, like they had been working together for years. The bond between them was strong, and Wren felt a deep sense of belonging, something he hadn't experienced in a long time.

As they reached the top, the caves came into view—dark, ominous openings in the rock face, their jagged edges glowing faintly in the last light of the day. A shiver ran down Wren's spine, but it wasn't fear. It was excitement.

"This is it," Alex said, his voice low but charged with anticipation. "The caves. We're close."

Adrian nodded, his eyes locked on the entrance. "Stay sharp, everyone. We don't know what we'll find inside, but whatever it is, it's the key to solving this mystery."

They descended toward the caves, the atmosphere around them growing heavier with each step. The trees at the base of the ridge seemed taller, their branches twisted in unnatural shapes, casting eerie shadows across the ground. But the team was undeterred.

When they finally reached the mouth of the largest cave, Wren felt his heart pounding in his chest. The air was cooler here, and the faint sound of wind echoed from deep within the cave's tunnels. It felt like the entire forest was holding its breath, waiting for them to make the next move.

Adrian turned to the group, his voice steady. "Alright, let's split up. We'll cover more ground that way. Wren, you're with me. Alex, take George and Emma. Ria, keep an eye on the entrance. If anything looks out of the ordinary, signal us."

Ria nodded, her eyes sharp and focused as she took her position at the cave's entrance.

Wren swallowed the lump in his throat, adrenaline coursing through him. *This is it. We're going in.*

Adrian led the way into the cave, his flashlight cutting through the darkness, illuminating the rough stone walls. Wren followed close behind, his own flashlight in hand, the beam dancing over the rock formations. The further they went, the quieter the outside world became, until all they could hear was the sound of their footsteps echoing through the cave.

"This place is huge," Wren whispered, his voice hushed in the cavernous space. "How are we supposed to find anything in here?"

Adrian glanced back at him, his eyes gleaming in the dim light. "We follow the clues. Stay close."

As they ventured deeper into the cave, Wren couldn't shake the feeling that they were being watched. It was as if the walls themselves were alive, pulsing with the energy of the mystery they were about to uncover. But despite the eerie atmosphere, Wren felt a surge of excitement. This was what he had always wanted—an adventure, a purpose.

Suddenly, Adrian stopped, his flashlight illuminating a strange set of markings on the wall. "Here," he said, his voice tense with anticipation. "This is it. This is what we've been looking for."

Wren moved closer, his eyes widening as he took in the symbols etched into the stone. They were ancient, worn by time, but there was no mistaking their significance. They had found something—something big.

"What does it mean?" Wren asked, his heart racing.

Adrian studied the markings for a moment, his brow furrowed in concentration. "It's a map. Or at least, part of one. Look—this symbol here, it matches the one we found on that old artifact last week."

Wren's excitement bubbled over. "So, we're on the right track. This is the key, isn't it?"

Adrian nodded, his eyes bright with determination. "Yeah. It's all connected. If we can decode this, we'll know exactly where to go next."

Wren felt a surge of pride. He had become a part of something bigger, something extraordinary. Together, they were solving a mystery that had stumped others for generations. He couldn't wait to see what they would discover next.

Suddenly, a sharp whistle echoed from the entrance of the cave. It was Ria's signal.

Adrian's eyes snapped toward the entrance, his expression serious. "Something's happening. We need to go."

Without hesitation, they turned and sprinted back toward the entrance, their flashlights bouncing off the walls as they ran. Wren's heart pounded in his chest, not with fear, but with exhilaration. They were on the verge of something incredible, and nothing was going to stop them.

As they reached the cave's entrance, Ria was standing there, her eyes wide with excitement. "You guys need to see this."

Wren followed Adrian out of the cave, his breath catching in his throat as he saw what Ria was pointing to.

The sky above the forest was glowing, a strange, ethereal light shimmering in the distance. It was unlike anything Wren had ever seen before—otherworldly, mesmerizing.

"This is it," Adrian said, his voice filled with awe. "This is what we've been searching for."

Wren felt a thrill run through him. They were on the brink of an incredible discovery, and he was right there with them—part of the team, part of the adventure. Together, they would uncover the truth behind the mystery, and nothing would stand in their way.

WREN'S EYES FLUTTERED open as the dream faded, the cool morning air drifting into the tent. For a moment, he lay there, the excitement of the dream still coursing through him. He had felt alive in that dream—part of something bigger than himself, part of a team.

As he sat up, the reality of the day settled in, but there was a renewed sense of purpose in his chest. The dream had felt so real, so vivid, and he couldn't help but feel that it was a sign of things to come.

He wasn't just some lost hiker anymore. He was part of something bigger now, part of a crew with a mission. And together, they were going to solve the mystery—whatever it took.

Wren laid still in the tent, his heart was racing from the dream he had just woken from. The vividness of it lingered—Adrian, Alex, Ria, George, and Emma by his side, solving mysteries and facing the unknown with courage. For the first time in what felt like forever, he wasn't alone, and the weight of his isolation seemed to lift from his chest. *I'm not that guy anymore*, he thought, his fingers absentmindedly tracing the edge of the blanket. *I'm part of something now.*

The world outside was silent, the night holding its breath, but inside, Wren's mind was alive with energy. His hands, which had once trembled with fear and desperation, were now steady, clenched in determination. He had a purpose now, a path forward. But there was something else stirring in him—something deeper.

"Ethan..." Wren whispered the name of his lost friend, barely loud enough to disturb the quiet. His voice was soft, almost reverent, as if speaking it too loudly might shatter the fragile hope that was growing inside him. *Where are you? Are you still out there somewhere?*

The dream had rekindled a fire inside him, one he thought had long been extinguished by fear. He had been surviving—barely scraping by in the wilderness—but now he was ready for more. He was ready to fight, to uncover the truth, and to find his friend, wherever he might be. *I'm coming for you, Ethan. I'm not giving up.*

He rolled onto his side, staring at the dim glow of the lantern's last flickers, feeling the weight of everything ahead of him. His whisper broke the stillness again, but this time, there was no hesitation in his voice.

"I can do this."

His mind was racing with the possibilities. *I can find Ethan. I can help Adrian and the others. I don't have to be afraid anymore.* The team had given him a lifeline, a sense of belonging he hadn't felt in years. It wasn't just about survival now—it was about redemption. *I'm not the scared, lost guy anymore. I'm going to do this. We're going to solve this mystery.*

He remembered the look on Adrian's face when he had offered him a spot on the team—how serious and confident he had been. Adrian had seen something in him, something worth fighting for, and for the first time, Wren believed it too. *I have a chance to prove myself now. To make up for the mistakes I made.*

Wren's hands tightened into fists. *No more running. No more hiding. This time, I'm going to face whatever comes.* The excitement bubbled up inside him again, that same excitement he had felt in the dream. But now it wasn't just a dream—it was real. And he was ready.

He let out a shaky breath, feeling the tension in his body ease, replaced by a sense of calm focus. "I've got this," he whispered, a small smile playing at the corners of his lips. "I've finally got this."

His thoughts drifted back to the team—Adrian's steady leadership, Alex's quick humor, Ria's sharp instincts, and Emma's practicality. They were strong, capable, and together, they could face whatever was waiting for them. *And now I'm a part of that.* The idea sent a surge of pride through him, something he hadn't felt in a long time. He wasn't just tagging along—he was an important part of this group.

He sat up slightly, the blanket falling from his shoulders, and stared at the faint outlines of the trees through the tent's flap. The darkness outside didn't seem so oppressive now. It felt like the calm before the storm, the quiet moment before something big happened.

"We're going to solve this," he whispered to himself again, as if speaking the words out loud would make them true. "We're going to figure it all out. The mystery, the caves, everything."

But his mind kept circling back to one thing. Ethan. The thought of his friend being out there somewhere, lost and alone, tugged at Wren's heart. He had let Ethan down once, but he wouldn't let it happen again. *I'm going to find you. I don't care how long it takes.*

His voice dropped to a determined murmur. "I'm coming for you, Ethan. Wherever you are."

Wren felt a strange sense of clarity, like everything in his life had been leading up to this moment. The fear that had once clouded his mind was gone, replaced by a burning desire to do something, to make things right.

"I'm not going to stop," he said firmly, his voice stronger now, filled with resolve. "I'll help them solve the mystery, and I'll find you."

He lay back down, but this time there was no nervous energy keeping him awake. His mind was quiet, but focused, every thought aimed at the adventure ahead. The thrill of discovery and the hope of finding his friend were intertwined now, propelling him forward.

"I can't wait for tomorrow," Wren whispered, feeling a smile spread across his face. He closed his eyes, the weight of exhaustion pulling him under again, but this time, his sleep was peaceful.

Because for the first time in a long while, Wren had something to fight for—and this time, he wasn't going to lose.

The first light of dawn crept over the horizon, casting soft golden hues across the campsite. A gentle breeze rustled through the trees, carrying with it the crisp smell of pine and dew-soaked earth. The once quiet and dark forest now seemed to stretch awake, birds chirping lazily as the sun started to bathe everything in warmth.

Wren stirred beneath the blanket, blinking as the sunlight filtered through the canvas of the tent. For a moment, he felt disoriented, the line between his vivid dream and reality blurred. But the warmth on his face and the soft sounds of the morning reminded him where he was. He wasn't lost. He wasn't alone. He was with them.

Adrian, Alex, Ria, George, Emma... The thought of being part of something filled his chest with a sense of belonging, one that felt unfamiliar but good. He smiled to himself, the lingering excitement from the dream still fresh in his mind.

As the camp stirred to life, the sound of zippers being pulled echoed through the clearing. Wren heard the low murmur of voices outside, and before long, Adrian's familiar voice called out.

"Morning, everyone!"

Adrian emerged from his tent, his face lit with the relaxed energy of someone who had slept well. He stretched his arms high above his head, the morning sun catching the edge of his smile. He spotted Wren, who was just crawling out of his tent, blinking against the light.

"Wren! Good Morning!" Adrian called cheerfully, his tone warm. "Sleep alright?"

Wren stood slowly, feeling the cool morning air wrap around him, but the chill wasn't uncomfortable. He nodded, offering a small smile. "Yeah... better than I have in days."

Before Wren could say more, the flap of another tent rustled open. Alex tumbled out of his ready-made tent with his usual swagger, rubbing his eyes groggily. His hair was a wild mess, and he yawned loudly as he stepped into the clearing, oblivious to the soft serenity of the morning.

"What's up, world?" Alex greeted the day like an old friend, his grin already forming as he stretched. Then, his eyes landed on Wren, standing in the middle of the camp, looking much more integrated than the haunted figure they had first encountered.

Alex stopped mid-stretch, his brows raising in surprise. "Well, well, well... look who's up and ready to roll." He shot Wren a grin, clearly pleased. "Feeling like part of the team already, huh?"

Wren chuckled nervously, his hands brushing over his ragged clothes. "Trying to. It feels... different today."

George emerged next, stepping out of his tent with his usual steady calm. He squinted at the sun, stretching his back as if to shake off the stiffness of the night. His gaze fell on Wren, and he offered a nod of acknowledgment.

"Morning, unknown," George greeted with a simple warmth. "Who are you, exactly?"

"Thanks, I'm Wren, and I guess I'm part of the crew now," Wren said, still a bit taken aback by the unexpected warmth he was receiving from everyone. "It's a long story about what happened yesterday—hard to explain right now." His eyes flickered with a hint of mystery, leaving everyone even more curious about how he ended up here.

Emma's tent rustled, and soon enough, she appeared, tucking her wild curls behind her ears as she stepped out into the morning light. She greeted everyone with a wave, her eyes quickly scanning the campsite as she adjusted to the daylight. Her gaze lingered on Wren, and her expression softened.

"Well, look at you," she said, her voice kind but teasing. "Looks like we've got a new morning person among us."

Wren couldn't help but smile at her easy humor. "I guess so."

Ria was the last to emerge, her steps quiet and precise as she stepped into the clearing. She had overheard everything Wren had shared with the others about himself, her curiosity had grown with each word. She took in the scene with her usual sharp eyes, and though she didn't speak right away, she gave Wren a nod of approval, her expression softening as well. "Hey, newbie. Are you feeling alright? Are you ready?"

Wren felt a swell of gratitude and surprise. They were all looking at him differently now—like he belonged. He wasn't just the lost, desperate guy from the night before. He was part of the group. And that realization made something warm spread through his chest.

"I am," Wren said, his voice more confident than he expected. "I'm ready."

The others exchanged glances, smiles spreading across their faces, the unspoken understanding between them thick in the air.

Adrian stepped forward, clapping Wren on the shoulder. "Glad to hear it. Today's the start of something big, and I'm glad you're with us, Wren."

Wren met his gaze, his heart swelling with a mix of excitement and resolve. "So am I."

"Everyone, meet Wren—a new addition to our crew, and from now on, part of this wild journey with us. And as for Alex, well, you probably already know him by now. He joined us just last night at the stroke of midnight, and he's the one who brought Wren in. So, things are about to get even more interesting!"

Everyone let out a collective sigh, some having finally dispelled their lingering doubts about Alex's unexpected return, while others wrestled with their apprehensions regarding the newcomer, Wren.

The morning sun continued to rise, casting the group in a warm, golden light, and for the first time, Wren felt like he was exactly where he was meant to be. Surrounded by the crew, he could hear snippets of their conversations as they prepared for their expedition, a mixture of excitement and trepidation buzzing in the air.

"Have you heard the legends about Xel Island?" one crew member asked, glancing at Adrian with a mix of awe and disbelief.

Adrian, who had been studying a worn map spread out on a makeshift table, looked up. "Legends? You mean the tales of disappearances, strange occurrences, and that whole 'island of shadows' nonsense?"

"Come on, it's not nonsense," the crew member protested, his eyes wide. "What about the stories of explorers who've gone missing? They say the island has a mind of its own!"

Wren leaned in, curiosity piqued. "Is it true? Has anyone really gone missing?"

Adrian sighed, folding his arms as he regarded the younger crew member. "True or not, the stories about Xel have persisted for generations. Explorers, treasure hunters—those who dared to set foot on its shores often didn't return. It's said the island plays with your mind, twisting your fears into reality."

"Twisting fears? What do you mean?" Wren asked, feeling a shiver run down his spine.

"The island is said to be alive in some way," Adrian continued, his voice steady but intense. "It draws people in, feeding on their hopes and dreams. Some have claimed to see visions, like a haunting reflection of their deepest regrets. It becomes a trap—a beautiful, seductive trap."

"Visions? Like what?" another crew member, Mia, piped up, her skepticism evident. "It sounds more like folklore than fact."

"Folklore? Perhaps. But every myth has a kernel of truth," Adrian replied, his gaze unwavering. "When I was studying the artifacts unearthed from the previous expeditions, many contained symbols linked to madness—markings that could drive a person to the brink if they dwelled on them too long. It's as if the island is a mirror reflecting back the worst parts of those who dare to approach."

"Just tell me we're not camping there," Mia interjected, her voice rising slightly. "I don't fancy becoming part of some ghost story."

"No, we're not on Xel Island," Adrian assured her. "We're in a safer location, just off the coast. We've set up camp on a small island that acts as a launch point for our explorations. The threats from Xel are less imminent here, but the air is still thick with its mysteries. Just being in the vicinity can feel like a weight on your chest."

"Then why bother? Why not just avoid the place altogether?" another crew member asked, skepticism evident in his tone.

"Because," Adrian said, his voice sharp and passionate, "curiosity drives us. The stories are powerful, and so is the promise of discovery. What if we could unravel the truth behind those legends? What if the island holds secrets that could change everything we know about history and ourselves?"

Wren felt a thrill run through him. "You really believe that?"

"Absolutely," Adrian replied, leaning closer to Wren. "But there's a fine line between belief and obsession. We must tread carefully. The more you dig into Xel's past, the more it pulls you in. I've spent years studying this island, and I've felt its allure firsthand. It's intoxicating."

"Intoxicating or not, I'm not losing my sanity over some myth," Mia replied, crossing her arms defiantly. "We need to keep our heads straight if we're going to explore these places. If there's even a hint of danger, we must be prepared."

"Preparation is crucial," Adrian agreed, nodding. "We'll run drills, develop protocols for maintaining our mental health while we work in the field. If any of us starts feeling overwhelmed, we'll pull back. It's essential to keep a level head."

"But what if the island is really that powerful?" Wren chimed in. "What if it does affect us in ways we can't control?"

"It's possible," Adrian admitted. "That's why I'm stressing the importance of teamwork. If one of us feels off, we'll communicate. We're stronger together."

"Yeah, right," Emma scoffed. "And what if it's already too late? What if we're already marked by the island just by being near it?"

"Enough of that," Mia snapped, her voice rising. "We're not going to entertain these thoughts. We're here to explore, not to let fear paralyze us. Let's focus on our mission and keep the legends where they belong—within the realm of stories, not reality."

"Exactly," Adrian agreed, raising an eyebrow at the doubter. "We respect the stories, but we don't let them dictate our actions. Knowledge is power. We're not going to let fear control us."

"I don't know, man," Alex replied, a hint of doubt still lingering in his voice. "You can't help but feel the tension. There's something unsettling about it."

"Every expedition carries a risk," Adrian countered, his voice steady and resolute. "That's the nature of discovery. The real danger lies in ignorance. We can't ignore the island's existence or its impact. We have to face it head-on."

"Let's not forget why we're here," Wren added, his tone more confident now. "This isn't just about fear; it's about understanding. If we want to uncover the truth, we have to confront the darkness."

Adrian nodded approvingly at Wren. "Exactly. We're explorers, adventurers. This is what we signed up for. We owe it to ourselves and to those who came before us to seek the truth, no matter how uncomfortable it might be."

"Alright, then," Mia said, her resolve returning. "If we're going to do this, let's commit to each other. We stay vigilant and watch out for one another. If we feel the island's pull, we speak up. Agreed?"

"Agreed," Wren replied, feeling a surge of camaraderie.

"Count me in," Ria said, a flicker of enthusiasm sparking in her eyes. "I didn't come here to back down now."

The air around them shifted, tension dissipating into a newfound determination. The sun's rays broke through the clouds, illuminating their camp as laughter began to replace the seriousness of the conversation.

"Let's make a pact," Adrian proposed, a smile creeping onto his face. "No matter what happens, we stick together. We face this as a team. If the island tries to play tricks, we'll call each other out. We'll share our experiences and confront them openly."

"Sounds like a plan," Mia replied, her tone lightening. "Let's tackle this challenge together. But I still want to keep my sanity intact!"

"Can't argue with that!" Wren chuckled, the weight on his shoulders lifting as he shared a smile with his new friends.

As the sun rose higher, the group returned to their tasks, but a sense of unity lingered in the air. Each member of the team felt the weight of the island's legend, but now they shared a common goal. They would explore the unknown together, and together they would face whatever mysteries Xel Island had in store for them.

The conversations continued to ebb and flow, moving from fears to plans, and as they worked, Wren couldn't shake the feeling that he was finally where he belonged.

"Hey, Wren," Alex called over. "How about you tell us a bit about yourself? We've shared our fears, but what about your story?"

Wren paused, feeling the gaze of his peers on him. "Well, it's a long one," he began, a slight nervousness creeping in. "I ended up here after some... difficult times. Let's just say I've learned a lot about facing fears."

"Facing fears, huh?" George chimed in. "Sounds like you've got some interesting tales of your own."

"Maybe," Wren replied, glancing at Adrian for encouragement. "But I'm more interested in hearing about all of you and your connections to Xel. Why did you come here? What drives you?"

"Well, for me," Mia said, her voice thoughtful, "it's the thrill of discovery. I've always been fascinated by ancient civilizations. Understanding how they lived and what they believed fascinates me. It feels like a treasure trove of knowledge waiting to be unlocked."

"Mine is more personal," Adrian added, the light in his eyes dimming momentarily. "My father was an archaeologist. He taught me everything I know. He had a fascination with places like Xel. I guess it's my way of honoring his memory, of continuing his work."

"That's powerful," Wren responded, feeling the weight of Adrian's words. "It's like you're carrying his legacy with you."

"Exactly," Adrian replied, his voice growing steadier. "This isn't just an expedition for me. It's about finding closure. Xel Island has always haunted my dreams, and I want to uncover its secrets, not just for myself, but for him."

The crew nodded in understanding, the atmosphere shifting again. "What about you, Wren?" Mia asked. "What drives you to be here?"

Wren hesitated, looking around at the expectant faces. "I guess... I've always been searching for a sense of belonging. After losing my family, I didn't know where to turn. I drifted for a while, but something about this crew feels right. Like I'm finally part of something bigger."

"Hey," another crew member interjected, his voice lighthearted, "we're all searching for something, right? Just remember, you're not alone anymore. We've got your back."

Wren felt a smile creeping onto his face, a warmth spreading through his chest. "Thanks, I appreciate that. I just hope I can contribute."

"You will," Adrian assured him. "Each of us brings something unique to this team. We'll figure this out together."

With the sun climbing higher in the sky, the conversations continued to flow, the group bonding over shared fears and hopes. Laughter rang out, and the initial tension surrounding Xel Island began to dissipate, replaced by a shared sense of purpose.

As the day wore on, the camp transformed into a bustling hub of activity. Crew members organized supplies, while others gathered in small groups, discussing strategies for their upcoming explorations. Wren found himself drawn into the conversations, his earlier apprehensions slowly melting away.

Hours passed, and the sun dipped high in the sky, casting a warm, golden glow across the camp. Wren glanced at Adrian, who stood at the center of it all, directing the team with an air of calm confidence.

"Hey, Adrian," Wren called, moving closer to the older man. "How do you stay so composed with all this pressure?"

Adrian turned, a slight smile tugging at his lips. "Experience, I suppose. Every expedition brings its own challenges. But I've learned that remaining level-headed is crucial. If I panic, the team will panic. Confidence breeds confidence, you know?"

"Yeah, I get that," Wren replied, feeling the weight of responsibility settling on his shoulders. "But what if something goes wrong?"

"Then we adapt," Adrian said, his tone steady. "This is uncharted territory. Flexibility is key. As long as we communicate, we can handle anything that comes our way."

Wren nodded, feeling a renewed sense of determination. "Thanks, Adrian. That really helps."

"Just remember," Adrian added, a glint of mischief in his eye, "fear is just excitement in disguise. It means you care about what's happening. Embrace it, and let it fuel you."

As the sun began to set, the camp was alive with energy, and the conversations shifted from fear to laughter, the crew members joking about their impending adventures on Xel Island.

"Hey, how about a toast?" Mia suggested, raising her water bottle high. "To new beginnings, to exploration, and to facing our fears!"

Wren joined in, raising his own bottle. "And to teamwork! We're in this together!"

The crew cheered, their voices ringing out as they clinked their bottles together, the sound resonating with camaraderie and hope.

As the night descended, the stars began to twinkle overhead, casting a serene glow over the camp. Wren felt a sense of peace wash over him. He was surrounded by a group of people who understood the weight of their mission, who were willing to face the unknown together.

"Hey, do you think we'll really uncover the secrets of Xel?" Wren asked, breaking the silence as they settled around the campfire.

Adrian leaned back, staring into the flames. "I believe we will. The truth is out there, waiting to be discovered. And who knows? Maybe we'll uncover something that challenges everything we thought we knew."

"Or we might just find a bunch of old rocks," Mia joked, laughter bubbling up around the campfire.

"But what if those rocks tell a story?" Adrian countered, his voice rich with passion. "What if they reveal connections to civilizations we thought were long lost? Every piece of history has a voice waiting to be heard."

Wren gazed into the fire, feeling the flames flicker in rhythm with the growing anticipation in his chest. "I want to hear those voices," he said softly. "I want to know their stories."

"Then we will," Adrian promised, his tone unwavering. "Together."

As the fire crackled and the sun shone above, Wren knew this was just the beginning. The crew may have been filled with uncertainty and fear, but they also carried hope. And with that hope came the strength to face whatever lay ahead, even if it meant confronting the mysteries of Xel Island itself.

Adrian stood tall before his assembled team, his presence both commanding and reassuring. His broad shoulders squared and his eyes, sharp and focused, swept over the group, gauging their expressions—curiosity mixed with apprehension, anticipation palpable in the air. It was a moment of quiet before the storm of activity that lay ahead.

"I have devised a plan we need to execute," he declared, his voice steady and resonant. "I'll discuss the details in an hour or two. But first, I urge you all to take a moment to enjoy your meals."

As his words echoed around the room, a collective sigh of relief surged through the group. They turned to the long table, where an inviting spread of food awaited them: steaming bowls of hearty stew, freshly baked bread, and vibrant salads glistening with dressing. The comforting aroma wafted through the air, drawing everyone closer.

Emma, the spirited young woman with bright eyes and an infectious smile, felt her stomach rumble in agreement. She scanned the room, watching as her comrades filled their plates and settled into groups, laughter spilling over like the contents of a well-loved pot. In the midst of this camaraderie, her gaze drifted toward Wren, the new guy who had recently joined their ranks.

Wren stood slightly apart from the throng, his lean frame rigid, as if he were unsure how to blend into this newfound chaos. His dark hair fell over his forehead, partially shadowing his deep brown eyes, which reflected an inner turmoil she couldn't quite place.

Emma felt a pull of empathy towards him; she remembered her own first days here, where the whirlwind of voices and laughter had both exhilarated and overwhelmed her.

Determined to make him feel welcomed, Emma made her way through the bustling crowd, her heart racing slightly as she approached Wren. "Hey there," she greeted, her voice light and inviting. "What do you think of the food?"

Wren looked up, surprise flickering across his face, and managed a small smile. "It looks good," he replied, a hint of hesitation in his tone.

Emma sensed his guardedness and decided to delve a little deeper. "Do you want to grab a plate together? I'd love to hear more about you."

Wren hesitated, his eyes darting back to the lively group. "Sure, I guess," he finally said, his voice low.

They walked to the table side by side, the atmosphere around them buzzing with chatter and laughter. Emma ladled a generous portion of stew into her bowl and handed Wren the breadbasket, encouraging him to take what he liked.

"So, Wren, I was curious about your childhood," Emma began, her tone gentle but inquisitive. "What was it like for you growing up?"

Wren's expression shifted, his guarded demeanor cracking slightly as he considered her question. Memories flitted through his mind, bright and warm, then dark and cold, like flickering candlelight in a storm. He took a deep breath, feeling the weight of his past press against him. "I lived happily with my family until a flood took them away from me forever," he confessed, the words spilling out in a rush, tinged with an underlying sorrow that hung heavily in the air.

Emma's heart sank at the revelation, empathy flooding her being. "I'm so sorry to hear that, Wren," she said softly, her voice barely above a whisper. "That must have been incredibly hard for you."

"It was," he admitted, his gaze drifting as he relived that fateful day. "I remember the storm warnings on the radio, the way the skies darkened, and the winds howled like they were mourning something. We were trying to stay calm, but as the waters rose, panic set in."

Emma could see the pain etched on his face, and she wished she could take it away. "What happened next?" she urged gently, wanting him to share, to lighten the burden he carried.

Wren swallowed hard, the memories flooding back with unrelenting clarity. "We tried to evacuate, but the water rose too quickly. I lost my family that day… I was only a child, and I didn't understand. One moment, we were together, and the next, I was alone—floating on a piece of debris, watching as everything I loved was swallowed by the raging river."

Emma felt her throat tighten, unable to imagine the horrors he had endured. "That's… unimaginable. I can't even begin to understand how you must have felt."

Wren nodded, his voice thickening with emotion. "After that, my friend Ethan took me in. His family was kind and understood my situation. They opened their home to me when I had nowhere else to go. For that, I will always be grateful."

"Ethan sounds like a true friend," Emma said, her admiration for the boy growing as she listened.

"He was more than a friend," Wren said, a small smile breaking through his sadness. "He became my family. His parents treated me as their own, offering me comfort in a time of chaos. They helped me through the darkest moments."

"What about school? Did you get to go?" Emma asked, genuinely interested in his journey.

Wren shook his head, his expression sobering. "They wanted to, but their finances were limited. They couldn't afford to send me to school, and that was difficult to come to terms with. I had a hunger for knowledge, but I had to learn differently."

"Did you and Ethan find ways to learn?" Emma inquired, intrigued by the resilience of their bond.

"Yes, we did," Wren replied, a spark igniting in his eyes. "Ethan was resourceful. He would teach me what he learned in school and we would read books together. We explored the world around us, discovering new things and inventing games to keep our minds active."

"I can't imagine how strong you had to be, Wren," Emma said, her admiration for him deepening.

Wren shrugged, his modesty shining through. "We just made the best of what we had. I think that's what kept me going. We were just kids trying to find joy in the little things. We built treehouses and spent summers wandering through the woods, losing ourselves in our imaginations."

Emma could picture it vividly, the laughter of two boys echoing in the trees, their carefree spirits untouched by the hardships of life. "That sounds beautiful," she said, her heart swelling at the thought of their adventures. "What was the best memory you shared?"

Wren's face lit up as he recalled a particular moment. "We once decided to build the biggest fort we could. We scavenged materials from all over the neighborhood—old blankets, wooden pallets, and even furniture that people were throwing away. It took us weeks, but it was magnificent. We decorated it with fairy lights and called it our secret hideaway."

"I love that!" Emma exclaimed, grinning at the image of two boys in a glowing fort. "Did you spend a lot of time there?"

"Every moment we could," Wren said, his voice filled with nostalgia. "We would sit inside, sharing our dreams, pretending we were on grand adventures. We believed nothing could tear us apart."

"What happened next?" Emma asked, sensing the shift in his mood.

"Eventually, we came here for a hiking trip," Wren continued, the joy in his voice waning. "We thought it would be another adventure, but we got separated during one of the hikes. I kept calling for him, but the forest swallowed my voice. I waited for hours, hoping he would return, but he never did."

Emma's heart broke at the weight of his words. "You lost him," she said softly, realizing the depth of his pain.

"Not in the same way," Wren replied, his gaze heavy. "But yes, I lost him. It felt like I was drowning again, adrift in uncertainty. It's been hard, adjusting to life without him. I miss him every day."

Emma reached out, placing a comforting hand on Wren's arm. "You're not alone anymore," she said, her voice firm yet gentle. "We're all here for you. You have a family now, even if it looks different."

Wren's eyes glistened with unshed tears as he absorbed her words. "Thank you, Emma. That means more to me than you know."

5
The Beginning Of The Search

The sounds of laughter and conversation swelled around them, pulling them back into the present. Adrian, noticing the gathering crowd, stepped forward to address the group.

"Alright, everyone! I hope you've all enjoyed your meals. It's time to shift our focus to the mission at hand," he announced, his voice rising above the din.

Excitement rippled through the group as they turned their attention back to Adrian, eager to hear what he had planned. Emma felt a rush of anticipation as the atmosphere shifted from the warmth of shared meals to the seriousness of their purpose.

"I need each of you to contribute your strengths," Adrian continued, pacing the room with the authority that came so naturally to him. "We have much work to do, and each one of you plays a crucial role in this mission."

Emma glanced at Wren, her heart swelling with pride as Adrian outlined their tasks. "Wren, I want you to help organize the logistics of our supply gathering. Your resourcefulness will be invaluable," Adrian said, locking eyes with Wren.

Emma could see Wren's surprise, his eyes widening as Adrian acknowledged him in front of the group. "Emma," Adrian continued, "your ability to connect with people and also your knowledge about technology is vital. I want you to take charge of outreach."

Nodding, Emma felt the weight of responsibility settle on her shoulders, but she also felt empowered. She glanced at Wren, who was visibly moved by the recognition.

Then Adrian continued to address others about their job.

"George," Adrian called, his tone commanding yet encouraging. "I need you to work with Ria on reading the maps. Your expertise will be invaluable as we navigate our way forward."

George straightened, a spark of enthusiasm igniting in his eyes. "You can count on me, Adrian. Ria and I will ensure we have the best route planned out."

"Excellent," Adrian replied, a hint of a smile crossing his face. "And Alex, I'll need you to assist me and Mia in strategizing our next moves."

"Got it," Alex replied, leaning forward, his interest piqued. "What's the plan, Adrian?"

Adrian took a deep breath, gathering his thoughts before unveiling the mission. "Our primary objective is to travel to the West Indies and locate the sailor known for his expertise in navigating the treacherous waters surrounding Xel Island. He's reputed to be the key to finding safe passage."

Mia, sitting nearby, chimed in, her curiosity bubbling over. "But why is this sailor so important? What does he know that we don't?"

"He possesses knowledge of the hidden routes and the dangers that lurk in those waters," Adrian explained, his voice steady and filled with conviction. "Without his guidance, we risk losing our way or encountering obstacles we're ill-prepared for."

George furrowed his brow, considering the implications. "And once we reach Xel Island, what then? Are we sure it's safe?"

Adrian's gaze hardened with determination. "That's the challenge we must face. Xel Island is rumored to be fraught with dangers, from rugged terrain to unexpected wildlife. But if we stick together and remain vigilant, I believe we can overcome whatever lies ahead."

"Together," Ria echoed, her eyes sparkling with determination. "We've faced challenges before, and we've always come through stronger."

"That's right," Adrian affirmed, his voice rising in intensity. "We are not just individuals; we are a team. Each of us brings unique strengths to the table. If we combine our efforts, we can face any challenge this island throws at us."

Mia nodded, her heart swelling with confidence. "I'm ready for whatever comes our way. We can do this!"

"Exactly," Adrian said, his energy contagious. "Now, let's finalize our preparations. We'll leave at dawn, so everyone should be well-rested and ready to go."

As the team dispersed, excitement mixed with apprehension buzzed in the air. Conversations sprang up, voices overlapping as plans were discussed. George approached Ria, enthusiasm etched on his face. "Alright, let's tackle these maps. I'll take the lead, but I want to hear your ideas too."

Ria smiled, her confidence bolstered by his approach. "Absolutely! We can create a strategy that will guide us effectively."

Meanwhile, Adrian pulled Alex and Mia aside. "I appreciate your help with the planning. It's crucial we anticipate any potential roadblocks."

Alex nodded, his brow furrowed in concentration. "What specific challenges do you foresee?"

Adrian leaned in, his voice lowered to a conspiratorial whisper. "We need to consider the island's geography, weather patterns, and any possible encounters with wildlife. I've heard tales of ferocious creatures that roam the island."

Mia shuddered slightly. "I'll admit, I'm a bit nervous about that. But I also know we have each other's backs."

"Exactly," Adrian replied, a fire igniting in his voice. "Our unity is our strength. If we stick together and watch out for one another, we can handle anything. Trust in your training, and trust in each other."

"Let's make sure we have enough supplies too," Alex suggested, his mind racing with possibilities. "We'll need food, water, and tools for navigation."

Adrian nodded, appreciating Alex's practicality. "Good thinking. Let's compile a list tonight, and order online, so we're fully equipped for our journey."

As they strategized, a sense of camaraderie enveloped them, binding them closer together. They could feel the weight of the mission ahead, but it only fueled their determination. Each member of the team was vital, each person's strengths complementing the others.

As the sun began to set, casting long shadows over their gathering, Adrian felt a renewed sense of purpose. They were stepping into the unknown, but he had faith in their unity and resolve.

"Tomorrow marks the beginning of a new adventure," he declared, looking around at the faces of his friends. "Together, we will conquer Xel Island and emerge stronger than ever!"

Cheers erupted from the group, their voices rising in a chorus of determination. The challenges ahead were daunting, but the fire in their hearts burned brighter than any fear.

And as time rolled over, they prepared for their journey, ready to face whatever awaited them on the horizon, united as one.

Then the site began to empty, yet Emma and Wren lingered, caught up in the moment. "I can't believe how far we've come," Emma remarked, looking around at the remnants of their gathering—the half-eaten food, the scattered papers with plans and ideas. "It feels like just yesterday we were all strangers."

Wren smiled, a sense of warmth blooming within him. "It really does. I didn't expect to find a place where I belong so quickly."

"Neither did I," Emma admitted, feeling a flutter of excitement. "It's amazing how we've connected despite our different backgrounds."

Wren shifted slightly, contemplating her words. "Do you ever think about what you want in the future?"

Emma's heart raced at the question. "All the time. I want to make a difference, to create something that lasts. I want to help people, just like you're doing now."

Wren met her gaze, sincerity written across his features. "You're doing just that, Emma. You've already made a difference in my life."

The two exchanged smiles, their bond solidifying with each passing moment. As the sun dipped below the horizon, painting the sky in hues of orange and pink, the warmth of companionship enveloped them.

The soft rustling of leaves and the distant calls of wildlife surrounded them, creating a serene ambiance. Emma leaned back against the log they were sitting on, feeling a profound sense of peace wash over her.

"We've come a long way," she said softly, her heart swelling with hope. "I can't wait to see what the future holds for all of us."

Wren nodded, a flicker of optimism igniting within him. "Me too, Emma. It feels like a new beginning."

As darkness enveloped the campsite, the stars began to twinkle overhead, a breathtaking display that mirrored the possibilities lying ahead. Emma and Wren continued to talk, their voices weaving through the night, sharing dreams, aspirations, and stories of resilience.

In that moment, surrounded by the glow of friendship and the promise of tomorrow, both Emma and Wren understood that despite the shadows of their pasts, they were embarking on a journey filled with hope and determination. Together, they would face whatever challenges lay ahead, hand in hand, ready to create their own destiny.

Adrian sat cross-legged on the floor of his tent, the muted glow of his laptop reflecting off his furrowed brow. The cool evening air slipped in through the open flap, but the outside world barely registered as he scrolled through an avalanche of rumors, gossip, and exaggerated headlines under the ever-growing #XelScares hashtag. His eyes darted from one sensationalized post to the next, a tangled web of hysteria woven across social media feeds that seemed to thrive on every click, every retweet. He muttered to himself, shaking his head at how far people would go for a shred of internet fame.

"The lies people invent just to hit that monetization goal," Adrian grumbled under his breath, fingers tapping absently on the keyboard. The sheer volume of garbage he had to sift through was staggering, each post more ridiculous than the last. Some of them were so poorly constructed, it was almost laughable—obvious hoaxes made by people looking to cash in on the fear surrounding Xel Island. They lacked even a shred of subtlety, their fakeness shining through like a neon sign.

Still, a few posts stood out, crafted so cleverly that, for a moment, even Adrian felt the faint tug of belief. There was something sinisterly captivating about the island's lore, even when wrapped in lies. One post, in particular, made him pause, the words sinking into him with a chilling intensity: *"Xel Island, the notorious site once explored by the fearless siblings Georgia and Marcus, has now claimed another life. The island's cursed grip tightens..."*

He stared at the screen, his pulse quickening despite himself. It was absurd—he knew that. But the way the sentence was phrased, the way it insinuated something dark and foreboding lurking in the shadows, made his breath catch for just a second. He could almost picture the island itself, shrouded in mist, whispering secrets to those foolish enough to listen.

"Ridiculous," Adrian muttered, snapping himself out of it. His rational mind quickly took over as he dove into the comment section, scrolling past the responses of people either buying into the lie or debunking it with ease. It didn't take long to confirm that this, too, was just another fabrication—another cheap ploy for attention. Satisfied that there was no truth to be found here, Adrian closed the tab.

But his purpose for being glued to the screen wasn't to get lost in social media nonsense. There was a reason he had his laptop open in the first place, and it had nothing to do with the spiraling rumors surrounding Xel Island. No, his goal was something more practical, more immediate. He had to book their flights. Their journey to the West Indies was looming, and with every second ticking by, the need to secure a plan became more urgent.

With a few quick keystrokes, Adrian turned his focus to finding available flights. He pulled up several different travel sites, eyes flicking between tabs as he hunted for open seats. Every time he thought he'd found something, the page would refresh, showing either sold-out flights or an increase in ticket prices. Frustration built up in his chest as the process dragged on longer than he anticipated.

"Come on, there's got to be something," he muttered, his frustration seeping through clenched teeth. He had been searching for nearly an hour, and every time he thought he was getting close, he hit another dead end.

The irony of it all was that while social media exploded with fabricated stories about a supposedly cursed island, here he was, struggling with the very real logistics of simply getting there. The gap between reality and fiction never seemed wider. But then, at last, his persistence paid off. A handful of empty seats popped up on a flight that fit their schedule, and Adrian wasted no time grabbing them.

He exhaled sharply, a mixture of relief and excitement washing over him as the confirmation page appeared on the screen. Finally, something tangible, something real. The tickets were booked. A surge of anticipation thrummed in his veins. This was it. They were going to the West Indies. He stared at the confirmation email for a moment, a small smile tugging at the corner of his mouth. The journey that lay ahead was going to be something else—he could feel it. But even in his quiet excitement, Adrian didn't see the need to make a big deal out of it.

No fanfare. No gathering the group for some dramatic reveal. He wasn't that kind of guy. Instead, he opted for his usual understated approach. Grabbing his phone, he quickly typed out a message to the others. No frills, no excessive explanation. Just the essentials.

"Everyone, be ready tomorrow. We're headed somewhere connected to the island. Pack your things and get a good night's sleep."

The message was sent with a simple tap of his finger, disappearing into the ether to reach the rest of the team. They'd all been preparing for this for some time now, but he didn't see the need to stir up more excitement than necessary. Better to let them sleep easy tonight, without the weight of expectations hanging over their heads.

He leaned back against the canvas wall of his tent, staring at the ceiling for a moment as the adrenaline of the evening began to ebb away. Tomorrow was going to be a big day, and the thought of what lay ahead swirled around in his mind. His thoughts drifted to the island once again—the real one, not the dramatized version plastered across social media.

Xel Island had become something of a myth, shrouded in rumours, mysteries, and exaggerated tales that turned it into more of a supernatural entity than a geographical location. Adrian wasn't one to buy into such things easily, but he couldn't deny the allure that the island seemed to hold over people. Stories of Georgia and Marcus's ill-fated expedition, the whispers of unexplained phenomena, and the strange disappearances that cropped up whenever anyone got too close... it was hard not to let those ideas creep into the corners of his mind, even if he kept them at bay with logic.

But the truth of the matter was, the island was real, and they were going to be standing on its shores soon enough. He had no doubt that whatever awaited them would be far more grounded in reality than the fantastical nightmares conjured up online. Still, the lingering unease, the flicker of doubt that came with the unknown, gnawed at him quietly in the back of his thoughts.

Adrian pulled himself back into the present. Dwelling on what-ifs wouldn't get him anywhere, and besides, tomorrow would be here soon enough. For now, he needed to sleep, to rest and gather his strength for whatever awaited them.

He powered down his laptop and set it aside, the darkness of the tent now illuminated only by the dim glow of the moon filtering through the fabric walls. The quiet of the night settled around him like a blanket, the hum of distant insects and the occasional rustling of leaves in the wind lulling him into a sense of calm.

While Adrian busied himself with logistics, tucked away in his tent and preoccupied with booking their flights, Ria and George were in a world of their own. Their tent was softly lit by a lantern, casting a warm glow over the two of them as they lounged on a makeshift bed of sleeping bags and blankets. It was a rare moment of peace amid the chaos that had surrounded their lives lately, and they had slipped easily into the comfort of each other's arms, reliving the closeness they had cherished in the early days of their marriage.

Ria was nestled against George's chest, her head resting in the crook of his neck. His arms were wrapped around her, strong but gentle, the kind of embrace that felt like home. Outside, the night air was cool, but inside their small sanctuary, it was warm—more from the heat between them than the actual temperature. They shared soft kisses, the kind that carried the weight of a thousand unspoken words, and with each touch, memories of their past together drifted to the surface like whispers of a life they had barely had the time to relive lately.

"I was just thinking," Ria murmured, her voice barely above a whisper as she traced a slow pattern on George's chest with her fingers, "about that time we went to the lake after our wedding. Do you remember?"

George chuckled softly, the sound a low rumble that vibrated through her. "How could I forget? You were so determined to row that boat by yourself."

Ria smiled against him, tilting her head back to meet his gaze. "I was not determined. I was curious. There's a difference."

"Right," George teased, his lips brushing her forehead. "Curious enough to almost capsize us both."

She playfully swatted at him, her laughter filling the space between them. "You were supposed to help me, but you were too busy laughing at my attempts."

"How could I not?" George grinned, pulling her closer. "You were adorable, getting all flustered every time the boat rocked. You kept telling me you had it under control, even though the oars were going in completely opposite directions."

Ria couldn't help but laugh at the memory. It had been one of those perfect days, filled with sunshine and laughter, the water sparkling like diamonds beneath a clear blue sky. They had decided, on a whim, to take a day trip to the countryside, just the two of them. It was meant to be a break from the whirlwind of family visits and post-wedding formalities—a chance to just be together without the noise of the world around them.

They had stumbled upon the lake by accident, a hidden gem tucked away behind a grove of trees. It was secluded, quiet, with a small wooden dock that led out to a handful of rowboats tied to posts. Ria had been the one to suggest they take one out on the water, her eyes lighting up with excitement at the prospect of doing something new, something spontaneous.

"I remember how peaceful it was," she said softly, her voice carrying a note of nostalgia. "Just the sound of the water lapping against the boat and the birds in the distance. It felt like we were the only two people in the world."

George's smile softened as he looked at her, his thumb tracing a gentle line along her jaw. "It was perfect, wasn't it? No distractions, no interruptions—just us."

She nodded, her mind drifting back to that golden afternoon. They had spent hours on the water, the boat lazily drifting under the sun as they talked about everything and nothing. The future had seemed so full of possibilities then, each one as bright as the sunlight that danced on the surface of the lake. They had shared stories, dreams, and hopes, their laughter carrying across the water like music.

"I remember you told me that day," George said, his voice low and full of affection, "that you wanted us to keep doing things like that. Little adventures. Even when life got busy."

"And look at us now," Ria teased lightly, though her words were tinged with a certain fondness. "In the middle of an adventure, surrounded by mystery and danger. I suppose we got more than we bargained for."

George chuckled, pressing a kiss to her temple. "I wouldn't trade any of it, though. As long as I'm with you, it's worth it."

Ria's heart fluttered at his words, her hand coming up to cup his cheek. There was something so sincere, so grounding about the way George spoke to her. Even after all the excitement and uncertainty that had filled their lives lately, moments like this—just the two of them—reminded her of what truly mattered. The world could turn upside down, but as long as they had each other, they would always find their way.

"Do you remember what you said to me that day?" George asked, his voice a soft murmur.

Ria thought for a moment, her brow furrowing slightly as she tried to recall. There had been so many conversations, so many words exchanged in the quiet of that afternoon.

"You said you'd never let anything come between us," George reminded her, his gaze searching hers. "That no matter what happened, we'd always make time for each other."

Ria smiled, her eyes glistening with emotion as the memory settled over her. "And I meant it. I still do."

They shared a kiss then, slow and tender, the kind of kiss that felt like a promise—a reaffirmation of everything they had built together. It was moments like this, when the world around them faded away, that Ria knew their love was stronger than anything life could throw at them. No matter how chaotic things got, they would always have this—a love that was steady, unwavering, and constant.

As they pulled apart, George rested his forehead against hers, his breath warm against her skin. "I love you, Ria."

"I love you too," she whispered, her voice full of affection. "More than you know."

They stayed like that for a while longer, wrapped up in each other, the outside world distant and irrelevant. But eventually, reality came knocking in the form of a notification sound from George's phone. The peaceful bubble they had created for themselves popped as he reached for the device, unlocking the screen to reveal the message Adrian had sent.

Ria sighed softly, pulling herself away from George's embrace just enough to read the message over his shoulder. "*Everyone, be ready tomorrow. We're headed somewhere connected to the island. Pack your things and get a good night's sleep.*"

"Well," George said with a sigh, "so much for a quiet night."

Ria smiled at him, though there was a flicker of disappointment in her eyes. "We knew it was coming. We'll have plenty of time later for us, right?"

George nodded, pressing one last kiss to her forehead before they both reluctantly got up to gather their things. Their peaceful evening was over, but the memory of their time together lingered in the air like the scent of jasmine, sweet and enduring.

As they packed their bags in silence, the glow of their earlier conversation stayed with them. They knew that no matter what awaited them tomorrow—no matter what the island had in store—this love, this connection between them, was their anchor. And once the storm of the island had passed, they would hope to return to these quiet moments, to each other, and the world would feel whole again.

Meanwhile, in a tent not far from George and Ria's, Emma and Wren were nestled in their little world, immersed in a vibrant conversation that flowed effortlessly between them. Though they weren't sharing the same space as their friends, the connection they were building felt equally significant. Their phones lit up the dim interior, the glow illuminating their faces as they laughed and shared stories late into the night.

"Can you believe how ridiculous that last post about the island was?" Wren chuckled, his eyes twinkling with mischief. "I mean, *haunted squirrels*? Seriously?"

Emma giggled, leaning back against the tent wall. "Right? I almost choked on my snack when I read that. Who comes up with these things? It's like they're trying to outdo each other with sheer absurdity."

Wren shrugged, a playful smile dancing on his lips. "Maybe it's a competition. The more outrageous, the better the engagement?"

"Or maybe they just have too much time on their hands," Emma replied, rolling her eyes. "I mean, if I had that kind of creativity, I'd write a novel instead. Or at least a short story that doesn't involve *haunted squirrels*!"

As they continued their light-hearted banter, the bond between them deepened with each shared laugh, each playful jab. There was a familiarity growing, a sense of comfort that enveloped them like a warm blanket on a chilly night. They traded stories of their past adventures, weaving in and out of memories that painted a vivid tapestry of their lives.

"Do you remember that camping trip we took last summer?" Wren asked, his expression turning nostalgic. "The one where we got lost for hours?"

Emma's eyes sparkled with amusement as she recalled the chaos of that day. "Oh, how could I forget? You insisted on taking the 'shortcut' through those woods, and we ended up in a completely different campsite! We didn't even have a map!"

Wren laughed, the sound echoing in the confined space. "But we made it back eventually! And when we found that gorgeous lake at sunset? Totally worth it!"

Emma nodded, a soft smile gracing her lips as she envisioned the serene scene they had stumbled upon. "That was magical. Just the two of us, watching the sun dip below the horizon, painting the sky in shades of orange and pink. I'll never forget how peaceful it felt."

"It was one of those moments that makes you realize how beautiful the world can be," Wren said, his tone turning more serious. "Just being out there, away from everything... it felt liberating."

Emma felt a flutter in her chest at his words, the sincerity behind them pulling her in closer. "Yeah, and to think we almost missed it because of your terrible sense of direction!"

Wren feigned offense, clutching his heart dramatically. "Hey! My sense of direction is *flawless*—when I'm not following your *absolutely insane* suggestions!"

They erupted into laughter, their teasing a playful rhythm that felt natural. It was moments like these, amidst the chaos of their lives, that grounded them both, reminding them of the joy in shared experiences.

However, their lighthearted reverie was abruptly interrupted by the familiar sound of a notification chiming from Wren's phone. He glanced down, and his expression shifted from amusement to curiosity as he read the message from Adrian.

"Looks like the others are getting things organized," he said, a hint of disappointment creeping into his voice. "Adrian just sent a message."

"What does it say?" Emma asked, leaning in closer, her interest piqued.

"*Everyone, be ready tomorrow. We're headed somewhere connected to the island. Pack your things and get a good night's sleep.*" Wren relayed, the excitement tinged with an underlying sense of urgency.

Emma's heart raced a little at the news, the reality of their upcoming adventure hitting her all at once. "Well, I guess that means we should start packing up, huh?"

"Yep," Wren replied, trying to mask his reluctance as he slid his phone into his pocket. "Time to say goodbye to our cozy little chat for now."

They both stood up, shaking off the comfortable lethargy that had settled over them. The mood shifted from relaxed camaraderie to purposeful movement as they began gathering their belongings. They rummaged through their bags, tossing clothes, toiletries, and essentials into an organized chaos that reflected their shared urgency.

"You know," Emma said, folding her clothes with meticulous care, "it's moments like this that make me appreciate what we have—this whole experience, the friendships, the adventures. It's nice to know we're all in it together."

Wren paused, glancing over at her with a soft smile. "Absolutely. And even if we're dealing with some strange rumors, we have each other's backs. That's what matters."

As they finished packing, they couldn't help but feel the thrill of anticipation coursing through them. The night may have been drawing to a close, but a new day awaited them—one filled with unknown possibilities and shared adventures. They exchanged a knowing glance, the excitement palpable in the air.

Outside their tent, the stirrings of the others began to emerge. The quiet of the night was interrupted as sounds of rustling fabric and muted conversations filtered through the canvas walls. The energy was shifting, a ripple of excitement spreading among the group.

While Emma and Wren finished securing their bags, they could hear snippets of conversation drifting in from the nearby tents. The others were awakening from their restful state, curiosity and anticipation overriding their previous fatigue. One by one, they emerged from their tents, groggy but eager, stretching as they adjusted to the cool night air.

"Did you see the message?" someone called out, excitement bubbling over. "What's going on?"

"Adrian booked the tickets! We're heading to the island tomorrow!" Wren shouted back, a grin breaking across his face.

The energy shifted as the news spread. Conversations erupted, a chorus of voices filled with excitement and questions. Each person hurriedly packed their belongings, the sense of urgency propelling them into action.

"Did anyone else get that crazy post about haunted squirrels?" a voice chimed in, prompting laughter among the group as they shared their thoughts on the absurdity of the rumors.

With every passing moment, the anticipation built, electrifying the atmosphere. Emma watched as the group transformed from sleepy campers into an energized team, each individual contributing to the buzz of excitement.

Wren caught her gaze and grinned. "See? We're all in this together, just like we said."

"Yeah," Emma agreed, her heart swelling with warmth at the sense of camaraderie surrounding them. "This is going to be amazing."

With the last of their bags zipped up, they prepared for whatever awaited them at the island. The night's adventures were behind them, but new horizons were on the horizon, full of promise and shared experiences waiting to unfold.

Tomorrow, they'd take the first step toward unraveling the truth behind Xel Island—whatever that truth might be. But tonight, Adrian allowed himself the brief luxury of simply closing his eyes and breathing in the stillness, his mind drifting toward sleep, even as the thrill of what was to come simmered just beneath the surface.

In the early hours of the morning, before the sun had fully risen to chase away the remnants of the night, Adrian was the first to wake. He blinked against the soft glow of the lanterns, his mind stirring as he took in the faint sounds of the campground. Birds chirped in the trees outside, and the crisp air hinted at the promise of a new day. Adrian stretched and rubbed the sleep from his eyes, a sense of excitement bubbling within him as he recalled the day's plans.

He carefully rose from his sleeping bag, making sure not to disturb the others still nestled in their tents. The quietness of the morning was a welcome contrast to the chatter and laughter of the previous night. Adrian stepped outside, inhaling deeply the fresh morning air, which carried with it a hint of dew and the earthy scent of nature awakening.

As the sun began to peek over the horizon, casting a warm golden light over the campsite, Adrian took a moment to savor the stillness. He felt a thrill of anticipation coursing through him—today was the day they would embark on their adventure to the West Indies. His thoughts raced ahead to the vibrant beaches, the crystal-clear waters, and the memories they would create together.

Not long after, the sound of rustling fabric and muffled yawns began to emerge from the other tents. One by one, his friends stirred to life, each waking up in their own unique way.

From the tent adjacent to Adrian's, George poked his head out, tousled hair sticking up in every direction. "Morning, sunshine!" he called out, a sleepy grin spreading across his face as he squinted against the sunlight.

"Morning!" Adrian replied, chuckling at George's disheveled appearance.

Ria, who had been lying next to George, emerged from the tent, her eyes still half-closed. "What's all the racket?" she mumbled, stifling a yawn.

"Just the dawn chorus," Adrian teased, waving his arms dramatically as if conducting an invisible orchestra. "Welcome to the great outdoors!"

"Very funny," Ria shot back with a sleepy smile, rubbing her eyes and slowly waking up.

Next to their tent, Emma and Wren emerged, looking slightly more put together than George. Emma smiled brightly, her hair catching the light as she stepped into the morning. "What's on the agenda for today?" she asked, stretching her arms overhead.

"Adventure awaits!" Adrian exclaimed, his excitement infectious. "We're heading to the West Indies today!"

"What?" Wren exclaimed, raising an eyebrow. "You're not kidding, are you?"

"Nope! Adrian booked the tickets last night," Ria confirmed, a grin spreading across her face.

"Awesome! Let's get moving, then," Emma replied, her enthusiasm palpable. "I can't wait to feel the sun on my skin and sink my toes in the sand."

As they all began to shake off the remnants of sleep, Alex poked his head out of the tent he shared with Mia. "What's going on? Did I miss something?" he asked, confusion etched on his face.

"West Indies!" Adrian shouted, unable to contain his excitement. "We're flying there today!"

"Wow, that sounds incredible!" Mia exclaimed, her eyes lighting up as she joined the group outside. "I can't believe we're actually doing this!"

"Let's hurry up and pack, then," George suggested, his voice brimming with energy now that the idea of adventure was upon them. "We don't want to miss our flight!"

With a shared sense of urgency, the group scattered to gather their belongings. Tents were unzipped, bags were flung open, and clothes were hastily shoved inside. The atmosphere was charged with a mix of excitement and determination as they worked together, moving swiftly to ensure they were ready to leave.

"Hey, don't forget the sunscreen!" Emma called out, her voice cutting through the bustle. "I don't want to look like a lobster by the time we land!"

"Got it! I'll take care of it!" Adrian replied, quickly grabbing the bottle and tossing it into his bag.

Mia, in her own little corner, was checking her belongings, making sure she had everything she needed. "Is everyone packed?" she asked, her brow furrowed with concentration.

"Almost!" Ria shouted back, wrestling with her sleeping bag, which seemed to have a mind of its own.

Once they had gathered their things and ensured nothing was left behind, they made their way to the designated meeting point—a large, flat rock that served as their makeshift gathering space. The sun was climbing higher in the sky, casting a warm glow over the campsite.

"Alright, let's do a headcount," Adrian said, assuming the role of the unofficial leader. "Everyone here?"

"Present!" George saluted dramatically, earning a laugh from the group.

"Ready to conquer the day?" Wren asked, a twinkle of mischief in his eye.

"Always!" Emma replied, her voice ringing with enthusiasm.

Adrian grinned, feeling a surge of happiness as he looked at his friends. "Great! Let's get going, then. We have a flight to catch!"

As they started down the path that led to the airport, the group was buzzing with conversation, exchanging excited remarks and speculating about the adventures that awaited them. The cool morning air filled their lungs as they walked, the scenery transforming around them from the secluded campsite to the vibrant hustle and bustle of the airport.

"What do you think the first thing we should do when we get there?" Alex asked, glancing at Adrian with curiosity.

"I think we should hit the beach immediately!" Adrian declared, a playful grin on his face. "Sun, sand, and surf!"

"Count me in! I can't wait to dive into the ocean," Mia chimed in, her enthusiasm infectious.

"What if we have to check into our accommodations first?" Ria reminded them, a thoughtful expression on her face. "We might want to drop off our bags before we hit the waves."

"Good point," George agreed. "But let's make it a quick drop-off! No dilly-dallying!"

As they approached the airport, the energy was electric. The sounds of engines roaring and announcements echoing through the terminal created an ambiance that was both familiar and exciting. Adrian led the way, his heart pounding with anticipation. He navigated through the airport, weaving through the crowd with ease as they followed closely behind.

Once they reached the check-in counter, Adrian took the lead once more. "Alright, let's get our tickets and check our bags," he instructed, pulling out the confirmation email he had saved on his phone.

The process went smoothly, and soon enough, they had their boarding passes in hand. Adrian couldn't help but feel a surge of accomplishment as he looked around at his friends, each of them buzzing with excitement.

"Now that that's done, let's find some coffee or breakfast," Emma suggested, her eyes bright with energy. "I don't know about you all, but I need fuel for this adventure!"

"Great idea!" Wren agreed, and they all started to move toward a small café just inside the terminal. The smell of freshly brewed coffee wafted through the air, mingling with the sweet scent of pastries, making their mouths water.

As they settled into a cozy corner table, they eagerly placed their orders. "I'll have a large coffee and a chocolate croissant, please," Adrian said, handing over his money with a grin.

"I'll just have a muffin," Mia said, glancing over the pastry display with indecision. "Actually, make that two muffins. One for now and one for later!"

The others laughed at her enthusiasm. "Smart choice!" Wren teased, giving her a playful nudge.

As they waited for their food, the conversation flowed effortlessly. They shared stories of past travels, reminiscing about hilarious mishaps and unforgettable experiences.

"Remember when we got lost in that city in Europe?" Alex said, laughter bubbling up as he recalled the memory. "We wandered around for hours trying to find our hotel, only to realize we had been two blocks away the entire time!"

"Right! And didn't you insist we ask for directions from that random street performer?" George added, shaking his head. "I thought we were doomed!"

"I thought he was going to lead us into a trap!" Adrian laughed. "But it turned out he was a good guy—just a little too obsessed with juggling flaming torches!"

As their food arrived, they dug into their breakfast, enjoying the deliciousness of pastries and the warmth of fresh coffee. The ambiance of the café buzzed with laughter and chatter, a fitting prelude to the adventure that lay ahead.

After their meal, they made their way to the boarding gate, adrenaline coursing through them as they prepared to board the flight. Adrian glanced around, taking in the energy of the crowd—families, solo travelers, and groups of friends, all embarking on their own journeys.

"Alright, everyone! Get ready!" Adrian called out, rallying the group as they approached the gate. "This is it!"

The excitement was palpable as they presented their boarding passes and made their way down the jet bridge. Adrian felt a rush of exhilaration, and he couldn't help but smile as they stepped onto the plane.

Once they found their seats, settling in and buckling their seatbelts, the reality of their adventure began to sink in. The plane's engines roared to life, and as they taxied down the runway, Adrian exchanged glances with his friends, each face lit up with anticipation.

"Ready for takeoff?" Ria asked, her eyes sparkling.

"Ready!" everyone chimed in unison, their voices full of enthusiasm.

As the plane lifted off the ground, leaving behind the familiar landscape, Adrian

felt a wave of emotion wash over him. They were officially on their way to the West Indies, and the possibilities stretched out before them like the vast ocean below.

With the clouds surrounding them, they shared excited whispers, counting down the hours until they would touch down on the sandy beaches they had all dreamed about. Adrian couldn't wait to dive into the adventures that awaited them, ready to create unforgettable memories with his closest friends.

The flight seemed to fly by as they engaged in conversations filled with laughter and anticipation. They played games, shared funny stories, and made plans for their time in the West Indies.

"First on the agenda: beach volleyball!" Wren declared, a competitive glint in his eye.

"Definitely! But only if you promise not to throw sand in my face again," Emma retorted, a mock glare directed at Wren.

"I can't make any promises!" he laughed, his charm infectious.

After several hours, the captain's voice came through the intercom, announcing that they would be landing soon. The group looked at each other with wide eyes, excitement bubbling over as they prepared for their arrival.

As the plane began its descent, Adrian gazed out the window, marveling at the view of turquoise waters and palm-fringed beaches that stretched out beneath them. This was it—the West Indies!

"Look at that water!" Mia exclaimed, her voice filled with awe. "It's so beautiful!"

"I can't believe we're finally here!" Ria added, her eyes gleaming with excitement.

Once the plane touched down and came to a stop, the group erupted into cheers, their anticipation reaching its peak.

As they disembarked, the warmth of the sun enveloped them, and they stepped into the vibrant atmosphere of the West Indies. Adrian took a deep breath, savoring the scent of salt in the air and the thrill of adventure in his veins.

"Let the adventure begin!" he proclaimed, leading his friends into the unknown, ready to embrace every moment together.

As the plane touched down and rolled to a stop at the vibrant airport, Adrian and his friends could barely contain their excitement. The cabin doors opened, releasing a rush of warm, salty air that swept through the aisles, igniting their senses. The faint hum of island music wafted in, adding to the infectious energy of their arrival.

"Welcome to the West Indies!" Adrian exclaimed, beaming as he stood up, ready to disembark. "Let's do this!"

With their bags in tow, they made their way down the jet bridge, their hearts racing with anticipation. As they entered the airport terminal, the lively atmosphere engulfed them. Colorful banners hung from the ceilings, and the walls were adorned with vibrant artwork depicting the lush landscapes and rich culture of the islands.

"Can you believe we're finally here?" Mia said, her eyes sparkling with wonder. She glanced around, taking in the sights and sounds. "It's even more beautiful than I imagined!"

Adrian nodded, feeling a surge of excitement. "Let's get through customs and then we can find a taxi to take us to our hotel."

They moved quickly through the airport procedures, navigating the lines at customs with a mix of enthusiasm and impatience. Adrian led the way, waving his passport with confidence as they approached the officers.

"Is everyone ready?" he asked, glancing back at the group.

"Ready!" came the chorus of responses.

The customs officers greeted them with friendly smiles, and before long, they had cleared the checkpoint. As they stepped into the main terminal, the sounds of laughter and chatter filled the air, blending with the faint melodies of local musicians playing nearby.

"Alright, let's find a taxi," Adrian said, feeling a rush of adrenaline. He spotted a row of taxis waiting just outside the airport's entrance. The sun beamed down brightly, casting a warm glow over everything.

"Who wants to take the front seat?" George asked, nudging Ria playfully.

"I'll go! I want to see everything up close," Ria replied, her excitement contagious.

"Alright, let's pile in!" Adrian called out, gesturing for everyone to follow him. They hurried toward the taxis, the anticipation of their first ride on the island making them giddy.

As they approached a taxi, a friendly driver greeted them with a broad smile. "Welcome! Where do you want to go today?" he asked, his accent rich and melodic.

"Can you take us to the best hotel nearby?" Adrian replied, his enthusiasm bubbling over. "We're looking for a place to stay for a few days."

"Absolutely! I know just the spot," the driver said, helping them load their bags into the trunk. "You're going to love it. The beach is just a short walk away."

As they settled into the back of the taxi, the group couldn't contain their excitement. Adrian slid open the window, allowing the warm breeze to rush in. "This is amazing!" he shouted over the roar of the engine.

The driver navigated through the bustling streets, and the scenery outside transformed into a beautiful display of palm trees, colorful buildings, and friendly locals going about their day. The vibrant colors of the island were mesmerizing, and Adrian couldn't help but grin as he took it all in.

"Look at that!" Emma pointed out the window, her voice filled with awe as they passed a beach lined with golden sand. "We need to hit that beach as soon as we check in!"

"Definitely!" Wren agreed, leaning forward in his seat. "I can already feel the sun on my skin!"

As they drove, the driver shared stories about the island, pointing out landmarks and hidden gems. "You're going to love the local cuisine. Try the jerk chicken—it's a must!" he advised, his enthusiasm palpable.

"Now you've got my attention!" Mia replied, her mouth watering at the thought of delicious food. "I can't wait to dive into the local flavours!"

Finally, after what felt like a whirlwind of excitement, the taxi pulled up to a charming hotel nestled among lush greenery. The building was adorned with vibrant flowers, and the sound of waves crashing against the shore could be heard in the background.

"Here we are!" the driver announced, parking the taxi with a flourish. "Enjoy your stay!"

They quickly hopped out, adrenaline coursing through their veins as they took in their surroundings. The hotel exuded a warm, inviting vibe, with friendly staff welcoming them at the entrance.

"This place looks amazing!" Ria said, her eyes wide with delight as she admired the tropical decor.

Adrian approached the front desk, eager to check in. "I would like to have a reservation under my name," he said, flashing a friendly smile at the receptionist while handing over the required cash.

"Welcome! Let me get that for you," the receptionist replied, her demeanor warm and inviting. She typed into the computer, her fingers flying across the keys. "Ah, yes! Here it is. You'll be in room 205. Enjoy your stay!"

With their keys in hand, the group headed toward the elevators, excitement bubbling within them. "I can't believe we're finally here!" Adrian said, bouncing on his heels. "This is just the beginning!"

As they reached their floor, they eagerly opened the door to their room, stepping inside to find a cozy space adorned with colorful island decor. The sound of the waves outside created a soothing backdrop, and the scent of fresh flowers filled the air.

"Wow, this is beautiful!" Emma exclaimed, taking in the view from the balcony that overlooked the beach.

"Look at that view!" George shouted, racing over to the sliding glass door. He stepped outside, letting the warm breeze wash over him. "I'm already in love with this place!"

"Let's unpack and freshen up quickly," Adrian suggested, feeling the urgency of their excitement. "We don't want to waste any time!"

As they all busied themselves unpacking and settling in, the atmosphere was electric with anticipation. Adrian could hardly focus on his tasks, his mind already racing ahead to the beach, the sun, and the adventures that awaited them.

"Can we please go to the beach now?" Mia pleaded, her eagerness palpable as she flitted about the room.

"Let's do it!" Adrian replied, determination in his voice. "We'll head to the beach, soak up the sun, and then figure out what to do next."

In a flurry of energy, they quickly changed into their beachwear, excitement radiating from each of them. Once ready, they gathered their beach towels, sunscreen, and a few snacks to take along.

"Beach time!" Ria cheered, pumping her fist into the air as they made their way out of the hotel.

The beach unfolded before them like a living postcard, a breathtaking expanse of golden sand kissed by the gentle caress of the turquoise waves. The sun hung high in the azure sky, casting a warm, golden glow that danced across the water, creating sparkling diamonds that twinkled with every ripple. Palm trees swayed gracefully in the light breeze, their fronds rustling softly, whispering secrets of the island to those who would listen.

As they approached the shoreline, the intoxicating scent of salt and sun warmed their senses, mingling with the faint, sweet aroma of tropical flowers that dotted the landscape. The soft, powdery sand slipped through their toes, warm and inviting, offering a comforting embrace that beckoned them to wander further along the shore.

The rhythmic sound of the waves breaking against the shore provided a soothing soundtrack, a natural melody that harmonized with the cheerful laughter of beachgoers enjoying the sun-drenched day. Children splashed in the shallow waters, their delighted squeals blending with the distant notes of steel drums played by a local band, infusing the air with a festive spirit.

As Adrian and his friends stepped onto the beach, they felt an exhilarating rush of freedom. The vast expanse of the ocean stretched endlessly before them, a brilliant canvas of deep blues and greens, inviting them to explore its depths. Each wave rolled in with playful enthusiasm, leaving behind frothy white lace that shimmered in the sunlight before retreating back into the embrace of the sea.

Nearby, colorful beach umbrellas dotted the landscape, providing cheerful spots of shade for sunbathers lounging on beach towels, each one lost in a book or enjoying a refreshing drink. The occasional seagull swooped down to investigate, adding a touch of whimsy to the scene.

Adrian felt a sense of wonder wash over him as he surveyed the beauty around him. This beach was not just a destination; it was a paradise, a vibrant escape from the ordinary. It promised laughter, adventure, and memories waiting to be made. The allure of the ocean called to him, its waves whispering sweet promises of exploration and fun. With his friends by his side, he was ready to dive headfirst into this slice of heaven, embracing every moment of their time in the West Indies.

As the golden sun arched high in the sky, casting a warm glow over the beach, the group gathered near the sand court, their energy palpable. The soft sound of waves crashing against the shore formed a rhythmic backdrop, a natural soundtrack to the excitement that bubbled within them.

"Alright, team captains!" Adrian announced, his voice booming with enthusiasm as he pointed to George and Ria, the two natural leaders among the group. "Time to pick your players for some beach volleyball! Let's see who's got what it takes!"

"Ladies first!" George declared with a playful grin, gesturing to Ria, who feigned a dramatic sigh before narrowing her eyes playfully at her choices.

"Okay, okay! I'll take Emma!" Ria said, a smile breaking across her face as she claimed her friend. Emma jumped up and down, her excitement infectious.

"Nice pick! I'll take Wren!" George shot back, his eyes gleaming with competitive spirit. Wren raised his arms in triumph, ready to bring his A-game.

Ria quickly followed with, "Then I choose Mia!"

"Wow, leaving Alex and Adrian for last, huh?" Alex quipped, crossing his arms dramatically while feigning hurt.

"Sorry, guys! Just saving the best for last!" Ria laughed, and the group burst into laughter at her playful banter.

"Alright, Adrian! You're with me!" George exclaimed, snatching up the last player, sealing their fates in the match.

"May the best team win!" Adrian said, determination shining in his eyes. He clapped his hands together, shaking off the lighthearted tension as they lined up on opposite sides of the net.

With the teams set—Ria, Emma, and Mia on one side, and George, Wren, and Adrian on the other—the air was thick with anticipation. The sun glinted off the sand, creating a shimmering effect that mirrored the excitement in the players' hearts.

"Let's do this!" Ria shouted, tossing the ball high into the air before serving it over the net with a powerful swing. The ball soared, cutting through the warm air, and landed with a soft thud on the sand just past Adrian, catching him slightly off guard.

"Nice serve!" George complimented, clapping for Ria as the game kicked off.

With renewed energy, Adrian sprinted to the ball as it rolled back into play. He deftly set it up for George, who spiked it with a fierce swing, sending it flying over to Ria's side.

"Watch out!" Emma yelled, diving to the sand just in time to prevent the ball from hitting the ground. With her quick reflexes, she managed to keep the play alive, sending it soaring back across the net.

The game intensified, filled with laughter, shouts, and playful taunts echoing off the beach. Each serve, each dive, each point brought a wave of exhilaration that surged through them, igniting their competitive spirits.

"Let's go, team!" Adrian cheered, rallying his teammates. "We've got this! Keep your eyes on the ball!"

The ball sailed back and forth, and the sun began to dip slightly in the sky, painting the horizon with hues of orange and pink. The game became a delightful chaos of laughter and quick movements, with sandy feet digging into the soft ground as they chased the ball.

"Get it, Wren!" George yelled as Wren lunged forward, his hair whipping around as he sprinted after the ball. He leapt, arms outstretched, connecting with the ball just in time, sending it careening back to the opposite side.

"Too slow!" Ria teased, a grin lighting up her face as she dove for the ball, narrowly missing it as it bounced off her fingertips. "Nice shot, Wren!"

"Don't get cocky, Ria!" Wren called out, a cheeky grin spreading across his face. "This is just the beginning!"

As the game wore on, they paused briefly for water, the sun beating down mercilessly but only adding to their energy. "We should do this every day!" Emma suggested, her cheeks flushed from the excitement and exertion.

"I'm all for it! Just let me know when to bring the sunscreen!" Adrian joked, eliciting laughter from the group.

Once refreshed, they dove back into the game, the friendly competition heating up. With each point scored, they exchanged cheers and high-fives, their camaraderie deepening with every laugh and playful jab.

"Okay, last point wins!" Adrian declared, determination glinting in his eyes as he positioned himself at the net. "Let's finish strong!"

The ball soared through the air again, each player now fully in tune with the game. Ria served it over with fierce intensity, and the rally began.

Adrian set it up for George, who slammed it over the net, but Emma was quick, leaping up to block it. The tension in the air grew thick as the ball ricocheted back and forth, players diving and scrambling in a flurry of sand and laughter.

Finally, after a tense exchange, Wren scored the winning point with a beautiful spike that sent the ball landing just inside the boundary, prompting cheers of joy and playful groans of defeat from the other side.

"Victory!" Wren shouted, arms raised in triumph, a wide grin plastered across his face.

"Alright, alright! You got us this time," Ria conceded, a playful smirk on her lips. "But just wait until the rematch!"

The sun began to set, casting a warm golden hue over the beach, and as the group huddled together, they reveled in the shared joy of the game. Sand clung to their skin, laughter filled the air, and the taste of victory lingered sweetly on their tongues.

"Let's head to the water and cool off!" Adrian suggested, and the group eagerly agreed. They sprinted toward the waves, laughter echoing as they splashed into the refreshing ocean, the day transforming into a cherished memory that would linger long after the sun dipped below the horizon.

With the exhilaration of the volleyball match still buzzing in their veins, Adrian and his friends sprinted toward the ocean, laughter bubbling from their lips as they dove into the inviting waves. The cool water enveloped them, refreshing and invigorating after the heat of the beach.

"Ahh, this feels amazing!" Emma squealed, her voice barely rising above the sound of the crashing waves as she splashed water playfully at Mia.

"Watch out!" Mia squealed, dodging Emma's playful attack before diving under the surface. As she emerged, droplets of water glistened in the sunlight, and her laughter blended harmoniously with the rhythmic sounds of the ocean.

"Come on, let's ride some waves!" Adrian shouted, leading the charge deeper into the water. The waves rolled in steadily, and the group began to jump and dive, timing their movements with the incoming swells. They were a whirl of energy, excitement, and camaraderie, enjoying the freedom that only the ocean could provide.

"Catch me if you can!" Wren yelled, swimming out a little farther, his competitive spirit flaring up once again.

"Not a chance!" George replied, playfully splashing Wren before diving under a wave to swim faster. The water felt liberating as they splashed about, their joy radiating under the sun, making them feel weightless.

After an exhilarating half-hour of riding the waves, they finally paddled back toward the shore, reluctantly leaving the cool embrace of the water. "Alright, let's head back and get cleaned up!" Adrian suggested, his voice slightly breathless but brimming with excitement.

"Good idea! I'm starving!" Emma replied, shaking her head to rid it of excess water, her hair flicking droplets everywhere.

As they made their way back across the sandy beach, the sun began its descent toward the horizon, painting the sky in hues of orange, pink, and gold. The breathtaking view created a perfect backdrop for the memories they were creating, a reminder of the magic of the moment.

"Can we take a quick picture before we head up?" Mia asked, pulling out her phone with eager anticipation. "I want to capture this incredible day!"

"Absolutely! Let's get a group shot!" Adrian replied, a broad smile spreading across his face as they all gathered together. They struck playful poses, the camera clicking repeatedly as laughter filled the air.

"Okay, now a serious one! Everyone, look at me!" Mia instructed, trying to stifle her laughter. They all managed to compose themselves for a moment, holding their poses before erupting into giggles once again.

"Alright, let's go before I get sand in my shoes again!" Ria said, wiggling her toes dramatically as they started walking toward their hotel.

Once inside their hotel room, they quickly freshened up, the atmosphere buzzing with energy as they changed out of their sandy swimsuits into comfortable, stylish attire suitable for dinner.

"What do you think? Does this look alright?" Adrian asked, stepping out of the bathroom in a casual shirt and shorts, a hint of nervousness in his voice as he twirled in front of the mirror.

"Looking good, Adrian! You're ready to impress!" Wren teased, adjusting his own shirt with a mock-serious expression. "Just don't steal all the attention."

"Easy for you to say! You're the one with the beach hair model look going on," Adrian shot back, laughing.

"Thanks, man! I'll take that as a compliment," Wren said, puffing out his chest and striking a pose.

Finally, they were ready, and the group made their way to the buffet, the aroma of delicious food wafting through the air, tantalizing their appetites. As they entered the dining area, they were greeted with a vibrant spread that showcased the rich culinary traditions of the islands.

"Wow! Look at all this food!" Emma exclaimed, her eyes wide as she scanned the array of colorful dishes, from fresh seafood to local delicacies. "I don't even know where to start!"

"Let's make a plan! We should all try a little bit of everything," George suggested, rubbing his hands together in excitement.

"I'm definitely getting some jerk chicken!" Adrian declared, already moving toward the serving line. "And maybe some plantains—those are a must!"

"Don't forget the fried fish! It's supposed to be amazing!" Ria chimed in, following Adrian as they filled their plates with mouth-watering selections.

They all piled their plates high, laughter and chatter mixing as they gathered around a large table by the window. The sunset created a picturesque backdrop, illuminating the room with a warm golden glow, enhancing their dining experience.

"Alright, let's dig in!" Adrian said, lifting his fork triumphantly. They all clinked their glasses together, a celebratory toast to their first night on the island.

As they sampled the various dishes, their conversations flowed freely, punctuated by exclamations of delight and laughter. "This jerk chicken is incredible!" Mia said, her eyes sparkling with enthusiasm as she savored the flavors.

"Seriously, I could eat this every day!" George agreed, stuffing his mouth with a generous portion of fried fish.

"And this coconut rice? Wow!" Emma added, her taste buds dancing as she took another bite. "We need to learn how to make this back home!"

"Good luck getting the ingredients! It won't be the same," Adrian teased, a playful smile on his lips. "You've got to come back here to enjoy it!"

Their meal continued with lively banter and shared stories of past adventures, a delightful fusion of flavors and friendship. The sun dipped lower on the horizon, casting a beautiful orange glow that danced through the dining room.

As the group finished their meals, Ria leaned back in her chair, a satisfied smile on her face. "I don't know about you guys, but this has been one of the best days ever."

"I completely agree! From the beach to the food—it's all been perfect," Wren said, raising his glass in a toast once more.

"Here's to more adventures!" Adrian exclaimed, grinning widely. "We've got plenty more to explore!"

With laughter and excitement still bubbling in their hearts, they savored the moment, knowing this trip was just beginning. The atmosphere was charged with anticipation for what awaited them next, a promise of memories yet to be made under the West Indian sun.

After indulging in their sumptuous meal, Adrian glanced at the time and noticed the sun was beginning to set, painting the horizon with vibrant hues of orange and pink. The invigorating day had left them all pleasantly fatigued, their energy reserves running low.

"Alright, team," Adrian declared, leaning back in his chair, a satisfied smile on his face. "Before we head out to find the old sailor, how about we take a breather? Let's rest for an hour to recharge."

"Great idea!" Emma exclaimed, stifling a yawn. "I could use a quick nap to recover from all that sun and excitement."

"Same here!" Ria chimed in, her eyes sparkling with anticipation for what lay ahead but also heavy with the need for a little rest. "We've got a big adventure to tackle."

George nodded in agreement, stretching his arms above his head. "I don't want to miss anything tonight, but I definitely need to recharge my batteries. Count me in!"

"Alright, then it's settled!" Adrian replied, clapping his hands together. "We meet back here in an hour. Set your alarms if you need to!"

As they gathered their things, the group began to disperse, each finding their own cozy corner of the bed in the room to unwind. Adrian plopped onto the large, inviting bed, sinking into the plush comfort of the pillows. He closed his eyes, letting the soft sounds of the waves crashing outside lull him into relaxation.

Meanwhile, Emma settled into a chair by the window, enjoying the soft breeze that drifted in. She pulled out her phone, scrolling through the photos they had taken earlier, reliving the laughter and joy of the beach volleyball game. "I can't believe how much fun we had! This trip is already incredible!" she murmured to herself, her heart swelling with gratitude.

Across the room, Ria and Mia were sprawled on the same bed, chatting softly about the day. "I can't wait to meet this old sailor. I've heard so many legends about him," Mia said, her eyes gleaming with curiosity.

"Me too! I hope he has some wild stories to share," Ria replied, resting her head on her palm. "I'm sure he's seen a lot out here, especially with all the adventures he's had at sea."

"I wonder what secrets he holds," Mia mused, her thoughts drifting to the possibilities of their encounter. "It feels like we're part of some grand adventure, doesn't it?"

"Absolutely! We're like explorers on a quest for treasure," Ria laughed, a glint of excitement in her eyes. "And who knows, maybe he'll share some hidden gems about the island itself!"

Meanwhile, in the other corner of the room, Wren and George were engaged in a light-hearted conversation. "So, what's your guess about this old sailor?" Wren asked, leaning against the wall. "Do you think he's a grizzled old man with a parrot on his shoulder?"

"Or maybe he's a retired pirate!" George added, his voice dripping with mischief. "He could tell us tales of buried treasure and sea monsters!"

"Or he's just a regular guy who happens to know a lot about the ocean," Wren replied, chuckling. "But where's the fun in that? I like the idea of a pirate!"

As the day deepened and the sound of the ocean's gentle waves crashing against the shore created a serene backdrop, the group gathered in the small room. The earlier excitement had faded into a tranquil calm, and everyone settled into quiet, reflective conversations. The atmosphere was warm, intimate, and peaceful, as though the day's adventures had bonded them even closer. They shared small jokes, reliving the best moments of the day—particularly the beach volleyball match, which brought out the most laughter.

"I still can't believe George missed that serve," Wren teased, a mischievous grin on his face.

"Oh, come on! It was one time!" George replied, shaking his head, though his own chuckle betrayed him. "You were no MVP either, by the way."

"I'll admit it," Wren said, leaning back and stretching his arms. "But it was fun, and that's what counts, right?"

"Right," Ria agreed, resting her head on George's shoulder, her voice a soft hum of contentment. "We needed this—something easy, fun. It's been a while since we all just... relaxed like this."

Emma, sitting beside Mia, nodded in agreement. "I think today, until now was perfect. And the next few hours will be another adventure. Who knows what the sailor will tell us?" she mused, her eyes half-closed, already halfway to dreamland.

Mia shifted slightly, making room on the already cramped surface. "We've got a lot of ground to cover after our sleep," she added, adjusting her legs under her. "I hope we all get some decent rest tonight."

Adrian glanced around the room, noticing how everyone had unconsciously gravitated closer to each other as the conversations wound down. The limited space wasn't ideal, but the camaraderie more than made up for it. The room was small, dimly lit, and cozy, the perfect setting to end a long, exciting day.

"Speaking of rest, we should get some sleep soon," Adrian suggested, stifling a yawn. "We've got a long day ahead of us, and I'm sure we'll need our energy for whatever we uncover."

The others nodded in agreement, the fatigue of the day finally catching up with them. However, as they began to settle in, it became abundantly clear that the space wasn't going to be nearly enough for them to sleep comfortably. The beds were small, and there weren't enough for everyone to spread out.

"Looks like we'll have to get a little creative with our sleeping arrangements," George remarked, glancing around with a smirk. "Not exactly a five star setup, is it?"

Ria laughed softly, already leaning into him. "It's fine. I don't mind at all," she whispered, resting her head in his lap, a soft smile playing on her lips. George's hand instinctively came to rest on her shoulder, the gesture natural and comforting.

On the other side of the room, Wren and Emma exchanged a glance, silently agreeing to follow suit. Emma curled up, laying her head on Wren's lap, her fingers absentmindedly tracing circles on his knee. Wren smiled down at her, his arm draping casually over her as they both relaxed into the moment.

"This works," Emma murmured, her voice heavy with sleep. "Not the most luxurious setup, but I think it'll do."

"Could be worse," Wren replied, a chuckle in his tone. "As long as you're comfortable."

Mia and Adrian, though not as coupled up as the others, found their own makeshift sleeping spots. Mia tucked herself into a corner, using a jacket as a pillow, while Adrian stretched out on the floor, one arm resting behind his head as he stared up at the ceiling.

"Well, at least everyone's got a spot," Mia noted, her voice soft as she settled into her place. "The Next few hours will be some long hours, but I'm excited. I think that old sailor has some real stories to tell."

"Yeah," Adrian agreed, closing his eyes, though the anticipation of the coming hours lingered in his mind. "It's going to be an adventure for sure."

Despite the less-than-ideal sleeping conditions, the room was filled with a sense of peace and comfort. The gentle breathing of their companions, the rhythm of the ocean outside, and the closeness of their bonds created a calm, soothing atmosphere.

Ria, nestled against George, felt her eyelids grow heavy, lulled by the warmth of his body and the security of the moment. She was drifting off, her thoughts fading into dreams, when she felt George shift slightly beneath her.

"Comfortable?" he whispered, his voice low.

"Mm-hmm," she murmured, her hand resting lightly on his chest. "Perfect."

On the other side of the room, Emma, her head still in Wren's lap, was also on the verge of sleep. "You okay?" Wren asked softly, his fingers lightly brushing through her hair.

"Yeah, more than okay," Emma replied, a sleepy smile crossing her face. "Goodnight."

Wren smiled, leaning his head back against the wall. "Goodnight, Em."

As the room fell into a soft silence, broken only by the rhythmic breathing of the group and the occasional creak of the old hotel walls, the peace of the day wrapped around them like a comforting blanket. The air was filled with a deep sense of connection, of shared adventure, and of the quiet certainty that, no matter what the next day brought, they would face it together.

And with that, one by one, they all slipped into sleep, the weight of the day's adventures and the promise of the next hour lulling them into restful dreams.

Adrian was abruptly pulled from his sleep by the sharp, relentless beeping of his alarm. His eyes fluttered open, the grogginess weighing him down for a moment as the darkness of the early morning filled the room. He blinked a few times, adjusting to the dim light filtering in from the windows. The alarm was persistent, pulling him back to reality faster than he would have liked.

He reached over to silence it, the beeping cutting off instantly, leaving the room in an eerie quiet, save for the sound of soft breathing from the others. Adrian stretched his arms above his head, his muscles tight from sleeping on the floor. He glanced around, realizing the day ahead was waiting for them. The old sailor's tales, the secrets of the island—all of it was just beyond the horizon, and they needed to get moving.

"Time to wake up," Adrian muttered to himself before standing up. His voice was still hoarse with sleep, but his mind was quickly shaking off the fog. He looked at his friends, all curled up in their makeshift beds, still lost in their dreams. Ria was nestled in George's lap, and Emma and Wren were similarly intertwined, their bodies slack with peaceful rest. Mia was in the corner, her jacket rolled into a makeshift pillow, her face soft in sleep.

"Alright, rise and shine, everyone," Adrian called out, his voice louder now, cutting through the quiet. He clapped his hands once, the sharp sound startling Ria and George awake first.

George stirred, blinking rapidly. "What time is it?" he asked, his voice thick with sleep.

"Early," Adrian replied with a smirk, grabbing his bag and beginning to pack his belongings. "Time to get dressed and hit the road. We've got an old sailor to find, remember?"

Ria sat up, rubbing her eyes and looking over at George, who groaned as he shifted to get comfortable. "Already?" she asked, though the excitement in her voice betrayed her weariness. "Didn't we just fall asleep?"

Adrian chuckled. "Yeah, but the island waits for no one. We've got a long day ahead."

Emma was the next to stir, stretching her legs out from Wren's lap. "Five more minutes?" she mumbled, shielding her eyes from the faint light starting to peek through the windows. Wren, still half-asleep, blinked blearily and smiled at her.

"Nope," Adrian said, crossing the room and tapping her on the shoulder lightly. "Up and at 'em. We need to be out of here soon."

Emma groaned but slowly sat up, brushing her tangled hair away from her face. Wren stretched out his arms, yawning as he straightened his back. "Fine, fine, I'm up," he said, grinning lazily.

"Come on, guys," Mia finally chimed in from her corner, already sitting up and rubbing the sleep from her eyes. "If Adrian says it's time, it's time. Let's get moving." She started folding her jacket and gathering her things, her movements quick and efficient despite her tiredness.

George reluctantly disentangled himself from Ria, rolling his shoulders as he stood. "Alright, alright, I'm up. Let's do this."

In a flurry of sleepy yet determined movement, everyone began to gather their belongings, pulling on fresh clothes and making themselves as presentable as possible given the early hour. Ria tossed George his shirt, which had been draped over the edge of the bed, and he caught it with a playful smirk.

"Thanks, love," he said, pulling it on.

Emma and Wren helped each other find their things, exchanging quiet remarks about how little sleep they'd gotten, but there was an undeniable spark of excitement in their eyes. The day ahead held too much promise to let exhaustion dampen their spirits.

Adrian, already dressed and ready, stood by the door, checking his watch. "Alright, ten minutes, people. We've got a tight schedule. Don't want to miss our chance to track down that sailor."

"Yeah, yeah, we're coming," George muttered, slipping into his shoes.

Ria pulled her hair into a quick ponytail, glancing at Adrian. "What's the plan once we get out of here? Straight to the docks?"

"Exactly," Adrian confirmed. "The sooner we find him, the better. I want to hear what he has to say before the day really kicks off."

Within minutes, everyone was packed and dressed, the room quickly emptying as they filed out, leaving behind the warmth of their brief rest. The hotel's hallway was quiet, the faintest hints of dawn creeping through the windows as they made their way downstairs.

"Alright, adventure time," Mia said, a grin spreading across her face as they stepped into the cool morning air. The world outside was just beginning to wake up, the island still shrouded in the calm before the day's activities would take over.

Adrian took a deep breath, feeling the crispness of the ocean air fill his lungs. "Let's go," he said, leading the group down the quiet street toward their next destination.

They piled into a taxi, the driver nodding silently as Adrian gave him instructions. The sound of the engine humming to life cut through the stillness, and soon, they were heading off, the excitement building once again as the promise of adventure loomed on the horizon.

Adrian, still brimming with confidence as they arrived at the docks, according to the suggestion of himself, stepped out of the taxi with a sense of purpose. The sea breeze was stronger here, carrying the scent of saltwater and damp wood. All around them, boats rocked gently in the harbor, tied to their moorings, while a few fishermen and sailors went about their business, hauling gear or preparing to set off. The early morning light reflected off the water, casting shimmering patches across the surface.

He glanced back at the group, his eyes bright with the anticipation of finding the old sailor. "Let's start here," he said, nodding toward a cluster of boats anchored along the pier. "Someone must know where he is."

The others followed, their steps echoing faintly on the worn wooden planks of the dock. George was busy looking around, taking in the sight of the boats, while Ria held his hand, curious but clearly sensing the tension in the air. Emma and Wren lagged behind a bit, still waking up, while Mia walked close to Adrian, eyes scanning their surroundings with sharp curiosity.

Adrian approached the first sailor he saw, a grizzled man cleaning his boat. He wore a faded cap, and his sun-weathered skin suggested years of experience at sea. Adrian gave a polite smile and spoke in a friendly tone. "Excuse me, sir. We're looking for someone—a sailor who knows about Xel Island. Could you point us in the right direction?"

At the mention of Xel Island, the man froze. His eyes flickered with something—fear, unease, maybe even recognition—but whatever it was, he masked it quickly. He didn't answer immediately, just kept scrubbing the deck of his boat, his movements now more mechanical.

Adrian frowned slightly but tried again. "We're just trying to find some information. It's important."

The man finally looked up, his eyes cold. "I don't know what you're talking about," he muttered, turning his back on them and returning to his work. "And I suggest you stop asking."

Adrian was taken aback by the abruptness of the response, but he wasn't about to give up so easily. He turned to another sailor, this one a younger man, unloading crates of fish. "Excuse me, do you know anything about Xel Island? We're trying to find a sailor who—"

Before he could finish, the young man's face paled, and he quickly shook his head. "No, no, I don't know anything about that. And if you're smart, you won't go looking for it either."

Ria, overhearing the conversation, raised an eyebrow and leaned in toward George. "What's with these people? They look terrified."

"Maybe Xel Island has a bad reputation," George suggested, though he didn't sound entirely convinced.

Adrian pressed on, moving to a small group of fishermen standing near the edge of the pier. "We're looking for a sailor who can tell us about Xel Island," he said, his voice more insistent this time. "Can anyone help us?"

The fishermen exchanged nervous glances, and one of them—a tall man with a scar running across his cheek—stepped forward.

"You'd best leave that alone, friend," he said in a low, gravelly voice. "No good comes from asking about that place."

Adrian squared his shoulders. "Why? What is it about Xel Island that has everyone so spooked?"

The scarred man didn't answer immediately. Instead, he looked out toward the horizon, where the island itself might have been visible if not for the morning mist hanging over the water. His lips tightened, and for a moment, it seemed like he might say something important.

But then, just as quickly, he shut down. "I've said too much," he muttered, turning away and disappearing into the nearby boathouse.

Adrian's frustration mounted. Every time the name "Xel" was mentioned, it was as if a wall of silence went up. Fear and discomfort were etched on the faces of every sailor they approached, and the more they pushed for answers, the more the locals seemed to retreat.

George stepped up beside Adrian, lowering his voice. "It's like they're afraid of something... or someone. Maybe this island has a darker history than we realized."

Adrian clenched his jaw, feeling the weight of the situation. He wasn't one to back down easily, but the resistance was stronger than he had anticipated. "There's got to be someone who will talk," he said quietly, scanning the dock once more. "Someone who knows."

"Maybe the old sailor is our only chance," Mia added, watching as yet another group of sailors turned their backs on them as soon as they heard the word "Xel."

Ria, who had been mostly quiet, finally spoke up. "Do you think it's dangerous? I mean, really dangerous? The way these people are reacting... it feels like more than just rumors."

Adrian's face hardened. "We won't know until we find him. But I'm not giving up. We didn't come all this way to be scared off by a few frightened sailors."

He walked further down the dock, determined to keep trying, though every interaction left them with the same result: fear, avoidance, and silence. The name "Xel" seemed to carry an unspoken curse, a weight that none of the locals were willing to bear.

Finally, Adrian stopped, feeling the frustration build inside him. "We're not going to find anything here," he admitted, looking back at the group. "But I'm not leaving without answers. If no one will tell us about Xel Island here, we'll have to find another way."

Wren sighed, running a hand through his hair. "We'll figure it out. Let's just keep asking around, or maybe someone in town will know something."

Adrian nodded. "Yeah, we'll keep looking. But I've got a feeling that whoever this old sailor is, he's the key to all of this. We just have to find him."

As they left the docks, Adrian couldn't shake the nagging feeling that something was deeply wrong. The fear in the eyes of those they had spoken to wasn't the result of idle superstition—it was real, and it had shaken him more than he cared to admit.

As they walked away from the docks, their frustration hung in the air like a thick fog. The group's mood had shifted from excitement to quiet determination, and though no one said it aloud, the eerie reluctance of the sailors had cast a shadow over their quest. Adrian, still processing the reactions they had just encountered, motioned toward the waiting taxi. The driver, an older man with a weathered face, was leaning against the side of his cab, smoking a cigarette, watching them with mild curiosity.

Adrian gave a tight smile as he approached the car. "Looks like we're not getting any answers here," he muttered under his breath.

He glanced back at the group, all of them looking slightly dejected after the morning's failures.

Ria let out a small sigh and leaned against George. "So, what now?" she asked softly.

Adrian turned toward the driver, who extinguished his cigarette under his boot, and asked, "Can you take us to another dock? Somewhere else where sailors gather? We need to keep searching."

The driver gave a slow nod. "Sure, there's another one about twenty minutes from here. You're looking for someone in particular?"

Adrian hesitated, then shook his head. "Just need some more information. Someone's bound to talk."

"Good luck with that," the driver said, his voice gruff but not unkind. "Get in, I'll take you there."

Everyone piled into the taxi again, a quiet tension filling the car as they drove through the town, the streets still mostly quiet in the early hours. The occasional vendor setting up stalls for the day or a few locals walking their dogs passed by, but otherwise, the island seemed peaceful, unaware—or perhaps willfully ignorant—of the shadows lurking around the name "Xel."

When they reached the next dock, it was clear it was smaller than the first, less bustling, with fewer boats moored along the pier. Adrian stepped out first, scanning the area. He felt the weight of time slipping away, but he pushed forward, motioning for the others to follow.

They repeated the process—asking questions, probing for any clues about the old sailor and Xel Island—but again, they were met with the same apprehension. The sailors here were fewer in number, but the fear was the same, an unspoken dread whenever the name "Xel" crossed their lips.

Finally, after what felt like the hundredth refusal, they approached a young man who appeared to be finishing up some maintenance on his small fishing boat. He didn't seem as hardened as the older sailors, his face more open, though the moment Adrian mentioned Xel Island, the familiar tension appeared in his posture.

"I don't know much about that," the young sailor said, rubbing the back of his neck nervously. His eyes darted around as though searching for a way out of the conversation. "People don't talk about that island."

Adrian, sensing a potential breakthrough, softened his approach. "We're not here to stir up trouble. We just need to find someone who knows more. Someone mentioned an old sailor—someone who might know the island better than anyone else."

The young man bit his lip, clearly torn between saying nothing and giving away too much. Finally, after a moment's hesitation, he leaned in a little closer, his voice barely above a whisper. "Look, I don't know much, like I said. But there's an old sailor... some folks say he's been around longer than anyone remembers. You might find him in the market—sometimes he's there. Or... he could be at the post office. I've heard he goes there often, mailing letters to his daughter, who went missing a long time ago. That's all I know."

Adrian's heart leaped at the hint of useful information, and he nodded gratefully. "The post office or the market, you said?"

The young sailor nodded quickly, clearly eager to end the conversation. "Yeah. But be careful. People around here don't like talking about that stuff for a reason."

"Thank you," Adrian said, turning to the others with a flicker of hope in his eyes. "Looks like we might have a lead."

Mia, who had been standing nearby, let out a small sigh of relief. "Finally. Maybe now we'll get some real answers."

George clapped a hand on Adrian's shoulder. "Nice work. Let's hope this old sailor knows what we're after."

The taxi driver, who had been watching the interaction from a distance, raised his eyebrows as they approached. "Any luck?"

Adrian nodded. "Take us to the market first."

The driver nodded and gestured for them to get back into the car. "Market's not far. Let's hope you find what you're looking for."

As they drove off toward the market, the sun was rising higher in the sky, casting long shadows on the narrow streets. The market would be bustling soon, full of life and color, but Adrian couldn't shake the unease in the pit of his stomach. The sailor's warning echoed in his mind: people didn't talk about Xel for a reason.

Whatever they were about to uncover, he knew it wouldn't be simple. But now, there was no turning back. The mystery of Xel Island, and the old sailor who might hold the key, was within their grasp.

As the taxi wound its way toward the market, the roads transformed from the tranquil lanes of the docks to a bustling thoroughfare alive with energy. The asphalt, cracked and uneven, reflected the morning sun, and the scent of the sea gradually gave way to an array of more pungent aromas—fried street food mingling with the earthy notes of spices and the unmistakable smell of sweat from the throngs of people.

The further they drove, the more the chaos enveloped them. Colourful stalls began to line the roads, their awnings flapping slightly in the breeze. Vendors shouted their wares, hawking everything from fresh produce to handmade crafts. Adrian's heart raced in anticipation, the lively atmosphere invigorating him despite the less-than-pleasant smells wafting through the open windows of the taxi.

"Look at all those stalls!" Mia exclaimed, her eyes wide with excitement. "It's like a festival!"

"Yeah, if only the smell was better," George joked, scrunching up his nose as they passed a particularly pungent seafood stand.

Ria chuckled, elbowing him gently. "Come on, it adds to the experience. You can't have a market without a little chaos."

"Chaos is one way to put it," Adrian muttered, scanning the streets as they finally approached their destination. The taxi lurched to a stop, and the group spilled out onto the crowded street, instantly enveloped by the hustle and bustle.

The market was a whirlwind of sound and movement. The air buzzed with conversations, laughter, and the occasional shout of a vendor trying to draw attention. Stalls filled with bright fruits, woven baskets, and colourful trinkets cluttered the narrow pathways, forcing the group to weave in and out of the throngs of people. Adrian felt his heart race with the possibilities that lay ahead but was equally aware of the overwhelming sensory overload.

"Stick close together!" Adrian called over the cacophony, his voice almost swallowed by the din of the market. "We don't want to lose anyone in this crowd."

"Right behind you!" Emma shouted back, her eyes darting between the stalls, clearly fascinated by the vibrant chaos around her.

Despite the excitement, a sense of urgency hung in the air as they began their search. They navigated through the crowd, the path beneath their feet uneven with cobblestones and dirt, which made each step feel precarious. A pungent odor permeated the air, a combination of spoiled food and sweat that mixed with the sweetness of ripe fruit, creating an almost unbearable stench.

"Ugh, it smells terrible here!" Wren remarked, wrinkling his nose in disgust. "Why is it so messy?"

"It's a market, not a museum," Adrian replied with a wry grin. "People are here to buy and sell, not clean up."

"Still, you'd think they'd have some standards," Wren muttered, though a small smile broke through his irritation.

As they pressed on, they stopped at various stalls, each vendor more eager to sell than the last. They posed questions about the old sailor, hoping for any scraps of information that might lead them to her. However, every inquiry was met with dismissive waves or nervous glances.

"Excuse me," Adrian approached a stout woman selling brightly colored fabrics. "We're looking for an old sailor. Have you seen her around?"

The woman looked him up and down, her expression revealing her skepticism. "Sailors? You think they come here?" She shook her head, dismissing him with a wave of her hand. "You'll have better luck asking the ghosts."

Adrian exchanged glances with the others, his frustration growing. "Thank you," he said tersely, moving on.

As they continued searching, they encountered a group of locals gathered around a makeshift bar, their laughter ringing out. Adrian decided to approach, hopeful. "Hey, we're trying to find an old sailor—might you have seen him?"

One man, his shirt unbuttoned and his demeanour relaxed, raised a glass in a mock toast. "Old sailor? The only old thing around here is my last drink." His friends erupted into laughter, but Adrian pressed on.

"Come on, we really need to find him," Adrian insisted, trying to convey the urgency of their quest. "He might know something about Xel Island."

"Xel?" The laughter died down, and the group's mood shifted, shadows crossing their faces. "Best leave that alone, mate. Bad news, that island."

"Do you know where the sailor is or not?" Ria interjected, her patience waning.

"Why would we help you?" the man replied, now defensive. "What's in it for us?"

George stepped in, clearly frustrated. "We're just asking for a little information. If you don't know anything, that's fine, but there's no need to be rude."

"Rude? You're the ones looking for trouble," the man sneered, turning his back on them.

"Let's just go," Mia said, glancing around at the growing crowd, the loud noises pressing in on them. "This isn't getting us anywhere."

"Yeah, but we can't give up yet," Adrian insisted, refusing to let their spirits deflate. "There has to be someone here who knows something. We just need to keep looking."

They moved deeper into the market, their enthusiasm dampening with each passing moment as they encountered more dismissals and nervous glances.

Ria stopped at a stall selling local spices, drawn in by the vibrant colors and strong scents. "Maybe they know something?" he suggested, her optimism flickering.

Adrian nodded, making his way over to the stall. "Excuse me!" he called to the vendor, an older man with a long grey beard and kind eyes. "We're looking for an old sailor. We heard he might come here sometimes."

The vendor paused, glancing around as if checking for eavesdroppers. "Sailor? What sailor?" His voice dropped to a whisper, as if he feared being overheard.

"The one who might know about Xel Island," Adrian said, lowering his voice as well. "We really need to find him."

The vendor hesitated, his eyes darting to the bustling crowd. "You don't want to be involved with that. He's not someone you want to seek out. Best forget about him and leave this island."

Adrian pressed. "Please, we just want to help."

With a sigh, the vendor leaned closer, his voice barely audible above the market's noise. "If you're set on finding her, try the post office. He goes there every day to send letters to her daughter. But be careful. People are watching."

"Thank you!" Adrian exclaimed, a rush of gratitude washing over him. He turned back to the group, determination renewed. "Let's head to the post office!"

As they navigated their way back through the market, a newfound urgency propelled them forward. They dodged shoppers, weaving in and out of the stalls. The noise seemed louder now, the air thick with anticipation.

"Do you think he'll really be there?" Emma asked, her voice barely rising above the clamour.

"Only one way to find out," Adrian replied, his heart racing with the thrill of possibility.

They exited the market, the chaotic noise subsiding slightly as they stepped into the quieter streets. The post office was just a short walk away, and as they approached, Adrian couldn't help but feel a mix of excitement and trepidation. Would the old sailor be there? Would he be willing to share his knowledge?

The building was unassuming, a simple structure with peeling paint and a faded sign. A small queue of locals was gathered outside, some chatting animatedly while others waited patiently. The atmosphere was tense, and Adrian felt a familiar flicker of unease as they entered the post office.

Inside, the smell of old paper mixed with the faint scent of ink and stamps. The air was thick with anticipation, and Adrian quickly scanned the room. Several clerks moved behind the counter, assisting customers, while others were busy sorting through letters.

"Now we just need to find him," Adrian murmured, glancing around.

"Maybe we should split up," George suggested. "We can cover more ground that way."

"Good idea," Ria agreed. "Just keep an eye out for each other."

As they began to separate, Adrian headed toward a small group of elderly patrons huddled together, sharing stories. He approached them, his heart pounding. "Excuse me, has anyone seen an old sailor? She comes here often."

One of the women, her silver hair tied in a neat bun, looked up at him, her eyes bright with curiosity. "An old sailor? What do you want with him?"

"We need to find him," Adrian said, urgency creeping into his voice. "It's important."

"He used to come here regularly," the woman replied slowly, a hint of nostalgia in her tone. "But it's been a while since I've seen him. I hope he's alright."

"Do you know where he might be?" Adrian pressed.

"Last I heard, he was spending time by the docks," another woman chimed in. "But you might be better off trying the market again. That's where she spent most of her time, sharing stories with anyone who would listen."

Adrian felt a sense of frustration rising. "We've already been to the market. Everyone there is terrified to talk about her or Xel Island."

The women exchanged glances, their expressions shifting to concern. "It's true, dear," the first woman said gently. "There's something about that island that brings fear to people's hearts. But if you really want to help him or get help, you might want to visit the old tavern near the docks. That's where sailors often gather."

Adrian nodded, thanking them for their help. He turned back to the others, who were regrouping, disappointment etched on their faces.

"Anything?" Ria asked, hope flickering in her eyes.

"They haven't seen him in a while," Adrian admitted, feeling the weight of their quest pressing down on him. "But they mentioned an old tavern near the docks. We should check it out."

"Alright, let's go!" George encouraged, rallying the group as they headed back outside. The sun hung high in the sky, casting a warm glow over the streets as they made their way to the tavern.

With each step, the anticipation grew, fueled by the uncertainty of what lay ahead. As they approached the tavern, a sense of determination surged within Adrian. They would find the old sailor, and together they would uncover the secrets surrounding Xel Island.

After settling the fare, they stepped out of the taxi and waved it off, watching as it merged into the flow of city traffic, a distant hum in the background. As the group waved off the taxi, they turned their attention to the winding path leading to the old tavern. The air buzzed with an undercurrent of excitement, and anticipation hung thickly around them. The atmosphere was charged, almost electric, as they walked in the setting sunlight.

As Adrian and his friends approached the old tavern, the structure loomed before them, weathered and charming in its own rugged way. The wooden beams, coated in a layer of faded paint, told tales of years gone by, while the creaky sign swung gently in the breeze, emblazoned with the name "The Wandering Mariner." A faint scent of saltwater wafted through the air, mingling with the earthy aroma of aged wood.

The tavern was nestled between a couple of bustling shops, its entrance adorned with colorful fishing nets and rusted anchors. A few locals lounged on the worn porch, exchanging stories as they sipped their drinks. The atmosphere buzzed with a sense of camaraderie, but as Adrian drew closer, he noticed a sudden commotion—a large crowd had gathered just outside the tavern.

Curiosity piqued, Adrian and his friends slowed their pace, instinctively drawn toward the scene. The crowd was clustered around a makeshift stage, a weathered crate serving as a platform. Shouts and laughter echoed through the air, but from their distance, they couldn't make out what was happening.

"What's going on over there?" Emma wondered aloud, glancing at Adrian.

"I have no idea," Adrian replied, squinting to see better. "But it looks like something interesting."

Despite their interest, they hesitated to push closer, unsure of the crowd's purpose. Instead, they stood back, exchanging glances filled with intrigue. The excitement in the air was palpable, but they knew they had a mission to complete: to find the old sailor who might hold the key to unraveling the mysteries of Xel Island.

"Should we check it out or keep looking for the sailor?" Wren asked, glancing between the tavern and the crowd.

"We can't get distracted," Ria said firmly. "We need to stay focused."

"Yeah, let's just keep our eyes peeled," George agreed. "The sailor's got to be around here somewhere."

With that, they turned their backs on the enticing spectacle and moved closer to the tavern, hoping their search would soon yield results.

The door of the old tavern creaked as Adrian gently pushed it further open, its old hinges groaning in protest. The dimly lit interior of the tavern greeted them with an eerie stillness.

The moment they stepped further into the tavern, an unsettling chill filled the air, cutting through the faint warmth that remained outside. The stillness was unnerving, every creak and groan of the old floorboards seeming to echo louder than it should, making them feel as though they weren't alone. Shadows clung to the corners of the room, and the dim light from the small windows barely penetrated the deepening darkness.

Adrian led the way, his hand instinctively reaching out to brush against the walls, as if the solid wood might anchor him. The others followed in tense silence, eyes darting around the tavern, alert to every subtle movement in the dark.

A sudden **clatter** broke the quiet, the sound of something heavy falling over in the back room, followed by a faint, distant scuffling. The group froze, each one exchanging uneasy glances.

"What was that?" Emma whispered, gripping Mia's arm.

"Probably just something knocked over by the wind," Adrian muttered, though his voice lacked conviction. "Stay close."

They moved further in, their footsteps hesitant and quiet, the sound of each step swallowed by the weight of the silence. The tavern felt like a forgotten relic—everything coated in dust, tables and chairs arranged as if waiting for patrons who never came. But something felt wrong, like they had stepped into a place where they didn't belong.

Without warning, the low groan of the tavern's wooden beams intensified, almost as if the walls themselves were tightening around them. Then, out of nowhere, a sharp screech rang out, like nails raking across metal, sending shivers down their spines.

Ria gasped, clutching Adrian's shoulder. "Did you hear that? That wasn't just a floorboard."

"Yeah, I heard it," George replied, his voice steady but his eyes wide with unease. "It sounded... close."

The sound came again, louder this time, almost like something dragging itself across the floor just beyond their vision.

Adrian swallowed hard. "We keep moving. We need to see if anyone's here. Let's check the back."

As they ventured deeper, a series of low, haunting whispers began to fill the air. At first, it was just a faint murmur, barely audible, but soon the whispers grew louder, circling around them, coming from every direction. The words were unintelligible, a jumble of breathy, disjointed phrases that seemed to be coming from nowhere and everywhere at once.

"What... what is that?" Mia's voice trembled as she tried to pinpoint where the whispers were coming from.

"I don't like this," Emma whispered. "This place feels wrong."

Suddenly, a sharp bang echoed from the far end of the room, like a door slamming shut with force. The group jumped, eyes wide as they instinctively stepped back, their nerves fraying with each strange occurrence.

"Maybe we should leave," Ria suggested, her voice thin. "Something's off about this place."

Just as they considered retreating, there was a loud **crash** from above them, followed by the distinct sound of footsteps pacing overhead—heavy, deliberate steps, as if someone or something was moving around in the upper floor of the tavern.

"They didn't say there was a second floor," Wren said in a low voice, looking up at the ceiling. The steady thud of footsteps continued, slowly moving across the floorboards above, the rhythm unnervingly deliberate.

Adrian glanced around, searching for a staircase. "We need to check it out."

"No way," Emma replied, shaking her head. "There's no one here. There **can't** be. We're hearing things."

Another set of heavy footsteps echoed from the far side of the tavern, closer now, as if something was coming down the stairs. The group tensed, hearts pounding as the door to the back room creaked open slowly, revealing nothing but a yawning void of darkness.

"Who's there?" Adrian called, his voice echoing in the eerie quiet, but no answer came. Only the sound of something scraping across the floor, like a dragging limb.

Suddenly, a high-pitched wail cut through the air, followed by the sound of skittering movement. It was erratic and frantic, like something trying to escape. Adrian pushed through the fear gnawing at his mind and stepped closer, the others trailing behind him reluctantly. The noise grew louder, almost feral, filling the space with a chaotic energy.

"What is that?" George whispered, his face pale, but before anyone could answer, the source of the terrifying noises revealed itself—a blur of movement shot out from behind an overturned chair, and two black cats darted across the floor, hissing wildly.

The group froze in shock, staring at the cats as they scattered, their wide, glowing eyes reflecting the dim light. The animals raced toward the back of the tavern, disappearing into the shadows.

"Are you kidding me?" Mia let out a nervous laugh, her hand pressed to her chest. "It was just—cats?"

"That was it?" Emma asked, her voice shaky, relief flooding through her as she slumped against the wall. "I thought we were about to die."

Adrian exhaled, running a hand through his hair. "Just two cats."

"Those weren't normal cats," Ria muttered, glancing uneasily around the tavern. "Something still feels off."

Despite the tension easing, the eerie atmosphere lingered. The whispers had stopped, but the weight of the tavern's strange energy still clung to them. They all shared a glance, silently agreeing that this was no place to linger.

"We should get out of here," Wren said, already moving toward the exit. "The sailor's not here, and I don't want to stick around to find out what else might be."

As they hurried out of the tavern, the cold air from outside rushed to meet them, clearing away the heaviness that had pressed down on their chests inside.

"I don't ever want to set foot in there again," Emma muttered, glancing back at the worn sign of the tavern.

"Agreed," Adrian said, though the unsettling feeling lingered in the back of his mind. The old sailor wasn't here, but this wasn't the end of their search—or the strange things they might encounter on the way.

The group stood just outside the old tavern, shaking off the unsettling atmosphere they had just escaped. Yet, even as they tried to regain their composure, their eyes were drawn to a commotion in the distance. A large crowd had gathered nearby, and an unsettling buzz of whispers filled the air, mingling with gasps and cries.

"What's going on over there?" Mia asked, her brow furrowed in curiosity.

Adrian turned to the group, his heart quickening with a mix of dread and anticipation. "Let's check it out. Maybe someone has seen the old sailor."

As they made their way through the throng of people, the crowd grew denser, a palpable tension hanging in the air. The murmur of voices turned into anxious whispers, and an oppressive feeling settled in the pit of Adrian's stomach. He felt uneasy as he pushed forward, the crowd parting reluctantly to let them through.

The closer they got, the more they realized that something was terribly wrong. The atmosphere shifted from curiosity to horror, and a sense of foreboding hung thickly around them. When they finally reached the front of the crowd, what lay before them was nothing short of horrific.

The body of the old sailor lay sprawled on the ground, blood pooling around him in a dark, macabre halo. His face was a grotesque mask of terror, and his skin was marred with deep cuts and gashes, each one telling a story of violence and brutality. The sight was enough to make even the bravest among them recoil in horror.

"Oh my God..." Ria gasped, her hands flying to her mouth as she fought to keep her composure.

"What happened?" George murmured, his face pale as he stared at the scene before them.

Adrian felt a cold sweat trickle down his back as he surveyed the chaos. The crowd was a mass of terrified faces, some weeping openly, while others stood in stunned silence, unable to comprehend the brutality of what had just occurred.

"Is this the old sailor?" Emma asked, her voice shaking, unable to tear her eyes away from the grotesque sight.

Before Adrian could answer, he noticed a young woman sitting on the ground, her back against a weathered wall. She looked to be around twenty-three, her hair disheveled and her clothes rumpled. Tears streamed down her cheeks, mingling with the dirt on her face. She was staring blankly at the scene, her expression one of utter despair.

"Someone should talk to her," Wren suggested, his voice hushed as he pointed toward the girl. "She might know something."

Adrian nodded, a feeling of urgency washing over him. He stepped forward, his heart racing as he approached the grieving woman. "Excuse me," he said gently, crouching down to her level. "Are you okay? Do you know what happened?"

She looked up at him, her eyes red and swollen from crying. "It's... it's terrible," she stammered, her voice breaking. "I was just... just here to see him. I didn't think..." She choked on her words, tears spilling over as she buried her face in her hands. "He was a good man. He didn't deserve this."

"Do you know who did this?" Adrian asked, his voice steady, though inside he felt a storm of emotions.

The girl shook her head violently, grief stricken. "No... I don't know. I just found him like this when I arrived. I—I thought he was just sleeping at first... but..." Her voice trailed off, and she broke into another wave of sobs.

Adrian felt a pit form in his stomach. The brutality of the old sailor's murder weighed heavily on him, and he could only imagine the turmoil swirling in the young woman's heart. "I'm so sorry," he said softly, wanting to offer comfort but unsure how.

Ria joined them, kneeling beside the girl. "What was his name?" she asked gently, hoping to connect with her somehow.

"Captain Eliah," the woman said, her voice shaky as she wiped her eyes with the back of her hand. "He took care of me when I had lost my mother's care forever... I was supposed to meet him today. I thought we'd go sailing. He loved the sea."

Mia leaned closer, feeling a deep sense of sympathy for the young woman. "What happened to him? Did you see anything unusual?"

"I... I don't know," the girl replied, shaking her head. "I was in town. I came here as soon as I heard the news. I just wish I had been here sooner." She took a shuddering breath, her sobs mixing with the sound of the crowd around them.

"Do you think someone wanted to hurt him?" Adrian pressed, trying to understand the situation.

"I don't know," she whispered, her voice barely audible over the rising murmur of the crowd. "But he always said the sea held secrets... I never understood what he meant until now."

Adrian felt a chill creep down his spine as he considered her words. The sailor's death was not just a tragic accident; it felt like a dark omen, something that echoed the dangers they had faced in their search for him. The weight of the situation settled heavily on him as he glanced back at the crowd, their expressions ranging from shock to fear.

"I'm so sorry for your loss," Ria said softly, placing a comforting hand on the girl's shoulder. "We'll help you find out what happened. You're not alone."

"Thank you," the girl murmured, her voice still shaky but a flicker of gratitude shining through her pain. "I just want to know why... why someone would do this to him."

Adrian stood up, his resolve strengthening. "We will get to the bottom of this. We'll find out who did this to Captain Eliah and why. He deserves justice."

As the group stood frozen in horror at the scene before them, a wave of whispers rippled through the crowd like a chill wind. Eyes widened in disbelief and fear as the gravity of the murder settled over them. People began to huddle together, exchanging hurried, anxious glances, their voices barely above a murmur.

"Did you see how he was cut?" one man whispered, his voice trembling. "It was like something out of a nightmare."

"Who could do such a thing?" a woman replied, clutching her companion's arm. "What kind of monster would kill an old man like that?"

"I heard he was a sailor, someone said he knew too much," a voice piped up from the back of the crowd, its tone laced with accusation. "They say he had secrets—dark ones."

"Secrets?" another voice chimed in, intrigued yet apprehensive. "What do you mean? Do you think it was someone from the island?"

The crowd swelled with tension as speculation ignited a fire of rumors. Faces turned towards each other, expressions shifting from shock to suspicion, fear hanging palpably in the air.

"Maybe it was revenge," a burly man muttered, glancing nervously around. "You know how sailors can be. They have their enemies."

"Or maybe it was something supernatural," an older woman suggested, her voice quavering with dread. "They say the sea can take a man's soul if he's not careful. What if he angered the spirits?"

"Spirits? Please!" scoffed a younger man, rolling his eyes. "This is a murder, plain and simple. There are no spirits involved—just a coward hiding in the shadows."

The conversations became more animated, and the crowd shifted, forming a chaotic web of emotions. Adrian felt a knot tighten in his stomach. The more they whispered, the more the atmosphere darkened, each new speculation adding to the weight of dread hanging over the group.

"Let's not jump to conclusions," he called out, trying to bring some semblance of calm. "We need to focus on what happened here and find out who did this."

But his voice was drowned out by the rising murmurs of the crowd, their eyes filled with a mix of fear and curiosity. "What if the old sailor knew something? What if he was trying to tell us?"

"Maybe we should leave," Emma suggested, glancing nervously at the bloodstained ground. "This doesn't feel right."

"No!" Adrian replied, a surge of determination pushing him forward. "We can't just turn away. This isn't just about us anymore. This poor man deserves justice, and we need to find out the truth."

As the whispers continued, a few individuals in the crowd exchanged knowing glances, and a sense of unity began to form among them. They were bound not just by fear but by a shared desire for answers, an unspoken pact igniting within the throng. As the chatter around her began to swell, the young lady felt an overwhelming rush of emotion. She sank to the ground once more, settling beside the lifeless body of the old sailor. The weight of her sorrow enveloped her, grounding her in a moment that felt suspended in time.

In this quiet scene, her grief contrasted starkly with the lively conversations surrounding her, highlighting the deep sense of loss she experienced amidst the chaos.

"What's the story behind this sailor?" Ria asked, her voice steady yet laced with curiosity. "If we're going to figure this out, we need to know who he was."

"I overheard him talking to someone last week," a woman in the crowd offered hesitantly, her voice rising above the chatter. "He mentioned something about an old treasure…something hidden on Xel Island."

The crowd quieted for a moment, hanging onto her words. "What treasure?" someone called out, igniting a renewed sense of interest.

The woman shrugged, her eyes darting nervously. "I don't know. He was just mumbling to himself at the tavern about legends and lost ships."

"Lost ships?" Wren echoed, stepping closer to the woman. "Do you remember anything else?"

"I didn't pay much attention," she admitted, shaking her head. "But it sounded like he was worried…like someone was after him."

The revelation sent another wave of whispers rippling through the crowd, excitement mixed with dread. Adrian felt the adrenaline rush through him. "We need to dig deeper," he said firmly. "If there's a treasure involved, it could lead us to the answers we're looking for."

As the crowd buzzed with anticipation, Adrian turned back to the young woman, still sitting on the ground, her face a mask of grief and confusion. "We're going to figure this out," he promised her softly. "You're not alone in this."

With a renewed sense of purpose, the group began to strategize, their minds racing with possibilities. The whispers in the crowd faded into the background, replaced by the determination to uncover the truth behind the sailor's brutal murder and the secrets that might still lie hidden within the shadows of Xel Island.

Adrian took a deep breath, feeling the weight of the moment settle upon him as he knelt beside the young woman once more. The crowd buzzed around them, but at that moment, it felt as if they were encased in a bubble, isolated from the horror surrounding them. "We need to know," he said gently. "What was your connection to Captain Eliah?"

The girl looked up, her tear-stained face contorted in a mix of sorrow and uncertainty. For a moment, she hesitated, her gaze flickering toward the grim scene before her. Finally, she whispered, "I'm... I'm his daughter."

The admission hung in the air like a heavy fog, and the murmurs of the crowd faded into a hushed silence. "His daughter?" Ria echoed, her voice a mixture of surprise and compassion. "But... we thought he didn't have any family except his lost daughter."

"I was lost to him," the girl continued, her voice trembling. "When I was young, there was an accident. I was taken away, and he was forced to hide me to keep me safe. He would send me letters, telling me about his life and the sea, but he never wanted me to come back... until now."

"Until now?" Adrian repeated, his mind racing. "What do you mean? Did he want to reunite with you?"

She nodded, fresh tears spilling down her cheeks. "He wrote to me just a few days ago, saying he was finally ready to bring me back. He wanted me to meet him here, at the tavern. He thought it was safe, but..." Her voice cracked, and she covered her face with her hands, the weight of her loss crashing down on her like a wave.

"I'm so sorry," Emma said softly, kneeling beside her. "But why did he keep you hidden? What was he afraid of?"

The girl took a shaky breath, wiping her eyes. "There were people... people who wanted him to stay silent. He was afraid they would come after me if they found out he had a daughter. He thought it would be safer for me to live far away, away from the dangers of his life as a sailor."

"Did he mention anything specific? Any names or places?" Wren asked, leaning closer, his expression serious.

She shook her head, frustration mixing with her grief. "No. He always wrote in riddles, like he was afraid of being discovered. But he did mention Xel Island—a place where he had buried secrets, where he believed he could keep me safe."

Adrian's heart raced at her words. "Secrets?" he repeated, feeling a connection forming between the sailor's past and the chaos unfolding in front of him. "What kind of secrets?"

"I don't know!" she cried, her voice rising in panic. "All I know is that he was worried. He had made some enemies, and he believed that Xel held the answers to what happened to our family. I didn't know what to believe until now."

The group exchanged glances, a sense of urgency filling the air. "If he was murdered because of those secrets, then we have to find out what they are," Adrian stated, his determination steeling. "For your sake and for the sailor's memory, we need to dig deeper."

"Yes," Ria added, her eyes fierce with resolve. "We need to uncover the truth. If someone is out there willing to kill for it, then we need to find them first."

The young woman looked at them, her eyes wide with hope. "You really think you can help me? Find out who did this?"

"We will," Adrian assured her, standing up with newfound purpose. "But we need to start with the letters he sent you. Do you have any of them?"

She nodded, her expression shifting from despair to determination. "Yes, I kept every one. They're all I have left of him."

"Then let's go somewhere private," George suggested, glancing back at the crowd still murmuring about the gruesome scene. "We need to talk this over and figure out our next steps."

As the group formed a small circle around the young woman, Adrian felt a flicker of hope in the midst of the horror. Together, they would hope uncover the secrets of the old sailor, face whatever dangers lay ahead, and bring justice to his memory—if it was the last thing they did.

Adrian, his voice calm but firm, approached the young lady still seated by the old sailor's body. "I know this is difficult, but we need to understand more. Would you allow us to come to your place and look through any letters he might've left? We can also talk about what happened... piece things together."

She glanced up, eyes swollen with tears, and after a heavy pause, gave a soft nod.

Before they prepared to leave, Adrian gently asked, "What's your name?"

"Clara," she whispered, barely audible above the hum of the city.

With that, they rose and made their way to her current residence, a modest house she'd just purchased the day before. The small home stood in a quiet, almost forlorn part of town, tucked away from the bustling streets. The building itself was quaint, its walls worn and its surroundings empty, as if it had been forgotten by time. A single tree cast a shadow over the entrance, adding to the sense of isolation. There was a certain stillness about the place, a quiet that echoed the loneliness of its new inhabitant.

Adrian, Clara, and the rest of the group stood in front of the house, the fading light of the day casting long shadows over the old, weathered building. The house itself was unremarkable, a modest structure with peeling paint and worn edges that suggested years of solitude. The silence in the air was heavy, filled with the tension that had been building since the moment they met Clara, now amplifying as they stood before her home.

"Are you sure this is the place?" George asked, eyeing the old, locked door. The metal chain that bound it glinted in the fading sunlight, rusted but firm, sending a signal that it hadn't been opened in a while.

Clara stood still for a moment, her eyes fixed on the house, as though she were bracing herself for what was to come. The others exchanged glances, their curiosity piqued. Ria, standing beside Adrian, noticed Clara's hands. They were empty—no keys, no bags. Nothing to indicate she could easily open the door that stood before them, locked as tightly as it was.

"How are we going to get inside?" Mia asked, her voice soft, but laced with a hint of anxiety.

"That's a good question," Wren added, crossing his arms. "Clara, do you have a key?"

Clara's lips curved into the faintest trace of a smile, but her eyes held a mixture of sorrow and nostalgia. "It's not exactly with me," she said quietly, stepping toward the side of the house.

"What does that mean?" Adrian muttered under his breath, watching as Clara moved away from the group. She walked slowly, purposefully, toward a vacant patch of soil near the house. The earth looked undisturbed, almost natural, as though nothing had ever been hidden beneath its surface.

George raised an eyebrow. "What's she doing?"

"Looks like she's digging for something," Ria said, her voice curious but steady.

Clara dropped to her knees without hesitation and began digging into the soil with her bare hands. The sound of her fingers clawing through the earth echoed faintly in the stillness of the air, creating an almost rhythmic pattern as dirt flew up in small clumps. Her movements were practiced, deliberate, as though she had done this a hundred times before. The others watched in silence, their confusion growing.

Adrian leaned closer, his eyes narrowing. "She's digging for a key?"

"She buried it," Mia whispered, realization dawning on her.

The more Clara dug, the more it became clear that something was buried beneath the surface. After a few moments, her fingers brushed against metal, and with a soft grunt, she unearthed a small, weathered box. She opened it carefully, and inside, nestled among the dirt and small stones, was a single, rusted key.

Clara held it up, her fingers trembling slightly. "This is the key to the house," she said softly, her voice almost drowned by the weight of the moment.

Adrian blinked in surprise, his gaze flicking from the key to Clara's face. "You buried it?"

Clara nodded, standing up and brushing the dirt from her hands. "It's safer this way. There are things inside this house that no one was meant to find. Secrets my father kept hidden. Secrets that he didn't want the world to know."

The gravity of her words sank in, and the group fell silent for a moment, absorbing the reality of the situation. This wasn't just a simple house—it was a vault for memories, for the forbidden secrets of her father's past.

"Let's not waste time," Adrian said firmly, cutting through the silence. His eyes, once filled with questions, were now focused. They had come too far to stop now.

Clara walked back to the front door, the others trailing behind her, the air around them charged with tension. She slid the rusted key into the lock, the metal grinding against metal in a sound that felt far too loud in the silence of the evening. After a brief struggle, the lock gave way with a click, and the chain fell loose from the door.

Clara hesitated for a moment, her hand hovering over the doorknob. Adrian watched her closely, sensing the weight of her hesitation. The door wasn't just a barrier to her home; it was a barrier to her past, one she hadn't stepped through in a long time.

"You okay?" Ria asked softly, her voice gentle, full of understanding.

Clara nodded, though the expression on her face said otherwise. "I haven't been inside since... well, since everything happened."

Adrian stepped forward, placing a reassuring hand on her shoulder. "We're here with you. You don't have to do this alone."

With a deep breath, Clara turned the doorknob and pushed the door open. The hinges groaned in protest as the door swung inward, revealing a dark, musty interior. The stale air hit them immediately, thick with dust and the scent of things left untouched for far too long.

The house was cloaked in shadows, the only light coming from the last rays of the setting sun filtering through the grime-covered windows. The furniture inside was sparse—an old wooden table, chairs that looked like they hadn't been sat in for years, and a fireplace with a stack of logs that had long since decayed.

They stepped inside cautiously, the wooden floor creaking beneath their weight. Every step felt heavy, each creak sending small vibrations through the still air.

"This place feels frozen in time," George remarked, his voice low. "Like no one's been here for ages."

"No one has," Clara replied, her eyes scanning the room. "My father didn't want anyone here. Not even me."

Adrian turned to Clara, his gaze intense. "What did your father hide here?"

Clara's eyes flickered toward a door at the far end of the room. "There's a room in the back. He always advised me to keep it locked, said it was for his eyes and the future's fate only. But I know there's more. I found letters... things he was never able to say to me directly and also some which I couldn't understand very well."

The air grew thick with unspoken questions, the tension in the room almost palpable. "Then that's where we start," Adrian said firmly, his eyes locked on the door at the end of the hall.

Clara hesitated for a moment, then nodded, leading the group toward the room that held the secrets they had been searching for.

As they moved through the house, the floor creaked beneath their feet, and the walls seemed to close in around them, as if the house itself was aware of the secrets it contained. The room at the back loomed ahead, its door old and worn, yet sturdy, as though it had been built to withstand the passage of time—and the prying eyes of the curious.

Clara reached for the doorknob, but before she could turn it, she paused, her breath catching in her throat. The weight of everything—her father's past, her own hidden identity, and the mystery that tied it all together—hung heavy in the air.

Adrian, sensing her hesitation, placed a hand on her shoulder. "Whatever's behind that door, we'll face it together."

With one final deep breath, Clara turned the knob and opened the door, revealing a darkness deeper than the shadows that had filled the rest of the house. They stepped into the room, their hearts racing, knowing that they were one step closer to the answers they sought—and the danger that came with them.

As Clara pushed open the door, the group stepped into a dimly lit room that seemed untouched by time. Dust particles floated lazily in the stale air, illuminated by the fading light that seeped through the cracks in the windows. The walls were lined with shelves full of old, weathered books, and a single wooden table sat in the middle of the room, its surface worn from years of use.

Adrian, George, Ria, Emma, Wren, and Mia all moved cautiously, their eyes scanning the room, feeling the weight of the past hanging in the air. This room was different from the rest of the house—there was something sacred about it, as though it had been a private sanctuary for Clara's father.

Clara entered behind them, her footsteps soft, yet purposeful. She seemed both relieved and tense at the same time, as if bringing them into this space was both cathartic and painful. She closed the door behind her, sealing them inside this quiet chamber of secrets.

"I'll make some tea and get us something to eat," Clara said, her voice steady but with an undercurrent of emotion. "You've come a long way. I'll be right back."

The group exchanged silent glances as Clara left the room, her figure vanishing into the darkness of the hallway. They heard her moving around the house, the sounds of cabinets opening, water running, and the clink of dishes echoing faintly in the still air.

Adrian took a deep breath, breaking the silence between them. "This place... it feels like it's holding something back, doesn't it?"

George nodded, eyes flicking toward the shelves. "Like it's trapped in a different time, waiting for someone to uncover it all."

"Do you think the letters will have answers?" Ria asked, her voice barely above a whisper. "About what happened to her father? Why he kept her hidden?"

"They have to," Mia replied softly. "It feels like everything is tied to those letters."

Before they could speculate further, Clara returned, carrying a tray filled with cups of tea and a few simple plates of food—bread, cheese, and some fruit. She placed the tray on the table with practiced ease, her expression calm but distant. "It's not much, but please, help yourselves," she said, gesturing to the food.

The group sat around the table, taking the offered food in quiet gratitude. There was something surreal about sitting in that room, sharing a meal, knowing that the answers they sought were so close, just beyond their reach.

As they ate, Clara disappeared again for a few minutes, and when she returned, she was carrying a small wooden box in her hands. It was old, worn at the edges, with intricate carvings of waves and a ship etched into the surface. Her expression was somber as she placed the box on the table in front of them.

"These are the letters," she said quietly, her voice laced with emotion. "Every letter my father ever sent me. He never wanted me to visit him in person. He said it was too dangerous... but now, I think there was more to it than just keeping me safe."

She opened the box with careful hands, revealing a stack of aged letters tied together with fraying twine. The group stared at the letters, the weight of their importance sinking in. They represented years of communication between father and daughter, the only connection Clara had to a man she barely knew.

Clara untied the twine, her hands trembling slightly as she handed the first letter to Adrian. "I think it's best if we read them together. Maybe you'll see something I missed."

Adrian took the letter carefully, the delicate paper crinkling slightly under his touch. The others leaned in closer as he unfolded it, his eyes scanning the words written in neat but hurried handwriting. The ink had faded over the years, but the message was still clear.

My Dearest Clara,

I hope this letter finds you well. I must apologize for the distance I've kept, but you must understand it is for your safety. The world I'm involved in is not a place for you. There are forces at play that go beyond anything you could imagine. Trust me when I say you are better off far away from it all.

Adrian paused, glancing at Clara, who was staring at the letter with a mix of sadness and confusion. "What forces was he talking about?" he asked, his voice low.

Clara shook her head. "He never explained. Every letter was like that—vague, filled with warnings and apologies. I thought he was just being overly protective."

"There's more," Ria urged. "Keep reading."

Adrian nodded and continued.

There is something I've kept hidden, not just from you, but from everyone. The island... Xel. It holds secrets that are too dangerous for the world to know. I've spent my life trying to keep them buried, but now... now, I fear they are surfacing again.

George's eyes widened. "He knew about Xel Island? He knew something was wrong?"

"Apparently," Wren murmured. "What could be so dangerous that he'd keep Clara hidden for her whole life?"

Clara swallowed hard, her hands clenching into fists. "I never understood why he couldn't tell me. It felt like he was always keeping me in the dark, always protecting me from something I couldn't see."

Adrian continued reading, his voice growing more intense with every word.

If you ever come to find me, there are things you need to know. The truth lies buried in the island, in places only I can show you. But it is not safe. There are people who will stop at nothing to uncover what I've kept hidden. They killed for it before... they will kill again.

A tense silence followed, the weight of the revelation pressing down on them all. The room felt even smaller now, the air thick with the danger that loomed over Clara and her father's legacy.

"Who's after this secret?" Ria asked, her voice filled with concern. "Who killed him?"

"I don't know," Clara said, her voice cracking with emotion. "I don't know who would have done this, but I'm starting to think it was because of what he knew—about Xel Island."

"We need to go there," Adrian said firmly, his mind racing. "We need to find out what your father was trying to protect."

Clara hesitated for a moment before nodding. "Yes. But be careful. My father spent his life keeping those secrets buried... and now, it's up to us to find out why."

Adrian carefully placed the first letter down on the table, the weight of its words still hanging heavily in the room. Clara's eyes lingered on it for a moment longer before she reached into the wooden box and pulled out another letter, her hands trembling slightly as she unraveled the twine.

"This one... this was the last letter he ever sent me," she whispered, her voice barely audible. Her expression was a mix of grief and anticipation, as though the letter might contain the answers she'd spent years longing for, but also the final blow to the hope she had been desperately clinging to.

The group gathered closer, their breaths held in anticipation. Adrian took the letter gently from her hands, the fragile paper crackling as he unfolded it. The ink had faded with time, but the hurried strokes of Clara's father's handwriting were clear, each word etched with urgency and sorrow.

Adrian began to read aloud, his voice low but steady.

My dearest Clara,

By the time you receive this, I fear it may already be too late for me. I have always tried to protect you from the darkness that surrounds me—the darkness that comes from the secrets of Xel Island. I've kept them buried for years, but now the truth is clawing its way back into the light, and with it, death follows.

Adrian paused, the weight of the words heavy on his tongue. The room grew colder, and Clara's breath hitched, her eyes glistening with unshed tears.

There are names you must know, my daughter. Victor, Marcus, Logan, Georgia, and many more—they all died because of these secrets. Each of them believed they could overcome the curse of Xel. They believed in their own strength, their self-confidence driving them forward. But it wasn't enough. The island does not forgive arrogance.

Clara's face paled as she listened to the names, each one carving a deeper wound into her heart. Adrian glanced at her, knowing the weight of hearing these names—names of people her father knew, people who had once lived and breathed, now reduced to tragic casualties of a terrible secret.

Ria placed a hand on Clara's shoulder, her touch gentle, but Clara couldn't pull her eyes away from the letter. "Victor, Marcus... they were his friends, weren't they?" she whispered, her voice trembling. "They died for him. For this secret."

Adrian continued, his own throat tightening as he read.

They were brave, all of them. They believed in themselves, believed they could protect the world from what Xel holds. But the truth is, none of us can escape the consequences of the island's secrets. Their confidence was their undoing. And now, I fear I am next.

Clara stifled a sob, her shoulders shaking as she tried to keep her emotions in check. But her eyes, red-rimmed and filled with anguish, betrayed the grief and fear building inside her. Each word felt like a dagger twisting in her chest.

Adrian's voice softened, his own heart heavy as he reached the final lines.

I want you to know, Clara, that keeping you safe has been my only goal in this life. But I cannot run from the island's curse forever. I know they will come for me, as they came for my friends. But before my time runs out, I want to see you one last time. I want to look into your eyes and tell you that I'm proud of the woman you've become. I want you to know that despite everything, you were the best thing that ever happened to me. If I don't get that chance... know that I loved you more than words can say.

Stay far away from Xel, my darling. It will only bring you pain. But if you must seek the truth... know that it comes with a heavy cost.

The letter ended there, the finality of the words striking like a hammer against stone. Clara's face crumpled, and she buried her face in her hands, her sobs breaking the silence that had settled over the room.

"He wanted to see me," she whispered, her voice barely audible between sobs. "He knew... he knew he didn't have much time, but I never came. I never got to say goodbye."

Adrian's heart clenched as he watched her. The letter had unraveled everything—her father's hidden fears, his regrets, and the desperate hope that he might see his daughter one last time. And yet, that hope had gone unanswered, leaving Clara to grapple with the weight of what could never be.

Ria moved closer, wrapping her arms around Clara, pulling her into a comforting embrace. "Clara, this isn't your fault," she murmured. "He was trying to protect you. You couldn't have known."

"But I could've been here," Clara choked out. "He asked to see me, and I... I didn't come. He died alone because of me."

Adrian felt the guilt radiating off her, a crushing wave of pain that seemed to echo the helplessness they all felt. There were no words that could heal that wound, no reassurance that could erase the regret she carried.

"He loved you," Adrian said softly, his voice gentle yet firm. "That's clear in every word he wrote. He did everything he could to protect you, and he died with that love. He didn't die because you weren't here, Clara. He died knowing he did what he had to—to keep you safe."

Clara's sobs quieted, though her grief remained palpable. She wiped her tears away, her hands trembling. "I want to finish what he started," she said, her voice shaky but resolute. "I want to know why they died. Victor, Marcus, Logan, Georgia—why did they all die for Xel? What was worth all this sacrifice?"

Adrian exchanged a glance with the others, each of them feeling the weight of Clara's resolve. This was no longer just about uncovering secrets—this was about honoring the memory of those who had died protecting them.

"We'll figure it out," Adrian promised. "Together. We'll find the truth. Your father's story doesn't end here."

Clara nodded, her expression a mixture of pain and determination. The grief still clung to her, but beneath it, a fire had been lit. She wasn't going to let her father's death be in vain. Not now.

With a final glance at the letter, Adrian folded it gently and placed it back in the box. The room remained heavy with unspoken words, the shadows of the past still hanging over them. But as they sat together in the silence, they knew their journey had taken on new meaning.

For Clara. For her father. And for the lost souls of Xel.

As Clara took a moment to compose herself, she reached back into the box, her fingers brushing over the letters with reverence. But just then, something slipped from her grasp and fluttered to the floor with a soft thud. The sound broke the heavy silence, drawing everyone's attention to the piece of paper that had fallen out.

"What was that?" Adrian asked, his curiosity piqued.

Clara looked down, her brow furrowing. "I don't know. It must have been stuck." She reached down to retrieve the letter, her fingers trembling slightly as she picked it up.

The paper was old and yellowed, the edges frayed and worn, as if it had been pulled from the depths of time itself. Clara unfolded it carefully, revealing an additional note that seemed to have been written in haste. The handwriting was less tidy than the previous letters, as though the author had been pressed for time, the letters scrawled with urgency.

"What does it say?" Wren asked, leaning forward, his eyes locked on the page.

Clara squinted at the dim light, her heart pounding as she began to read aloud:

To whom it may concern,

If you are reading this letter, then it means I am gone, and you are in grave danger. There are forces at play that cannot be ignored, and you must heed my warning. The island of Xel is not just a place of mystery; it is a breeding ground for evil, and it demands a price for those who dare to trespass.

The air in the room felt heavier, the oppressive atmosphere thickening as Clara's voice trembled with each word she read.

Those who seek the truth are often met with despair. Victor, Marcus, Logan, Georgia—they were all drawn to Xel by their own ambitions, their own desires for power and knowledge. But ambition blinds the heart to the perils of the past, and it can lead to ruin. They believed they could conquer their fears, that they were strong enough to handle whatever secrets the island held. They were wrong.

Adrian exchanged worried glances with the others, the gravity of the letter settling over them like a dark cloud. Clara's hands shook as she continued to read.

You are not safe here. The island knows who you are and what you seek. It has eyes everywhere. It watches, it waits, and it will come for you. I cannot say who it is that hunts you, but they are relentless and will stop at nothing to keep the secrets buried.*

"Secrets," Ria echoed, her voice barely above a whisper. "What secrets?"

If you find this letter, do not go to Xel. Leave this place behind. Do not put yourself in danger for a truth that will only lead to more pain. The shadows of the island are long, and the darkness will consume anyone who dares to delve too deeply. There is no treasure worth the price of your life.

With every sentence, the atmosphere around them grew darker, the words weaving a tapestry of dread that filled the room with an impending sense of doom.

I fear for you, for anyone who steps foot on that cursed land. I wish I had the courage to tell you the truth before it was too late, but now I can only beg you to turn back. I hope you find the peace I could not. Stay away from Xel Island and the horrors that dwell there. You will not survive.

Clara's voice faltered as she finished reading, her heart racing. The silence that followed was thick and oppressive, the weight of the letter's contents heavy on their minds.

"What the hell?" George murmured, his face pale as he processed the ominous warnings. "This is a lot to take in."

"This... this is terrifying," Mia said, her voice shaky. "If what he says is true, then we're in more danger than we thought."

Adrian felt a chill run down his spine, his mind racing. "But we can't just turn back now. Clara deserves to know the truth about her father, and we need to uncover whatever secrets are tied to Xel Island."

"Are you serious?" Emma replied, eyes wide with disbelief. "After reading this? We have to consider our safety. If there's even a chance this is true..."

"Every moment we hesitate puts us closer to danger," Clara said, her voice rising above the doubt. "My father believed in uncovering the truth, and I can't let fear dictate my life any longer. We owe it to him to find out what happened."

Adrian nodded, a fierce determination building within him. "Clara's right. We need to keep pushing forward. We can't let his death be in vain. We'll face whatever comes together."

The tension in the room hung heavy as they weighed the risks against the resolve in their hearts. The letter's horrifying warnings echoed in their minds, but with each passing moment, they felt a sense of unity and purpose solidifying their resolve.

"Then we need a plan," Ria said, her voice steady now. "We can't just go in blind. We need to gather information, find out what we're up against, and prepare ourselves for the journey ahead."

"Agreed," Wren added. "We should head back to town, speak to the locals, and see if anyone knows more about the island or the threats surrounding it."

Clara wiped the remaining tears from her face, her expression shifting from sorrow to determination. "Let's find the answers. I'm not afraid to face whatever's out there. I want to know the truth."

With a collective nod, the group steeled themselves for the challenges that lay ahead. The darkness of the unknown loomed, but their hearts burned with the fierce flame of hope and solidarity. Whatever secrets Xel Island held, they would face them together.

As the weight of their resolve settled into the air, Clara's expression shifted. The determination that had ignited her spirit moments before began to flicker like a candle in a storm. Her brow furrowed as she looked down at the letters, the truth of her father's warnings echoing in her mind.

"Wait," she said suddenly, her voice trembling as she stepped back from the group. "No. I can't do this."

The sudden change in her demeanor caught everyone off guard. Adrian furrowed his brow in confusion. "Clara, what do you mean? We're in this together. We can figure it out."

Clara shook her head, her hands gripping the edge of the table as she fought to steady herself. "No, you don't understand. My father's words... he wrote those letters for a reason. He warned me not to go to Xel Island. He said it wasn't safe for me—"

"But you said he wanted to see you!" Ria interjected, her voice filled with urgency. "This is your chance to learn about him and what he was protecting you from."

"Exactly!" Adrian added, stepping closer. "You deserve to uncover the truth about your father. We can help you."

Clara took a deep breath, her heart racing as she wrestled with the conflicting emotions swirling inside her. "But what if he was right?" she said, her voice breaking. "What if I'm not strong enough? What if I put all of you in danger by going after this? What if... what if I end up just like him?"

The room fell silent, the weight of her words settling heavily around them. The air felt thick with tension, and Adrian's heart sank as he realized the fear that gripped her was overpowering her desire for answers.

"Clara," he said gently, "we're stronger together. Your father's warnings don't mean you have to run away from the truth. You have the chance to find out who he was and what he kept hidden. You owe it to him to try."

She shook her head vehemently, tears welling in her eyes again. "I owe it to him to stay away! He sacrificed so much to keep me safe. I can't just ignore that. He had his reasons for wanting me to stay away from Xel, and I can't disregard that now. I can't put you all in danger for my curiosity."

"Clara," Mia pleaded, stepping forward. "You can't let fear control your choices. If you do, your father's sacrifices will have been in vain. This is about more than just finding the truth; it's about honoring his memory and his love for you."

But Clara looked between them, her heart heavy with indecision. "I can't," she whispered. "I can't go back there. I won't put any of you at risk."

Adrian felt a surge of frustration mixed with compassion. He understood her fears, but the thought of abandoning their mission felt like a betrayal to everything they had fought for.

"Then let us decide together what to do next," Adrian said, his tone firm yet gentle. "You're not alone in this. You don't have to bear this burden by yourself."

"I just don't want to lose anyone else," Clara said, her voice breaking again. "I lost my father... I can't risk losing you too."

The group stood still, the silence stretching on as Clara's emotions swelled, battling between the desire for connection and the fear of the unknown. Adrian stepped closer, reaching out to her, but she took a step back, shaking her head as fresh tears spilled down her cheeks.

"Clara, please," Adrian urged, desperation creeping into his voice. "We're committed to this. If you don't want to come, that's your choice. But we're not giving up on you or the truth."

She hesitated, her breath hitching as she looked around at the faces of her friends—determined, fierce, willing to stand by her no matter the cost. But the weight of her father's warnings pressed heavily on her heart.

"I'm sorry," Clara finally said, her voice breaking with the weight of her decision. "I can't go with you. I have to stay here... away from Xel. I won't risk it."

As she spoke, the resolve that had filled the room shifted into something heavier, a quiet acceptance of the path she had chosen. Adrian felt the knot in his stomach tighten as he realized they were at an impasse. The bond of friendship was strong, but Clara's fear was even stronger, and it held her captive in a way that was impossible to break.

"Clara..." he began, but she held up a hand, silencing him.

"Please understand," she said, her voice filled with anguish. "I need to honour my father's wishes. I won't let his sacrifice be in vain by putting myself in danger. I need to let you go after the truth. I can't join you."

The group stood in silence, the reality of Clara's decision settling heavily on their hearts.

"I respect your choice," Ria said finally, her voice soft yet resolute. "But just know, Clara, we'll be back. We'll find the answers—together or apart. Your father's legacy deserves to be honored."

Adrian nodded, feeling a deep sense of loss at the prospect of Clara not joining them on their journey. "You'll always be a part of this, Clara. We'll carry your father's story with us, and we'll find the truth for you."

With that, Clara stepped back, her heart aching as she watched them. She wanted to go with them, to uncover the secrets her father had left behind, but the fear of the unknown held her tightly, anchoring her in place.

As they prepared to leave, the group exchanged glances, each one filled with unspoken promises. They would continue their quest, but the weight of Clara's absence would linger in the air, a reminder of the choices they all had to make.

"Be safe," Clara whispered, her voice trembling as they turned to leave. "And if you uncover anything... please come back and let me know."

Adrian nodded, his heart heavy. "We will, Clara. We promise."

And with that, they stepped forward to go out of the room, leaving Clara standing alone amidst the echoes of her father's warnings, the path ahead uncertain and fraught with peril.

As Adrian and the others moved toward the door, a sense of finality began to settle over the room. The heavy silence after Clara's decision still lingered in the air, a bittersweet mix of regret and understanding. Adrian could feel the weight of leaving Clara behind, but he respected her choice. Still, something about her father's letters gnawed at him—the warnings, the names of those lost, and the secrets surrounding Xel Island. They were so close to unraveling it all.

Just as he reached for the doorknob, a voice broke through the silence.

"Wait!" Clara's voice rang out, trembling but insistent.

Adrian froze mid-step, and the others turned, their expressions a mixture of confusion and curiosity. Clara stood in the middle of the room, her brow furrowed as though she had just remembered something crucial.

"I—I almost forgot," she stammered, rushing toward them, her hands trembling slightly. "There's something else. My father... he mentioned it in one of his last letters."

They all turned fully toward her now, their attention fully captured by the urgency in her voice.

"He wrote about the way to Xel Island," Clara continued, her words spilling out in a rush. "He said there's a specific route—one that isn't on any map, one that only sailors like him knew how to navigate. If you don't take the right way, you'll never find it. It's like the island... moves."

Adrian exchanged a glance with George, both of them understanding the gravity of what Clara was saying. The island wasn't just shrouded in mystery—it was intentionally hidden, almost as if it didn't want to be found.

"What did he tell you?" Ria asked, stepping forward, her eyes filled with curiosity and apprehension.

Clara took a deep breath and motioned for them to come back inside the house. "I'll show you."

They followed her back into the room, the air heavy with a renewed sense of anticipation. Clara went over to the box of letters, rummaging through it quickly before pulling out one particular letter. It was older, the edges yellowed with time, and the ink slightly faded, but it was clear that this letter held something important.

"I didn't understand it before," Clara said, handing the letter to Adrian, "but now it makes sense."

Adrian took the letter and unfolded it carefully. As he scanned the words, he could see her father's careful handwriting, each word deliberate, as though he had been cautious about who might one day read it.

Clara, if you ever decide to follow the path to Xel, there's only one way to reach the island. Many have tried, and many have failed, but there is a route known only to a select few—a route that changes with the tides and the wind. The island doesn't stay in one place. It shifts, hides itself from those unworthy of its secrets.

Adrian's heart raced as he continued to read.

You must leave from the southernmost dock, in a place called Coral's End. It's an old fisherman's port. No one there will speak of the island, but they know the waters. From there, sail northwest. You'll need to time your journey with the moon's highest point in the sky—when the moon is full, the island reveals itself.

"The moon," Wren murmured, leaning in to read over Adrian's shoulder. "He's saying the island only becomes visible at a certain time. That's why no one can find it."

Ria nodded, her voice quiet with realization. "It's hidden. A full moon is the only way to see it."

Adrian continued reading, his hands gripping the letter tightly.

But be warned, Clara. The waters between here and Xel are treacherous, and not just because of the currents. There are dangers there that no sailor will speak of—those who guard the island, who ensure its secrets remain buried. You must sail in silence, speak to no one, and trust only the moon to guide you. If you stray off course, you may never return.

The letter ended abruptly, the final words haunting in their warning. Adrian folded it slowly, the gravity of the situation sinking in deeper with every passing second.

"So, that's it," Mia said softly. "We have a way to the island, but it's dangerous. It's like the island is protecting itself."

Clara nodded, her face etched with both fear and resolve. "I didn't understand what he meant when I first read it, but now I see. He was giving me the key to finding the island. He knew I might try one day... even though he begged me not to."

"This Coral's End," George said, leaning against the table, deep in thought. "It sounds remote. Hidden. It makes sense. A place like that wouldn't attract attention."

Adrian folded the letter back up and handed it to Clara. "We'll go. We'll sail from Coral's End and find Xel."

Clara shook her head, her expression still conflicted. "I still can't go with you. I can't betray his final wish for me. But you... you have the strength to face whatever's on that island."

"We understand," Adrian said gently. "But we'll bring back the truth. We won't let his sacrifice be in vain."

Clara's eyes filled with gratitude and sorrow as she looked at them, the weight of the moment pressing down on her. "Thank you. I'll wait for your return. And please—be careful."

Adrian nodded, his determination solidifying. "We will."

With that, the group turned to leave again, but this time there was a sense of purpose driving them forward. Clara had given them the key to the journey ahead, and now, they had a path to follow.

As they walked away from Clara's house, the fading light of the evening cast long shadows across the ground. Their minds were filled with the warnings, the dangers, and the mysteries that awaited them on Xel Island. But one thing was certain—they were heading into the unknown, and whatever secrets the island held, they were determined to uncover them, no matter the cost.

6

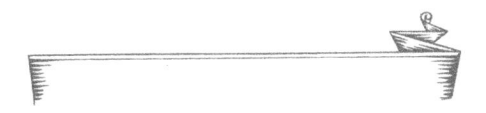

The Labyrinth of Shadows

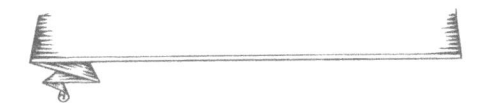

The group's journey began with an electric charge in the air, a restless energy as they made their way to the first stop on the road to Xel Island. Coral's End. The name had an ominous ring to it, but there was no turning back now. With Clara's instructions in hand and the weight of her father's warnings hanging over them, Adrian, George, Ria, Wren, Emma, and Mia pressed forward. Their destination was clear, but what awaited them there was anything but. They quickly hopped into a taxi that had been waiting, already parked and ready for passengers.

The road to Coral's End was rough, winding through narrow, dusty paths that seemed to shrink as they left the more populated parts of the West Indies behind. The further they travelled, the more isolated they became, the once-lively villages replaced by quiet, barren landscapes. The trees here were sparse, their branches gnarled and twisted as though they had weathered centuries of storms and survived by some dark magic. There was no sound but the wind and the occasional distant call of seabirds.

"This place feels like the edge of the world," Mia muttered, glancing out of the taxi window as the narrow road continued to snake along the coast.

"That's because it is," Wren replied, his voice quiet, as if afraid of breaking the eerie silence outside. "Coral's End isn't on any map for a reason. It's like we're heading straight into a ghost story."

"You're not helping," Ria said, but her nervous smile betrayed her unease.

Adrian, seated in the front passenger seat, remained focused, his mind turning over the instructions in Clara's letter. The moon would be full in just a couple of nights, and if they timed everything correctly, they'd have the chance to see Xel Island, to uncover its mysteries. But the warnings from Clara's father still lingered in his mind. *The waters are treacherous. There are dangers no one speaks of.*

He shook off the thought and leaned forward, speaking to the driver, an older man with graying hair who hadn't said much since they started the journey. "How much longer until we reach Coral's End?"

"Not long," the driver replied, his voice gravelly. "Maybe half an hour, but the place is strange. Folks don't go there much. You sure you want to head that way?"

Adrian exchanged a glance with George, who gave him a silent nod of reassurance. "Yeah," Adrian answered, his tone firm. "We're sure."

The driver shrugged, his weathered hands gripping the wheel a bit tighter. "Alright. But don't say I didn't warn you. Not much to see in Coral's End. Just fishermen and broken boats. And the sea's been rough lately—storms brewing on the horizon."

"Perfect," Emma muttered sarcastically from the back seat, drawing a small chuckle from Wren.

The landscape around them began to change as they neared Coral's End. The road became bumpier, the vegetation thicker but somehow less alive, as though the land itself was holding its breath. Dark clouds loomed in the distance, casting a strange, purplish hue over the late afternoon sky. The wind picked up, whipping through the branches and sending chills down their spines.

The driver pulled the car over at the edge of a steep cliff, where the road abruptly ended, leaving only a narrow path that descended toward a small, desolate village nestled by the water's edge. Coral's End. It was smaller than any of them had expected, barely a handful of buildings, most of them looking abandoned or forgotten by time. The sea stretched out beyond the village, vast and foreboding, the waves crashing violently against the rocky shore.

"This is where you get off," the driver said, nodding toward the path. "Coral's End is down there. If you need to leave, I'll be back tomorrow afternoon. But I doubt you'll be staying long."

"Thanks," Adrian said, offering a small smile, though his stomach churned with apprehension.

They climbed out of the car and stood at the edge of the cliff, staring down at the village below. The wind howled around them, carrying the salty tang of the sea with it, and in the distance, the roar of the waves was a constant reminder of the danger that awaited.

"That looks... welcoming," Mia said dryly, wrapping her arms around herself as a particularly strong gust of wind whipped through her hair.

"Let's just get down there and see what we're dealing with," George replied, hefting his backpack onto his shoulders. "No point in standing around here."

They made their way down the steep path, the ground uneven and rocky beneath their feet. The air grew heavier with each step they took toward Coral's End, as though the village itself was steeped in the weight of untold secrets. As they approached the first of the crumbling houses, they noticed the signs of neglect—peeling paint, broken windows, doors hanging on rusty hinges. There were no signs of life, only the distant sound of the sea.

"Doesn't look like anyone's been here in years," Wren remarked, glancing around.

"Except someone has," Adrian said, his eyes scanning the landscape. "Clara's father mentioned the fishermen. They're the ones who know the waters, who know the way to Xel."

"They don't look very chatty," Ria pointed out, gesturing toward the only sign of movement in the village—a small group of men standing near the docks, their weathered faces turned toward the sea, their bodies still and silent as statues.

Adrian frowned. "We need to talk to them. If anyone knows how to get to Xel, it's them."

As they approached the docks, the air grew colder, and the sea's roar became almost deafening. The fishermen didn't acknowledge them at first, their eyes fixed on the horizon as if they were waiting for something—something none of them wanted to see.

"Excuse me," Adrian called out, his voice carrying over the wind. "We need some information. About Xel Island."

At the mention of the island, the men finally turned to face them, their expressions hard and unfriendly. One of the older men, his skin leathery from years spent under the sun, stepped forward, his eyes narrowing with suspicion.

"You shouldn't be asking' about that place," the man growled, his voice as rough as the sea. "No good ever came from Xel."

"We don't have a choice," Adrian said, standing firm despite the growing sense of unease. "We need to get there."

The man's gaze flicked between them, his eyes dark and unreadable. "Ain't no one sane tryin' to get to Xel. You head there, you'll be lucky if the sea swallows you whole before the island does."

"What do you mean?" Mia asked, her voice tinged with fear. "What's on that island?"

The man didn't answer, but the silence that followed was more telling than any words he could have spoken. Behind him, the other fishermen exchanged uneasy glances, their eyes filled with a mix of fear and pity.

"Look," Adrian said, his voice steady but firm. "We're not here to mess around. We know the risks. We just need to know how to get there."

The old fisherman stared at them for a long moment before letting out a heavy sigh. "The only way to Xel is by moonlight. Full moon's in two nights. You'll need to leave from here, sail northwest, and pray the sea lets you pass. There's no map, no compass that'll help you. Just the moon and your gut."

Adrian nodded, grateful but wary. "Thank you."

The man shook his head slowly. "Don't thank me. Just remember what I said. Ain't no one come back from Xel the same."

With those ominous words ringing in their ears, the group made their way back from the docks, their minds racing with the reality of what lay ahead. The path to Xel was clear, but the dangers were only beginning.

The group walked away from the docks, the old fisherman's chilling words echoing in their minds. Adrian could feel the tension rising within them, each step pulling them closer to a point of no return. Coral's End, with its abandoned houses and lifeless air, had given them the final piece they needed: the way to Xel Island. But it had come with a warning that they couldn't ignore.

"We need to get ready," Adrian said, his voice clipped with urgency. "We only have two days until the full moon. We need supplies, we need a boat—everything."

"There's no time to waste," George agreed, picking up the pace. "If the old man's right, we're already on borrowed time."

"Did you see his face?" Mia asked, her breath quickening as they moved through the crumbling village. "It's like he's already written us off."

"We've got to stop thinking like that," Ria cut in, her voice sharp. "We made it this far. We've dealt with worse. The island is just another obstacle."

"But it's different this time," Emma muttered. "This place... it feels cursed."

Adrian didn't have time to argue. The air was thick with tension, and he could sense their growing fear. But fear wasn't an option. Not now. They had come too far to let it paralyze them. His mind raced as they walked—there was so much to plan, so much to organize. The fisherman's cryptic instructions played over and over in his head. The moon would be their only guide.

"Two days," he repeated, more to himself than to anyone else. "We need to gather whatever we can before we sail."

Wren, who had been silent up until now, quickened his steps to catch up to Adrian. "You think we'll even find a boat here? This place looks like it's been abandoned for years."

"We don't have a choice," Adrian replied, his tone hard. "There has to be something—anything that can get us to Xel. The fishermen will help us if we offer enough."

"They didn't seem too eager to get involved," Wren pointed out.

"They will," Adrian said firmly, his eyes narrowing. "We're not leaving without a boat."

They continued through the village, weaving through the empty streets, the eerie silence wrapping around them like a suffocating fog. It felt as if the entire place had been forgotten, as if it was a relic of a world long gone. But in two days, they would be sailing into the unknown.

"We should split up," Adrian said abruptly. "George and I will go talk to the fishermen again, see if we can convince them to loan us a boat. Ria, Wren, Mia, Emma—you gather whatever supplies you can find. Food, water, anything."

"Got it," George said, his voice tight with determination.

"We'll meet back here at sunset," Adrian continued, his mind already ticking through every possible scenario. "No wasting time. Let's move."

Without waiting for a response, Adrian and George broke off from the group, heading back toward the docks. The wind whipped around them, growing colder with every step as the sea roared in the distance. Adrian's heart pounded in his chest, adrenaline coursing through him as he replayed the old fisherman's words. There was no map. No compass. Only the moon.

They reached the docks again, the old fisherman and his crew still standing there like grim sentinels of a forgotten world. Adrian stepped forward, his shoulders squared, his jaw tight.

"We need a boat," he said, his voice commanding. "We're not leaving without one."

The old fisherman looked at him, his face hard and unreadable. "I told you—Xel's not a place you want to go."

"I understand the risks," Adrian replied, his voice steady. "But we're not asking for advice. We're asking for a boat."

The old man's eyes narrowed. "And what makes you think we'll give you one?"

George stepped up beside Adrian, his tone sharp. "You know the island. You know what's out there. If you don't help us, we're going to find another way—whether you like it or not. So either give us a boat or get out of the way."

The fisherman stared at them for a long moment, his expression unreadable. Finally, with a sigh, he nodded toward one of the smaller boats tied to the dock. "Take the skiff. It's old, but it'll get you there."

Adrian nodded, his pulse quickening. "Thank you."

The old man's face darkened. "Don't thank me yet. The sea is unforgiving. Xel isn't kind to those who seek its secrets."

Adrian didn't respond. He didn't need to. He and George turned and made their way back up the dock, the wind howling around them. They had their boat. Now, they needed to prepare for the rest.

Meanwhile, Ria, Wren, Mia, and Emma scoured the village for supplies. They moved quickly, searching through abandoned houses, prying open forgotten cabinets, and rummaging through whatever they could find. The village was eerily empty, each creak and groan of the old buildings echoing through the silence.

"There's hardly anything here," Wren said, frustration creeping into his voice as he tossed aside an empty crate. "This place has been dead for years."

"We don't need much," Ria replied, rifling through a drawer in the corner. "Just enough to get us through the journey."

Mia found a small stash of canned goods hidden in one of the cupboards, the labels worn and faded. "This should do for now," she said, her voice tight. "It's not much, but it's better than nothing."

Emma emerged from another house, a bundle of old rope slung over her shoulder. "I found some fishing gear. It might come in handy."

Ria nodded, her mind racing as they gathered what little they could find. The air around them was thick with tension, the weight of their mission pressing down on them like a storm cloud.

As the sun began to set, the group reunited near the docks, their supplies piled together in a small heap. Adrian and George returned with news of the boat, and though their faces were grim, there was a glimmer of hope in their eyes.

"We have what we need," Adrian said, his voice steady. "The skiff will be ready by morning. We leave at first light."

Everyone nodded, their hearts pounding with a mixture of fear and determination. The journey ahead was dangerous, the warnings still fresh in their minds. But they were ready. They had to be.

As the sky darkened and the first stars began to appear, Adrian looked out over the sea. The full moon would rise in two days, revealing the path to Xel.

The next day moved like a blur, every second filled with the urgency of preparation. The group, knowing that they had only one more day before they set sail, moved with relentless focus. Time felt like sand slipping through their fingers, and the weight of what lay ahead pressed on them heavily.

"Let's get everything in order," Adrian commanded, pacing back and forth at the small dock where their weathered skiff rocked gently in the waves. "We need everything packed and ready by tonight. We leave at dawn."

Ria and Mia were already sorting through the supplies they had gathered the day before. Mia worked quickly, her fingers nimble as she packed the canned goods into waterproof bags. "We've got enough food for about a week, maybe more if we ration carefully," she said, her voice quick, but calm.

Ria knelt beside her, tying off the rope they'd found the previous day. "It's not much, but we'll make do. I just hope we don't need this for anything more than securing the sails."

George hauled a heavy water container toward the boat, grunting as he set it down near the edge of the dock. "Fresh water's good for now. I filled these up at a nearby well, but once we're out there, we'll be at the mercy of the sea. We'll need to find a source when we reach Xel."

"If we reach Xel," Wren muttered, glancing nervously at the rolling waves. "The old fisherman wasn't exactly optimistic about our chances."

"Stop thinking like that," Adrian snapped, tightening the straps on the gear. "We're going to reach the island. And when we do, we'll need to be ready for whatever's there."

Wren sighed, shaking his head. "I'm just saying, we don't know what's waiting for us. If those fishermen are afraid of it, maybe we should be, too."

"We're prepared," Emma cut in, her voice sharp. "We've got food, water, and a boat. That's all we need right now."

Ria finished tying off the rope and stood, brushing the dirt from her hands. "Emma's right. We've come too far to start doubting now. We're heading to Xel whether we like it or not. The only thing left to do is make sure we're ready."

Adrian nodded, appreciating their resilience, but knowing that there was more to the preparation than just supplies. "Everyone's packed?" he asked, turning to the group. "Make sure you've got everything in order—clothes, maps, weapons if you've got them. We're not turning back once we leave."

George, ever the pragmatist, pulled a small knife from his belt and checked its edge. "I've got this. Not sure how much use it'll be, but I'm not going out there empty-handed."

"Same here," Ria said, pulling out a smaller, concealed blade from her pack. "You never know what we'll run into."

Emma was checking the fishing gear, her eyes scanning the horizon as she spoke. "We'll need to fish if we're out there longer than we expect. The sea's unpredictable—don't forget that. The moon might guide us to the island, but after that... we're on our own."

Adrian rubbed the back of his neck, feeling the pressure of leading this mission. "We're not just on our own," he said, his voice lowering. "We're heading into something that's killed people before. We need to stay sharp. No mistakes."

"Speaking of staying sharp," Mia chimed in, glancing at the small medical kit she was packing, "I've got basic first aid, but if something serious happens, we'll have to improvise. There's not much out here in Coral's End, and I doubt Xel will have a hospital waiting for us."

"Let's hope we don't need it," George muttered.

By midday, the skiff was nearly ready. The supplies were packed and secured tightly, and the group gathered at the dock, their eyes fixed on the small boat that would carry them to Xel.

"Here's the plan," Adrian said, his voice steady as he addressed the group. "We leave at first light tomorrow. We sail northwest, just like the fisherman said. The full moon will guide us to Xel. Once we're out there, we need to stay focused. No distractions, no panic. If we stick to the plan, we'll make it."

"Let's hope the moon doesn't have a mind of its own," Wren joked, though the nervous edge in his voice betrayed his unease.

Emma shot him a look. "This isn't a joke, Wren."

"I know," he muttered. "I just... never thought we'd be doing something like this. It feels surreal."

"We'll be fine," Adrian said, though the tension in his voice was palpable. "Just remember the goal. We're not just doing this for us. Clara needs answers about her father, and we need to know what's hidden on that island."

George nodded, his expression serious. "We owe it to Clara. But we also owe it to ourselves to stay alive. Let's not get careless out there."

As the sun began to set, casting long shadows over Coral's End, the group finalized their preparations. Each of them moved with purpose, a silent agreement among them that they were in this together, for better or worse.

"Tomorrow," Adrian said, looking at each of them in turn. "We set sail. This is it."

Mia pulled her jacket tighter around herself, the chill of the evening creeping in. "I can't believe we're actually doing this."

"We've been preparing for this since the moment we found those letters," Ria said, her voice strong. "Now it's time to see what's waiting for us on Xel."

With everything packed and ready, they gathered around the skiff one last time, the weight of the coming journey heavy in the air.

"We'll rest tonight," Adrian said, his voice calm but commanding. "At dawn, we sail to Xel."

No one needed to say anything else. They all knew the risks. They all knew what was at stake. As the last light of the day faded and the stars began to dot the sky, they dispersed to their tents, the silent understanding between them stronger than words.

Tomorrow, they would sail into the unknown. Tomorrow, they would face whatever Xel Island had in store for them.

As the night crept over Coral's End, the air thickened with anticipation. The small village, so quiet it felt as if it had been forgotten by the rest of the world, seemed even more still now. Inside their temporary shelter, Adrian and the others sat together, making the final preparations for their journey. Tomorrow, the sea would carry them to Xel Island—if the sea chose to show them the way.

Adrian stood by the door, watching the dark horizon where the waves crashed against the shore. His mind raced. No matter how many times he tried to push it down, doubt clawed at him. But there was no room for hesitation now.

"We need to be ready to move fast," Adrian said, breaking the tense silence. His voice was calm but charged with the weight of leadership. "We'll leave the minute the sun comes up. The winds will be with us, but the sea might not be. Stick to the plan."

Ria, leaning against the wall with her arms crossed, nodded. "Everything's packed. Food's secured, water's good. We're ready."

"We've checked the boat three times," George added, pacing as if he were trying to shake off the anxiety that simmered just below the surface. "It's old, but it'll hold. Barely."

Mia, sitting on one of the old chairs, looked up from the bundle of supplies she was tying together. "We'll make it. We've come too far to stop now."

Emma pulled her jacket tighter around her shoulders, her eyes flicking toward the window. "It's not the boat I'm worried about. It's everything after we set sail."

"Like what?" Wren asked, his usual sarcasm gone, replaced by genuine fear. "You mean the island, or whatever's guarding it?"

Adrian didn't answer right away. He could see the tension in everyone's faces, the worry gnawing at their confidence. But he knew the only way to get through it was to face it head-on. "We'll handle whatever comes. There's no turning back."

George stepped forward, his face hard. "What if we run into something we can't handle? What if the sea doesn't lead us where we need to go?"

"The fisherman said the full moon will guide us," Adrian replied firmly, though the doubt in his own voice was barely hidden. "We have to trust that. We sail northwest, keep our eyes on the moon, and trust that it'll show us Xel."

Mia shook her head, her fingers gripping the edge of her seat. "And if it doesn't? What then?"

"We'll find another way," Adrian said, refusing to let the fear creep in. "We always do."

The room went quiet again, the weight of the unknown pressing down on all of them. They'd faced challenges before—fear, uncertainty, danger. But this felt different. Xel Island wasn't just another mystery. It was something more.

"What if the island doesn't want to be found?" Emma asked softly, her voice breaking the silence. "What if it's not just the sea that's keeping it hidden? What if something—someone—wants to keep us out?"

Adrian locked eyes with her, knowing she was voicing the fear they all felt. "Then we'll deal with that when we get there."

Ria stood up from where she was leaning. "We've trained for this. We've been preparing for this ever since we found Clara's father's letters. We can handle whatever's waiting for us."

"We'll be smart about it," George said, his voice steadying. "We know what we're up against, or at least we have some idea. The island has killed before, but we're not walking in blind."

Wren exhaled slowly, rubbing his hands together as if trying to warm them against the chill that had settled in the room. "I just hope we don't become another name on the list."

"We won't," Adrian said, his voice sharp, cutting through the unease. "We're getting to that island, and we're finding the truth. For Clara. For her father. For all of us."

As the night wore on, they made their final checks. Ria went over the food and water once more, making sure everything was secured tightly. George inspected the ropes and sails, ensuring they were sturdy enough to withstand the journey ahead. Mia and Emma reviewed their medical supplies, making sure they were prepared for any injuries that might come. Wren, quieter than usual, kept pacing, his eyes darting toward the sea, as if expecting something to rise out of the waves.

Finally, after what felt like hours, Adrian called them all together again. "We're done here. Everyone get some rest. We leave at first light."

The group dispersed into their sleeping areas, though sleep wouldn't come easily for any of them. The sound of the sea, crashing against the rocks outside, filled the night with a constant reminder of what awaited them. Each of them lay awake, minds racing with thoughts of what tomorrow would bring.

Adrian, sitting by the window, couldn't shake the feeling of unease. The full moon was still a day away, but the tension in the air was already suffocating. He had led them this far, but the path ahead was full of uncertainty, and he knew he couldn't promise them safety.

But there was no turning back. Not now. They had to see this through.

As the night crept over Coral's End, the air thickened with anticipation. The small village, so quiet it felt as if it had been forgotten by the rest of the world, seemed even more still now. Inside their temporary shelter, Adrian and the others sat together, making the final preparations for their journey. Tomorrow, the sea would carry them to Xel Island—if the sea chose to show them the way.

Adrian stood by the door, watching the dark horizon where the waves crashed against the shore. His mind raced. No matter how many times he tried to push it down, doubt clawed at him. But there was no room for hesitation now.

"We need to be ready to move fast," Adrian said, breaking the tense silence. His voice was calm but charged with the weight of leadership. "We'll leave the minute the sun comes up. The winds will be with us, but the sea might not be. Stick to the plan."

Ria, leaning against the wall with her arms crossed, nodded. "Everything's packed. Food's secured, water's good. We're ready."

"We've checked the boat three times," George added, pacing as if he were trying to shake off the anxiety that simmered just below the surface. "It's old, but it'll hold. Barely."

Mia, sitting on one of the old chairs, looked up from the bundle of supplies she was tying together. "We'll make it. We've come too far to stop now."

Emma pulled her jacket tighter around her shoulders, her eyes flicking toward the window. "It's not the boat I'm worried about. It's everything after we set sail."

"Like what?" Wren asked, his usual sarcasm gone, replaced by genuine fear. "You mean the island, or whatever's guarding it?"

Adrian didn't answer right away. He could see the tension in everyone's faces, the worry gnawing at their confidence. But he knew the only way to get through it was to face it head-on. "We'll handle whatever comes. There's no turning back."

George stepped forward, his face hard. "What if we run into something we can't handle? What if the sea doesn't lead us where we need to go?"

"The fisherman said the full moon will guide us," Adrian replied firmly, though the doubt in his own voice was barely hidden. "We have to trust that. We sail northwest, keep our eyes on the moon, and trust that it'll show us Xel."

Mia shook her head, her fingers gripping the edge of her seat. "And if it doesn't? What then?"

"We'll find another way," Adrian said, refusing to let the fear creep in. "We always do."

The room went quiet again, the weight of the unknown pressing down on all of them. They'd faced challenges before—fear, uncertainty, danger. But this felt different. Xel Island wasn't just another mystery. It was something more.

"What if the island doesn't want to be found?" Emma asked softly, her voice breaking the silence. "What if it's not just the sea that's keeping it hidden? What if something—someone—wants to keep us out?"

Adrian locked eyes with her, knowing she was voicing the fear they all felt. "Then we'll deal with that when we get there."

Ria stood up from where she was leaning. "We've trained for this. We've been preparing for this ever since we found Clara's father's letters. We can handle whatever's waiting for us."

"We'll be smart about it," George said, his voice steadying. "We know what we're up against, or at least we have some idea. The island has killed before, but we're not walking in blind."

Wren exhaled slowly, rubbing his hands together as if trying to warm them against the chill that had settled in the room. "I just hope we don't become another name on the list."

"We won't," Adrian said, his voice sharp, cutting through the unease. "We're getting to that island, and we're finding the truth. For Clara. For her father. For all of us."

As the night wore on, they made their final checks. Ria went over the food and water once more, making sure everything was secured tightly. George inspected the ropes and sails, ensuring they were sturdy enough to withstand the journey ahead. Mia and Emma reviewed their medical supplies, making sure they were prepared for any injuries that might come. Wren, quieter than usual, kept pacing, his eyes darting toward the sea, as if expecting something to rise out of the waves.

Finally, after what felt like hours, Adrian called them all together again. "We're done here. Everyone get some rest. We leave at first light."

The group dispersed into their sleeping areas, though sleep wouldn't come easily for any of them. The sound of the sea, crashing against the rocks outside, filled the night with a constant reminder of what awaited them. Each of them lay awake, minds racing with thoughts of what tomorrow would bring.

Adrian, sitting by the window, couldn't shake the feeling of unease. The full moon was still a day away, but the tension in the air was already suffocating. He had led them this far, but the path ahead was full of uncertainty, and he knew he couldn't promise them safety.

But there was no turning back. Not now. They had to see this through.

Adrian drifted into an uneasy sleep, the gentle sounds of the exterior environment lulling him into a false sense of security. But as the darkness of night enveloped him, he was pulled into a nightmare that felt all too real, gripping him with its icy fingers.

He found himself standing on the edge of a vast, mist-shrouded shore, the salty air heavy with an unsettling silence. The moon hung high in the sky, its light casting eerie shadows that danced on the ground. But instead of illuminating a safe haven, the moonlight revealed twisted shapes, their outlines shifting and warping as if alive.

"Where am I?" he whispered, his voice echoing unnaturally. The wind howled around him, and he felt a cold chill creep up his spine.

Then, he heard it—a faint whispering carried by the wind. It was a voice he couldn't recognize, but it felt familiar, like a distant memory clawing its way to the surface. The whispers grew louder, merging into a cacophony that swirled around him, drowning out his thoughts.

"Turn back... leave now..."

Adrian spun around, trying to locate the source of the voice, but all he saw was the impenetrable fog thickening around him. Panic set in as the whispers escalated into frantic screams, piercing through the silence, demanding to be heard.

Suddenly, the ground beneath him trembled, and the sand shifted, revealing dark shapes rising from below. Faces—anguished, twisted, and contorted—emerged from the depths of the earth, their mouths open in silent screams. They clawed at the surface, desperate and pleading, as if begging him to help them.

"Get back!" he shouted, stumbling backward, heart racing as he felt their icy fingers brush against his ankles. The faces transformed into those of people he recognized—Victor, Marcus, Logan, Georgia—their eyes wide with terror, reflecting the very essence of fear.

"Adrian!" Victor screamed, his voice echoing in the darkness. "You have to help us! We're trapped here! We can't escape!"

"No! I can't!" Adrian shouted, panic rising in his chest. "I don't know how!"

With a sudden rush, the ground quaked violently, and the spirits surged forward, dragging him down into the sand. He felt himself sinking, the weight of their desperation pulling him deeper into the darkness.

"Adrian!" Ria's voice cut through the chaos, but it was faint and distant. "Adrian, wake up!"

The world around him distorted, colours swirling and blending into a nightmarish landscape. He was thrust into a labyrinth of twisted trees and gnarled roots, their branches clawing at him like skeletal fingers. Shadows danced menacingly between the trees, whispering secrets he couldn't understand.

"Run!" Adrian heard a voice shout, but it wasn't any of his friends. He turned to see a shadowy figure standing at the end of the path. The figure beckoned him forward, urgency etched into its movements.

Heart pounding, he sprinted toward the figure, but the path twisted and turned, disorienting him. The trees whispered his name, their voices melding into a chorus of despair. "Adrian, don't leave us! Don't forget!"

He felt a surge of dread clawing at his throat, suffocating him as he raced toward the figure. Each step felt heavier than the last, the ground beneath him shifting and writhing like a living entity.

Just when he thought he'd reach the figure, it vanished, swallowed by the darkness.

"No!" he yelled, spinning around, panic rising within him. He was alone now, surrounded by the echoes of his fears and the shadows of his past.

Suddenly, the whispers morphed into frantic laughter, echoing through the twisted forest. The laughter grew louder, resonating in his mind, taunting him. "You can't escape! You're one of us now!"

Adrian's breath quickened as he stumbled back, trying to find his way out. The shadows shifted, morphing into terrifying shapes that reached out for him, clawing at the edges of his sanity.

"Stop!" he shouted, desperation fueling his voice. "Get away from me!"

But the shadows only laughed louder, their voices a cacophony of mockery that filled his ears. "You think you can outrun your fate? You're already trapped!"

With every step, he felt the darkness closing in, suffocating him. He could hear the whispers of his friends, their voices mixed with the shadows, their fear wrapping around him like a vise.

Then, without warning, he stumbled into a clearing. The air shifted, and he found himself back at the shore, the moon glaring down at him like a malevolent eye. The water was churning violently now, waves crashing with fury as the spirits rose from the depths, their faces twisted in agony.

"Adrian!" Georgia's voice cut through the chaos, her eyes pleading as she reached out to him from the water. "Help us! Don't let us fade!"

"I can't!" Adrian cried, panic gripping his chest. "I don't know how!"

But as he looked closer, he realized the truth—each face belonged to someone lost, someone consumed by the island's darkness. It was the truth of Xel, the price paid for seeking its secrets.

The water surged higher, swallowing the spirits as they cried out, their voices blending into a symphony of despair. "You'll join us! You'll never leave!"

"No!" he shouted, stumbling backward, desperation fueling his movements. He turned to run, but the ground fell away beneath him, dragging him down into the abyss.

"Wake up! Adrian!" Ria's voice pierced through the nightmare, echoing in his mind like a lifeline.

Suddenly, he was jolted awake, gasping for breath, his heart racing as he found himself back in the room. The night was still, the gentle noises of the room grounding him, pulling him back from the edge of terror.

"Adrian!" Ria exclaimed, her face filled with concern as she leaned over him. "Are you okay?"

He looked around, the faces of his friends surrounding him, their expressions a mixture of worry and confusion. The moon hung low in the sky, illuminating the small house as the reality of the moment rushed back to him.

"What happened?" he asked, his voice shaky, drenched in sweat. "What did I say?"

"You were having a nightmare," George said, his tone serious. "You were screaming. We thought something was wrong."

Adrian took a deep breath, trying to shake off the remnants of the terrifying vision. "It felt so real," he said, his voice barely a whisper. "They were there—Victor, Marcus, Georgia. They were warning me about Xel."

"Warning you?" Emma asked, her brow furrowed in concern. "About what?"

"The island," he replied, still trying to catch his breath. "It's not just a place. It's... it's a trap. They were trapped there. They were trying to tell me to turn back."

"Turn back?" Ria echoed, her eyes wide with concern. "Adrian, we can't turn back now. We're committed to this."

"I know," he said, shaking his head, the weight of the nightmare still pressing on him. "But if they're trying to warn me..."

"Maybe it's a warning we need to heed," Wren chimed in, his voice steady. "But we can't let fear dictate our actions. We have to stay focused. Whatever we encounter, we'll handle it together."

Adrian nodded, the camaraderie of their group grounding him. He couldn't let the nightmare derail them. They had come too far, and the truth awaited them. They were bound for Xel Island, and despite the horrors that lay ahead, they would face them together.

"Alright," Adrian said, steeling himself. "Let's prepare. We'll stick to the plan and trust the moon. We can't let fear get in our way."

As they settled back into the rhythm of their journey, the tension that had gripped them began to ease. The stars twinkled overhead, and the trees gently rocked the house, a lullaby that coaxed them into a shared sense of purpose.

The nightmare had been a warning, yes, but it had also ignited something within him—a resolve to uncover the truth, no matter the cost. They would face Xel Island together, and whatever darkness awaited them, they would shine a light on it.

The moon was rising, and dawn was just around the corner. The island awaited, and they were ready to meet whatever lay ahead.

Adrian's breath came in quick, shallow gasps as he shook off the remnants of the nightmare, but the lingering fear clung to him like a heavy fog. Just as he began to regain his composure, the world around him shifted again, the familiar boat fading into a twisted reflection of the nightmare he had just escaped.

In an instant, he was back at the mist-shrouded shore, but this time, the sky was an unnatural shade of red, casting an eerie glow over everything. The whispers returned, louder and more insistent, filling his ears with a chorus of dread. Shadows flickered at the edge of his vision, darting in and out of the dense fog that enveloped the land.

"Adrian!" came a voice, echoing through the chaos. It was Clara's voice, but it was distorted, laced with panic. "You have to get out! They're coming for you!"

He spun around, heart racing, searching for her. "Clara! Where are you?" he shouted, but the fog swallowed his words, suffocating him. The ground beneath him trembled as dark shapes began to emerge from the shadows, shifting and writhing like nightmares given form.

The twisted faces of those lost to the island—Victor, Marcus, Georgia—materialized in front of him, their eyes wide with terror, mouths open in silent screams. They reached out with skeletal hands, trying to grasp him, pulling him closer to the abyss.

"Adrian, help us!" Victor cried, his voice a ragged whisper that cut through the howling wind. "We can't escape! You have to find a way to break the curse!"

"No!" Adrian shouted, stumbling back as the ground cracked open beneath him, revealing a churning void that seemed to pulse with darkness. He could feel the pull of despair tugging at him, threatening to drag him into the depths.

"Fight it!" Georgia's face contorted with pain as she reached for him. "You're stronger than this! You can break the cycle!"

Adrian's heart pounded in his chest as he struggled against the encroaching darkness. "I can't! I don't know how!" The voices of his friends melded with the cacophony of whispers, and the very air seemed to vibrate with their anguish.

Suddenly, the fog parted, and he found himself in a twisted version of the docks from Coral's End. The once-familiar place now lay in ruins, shattered boats bobbing in the water like ghostly remnants of forgotten dreams. The sea roared, waves crashing violently against the shore, sending sprays of saltwater that felt like daggers against his skin.

"Adrian!" Ria's voice called out, but the panic in her tone sent chills down his spine. "We need to get out of here! They're coming!"

He turned to see his friends standing at the edge of the docks, their faces pale and filled with terror. The shadows around them grew darker, swirling like a living entity, and Adrian felt a surge of panic rise within him. The darkness was alive, feeding off their fear, and it was closing in.

"Run!" he yelled, his voice raw as he sprinted toward them. The shadows lunged, snapping at his heels, and he could feel the icy breath of despair on his back, urging him to stop.

As he reached his friends, the shadows surged forward, reaching out with clawed hands. The air filled with the sounds of wailing and whispers, a cacophony that drowned out everything else. "You will join us!" they screamed, voices blending into a horrifying symphony of torment.

Adrian grabbed Ria's arm, pulling her toward the edge of the dock. "We need to jump!" he shouted, his heart racing as the darkness closed in.

"What about the boat?" Wren yelled, glancing back, panic etched on his face.

"Forget the boat! We have to get away from here!" Adrian insisted, feeling the weight of dread suffocating him.

In a moment of adrenaline-fueled desperation, they leaped off the dock, landing in the water with a splash that sent ripples cascading outward. The cold hit him like a shock, and he gasped, struggling to stay afloat as the shadows writhed and twisted above them, their ghastly forms looming like monstrous specters.

"Swim!" Emma yelled, panic in her voice. "We have to reach the shore!"

Adrian fought against the waves, pushing himself forward, but the darkness followed, clawing at his limbs with relentless ferocity. He could feel the chilling grip of despair wrapping around him, pulling him deeper into the abyss.

"No!" he gasped, kicking harder, adrenaline surging through his veins. "We won't let it take us!"

The water churned around them, dragging them down, but the voices grew fainter as they fought their way to the surface. They broke through the water, gasping for air, the cold sea enveloping them like a merciless embrace.

"Keep going!" Ria urged, her voice hoarse but determined. "We can't stop!"

Adrian looked back and saw the shadows lurking just below the surface, their eyes glowing with malevolence. He felt a surge of panic threaten to overwhelm him, but he shook it off, focusing on the shore that lay just ahead.

As they swam, the whispers transformed into angry roars, echoing in their ears. "You can't escape! You're ours now!"

With one final push, they reached the rocky shore, scrambling onto the land, gasping for breath as they collapsed on the wet sand. The moon hung high above them, casting a pale light that flickered as if it were mocking their desperate struggle.

Adrian rolled onto his back, panting heavily, his heart racing as the shadows receded, but the horror still lingered in his mind. "Is everyone okay?" he gasped, scanning the group.

"Barely," George replied, his voice shaky. "What the hell was that?"

"I don't know," Adrian said, still panting. "But we have to move. It's not done with us yet."

As they huddled together, the oppressive air thickened around them, and the darkness seemed to pulse in rhythm with their fear. The memories of twisted faces and anguished cries flooded Adrian's mind, a relentless reminder of the island's grip on their souls.

"We need to find shelter," Ria said, her voice steady, though he could see the tremors in her hands. "We can't let it get to us. We need to regroup, figure out what's happening."

Adrian nodded, pushing himself up and glancing around. The rocky shore was littered with debris, remnants of boats long forgotten. "There! We can take cover in that old boathouse," he said, pointing to a dilapidated structure nearby.

The group moved quickly, adrenaline fueling their movements as they darted toward the boathouse, their hearts pounding in their chests. As they entered, the scent of damp wood and decay filled their nostrils. The structure was barely standing, but it offered some semblance of safety.

"Shut the door!" Adrian barked, urgency lacing his voice. They hurried inside, slamming the door behind them and leaning against it, hearts racing.

"What was that?" Mia gasped, trying to catch her breath. "What was in the water?"

Adrian ran a hand through his hair, the panic creeping back into his chest. "It was the island. It was trying to pull us under. We need to stay focused and keep our heads clear. It feeds on fear. That's how it controls us."

"Then we can't let it win," Emma said, her eyes fierce. "We need to find a way to break its hold over us."

Ria nodded, taking a deep breath to steady herself. "Whatever happens next, we have to stick together. We can't let the shadows divide us."

The air grew heavy with tension as they took a moment to regroup. The haunting echoes of their nightmares lingered in the back of Adrian's mind, but he refused to let fear consume him. He had to be strong for them.

Suddenly, Adrian felt a sharp impact on his head, jolting him back to consciousness. *It had all been just another nightmare*, he thought. As he turned around, he noticed the others staring at him, their expressions a mix of concern and bewilderment, as if they were questioning whether he had lost his mind.

"Tomorrow, we set sail," Adrian said, his voice firm as he locked eyes with each of his friends. "We will find Xel Island, face whatever is there, and uncover the truth. We'll do it together."

The others, uninterested in probing Adrian about his condition, simply turned away and drifted back to sleep, leaving him wide awake and alone with his thoughts.

As the night deepened, the group settled into the cramped confines of the old house. The air was thick with tension, but exhaustion weighed heavily on their bodies. One by one, they closed their eyes, seeking refuge from the horrors that had invaded their dreams. But as Adrian drifted into a restless sleep, the shadows of the night continued to haunt him, swirling with whispers that echoed through his mind.

Just as dawn broke, a deep rumble shook the earth beneath them. Adrian bolted upright, heart racing as the sound reverberated through the walls. It was followed by a crack of thunder so loud it felt like the sky itself was tearing apart.

"Adrian!" Ria shouted, her voice filled with panic. "What was that?"

Adrian's mind was still foggy from sleep, but the immediate sense of danger jolted him awake. "I don't know! It sounded like—"

Before he could finish, another deafening clap of thunder rolled across the sky, followed by a torrential downpour that hammered against the roof of the boathouse. Rain pounded relentlessly, drowning out all other sounds, and the darkness outside thickened ominously. The wind howled, whipping through the cracks in the old wood, making it feel as if the storm were trying to invade their sanctuary.

"Get up! We need to move!" George shouted, scrambling to his feet. "This isn't good!"

"What's happening?" Mia cried, her eyes wide as she clutched her jacket around her. The storm was unlike anything they had ever experienced, wild and furious, a raging tempest that seemed to reflect the turmoil in their hearts.

"Everyone, grab your things!" Adrian barked, adrenaline surging through him as he forced himself to focus. "We can't stay here! We have to get to the boat before the storm gets worse!"

Ria grabbed her bag, the urgency in her movements echoing Adrian's. "We can't let the storm trap us here! We have to find a way to the skiff!"

The group moved quickly, scrambling out of the boathouse, rain soaking them instantly as they burst into the chaos outside. The world was transformed—the once serene shoreline now a maelstrom of water, wind, and darkness. Waves crashed against the shore with a ferocity that was terrifying, the sky roiling with dark clouds that churned and twisted like a living creature.

Adrian squinted against the rain, searching for the skiff. "It's over there!" he shouted, pointing toward the small boat that was bobbing violently in the churning water. It was tethered to the dock, but with the storm raging, it looked precarious, ready to break free at any moment.

"Move!" George yelled, pushing forward as they all sprinted toward the skiff, the wind tearing at their clothes and the rain blinding them.

"Adrian, we can't let it get away!" Emma shouted, struggling to keep her footing on the slick, muddy ground.

They reached the skiff, but as they did, another bolt of lightning illuminated the sky, momentarily blinding them. Adrian felt a surge of fear coursing through him. The storm was getting worse, and time was running out.

"Quick, untie it!" he barked, reaching for the ropes that bound the skiff to the dock.

Ria worked frantically beside him, hands shaking as she fumbled with the knots. "I can't get it! It's too tight!"

"Let me!" George pushed in, his hands moving quickly as the storm raged on. The wind whipped around them, making it nearly impossible to hear anything but the roar of thunder.

Just as George managed to loosen the knot, the boat lurched violently, the waves crashing against the sides. The force of the storm sent water sloshing over the edges, soaking them completely.

"Get in!" Adrian shouted, adrenaline pumping through his veins as he pushed George toward the boat. "Now!"

They scrambled aboard, each of them fighting against the elements as they climbed in. The skiff rocked wildly beneath them, the sound of wood creaking under the pressure of the waves sending a shiver down Adrian's spine.

"Everyone here?" he shouted, scanning the group as they settled into their places. The rain lashed against them, and he could barely see through the downpour. "Hold on tight!"

As he grabbed the oars, a deafening crack of thunder rang out overhead, and the sky erupted into a blinding flash of light. The storm surged, waves crashing higher, threatening to capsize the skiff.

"Adrian!" Ria screamed, her voice strained against the roaring wind. "We need to get away from the shore!"

"I know!" he shouted back, his heart racing. "We just need to get some distance from this storm!"

Adrian dug the oars into the water, pushing them forward with all his strength. The skiff lurched violently, nearly tipping as they fought against the surging waves. Rain dripped into his eyes, blurring his vision, but he pushed through, muscles straining against the relentless tide.

"Harder!" Wren yelled, panic creeping into his voice. "We need to get to deeper water!"

Adrian gritted his teeth, every stroke of the oars feeling like a battle against the storm. The wind howled around them, a malevolent force that sought to thwart their every movement. The sky above was a churning mass of darkness, the thunder rumbling like a beast awakened from a long slumber.

With every pull of the oars, they crept farther from the shore, but the storm showed no signs of letting up. Waves crashed against the sides of the skiff, spraying them with icy water.

"Keep going!" Emma shouted, her eyes wide with fear. "We can't stop now!"

But just as Adrian began to feel a semblance of progress, a massive wave loomed ahead, rising like a mountain from the depths of the sea. "Hold on!" he yelled, bracing himself as the wave crashed down on them.

The skiff was lifted and tossed violently, the boat tilting precariously as water surged over the edges. Adrian fought to keep his balance, desperately trying to keep the boat steady.

"Adrian!" Ria screamed as she lost her footing, slipping toward the edge. "Help!"

Without thinking, he lunged forward, grabbing her arm just in time. The force of the wave sent them both tumbling, but he held on, pulling her back just as another wave crashed over them, soaking them completely.

"Everyone, hold on!" Adrian shouted, adrenaline pumping as he struggled to regain control of the skiff. They were in the heart of the storm now, the wind howling like a banshee, the rain stinging like needles against their skin.

"Where do we go?" George yelled, trying to be heard over the chaos. "We can't see anything!"

Adrian squinted through the downpour, trying to navigate the turbulent waters. "We need to find the current! If we can ride it out far enough, we'll be safe!"

Suddenly, the boat lurched violently again, and another massive wave crashed over them, this time tipping the skiff dangerously to the side. Water poured in, and Adrian felt his heart race as he fought to keep them afloat.

"Bail out the water!" he yelled, but the command was drowned out by the storm's fury.

Adrian scrambled for the small bucket they had stashed in the boat. "Everyone grab something! We need to keep the water out!"

They worked frantically, bailing out the icy water as fast as they could, but the storm was relentless. The waves kept coming, pounding against the boat with unyielding force.

"Adrian! We can't keep this up!" Mia cried, her voice thick with panic. "We're going to sink!"

Just then, a blinding flash of lightning illuminated the world around them, and in that brief moment, Adrian saw the outline of Xel Island in the distance, shrouded in the storm's fury. It loomed like a dark specter, a promise of danger wrapped in mystery.

"Look!" he shouted, pointing toward the island. "There it is! We have to aim for it!"

"What? Are you crazy?" George yelled, his face pale. "That's where the storm is coming from!"

"It's our only chance!" Adrian shouted back, determination surging through him. "If we can reach the island, we might find shelter!"

"Hold on!" Ria yelled, gripping the sides of the boat as another wave slammed into them, sending them tumbling again.

Adrian adjusted the course, steering the skiff toward the ominous silhouette of Xel Island. The wind roared, a howling beast that threatened to tear them apart.

"Go, go, go!" he urged, pulling with all his might. "We can make it!"

With every stroke of the oars, they fought against the waves, determination pushing them forward. As they neared the island, the storm intensified, lightning striking dangerously close, illuminating the dark waters around them.

"Almost there!" Adrian shouted, hope igniting within him. "Just a little further!"

But the sea had other plans. Another wave crashed down, sending the skiff reeling sideways. Adrian felt himself losing grip, the boat tipping perilously as water surged in, flooding over the sides.

"Bail! Bail!" he cried, urgency filling the air. "We're not going down!"

In a last-ditch effort, they scrambled to keep the boat upright, adrenaline pumping through their veins. The island loomed closer, a dark shadow amidst the chaos, beckoning them with the promise of safety.

"Come on!" Adrian shouted, feeling the energy of the moment fueling him. "We're almost there!"

As Adrian and the others rowed fiercely toward Xel Island, the turbulent waves crashed around them, creating a chaotic symphony of water and wind. The silhouette of the island loomed closer with every desperate stroke of the oars, but just as hope began to swell within them, something strange happened.

"What the hell?" George exclaimed, his voice laced with disbelief. "Why does it feel like we're going backward?"

Adrian squinted through the relentless rain, focusing on the island that had seemed so near just moments ago. But now, it appeared to be moving further away, as if the very earth itself was mocking their efforts. "Keep rowing!" he shouted, confusion mingling with urgency. "We're not losing it now!"

Yet, despite their frantic efforts, the island seemed to pull away, the distance stretching unnaturally. The storm raged around them, but it was as if the island was surrounded by an invisible force, resisting their advance.

"Adrian, this is impossible!" Ria shouted, panic rising in her voice. "We're going as hard as we can!"

"I know!" Adrian yelled back, fear clawing at his chest. "Just keep pushing! We can't let this stop us!"

The water surged violently beneath them, churning like a beast awakened. The storm intensified, waves crashing higher, swirling around the boat as if trying to drag them back into the depths. The wind howled, carrying whispers that echoed in Adrian's mind, taunting him with every stroke.

"Row harder!" Emma cried, her face twisted with determination. "We can't let it win!"

But with every pull of the oars, the island continued to drift farther away, its outline blurring into the darkness, engulfed by the angry sea. "It's like it knows we're coming!" Wren shouted, his voice breaking with fear. "It doesn't want us here!"

Adrian could feel the panic rising within him, but he forced himself to focus. "There has to be something we can do! Keep rowing!"

As they fought against the storm, the waves crashed relentlessly, slamming into the sides of the skiff, soaking them through. Thunder rumbled overhead, a deafening roar that echoed the chaos around them.

Suddenly, a massive wave surged forward, higher than any they had encountered before, rising like a wall of water determined to crush them. "Brace yourselves!" Adrian yelled, but even as he shouted, he felt a sense of impending doom.

The wave crashed over them with a force that sent the skiff tumbling. Water flooded in, engulfing them as they were thrown into the icy depths. Adrian fought against the pull of the sea, gasping for breath as he surfaced, struggling to stay afloat.

"Adrian!" Ria screamed, her voice swallowed by the chaos. He turned to see her flailing in the water, fear etched on her face as the darkness threatened to drag her under.

"Hold on!" Adrian yelled, adrenaline surging through him as he fought against the waves. He swam toward her, reaching out as he felt the current pulling him back.

"Adrian, I can't!" Ria cried, panic lacing her voice. "It's too strong!"

But he wouldn't let go. He pulled her toward him, gripping her arm tightly as he tried to swim back to the skiff. "We're not giving up! We can make it!"

As they struggled against the powerful waves, Adrian glanced back at the island, now a distant shadow engulfed by the storm. It was as if the island had decided to abandon them, leaving them at the mercy of the furious sea.

"Push!" he yelled, forcing himself to focus on Ria. "We can do this together!"

With every ounce of strength he had left, he pulled them both toward the bobbing skiff, the small boat miraculously still afloat despite the chaos surrounding them. They reached it, and he heaved Ria up, scrambling after her as they clung to the sides, breathless and soaked to the bone.

The storm showed no signs of letting up, but with adrenaline coursing through him, Adrian clambered back into the skiff, pulling Ria in after him. They gasped for air, hearts pounding as they steadied themselves amidst the raging tempest.

"Is everyone okay?" Adrian shouted, glancing around. He felt a surge of relief as he saw the others making their way back to the boat, fear and determination etched on their faces.

"We need to get back to rowing!" George shouted, his eyes fierce. "If we don't, we'll be swept away!"

Adrian grabbed the oars, feeling the weight of the storm pressing down on them. "Row with everything you have! We're not giving up on this island!"

As they fought against the raging sea, the tension mounted, each stroke of the oars feeling like a battle against an unseen force. The waves crashed higher, threatening to capsize them again, but Adrian refused to back down. They were close—he could feel it.

"Just a little more!" he urged, heart racing as they pulled together, determined to break through the storm's grip. "We can reach it!"

But the island remained stubbornly out of reach, drifting further away as if it were playing a cruel game. With every stroke, the shadows around them deepened, the whispers growing louder, blending into the roar of the storm.

"Adrian, look!" Emma shouted, pointing toward the shoreline. "It's... it's gone!"

His heart dropped as he realized what she meant. The outline of the island had disappeared, swallowed by the tempest. "No! It can't be gone!"

"We have to get back to safety!" Ria cried, her voice rising in panic as another wave crashed over them, the force nearly capsizing the boat.

The storm raged on, a relentless beast that sought to drag them under. The whispers morphed into screams, taunting him with the reality of their situation. They were trapped in a nightmare with no escape.

Adrian dug his oars into the water, desperation fueling his every movement. "We're not giving up! We're going to find that island!"

With renewed determination, they fought against the waves, each stroke of the oars a testament to their resolve. The storm roared, but they would not be silenced. They were warriors against the elements, determined to conquer whatever lay ahead.

Then, just as despair began to creep back in, the clouds parted momentarily, revealing a glimmer of moonlight that pierced through the darkness. The water shimmered, reflecting the light as if the island were calling them back.

"There! The island!" Adrian shouted, pointing toward the flickering silhouette that began to reappear in the distance. "It's still there!"

With adrenaline surging, they pushed forward, the promise of Xel Island fueling their fight. The whispers grew quieter, replaced by the sound of the waves, the fear that had threatened to consume them now transforming into determination.

"Keep going!" George yelled, his voice fierce. "We're almost there!"

They rowed with all their might, the island drawing closer, its dark shape rising against the backdrop of the stormy sky. The fear that had threatened to tear them apart was replaced by a sense of unity, a shared goal that bound them together.

Adrian felt a surge of hope as they broke through the turbulent waters, the skiff cutting through the waves with renewed vigor. They would reach the island. They would face whatever awaited them, and they would do it together.

As they neared the shoreline, the shadows retreated, the storm beginning to lose its grip. They could see the sandy beach, a promise of safety in the chaos. The roar of the waves still echoed around them, but the island called out, pulling them forward.

"Almost there!" Adrian shouted, his heart racing with determination. "We can do this!"

With one final push, they reached the shore, leaping from the skiff onto the sand, breathless and soaked but filled with a newfound energy. The storm had tried to claim them, but they had fought back, refusing to let fear dictate their fate.

Standing on the shore of the Island, the moonlight illuminating the path ahead, Adrian took a deep breath, feeling the weight of the journey settle on his shoulders.

As Adrian and the others stumbled onto the shore, their hearts racing with adrenaline, they were met with a chilling realization. The storm that had threatened to drown them was still raging, the waves crashing violently against the rocks. The island, once a beacon of hope, now felt like a cruel mirage, taunting them with its distance.

"What the hell?" Adrian exclaimed, his breath hitching in confusion. "We're not at the island!"

"No, we're not," Ria replied, her eyes wide as she scanned the horizon, trying to make sense of their surroundings. "It's like the island is still out of reach!"

George, soaked to the bone, threw his hands up in frustration. "We fought through that storm, nearly drowned, and we're still stuck in this nightmare!"

Wren gritted his teeth, his frustration bubbling over. "What are we supposed to do now? The island was right there! It was calling to us!"

But Adrian's mind raced as he remembered the old sailor's words, the warnings that had echoed in his thoughts throughout the night. "We're not supposed to approach the island until the full moon," he said, his voice steady. "That's what he meant! It won't reveal itself until the moon is at its highest point."

"The moon," Mia echoed, her expression shifting from despair to a flicker of hope. "So we just have to wait? How long until then?"

Adrian looked up at the sky, trying to gauge the time. "It's only a few hours until the sun sets, but the full moon doesn't rise until midnight. We have to find a way to stay safe until then."

Ria nodded, a sense of determination creeping back into her voice. "We can set up a temporary camp here on the beach, keep watch. It's better than fighting the storm and getting swept away again."

"Good idea," Adrian replied, feeling the weight of leadership settle on his shoulders. "Let's gather what we can from the skiff and find a safe spot. If the island is going to reveal itself, we need to be ready."

As they worked together to secure their belongings, the storm began to shift, the wind howling like a beast in pain. They found a sheltered spot behind a cluster of rocks, where the waves crashed against the shore but the wind was somewhat muted. It was far from perfect, but it would have to do.

"Let's set up a fire," Wren suggested, rummaging through their supplies. "We can use it for warmth and light, and it might keep some of the wildlife away."

"Good thinking," Adrian agreed. "Everyone gather around while Wren and George work on the fire."

They huddled together, the weight of the storm still hanging over them. As they waited, the tension in the air was palpable. Fear lingered, but hope flickered in their hearts, fueled by the thought of reaching Xel Island.

"Do you think the old sailor's words are true?" Emma asked, her voice breaking the silence. "That the island only shows itself during a full moon?"

"I have to believe it," Adrian replied, his eyes fixed on the turbulent sea. "He warned Clara for a reason. If he knew it was dangerous, then we need to be cautious."

"Cautious is an understatement," George said, poking the fire as it began to catch. "This place feels wrong. It's like it's alive, watching us."

Adrian looked around, his heart heavy with the burden of their journey. "Whatever's on that island, we'll face it together. We've come too far to let fear hold us back. We owe it to Clara, to her father. We'll find out the truth."

As the sun began to dip below the horizon, casting long shadows across the beach, they settled around the fire, the flames flickering against the encroaching darkness. They took turns sharing stories, trying to keep the mood light despite the storm's oppressive presence.

Hours passed, the wind howling and the waves crashing violently, but they kept the fire burning, a small beacon of warmth and hope amidst the chaos. The tension in the air was thick, but they were united in their resolve to wait for the full moon.

Finally, as midnight approached, the storm began to ease. The wind softened, and the rain turned into a gentle drizzle. The clouds parted, revealing the moon—a brilliant silver orb that bathed the landscape in its ethereal glow.

"There it is," Adrian breathed, awed by the sight. "The full moon."

Ria's eyes sparkled with determination. "It's time. If the old sailor was right, then the island should reveal itself now."

They stood, hearts pounding as they turned their gaze toward the sea. The water shimmered in the moonlight, and for a moment, everything felt still. Then, slowly but surely, the silhouette of Xel Island began to emerge from the depths, the darkness lifting like a shroud.

"Look!" Mia gasped, pointing. "It's appearing!"

The outline of the island grew clearer, jagged cliffs rising above the waves, lush vegetation spilling over the edges. It was beautiful and haunting, a siren call that drew them in with a promise of secrets and danger.

"Let's get to the boat," Adrian said, his heart racing. "We can't waste any time!"

They hurried back to the skiff, the adrenaline coursing through them as they climbed aboard. The air was charged with electricity, and the island loomed closer, the very essence of adventure and fear wrapped up in its shadow.

"Get ready!" Adrian shouted, gripping the oars as they set off toward the island, the moon guiding their way. "This is it! We're finally going to uncover the truth!"

With each stroke of the oars, they propelled themselves forward, the darkness of the stormy night fading behind them. As they approached Xel Island, the whispers of the night transformed into a haunting melody, a sound that beckoned them closer, urging them to uncover the secrets hidden within its depths.

"We're almost there!" Ria called out, her eyes shining with determination.

Adrian felt the thrill of the moment surge within him as they closed the distance. "Prepare yourselves! Whatever's waiting for us on the island, we face it together!"

The boat skimmed across the water, the full moon illuminating their path, casting shadows that danced like specters on the waves. They were finally on the brink of discovering what lay within the heart of Xel Island, and as they approached the shore, the promise of adventure surged within them, stronger than any fear that threatened to hold them back.

After what felt like an eternity of battling the waves, their determination unwavering, Adrian and the others finally felt the skiff glide over the shallows. The roar of the ocean began to fade, replaced by the sound of the waves gently lapping at the shore.

"Hold on!" Adrian shouted, gripping the oars with fierce resolve. The boat pitched and rolled, but he maneuvered it expertly toward the sandy beach. The moonlight illuminated their path, revealing jagged rocks and foamy water.

"Almost there!" Ria called out, her excitement palpable as the silhouette of Xel Island loomed larger before them.

With one final, powerful stroke, they propelled the skiff forward, and it struck the sandy shore with a thud, the sudden stop jarring them but signaling their arrival.

"We made it!" George exclaimed, breathless as he scrambled to the edge of the boat.

They all jumped out, splashing into the shallow water, their hearts racing with adrenaline and anticipation. Standing on solid ground, they turned to gaze at the island, its dense foliage casting eerie shadows in the moonlight.

"Let's move quickly," Adrian urged, scanning their surroundings. "We don't know what's waiting for us here."

As they made their way onto the beach, the salty breeze whipped around them, carrying with it the promise of mystery and danger. They were finally on Xel Island, ready to uncover the secrets that lay hidden within its depths.

Then they stumbled onto the sandy shore of Xel Island, the adrenaline of their arrival surged through them. But the struggle of the night had taken its toll. One by one, they collapsed onto the ground, breathless and soaked from the ocean's grasp.

Adrian fell back against the cool sand, his chest heaving as he stared up at the night sky. The storm had vanished, leaving a tranquil darkness dotted with a thousand stars. The moon hung high above, casting a soft glow that bathed the island in silver light, illuminating the lush vegetation that bordered the beach.

"Wow," Ria breathed, lying beside Adrian, her eyes wide with awe. "Look at the stars. It's beautiful."

"After all that chaos, it feels surreal," Mia said, her voice a mixture of exhaustion and wonder as she leaned back, letting the soft sand cradle her. "I can't believe we're finally here."

"We made it," George echoed, glancing up at the sky, the tension in his body slowly melting away. "We survived the storm. This is our moment."

Wren, propped up on his elbows, looked around, absorbing the serenity that surrounded them. "It's quiet now," he remarked. "Almost peaceful."

Adrian closed his eyes for a moment, letting the calm wash over him. The horrors of the night felt distant, and for the first time since they had embarked on this journey, he allowed himself to breathe deeply.

"Just look at that," Emma said, pointing skyward. "The stars are so bright. It's like we've crossed into another world."

"Or another realm," Adrian added, his voice thoughtful. "This island holds secrets, and the sky is inviting us to discover them."

The group lay there, each of them lost in their thoughts, the vastness of the night sky stretching out above them. It was a moment of respite, a brief interlude before the challenges that lay ahead. As the gentle sound of the waves lapping at the shore filled the air, they found solace in the shared experience of reaching this place together.

But deep down, Adrian knew that the calm would not last. They had come to Xel Island seeking the truth, and the shadows of their fears loomed just beyond the horizon. Yet, for now, he allowed himself to relish the beauty of the moment, knowing it was a rare gift amidst the uncertainty of what lay ahead.

As the group lay sprawled on the sandy beach, the tranquility of the night wrapped around them like a comforting blanket. The stars twinkled brightly overhead, creating a stunning tapestry against the darkness. But even in this serene moment, there was an undercurrent of tension—a reminder that they were on Xel Island, a place steeped in mystery and danger.

Wren turned to Emma, who was lying next to him, her eyes reflecting the moonlight. "You know," he began, breaking the silence that had settled over them, "I never thought I'd be here, on an island that people only whisper about."

Emma smiled, her expression a mix of exhaustion and excitement. "Me neither. It feels unreal, like a dream I don't want to wake up from. But we've come this far, and we're finally facing the truth."

Wren shifted slightly, propping himself up on his elbow. "What do you think we'll find here? I mean, beyond the legends and all those stories we've heard."

"Honestly? I don't know," Emma replied, a hint of apprehension creeping into her voice. "I hope it's not just more nightmares. But something tells me that the island has its own secrets, and they're not going to reveal themselves easily."

Wren nodded, the weight of her words settling over him. "Do you think the darkness we saw in the water... do you think it will come back? Or was that just part of the storm?"

"I don't know," she admitted, shivering slightly as a cool breeze swept across the beach. "But whatever it was, it felt alive—like it was watching us. The island might have a mind of its own."

He frowned, concern etching lines on his forehead. "Let's just stick together, okay? If anything comes our way, we'll face it as a team."

"Agreed," Emma said, her smile returning as she reached out to squeeze his hand. "No matter what happens, we're in this together."

The others, still lost in their thoughts, began to drift off one by one, their bodies exhausted from the night's turmoil. The rhythmic sound of the waves lulled them into a deep sleep, their minds finally at ease after the chaos of the storm.

But as they surrendered to the night, unaware of the shadows that lingered just beyond the moonlight, a sinister presence stirred in the darkness around them. The air grew thick, a tension settling like a weight on the island.

Slowly, a pair of glowing eyes blinked open among the dense foliage nearby, piercing through the shadows with a predatory gaze. One by one, more eyes flickered to life, watching the sleeping group with a hunger that sent shivers through the night.

The eyes blinked in unison, glistening like distant stars, and the darkness pulsed around them, as if alive with anticipation. They were not alone on Xel Island, and the island was waking up.

As the darkness thickened, the sounds of the night faded away, replaced by the low, almost imperceptible whispers of the unseen. The eyes continued to watch, unblinking, their gaze fixed on the sleeping figures before them, waiting for the right moment to reveal themselves.

Unbeknownst to Adrian and his friends, the island held secrets deeper than they had imagined, and the horrors they had narrowly escaped were only the beginning. The night stretched on, thick with tension and promise, as the eyes blinked in the darkness, a silent promise of what was to come.

7

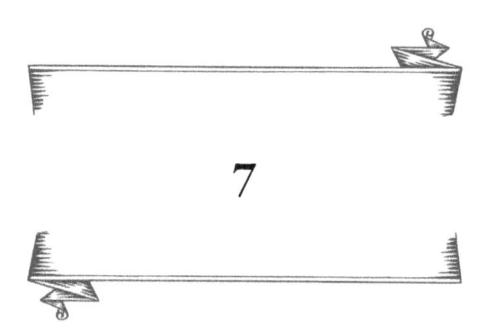

Lives Become Hard But...

As the night deepened, the gentle rhythm of the waves lulled Adrian and the others into a peaceful slumber. But unbeknownst to them, the island held its breath, waiting. From the dense underbrush surrounding the beach, a pair of wild creatures crept closer, drawn by the scent of the sleeping group.

With padded paws, they moved silently through the foliage, their bodies low to the ground, muscles coiled and ready to spring. Their fur blended seamlessly with the shadows, dark and sleek, and their eyes glowed with an unsettling light, reflecting the moon's silver sheen.

The first creature, a lithe figure with sharp features, sniffed the air, catching the scent of warmth and vulnerability. It paused, nostrils flaring as it drew closer to the sleeping humans. The second creature, larger and more muscular, followed closely behind, its breaths low and heavy, a deep rumble in the silence of the night.

As they approached the edge of the beach, the creatures paused, their eyes locked onto the group sprawled on the sand. They could smell the fear, the adrenaline still lingering in the air from the earlier storm. The larger creature stepped forward, its instincts battling with curiosity and caution.

Suddenly, the smaller one darted forward, nose close to Adrian's leg, sniffing intently. Adrian stirred slightly but remained asleep, oblivious to the danger so close at hand. The creature's breath ghosted over him, a chilling whisper that sent a shiver down his spine even in his dreams.

After a tense moment, the larger creature let out a low growl, an instinctual warning that echoed through the stillness. The smaller one hesitated, then backed away slowly, its senses alerting it to the risk of the unknown.

With a final glance at the group, the creatures melted back into the shadows, their forms disappearing into the underbrush as silently as they had arrived. But as they vanished, the whispers began, dark and echoing, weaving through the night like smoke.

"Fools," a voice hissed from the depths of the trees, dripping with malice. "They think they can trespass without consequence."

"Let them sleep," another voice replied, softer, almost seductive. "The island is hungry. It will feed."

The whispers continued, weaving tales of dread and warning, swirling around the slumbering figures like a sinister breeze. "They carry the weight of fear," a shadow murmured. "And fear is a feast for the island."

As the voices faded into the distance, the night sky above began to shift. The stars, which had twinkled softly in the aftermath of the storm, started to shine brighter, their light intensifying as if responding to the unseen presence that lurked nearby. But the moon, once a bright beacon, began to vanish behind a thick blanket of clouds, its glow dimming until it was nothing but a sliver of light, swallowed by darkness.

Adrian shifted in his sleep, a frown creasing his brow as if sensing something was amiss. The atmosphere around them thickened, wrapping them in a shroud of unease. The wind picked up, whispering secrets through the trees, and the night grew colder, a chilling reminder of the dangers that prowled just out of sight.

Suddenly, a rustle broke through the silence, sharp and quick. Adrian's eyes snapped open, and he bolted upright, heart pounding as he surveyed the darkness around them. "What was that?" he gasped, glancing at his friends, who were slowly awakening.

"What's wrong?" Ria asked, her voice groggy but filled with concern.

"I heard something," Adrian replied, straining his ears against the night. The whispers had receded, but the air was charged, heavy with an unseen tension.

Wren shook his head, rubbing his eyes. "It was probably just the wind. This place is crawling with sounds."

"Yeah, but it felt different," Adrian said, rising to his feet, the adrenaline coursing through him. "We're not alone."

As if on cue, the shadows around them flickered, and the air seemed to shift, a low growl reverberating through the darkness. The group froze, fear racing through them as they caught sight of something moving just beyond the treeline.

"Did you see that?" Emma whispered, her voice trembling as she pointed toward the dense brush.

Adrian squinted, trying to make out the shapes that danced at the edges of the moonlight. "We need to be careful," he warned, heart racing. "Whatever it is, it's watching us."

As they strained to see, the shadows began to shift again, and the creatures from before emerged from the darkness, their glowing eyes reflecting the meager light like specters from a nightmare. But now, they weren't alone. More eyes appeared, blinking in the night, each pair glistening with hunger and intent.

"Get back!" Adrian shouted, urgency gripping him as he stepped in front of his friends, ready to defend them.

The creatures advanced slowly, circling the group, their movements calculated, predatory. The whispers returned, louder now, a chaotic chorus echoing through the trees. "They can't stay. They must be consumed."

Adrian's heart raced as he grabbed a nearby rock, feeling the weight of it in his hand. "Stay together!" he shouted, panic edging into his voice. "Don't let them separate us!"

The group huddled closer, the tension palpable as the creatures drew nearer, their eyes glimmering like hungry stars. The wind howled, and the shadows closed in, the darkness threatening to engulf them.

"Adrian," Ria said, her voice trembling. "What do we do?"

He looked around, desperately searching for an escape, but the surrounding darkness felt suffocating. "We need to make a stand!" he declared, trying to summon courage in the face of impending doom. "If we fight together, we can drive them back!"

Suddenly, one of the creatures lunged, darting forward with incredible speed. The others followed, eyes gleaming with feral intent. The group flinched, ready to defend themselves as the darkness surged toward them.

In that moment, the remaining light of the moon flickered weakly, casting eerie shadows that danced around them. Adrian's heart raced as he braced himself, adrenaline pumping through his veins.

The shadows converged, but just as they were about to reach the group, the moon broke through the clouds, bathing the beach in brilliant light. The creatures recoiled, hissing and retreating into the depths of the forest as if the moonlight burned them.

"Now!" Adrian shouted, seizing the moment. "We need to get back to the boat! They don't like the light!"

With renewed determination, they sprinted toward the skiff, the adrenaline fueling their movements. The creatures hissed from the shadows, but they dared not venture closer to the moon's glow.

"Keep moving!" George urged, pushing ahead as they raced through the sand. "We can't let them regroup!"

The group reached the boat, scrambling aboard as the creatures slunk back into the darkness, their glowing eyes watching from the treeline.

Adrian's heart hammered in his chest as he clambered into the skiff, the safety of the boat offering a brief respite from the terror that lurked just beyond the light. "We need to get away from the shore!" he yelled, grabbing the oars once more. "Now!"

They quickly set to work, adrenaline surging as they pushed off from the beach, gliding into the churning water. The moon shone brightly now, illuminating their path as they paddled away from the island, the threat of the creatures still palpable in the air.

Breathless and shaken, they rowed with all their strength, the danger of the night pressing in around them. The stars shimmered above, brilliant and vibrant, but the darkness behind them still flickered with hidden eyes, waiting, watching.

"We can't let this island claim us," Adrian panted, focusing on the task at hand. "Whatever lurks in the shadows, we face it together."

As they rowed further into the night, the echoes of the whispers faded behind them, but the memory of the dark eyes remained etched in their minds. They had escaped for now, but the island was far from finished with them. The night was still young, and the darkness held many secrets yet to be revealed.

As they drifted farther from the shore, the soft glow of the moon illuminated the water around them, casting ripples of silver light that danced over the surface. The adrenaline of their escape began to wane, replaced by an overwhelming exhaustion that settled into their bones. The island's sinister presence lingered in the back of their minds, but they were grateful for the distance they had put between themselves and the dark creatures.

"We need to find shelter," Adrian said, looking over at his friends, who were breathing heavily, still shaken from the encounter. "Somewhere we can regroup and catch our breath."

Ria nodded, her eyes scanning the shoreline that was becoming a dim outline against the moonlight. "Let's look for a spot where we can hide from whatever that was. We can't let our guard down, but we need to rest."

After a few minutes of rowing, they spotted a cluster of trees further along the beach. The thick foliage provided a natural barrier against the wind and offered a sense of protection. Adrian steered the skiff toward the shore, the sand crunching beneath their feet as they disembarked and pulled the boat onto the beach.

"We'll camp here for the night," he decided, glancing around at the tall trees that loomed above them like sentinels. "It should keep us hidden."

As they settled under the shade of the trees, the sense of safety began to envelop them. The sounds of the waves crashing against the shore faded into a gentle lullaby, and the tension in their shoulders began to ease.

"We should take turns keeping watch," George suggested, stretching out against the cool sand. "I don't want to be caught off guard again."

"Agreed," Adrian replied, though exhaustion tugged at him. "But first, let's get some rest. We can't afford to fall asleep at the oars again."

The group nodded in agreement, and one by one, they settled beneath the trees, finding patches of soft ground to lie on. Adrian nestled himself against the thick roots of a tree, closing his eyes as the moonlight filtered through the leaves, casting gentle patterns on the ground.

Despite the haunting memories of the creatures lurking just beyond their view, sleep began to pull them under. The stress of the night melted away as their bodies sank into the earth, lulled by the rhythmic sound of the ocean in the distance.

Hours passed, and the island remained eerily quiet. The tension in the air shifted, and the moon continued its journey across the sky, illuminating the landscape with a silvery glow. The creatures they had encountered earlier had vanished, but the shadows felt thick and watchful.

Suddenly, Adrian was jolted awake by a rustling noise. His heart raced as he opened his eyes, immediately scanning the darkness around him. The shadows danced among the trees, and for a moment, panic gripped him.

"Did you hear that?" he whispered, sitting up quickly, trying to shake off the remnants of sleep.

Ria stirred beside him, her eyes blinking open. "What's wrong?"

"I thought I heard something," Adrian replied, straining to listen. The stillness of the night returned, but he could feel the weight of the silence pressing down on him.

The others began to wake, their faces marked with confusion. "What is it?" Wren asked, his voice thick with sleep.

"Just a noise," Adrian said, his instincts on high alert. He could feel the unease settle in the pit of his stomach. "But I can't shake this feeling that we're being watched."

They all sat up, the shadows around them feeling denser, almost alive. The soft sounds of the forest had returned, but there was an underlying tension that crackled in the air.

"I don't like this," Emma said, glancing over her shoulder at the trees. "I can't shake the feeling that those creatures could come back at any moment."

"Let's stay alert," Adrian urged, his voice steady despite the unease creeping in. "If they come back, we need to be ready."

Just then, a flicker of movement caught Adrian's eye, and he turned quickly to see a pair of glowing eyes peering at them from the darkness beyond the tree line. His breath hitched in his throat, and he felt the fear spiral back.

"There!" he hissed, pointing toward the eyes. "There's something out there!"

The group froze, their hearts pounding as they turned to face the source of the light. The shadows began to shift, the air thickening with tension. The eyes blinked slowly, and the creatures emerged from the darkness, their forms coiling and twisting like smoke.

"Stay together!" Adrian commanded, rising to his feet as the creatures approached. They had returned, eyes glistening with a hunger that was both frightening and enthralling.

"What do they want?" Mia whispered, her voice trembling as she clung to Ria.

Adrian took a step forward, heart racing but resolute. "We'll confront them. We're not going to show fear."

As the creatures moved closer, the moonlight glinted off their sleek bodies, revealing sharp features and gleaming fangs. But instead of lunging, they paused just beyond the trees, their eyes narrowing as they regarded the group.

"What do they want?" Ria repeated, her voice quivering with uncertainty.

Adrian could feel the weight of their stares, the hunger in the air. But then something shifted. The larger creature stepped forward, its gaze locked onto Adrian, and in that moment, he felt a strange connection, a flicker of understanding.

"Are you here to claim what is ours?" the creature hissed, its voice low and throaty, echoing with an otherworldly resonance. "Or have you come to beg for mercy?"

"Neither," Adrian replied, his voice steady despite the fear coursing through him. "We're here to find the truth about this island."

The creatures shifted, the air around them crackling with energy as they listened, their eyes glowing with curiosity. "Truth," the larger one echoed. "Many have sought the truth. Few have returned. What makes you different?"

"We've come to honour those who were lost," Adrian said, his heart racing. "We're not afraid of the darkness. We seek to understand it, to uncover its secrets."

The creatures paused, their expressions unreadable. The tension in the air shifted slightly, as if they were weighing his words.

"Very well," the larger creature said, its voice dripping with an ancient authority. "If you wish to uncover the truth, you must face the darkness that binds this island. But be warned: not all truths are kind. Are you prepared for what lies ahead?"

Adrian looked back at his friends, their faces reflecting a mix of fear and determination. He knew they had come this far, and there was no turning back now.

"We are," he said, his voice ringing with resolve. "We're ready to face whatever comes."

"Then follow us," the creature said, gesturing with a clawed hand. "The path to the truth begins in the heart of the island. But beware—the shadows will watch, and the darkness will test your resolve."

With that, the creatures turned and began to move deeper into the forest, their forms gliding silently among the trees. Adrian exchanged glances with his friends, feeling the weight of their decision settling in.

"Are we really doing this?" George whispered, his voice tight with anxiety.

"We have to," Adrian replied, steeling himself. "This is our chance to uncover the truth about Xel Island and the dangers that lie within. We'll face it together."

As they followed the creatures into the depths of the forest, the night closed around them, the shadows flickering like wraiths. The stars continued to shine above, and though the moon had begun to vanish behind a thick shroud of clouds, Adrian felt a flicker of hope in his heart.

They were stepping into the unknown, but they would confront whatever horrors awaited them on Xel Island, united and determined to uncover the secrets hidden in the darkness.

As Adrian and the group followed the eerie creatures into the dense forest, the air grew colder, and the darkness seemed to thicken with every step they took. The creatures led them silently, their glowing eyes the only guide through the twisted trees and tangled underbrush. The shadows clung to the corners of their vision, and though no words were exchanged, the group felt the weight of their decision pressing heavily on them.

The moon, once bright and silver, had nearly disappeared behind the shroud of clouds that now covered the sky. The stars still glittered above, but their light felt distant, almost unreachable, as if the island itself had swallowed up the night.

After what felt like an eternity of walking, the trees abruptly parted, revealing something strange ahead. A massive, towering structure loomed before them—a maze, its walls stretching up into the sky, their stone surfaces worn and ancient. The maze was impossibly large, winding far beyond what their eyes could see, disappearing into the horizon. It was both awe-inspiring and terrifying, a place where the path forward was as uncertain as their future.

Adrian stopped in his tracks, his breath catching in his throat as he stared up at the maze. "What... is this?"

The creatures halted as well, their glowing eyes turning back to meet his. "This is the test," the largest one hissed, its voice echoing through the clearing. "The heart of the island lies beyond this maze. If you wish to find the truth, you must pass through it."

Ria stepped forward, her brow furrowed in confusion. "A maze? What kind of test is this? How do we know it isn't a trap?"

The creature's eyes narrowed, and it smiled—a twisted, malevolent grin that sent a shiver down their spines. "All truths come with a price. And this maze… it does not forgive weakness. Those who enter must find their own way. Or be lost forever."

Wren took a step back, his face pale. "Wait, you're saying we have to go in there? That thing looks endless!"

Emma glanced at Adrian, her voice trembling slightly. "Do we have a choice?"

Before Adrian could answer, the largest creature—the leader—began to shift. Its body, once sleek and fluid like smoke, started to transform, taking on a new shape. The air around it crackled with energy as its form contorted, growing taller and more solid. In a matter of seconds, the creature had shed its shadowy form, revealing a tall, imposing figure—a man, with broad shoulders and muscular limbs. His skin was pale, almost translucent, and his eyes burned with an intense, unnatural light.

The transformation was so sudden, so violent, that the group barely had time to react before the creature-turned-human moved with lightning speed. With a snarl, the man grabbed Adrian by the collar and threw him forward with incredible strength, sending him hurtling through the air and crashing into the entrance of the maze.

"Adrian!" Ria screamed, rushing forward, but before she could reach him, the man turned and grabbed her too, tossing her effortlessly into the maze alongside Adrian.

One by one, the rest of the group was thrown into the labyrinth, their cries of shock and fear echoing off the ancient stone walls. The man moved with unnatural speed and power, his cold gaze devoid of any compassion. He hurled them into the maze as if they were nothing more than rag dolls, his strength far beyond anything they could have expected.

George, Wren, Mia, and Emma—all of them were flung into the maze's depths, their bodies colliding with the hard stone floors. The shock of the impact left them breathless, disoriented as they tried to regain their bearings.

Adrian groaned, pushing himself up onto his hands and knees, the world spinning around him. His body ached from the force of the throw, but he forced himself to focus, his eyes darting around. He could see the others scattered across the floor of the maze, some still struggling to get up, others already on their feet, panic etched on their faces.

"What the hell just happened?" George gasped, clutching his side as he stumbled toward Adrian. "That thing just turned into a person and—"

"He threw us in here," Adrian finished, his voice tight with anger. "He's testing us. This whole island is testing us."

Emma hurried to Ria's side, helping her to her feet. "Are you okay?"

Ria nodded, wincing as she straightened up. "I'm fine. Just... what is this place? How are we supposed to get out?"

Before Adrian could respond, Wren let out a strangled cry. "Guys... the entrance. It's gone!"

Everyone turned to look back at where they had been thrown in. The massive stone doors that had once marked the entrance to the maze were now gone, replaced by solid, seamless walls. There was no trace of the opening they had come through—no door, no path, nothing. It was as if the maze had swallowed them whole, trapping them inside.

Adrian's heart sank as he stared at the smooth stone wall. "No," he muttered, rushing toward it. He pressed his hands against the cold stone, searching for any sign of a seam or hidden mechanism. But there was nothing. The wall was impenetrable, as if the entrance had never existed.

"We're trapped," Mia whispered, her voice trembling as she backed away from the wall. "There's no way out."

Adrian clenched his fists, his mind racing. "There has to be a way. There's always a way."

George shook his head, his face pale. "This is insane. We can't just wander around in here forever. That thing—the man—he did this on purpose."

"We need to stay calm," Ria said, though her own voice wavered slightly. "There has to be a way through this. The island wants us to find something. This is part of the test."

Wren, pacing nervously, ran his hands through his hair. "A test? This isn't a test, Ria! It's a death trap! We could be stuck in here for hours—days—maybe even longer! We don't even know what's waiting for us around the next corner!"

Adrian turned to face the group, trying to steady his own breathing. The panic was rising quickly, and they needed to stay focused. "Listen," he said, his voice firm but not unkind. "We're in a maze, but we're not powerless. We've faced worse before, and we made it through. This is just another obstacle. If we stick together and keep our heads clear, we'll find a way out."

George crossed his arms, his expression doubtful. "You're talking like we have a choice. We don't even know how big this maze is. For all we know, it could be endless."

"We have to assume there's a way out," Adrian countered, his tone resolute. "That thing wouldn't have thrown us in here if there wasn't."

Emma, still shaken but thinking clearly, stepped forward. "Adrian's right. The island—it's testing us. This maze has a purpose. It's not about wandering aimlessly. We need to figure out what the test is, and then maybe we'll find a way through."

Ria nodded in agreement. "It's a puzzle. It has to be. If we think like that—if we approach it with the mindset of solving something instead of just escaping—we'll have a better chance."

Adrian felt a flicker of hope as the others seemed to calm down slightly, the fear giving way to determination. "Okay," he said, taking a deep breath. "Let's start by figuring out our options. We can't go back, so the only way is forward. But we need to be smart about this. Let's split up into pairs and explore different paths. We'll mark the walls as we go so we don't get lost."

"Wait," Mia said quickly, her eyes widening in alarm. "Split up? Are you sure that's a good idea? What if something's in here with us?"

Adrian hesitated, the weight of her words sinking in. "You're right," he admitted. "Splitting up could make things worse. We'll stick together. Safety in numbers."

George nodded, looking relieved. "Good call. I don't want to be wandering through this place alone."

Adrian glanced around, his eyes scanning the towering walls of the maze. "Then let's move. We've already lost too much time standing here. Keep your eyes open, and if anyone notices anything strange, speak up."

They began to walk, the cold stone walls towering above them, casting long, dark shadows in the pale moonlight. The maze felt alive—every turn, every corner seemed to shift slightly, making it impossible to tell if they were making progress or simply walking in circles.

As they moved deeper into the labyrinth, the oppressive atmosphere grew thicker, and the maze seemed to close in around them. The air was cold and damp, and the silence was deafening, broken only by the sound of their footsteps echoing off the stone.

"This place is massive," Wren muttered under his breath, glancing nervously over his shoulder. "How long do you think it goes on for?"

"No idea," George replied, his voice tense. "But we need to keep moving. Standing still isn't going to get us anywhere."

Adrian, leading the group, felt a growing sense of unease. The maze was disorienting, and the more they walked, the more he realized just how labyrinthine it truly was. Every corridor looked the same—narrow, twisting paths with walls that stretched up into the sky, blocking out any hope of seeing the horizon.

"We should've hit something by now," Ria said, her voice strained. "A clue, a sign—anything. It feels like we're walking in circles."

Emma nodded in agreement. "This isn't right. There's no way a maze like this could just keep going on and on without some kind of end. It has to be playing tricks on us."

Adrian stopped in his tracks, the realization hitting him like a ton of bricks. "That's exactly what it's doing."

The others turned to face him, confusion etched on their faces. "What do you mean?" Mia asked, her brow furrowed.

"The maze isn't just physical," Adrian explained, his voice gaining strength as he pieced it together. "It's messing with our minds. The island—this place—it wants us to feel lost. It's designed to disorient us, to make us think we're trapped."

"So what do we do?" George asked, frustration bubbling to the surface. "We can't exactly break through the walls."

"We have to stop thinking like this is a regular maze," Adrian said, his mind racing. "We need to approach it differently. If it's a test, then maybe it's testing more than just our ability to navigate."

Ria nodded slowly, understanding dawning in her eyes. "It's testing our resolve. Our ability to stay calm under pressure. It's not just about finding a way out—it's about proving we can keep it together."

Wren let out a nervous laugh. "Well, if that's the case, we're screwed."

"No, we're not," Adrian said firmly. "We just need to focus. We've already survived the storm, the creatures, and whatever else this island has thrown at us. This maze is just another obstacle."

Emma stepped closer to Adrian, her expression serious. "So how do we beat it?"

"We stay calm," Adrian replied, his voice filled with determination. "We keep moving forward, and we don't let the maze get to us. It's trying to make us panic, to lose our sense of direction. But if we stick together, we can outlast whatever it's throwing at us."

Mia, still shaken but feeling a surge of confidence from Adrian's words, nodded. "We can do this."

George clapped Adrian on the shoulder, his eyes bright with newfound resolve. "Lead the way, man. We trust you."

With a renewed sense of purpose, the group pressed on, their steps more sure and deliberate. The maze continued to twist and turn, but they moved with a quiet determination, refusing to give in to the fear and confusion that lurked in the shadows.

The night stretched on, the walls of the maze growing more imposing with each step they took. But despite the disorienting paths and the oppressive atmosphere, the group held strong, their faith in each other driving them forward.

And as they walked deeper into the heart of the maze, Adrian couldn't shake the feeling that they were on the verge of discovering something—something that lay just beyond the next turn, waiting for them in the darkness.

The truth of Xel Island was close. They could feel it.

As they moved deeper into the maze, Adrian's thoughts raced. *What am I doing? Am I leading them into danger?*

He stole a glance at Ria, her expression a mix of determination and uncertainty. *I have to be strong for them. They're counting on me.*

"What if we never find a way out?" George muttered, his voice barely above a whisper. The anxiety in his tone was palpable.

"Don't think like that," Emma replied, her eyes darting nervously around. "We will find a way. We have to."

Her optimism is refreshing, Adrian thought, feeling a flicker of hope. *But can we really trust this maze?*

"Did you see the way that creature transformed?" Wren asked, his voice laced with disbelief. "It was like something out of a horror movie."

What else is lurking in the shadows? Adrian wondered, feeling the weight of dread creeping in. *Are we ready for what's next?*

"We're stronger together," Ria said, her voice steady, though Adrian could sense her underlying fear. *She's right*, he thought. *We need to stay united.*

"We just have to keep moving," Adrian encouraged, though doubt gnawed at him. *Can I really keep them safe?*

"What if it's a trick?" George interjected, fear evident in his eyes. "What if we're just walking in circles?"

That's exactly what it wants us to think, Adrian realized, clenching his fists. *But I won't let this place win.*

"Remember, we have each other," Emma said softly, her gaze fixed on Adrian. "No matter what happens, we'll find a way."

Adrian nodded, drawing strength from her words. *She's right. We've faced worse together. I won't let fear dictate our fate.*

"Let's keep our wits about us," Adrian said, his voice firm. "Stay alert, and if you notice anything strange, speak up. We can't let this maze divide us."

They continued walking, the air thick with tension, but beneath the uncertainty, there was a shared resolve—a silent promise that they would face whatever challenges lay ahead together. As they turned another corner, Adrian's heart pounded, but he felt a surge of determination.

We will find the truth. We will escape this maze.

As they navigated the twisting paths of the maze, Adrian felt a mixture of fatigue and apprehension building within him. The stone walls seemed to close in, and just when he thought they might find a way out, they stumbled upon a junction, a wide-open space that split into three distinct paths, each one leading deeper into the darkness.

"What now?" Ria asked, her brow furrowing as she stared down each of the three corridors. "How do we know which way to go?"

Adrian stepped forward, glancing at each passage. The left path was shrouded in shadows, its entrance dark and foreboding. The middle path was faintly illuminated, a flickering light beckoning from deeper within. The right path was lined with strange symbols carved into the stone, glowing softly in the dim light, casting an otherworldly glow.

We're at a crossroads, literally and figuratively, he thought, feeling the weight of responsibility settle heavily on his shoulders. *This could change everything.*

"Which one feels right?" George asked, squinting at the options. "I don't like the idea of splitting up again, but we can't stand here forever."

Emma's voice trembled slightly as she pointed toward the middle path. "That light might mean there's something—or someone—there. It could be a way out."

"But it could also lead us into a trap," Wren interjected, his eyes darting nervously between the options. "We don't know what's down any of these paths."

We can't afford to make a mistake, Adrian thought, his mind racing. He could feel the tension rising within the group. *We need to trust our instincts, but the stakes are too high.*

"What about the right path?" Ria suggested, motioning toward the glowing symbols. "Those markings... they look ancient. Maybe they'll lead us to something important."

Adrian nodded, considering her words. *Ancient markings could be a clue. They might have significance in this maze. But what if they lead us further into danger?*

"Whatever we choose, we have to decide quickly," Emma urged, her voice steady but anxious. "The longer we stand here, the more vulnerable we are. We don't know what might be lurking in the shadows."

"What if we go left?" George suggested hesitantly, glancing toward the darkened corridor. "It's the least inviting. Maybe that's where the truth lies?"

Adrian felt the pull of the left path, a dark whisper in the back of his mind urging him to explore it. *But is that just fear? Or is it intuition?*

"No, we shouldn't choose fear," Ria countered, shaking her head. "We need to find a path that offers some semblance of safety. I'm with Emma. Let's follow the light."

Adrian felt the pressure mounting. *They're all looking to me for guidance*, he thought, anxiety churning in his stomach. *I have to make the right choice.*

"Okay, let's think this through," he said, his voice steady as he turned to face his friends. "The left path is dark and could be dangerous. The middle path has light, which could lead us to safety or something worse. The right path with the symbols might have meaning we don't yet understand, but it could also lead us to answers."

"What if we go for the middle path?" Wren suggested, his voice laced with urgency. "It could lead us out of this maze. We need to know where we're going, and that light looks like it could be a way forward."

But what if it's a lure? Adrian thought, feeling the weight of their potential choice hanging in the air. "We need to be cautious, but we also need to move forward. We can't let fear dictate our choice."

Ria took a deep breath, stepping slightly forward. "I vote for the middle path. We can't ignore the light; it might be the hope we need right now."

"Middle it is, then," Adrian said, his voice steady. "Let's stay together and proceed with caution."

As they stepped into the middle path, the flickering light grew brighter, illuminating their way. Adrian could feel a mix of excitement and dread as they moved forward, each step echoing against the stone walls. *Whatever lies ahead, we face it together*, he reminded himself, determination surging within him. *We're not just trying to survive; we're seeking the truth of this island.*

With their hearts pounding, they advanced into the unknown, the darkness behind them slowly swallowing the light of the junction, as they prepared to confront whatever awaited them deeper in the maze.

As Adrian and his friends ventured deeper into the middle path, the flickering light ahead grew brighter, illuminating the rough stone walls and casting long shadows behind them. The atmosphere felt thick with tension, and the air crackled with an electricity that made them all uneasy.

Suddenly, they rounded a corner and halted, coming face to face with a group of men. The figures were huddled together, their expressions vacant, eyes glazed over as if they were lost in a trance. It was an unsettling sight—these men looked innocuous at first glance, but there was something deeply wrong about them.

"What the hell?" George murmured, stepping cautiously forward. "Who are they?"

Before anyone could answer, one of the men turned to them, a wild look in his eyes. "We are the slaves of Xel!" he shouted, his voice a distorted echo. "We serve the island! We have no will of our own!"

The others joined in, chanting the words like a haunting mantra, their voices rising in a chilling chorus. "Slaves of Xel! Slaves of Xel!"

Wren's heart sank as he recognized one of the men, his friend Ethan, standing among the group. "Ethan!" he shouted, desperation seeping into his voice. "Ethan, can you hear me?"

Ethan's eyes flickered briefly with recognition, but the haze quickly returned, his expression slipping back into the vacant stare. "Wren... help us," he mumbled, his voice barely above a whisper. "We're trapped... slaves of Xel."

Adrian felt a surge of anger mixed with fear. "We need to get them out of here!" he shouted, stepping forward. "This isn't right. We can't let them remain like this!"

But before they could devise a plan, the group of hypnotized men turned toward them, their demeanor shifting from vacant to menacing. The haunting chant intensified, reverberating through the stone corridors.

"Slaves of Xel! Slaves of Xel!"

With a sudden roar, the men lunged forward, their movements swift and aggressive. Adrian barely had time to react as the first man charged at him, fists raised.

Adrian sidestepped the attack, adrenaline coursing through his veins. He quickly countered, landing a solid punch to the man's gut. The force of the blow sent him stumbling backward, but before Adrian could catch his breath, another man charged, tackling him to the ground.

"Get off me!" Adrian grunted, struggling beneath the weight of his attacker. He twisted, throwing an elbow into the man's side, forcing him to roll away.

"Wren, help me!" he shouted, adrenaline surging as he pushed himself up.

But Wren was already engaged in his own fight, grappling with Ethan, who had suddenly turned on him, fueled by the dark influence of the island. Wren's heart raced as he tried to reason with his friend, shouting over the chaos. "Ethan, it's me! You have to fight it!"

Ethan's face twisted in a snarl, his eyes flashing with anger. "I am not Ethan! I am the will of Xel!"

Wren ducked as Ethan lunged, narrowly avoiding a wild swing. He countered with a punch of his own, but it felt like hitting a wall. The strength of the hypnotized men was unnerving, their movements fueled by an otherworldly force.

"Stay back!" Wren shouted, but Ethan was relentless, striking with a speed and ferocity that took him by surprise.

Meanwhile, Ria and Emma fought side by side, fending off two men who had zeroed in on them. Ria swung her backpack like a weapon, catching one of the men across the face, sending him crashing into the stone wall. Emma grabbed a loose rock, using it to jab at the other man, who had been closing in on her.

"Get back!" Emma shouted, her voice fierce as she threw the rock, hitting him squarely in the chest. He stumbled back, momentarily disoriented.

"Nice shot!" Ria yelled, a fierce grin breaking through her anxiety.

"Keep moving!" Adrian shouted, dodging another attack as he threw himself to the side. He grabbed a nearby loose stone, swinging it at the next man rushing him. The stone connected with a sickening thud, sending the man reeling.

The fight raged on, the echoes of fists hitting flesh and bodies colliding with stone filling the narrow path. Shadows danced along the walls as the chaos unfolded, and the air grew thick with desperation.

"Adrian! Look out!" Ria shouted, but it was too late. A man lunged from the side, tackling Adrian to the ground once more. They rolled, grappling for control, but the weight of the attacker was overwhelming.

Adrian struggled, throwing punches, but the man was relentless, pressing down harder. *I can't let them win*, he thought, desperation clawing at his mind. He managed to slip an arm free and landed a brutal blow to the man's jaw, finally breaking free.

Gasping for breath, he pushed himself up, his eyes scanning the chaotic scene around him. He could see Wren still struggling with Ethan, his friend's wild swings barely missing him.

"Wren!" Adrian shouted, rushing to his side. "We need to get him away from here!"

Wren dodged another swing from Ethan and yelled, "I can't hold him forever! He's too strong!"

Adrian grabbed Ethan's arm, trying to wrestle him away. "Ethan! Fight it! We're your friends!"

Ethan hesitated for a split second, confusion flickering in his eyes, but the force of the island pulled him back, and he lunged again, this time aiming for Adrian.

"No!" Wren shouted, stepping in front of Adrian just in time. Ethan's fist connected with Wren's side, and he doubled over in pain, gasping for air.

"Wren!" Adrian shouted, feeling a surge of anger and panic. He couldn't lose his friend—not like this.

With a fierce yell, Adrian tackled Ethan from the side, knocking him off balance. They tumbled to the ground, and Adrian threw punch after punch, each hit fueled by desperation.

"Fight it, Ethan! You're stronger than this!" he yelled, but the words felt hollow against the chaos around them.

Ethan's eyes flickered again, a brief moment of clarity breaking through the darkness. "Adrian?" he murmured, his voice wavering. "Is that you?"

"Yeah, it's me! You have to break free! We need you!" Adrian pleaded, but the dark force surged back, twisting Ethan's features into a mask of rage.

"No! I am the will of Xel!" Ethan roared, throwing Adrian off him with a surprising burst of strength.

Adrian hit the ground hard, scrambling to get back up as Ethan turned, focusing on Wren, who was still trying to catch his breath. "Wren!" Adrian shouted. "Get out of the way!"

But it was too late. With a powerful shove, Ethan lunged again, tackling Wren and sending him crashing into the stone wall. The impact echoed through the maze, and Adrian's heart dropped as he watched his friend hit the ground.

"Wren!" he screamed, pushing himself to his feet, desperation fueling his every movement.

As Adrian raced toward them, the chaos around him intensified. The other men, still hypnotized, continued to fight with wild abandon, their eyes vacant, driven only by the will of Xel. Adrian felt the world around him blur as adrenaline surged through him, each heartbeat echoing like thunder in his ears.

He reached Wren just as he was struggling to rise, grabbing his friend's arm to pull him back to safety. "We have to get out of here! Now!"

But just as they began to move, the other men surged toward them, blocking their escape. The air was thick with tension, the darkness closing in, and Adrian felt the weight of their situation bearing down on him. *We can't let fear take us*, he thought fiercely, determination surging within him.

"Fight back! Don't let them win!" Adrian shouted, rallying his friends as they prepared to face the onslaught together.

The fight had only just begun, and they were determined to push through the darkness of Xel Island, united against the forces that sought to consume them.

The tension in the air was electric, a charged atmosphere thick with the scent of sweat and fear as Adrian and his friends prepared for the brutal fight that lay ahead. The men surrounding them, once innocuous and innocent, had transformed into relentless fighters—empty shells filled with the will of Xel.

"Get ready!" Adrian shouted, rallying his friends as the hypnotized men surged forward, fists raised and eyes burning with a fierce determination that wasn't their own.

With a primal roar, the battle erupted. Adrian dove into the fray, fists flying as he landed blow after blow against the first attacker. The sound of flesh hitting flesh echoed in the narrow corridor, each punch igniting the air around them. The adrenaline coursed through him like fire, and he felt alive—every nerve ending buzzing with the thrill of combat.

"Watch out!" Ria shouted, ducking just in time to avoid a wild swing from one of the men. She retaliated with a swift kick to his knee, sending him crashing to the ground with a pained yelp.

"Nice one!" Emma yelled, grabbing a loose stone from the ground and hurling it at another attacker. It struck him squarely in the head, knocking him off balance.

But there was no time to celebrate. Another man lunged at her, and she barely sidestepped in time, countering with a swift jab to his ribs. The man grunted in pain but kept coming, fueled by the darkness that controlled him.

"Adrian! I need help!" Wren called out, grappling with Ethan, who was still caught in the grip of the Xel will. Adrian turned just in time to see Wren's desperate struggle as he tried to subdue his friend.

"Ethan, please! Fight it!" Wren shouted, gripping Ethan's shoulders as they wrestled on the ground. But the dark influence pulsed through Ethan like a tide, overwhelming any glimmer of recognition.

"You don't understand!" Ethan spat, pushing Wren back with a sudden burst of strength. "I am the will of Xel! I serve the island!"

Adrian felt the world tilt as he witnessed the struggle. *This isn't Ethan; this is the island's puppet*, he thought, dread sinking deep in his gut. He couldn't let his friend slip away like this.

"Get away from him!" Adrian shouted, charging toward them. He reached Wren just as Ethan lashed out, throwing a wild punch that connected with Adrian's jaw. The force sent him stumbling backward, but he quickly regained his footing.

"Fight it, Ethan!" Adrian yelled, desperation lacing his voice. "You're stronger than this! Remember who you are!"

The fight raged around them, chaos reigning as fists flew, bodies collided, and the air filled with the sound of grunts and shouts. Ria and Emma fought side by side, defending against two men who were closing in on them, their vacant expressions twisted into grim determination.

"We can't keep this up!" Ria gasped, throwing a powerful kick that sent one of the men sprawling backward. "They just keep coming!"

"They're not stopping!" Emma shouted, dodging an attack and countering with a sharp jab. "What do we do?"

Adrian glanced around, heart racing. "We have to find a way to break their hold! If we can reach Ethan, maybe he can help us!"

But before he could make a move, another attacker barreled toward him, fists raised. Adrian sidestepped, dodging the blow, then retaliated with a powerful punch to the man's gut. He followed it up with an elbow strike to the back of the head, sending the man crashing to the ground.

Adrian's focus shifted to Wren, who was still wrestling with Ethan, desperation etched on his face. "Wren, get away from him!" Adrian shouted, but the chaos of the fight drowned out his words.

Wren, struggling against the strength of his friend, gasped for breath. "I can't! He's still in there! Ethan, you have to fight it! You're not a slave to this island!"

The words seemed to penetrate the fog surrounding Ethan, and for a brief moment, his eyes flickered with recognition. "Wren?" he murmured, confusion washing over his features. "What's happening?"

"Ethan! Please!" Wren shouted, desperation clawing at his voice. "Fight it! We're here to help you!"

But the moment was fleeting. The darkness surged back, and Ethan's expression twisted into a snarl. "No! I won't let you take control! I serve Xel!"

In a flash, Ethan swung his fist at Wren, connecting with a brutal punch that sent him sprawling to the ground. The impact echoed in the narrow space, and a gasp escaped Ria's lips.

"Wren!" she cried, rushing to her friend's side as he struggled to get up. The fight around them escalated, the remaining men closing in with fierce determination.

Adrian felt rage boiling within him as he charged at Ethan, fury driving him forward. "You have to snap out of it!" he yelled, throwing a hard punch that connected with Ethan's jaw, sending him stumbling back.

But the hypnotic hold of Xel was too strong. With a roar, Ethan retaliated, tackling Adrian and throwing him against the stone wall. Adrian gasped as the impact rattled his bones, but he quickly pushed himself back to his feet, determination surging within him.

"Enough of this!" he shouted, forcing his way through the chaos, grabbing Ethan's arm. "You're stronger than this darkness! Remember who you are!"

But Ethan, consumed by the will of Xel, shook him off and retaliated with a fierce kick, sending Adrian sprawling to the ground.

"Adrian!" Ria shouted, her voice tinged with panic as she watched her friend go down. She fought against the men closing in on her and Emma, adrenaline coursing through her veins as she threw a series of rapid punches.

"Don't let them take you!" Emma shouted, narrowly dodging an attack and striking back. "Fight!"

As the battle continued, blood began to splatter against the cold stone walls, the sounds of grunts and yells mixing with the echoes of their struggle. Adrian felt the weight of fear pressing on him, but he refused to give in.

He rose to his feet, determination burning in his chest as he re-engaged with Ethan. "I won't let you hurt your friends!" he shouted, throwing himself at Ethan once more.

Ethan roared, a primal sound that sent chills down Adrian's spine. He retaliated with brutal force, launching punches that felt like they could shatter stone. The sound of fists connecting with flesh echoed through the narrow corridor, a chorus of chaos and desperation.

Adrian ducked and weaved, his instincts kicking in as he fought against Ethan's onslaught. "You're stronger than this! Remember us!" he cried, trying to reach the part of Ethan that still existed beneath the darkness.

But Ethan was relentless, fueled by the will of Xel. He charged forward, pushing Adrian back as they fought for control. The shadows around them swirled, closing in as if the island itself were watching, waiting for the outcome of this brutal clash.

Wren, still struggling to rise, finally pushed himself to his feet, his eyes locked onto Ethan. "Ethan! I'm not giving up on you!" he shouted, his voice filled with raw emotion. "Fight it! You're my friend! I believe in you!"

Ethan hesitated, the fight momentarily draining from him as the remnants of his true self flickered through the chaos. But just as hope surged within Wren, Ethan snapped back, a chilling smile crossing his lips.

"Wren..." he said, voice dripping with menace, "you're just a fool who thinks he can save me."

With a sudden burst of energy, Ethan lunged at Wren, delivering a brutal punch that sent him sprawling back to the ground. The air was filled with shock, and the sound of Wren hitting the floor echoed painfully in the narrow corridor.

"Wren!" Adrian screamed, watching in horror as his friend fell, clutching his side in pain.

"You shouldn't have come here!" Ethan growled, his voice dark and twisted. "You will all become part of the island!"

The fight escalated further, becoming a frenzy of chaos as the remaining men lunged forward, attacking with primal ferocity. Adrian fought tooth and nail, throwing punches and kicks, desperately trying to protect his friends from the overwhelming darkness.

"Stay together!" Ria shouted, her voice fierce as she threw a punch at one of the attackers. "We can't let them break us apart!"

But as the fight raged on, Adrian could feel the tide turning against them. Blood and sweat mingled in the air, the cries of pain echoing around them as they struggled against the onslaught.

Adrian turned back to Wren, who was slowly rising again, determination flashing in his eyes. "Wren, stay down! You're hurt!" Adrian shouted, but Wren shook his head, his gaze fixed on Ethan, who was advancing again.

"I won't let him take you! I won't let you go!" Wren shouted, launching himself toward Ethan, fueled by desperation.

"Wren, no!" Adrian cried, reaching out in a futile attempt to stop his friend.

Wren charged forward, determination etched on his face. "Ethan! Fight it!" he yelled, trying to reach the part of Ethan that was still his friend.

But Ethan, consumed by the darkness, lashed out with a vicious punch that connected squarely with Wren's gut. The impact sent Wren sprawling against the stone floor, gasping for air as the pain radiated through his body. The world spun around him, and for a moment, he felt completely lost, the chaos of the fight fading into the background.

"Wren!" Adrian shouted, his heart dropping as he saw his friend crumple. The raw intensity of the moment struck him like a punch to the gut, and fear clawed at his insides. "Get up! You have to get up!"

Wren struggled, trying to catch his breath, but the darkness loomed over him. He could see Ethan, now a formidable shadow against the dim light, turning his attention back to the group, eyes blazing with a predatory glint.

"No!" Wren gasped, forcing himself to rise again, the pain shooting through him like fire. He pushed against the ground, gritting his teeth as he staggered to his feet. "Ethan, fight it! You're stronger than this! We're here for you!"

But Ethan's face twisted with rage, the flicker of recognition quickly replaced by the insatiable hunger of Xel. "You think you can save me? You're just a weakness!" he hissed, advancing menacingly, fists clenched.

Adrian stepped in front of Wren, anger and determination flooding through him. "You're not Ethan anymore! You're a puppet of this island!" he shouted, rage coursing through him. "We'll break this hold!"

With a primal roar, Adrian lunged at Ethan, throwing a series of punches that connected with brutal force. Each blow echoed through the narrow corridor, fueled by desperation and a fierce desire to save his friend.

Wren, still reeling from the earlier blow, watched helplessly as Adrian and Ethan clashed, the two locked in a brutal struggle. *I can't let it end like this*, he thought, heart pounding as adrenaline surged through him. *I have to fight back!*

Gathering every ounce of strength, Wren launched himself at Ethan again, joining the fray despite the pain radiating through his body. "Get away from him!" Wren shouted, his voice filled with fierce determination. He struck Ethan with a powerful punch, but the force of the impact was nothing compared to the darkness that clouded his friend's mind.

The fight escalated, chaos swirling around them like a living entity. Adrian and Wren fought side by side, each movement a desperate attempt to bring Ethan back from the brink. Ria and Emma held their own against the other men, throwing punches and kicks, their determination unwavering despite the odds stacked against them.

"Adrian! Watch out!" Ria shouted, her voice breaking through the chaos as she intercepted a charging man with a swift kick to his chest, sending him crashing backward.

Adrian caught a glimpse of Wren grappling with Ethan, the two locked in a fierce struggle. "Wren, be careful!" he yelled, feeling a surge of fear wash over him as he rushed to help his friend.

But just as Adrian reached them, Ethan broke free of Wren's grasp, eyes blazing with an unholy fury. "You can't stop me!" he roared, lunging forward and throwing Wren back with a savage blow.

Wren hit the ground hard, pain exploding in his ribs as he gasped for breath. "Ethan, please!" he cried, desperation filling his voice. "Fight it! Remember who you are!"

Ethan paused for a brief moment, the chaos around them fading into a blur as confusion flickered in his eyes. "Wren?" he murmured, his voice trembling, almost pleading.

"Yeah! It's me! Fight against Xel!" Wren shouted, pushing himself up despite the pain. "You're not alone! We're here for you!"

But before Wren could take another step, the darkness surged back, drowning out the flicker of recognition in Ethan's eyes. "No!" Ethan screamed, the voice now twisted and full of malice. "You're a weakness I won't tolerate!"

In an instant, Ethan lunged at Wren again, faster than before. Wren barely had time to react. "No! Ethan, please!" he cried out, but it was too late. Ethan's fist connected with Wren's chest, driving him backward with a brutal force.

Wren felt the breath knocked out of him as he collided with the stone wall, pain radiating through his body. He looked up just in time to see the fury in Ethan's eyes, the darkness consuming him completely. "You should have stayed away!" Ethan roared, advancing toward him.

"Ethan! Fight it! Remember your family! Remember us!" Wren pleaded, desperation coating his words as he struggled to regain his footing. But the darkness had taken hold, and Ethan was lost to it.

Adrian rushed forward, determination flooding his veins. "Wren, move!" he shouted, lunging at Ethan again. He threw himself between Wren and Ethan, fists raised, ready to defend his friend.

Ethan turned his rage toward Adrian, and the two collided with a ferocity that echoed through the maze. The sound of fists hitting flesh reverberated off the stone walls, a brutal symphony of chaos.

"Get away from him!" Adrian yelled, landing a powerful punch to Ethan's jaw, but the blow barely fazed him.

Adrian's heart raced as he struggled to overpower Ethan, fueled by desperation to save Wren. *I won't let this end like this! I won't lose another friend!*

The battle raged on, chaos swirling around them. Ria and Emma fought off the other men, their determination unwavering as they pushed back against the throngs of attackers.

"Keep fighting!" Ria shouted, her voice a beacon amidst the chaos. "We can't let them take us down!"

But the odds were against them. The hypnotized men were relentless, moving like a swarm, fueled by the dark influence of the island. Adrian felt the weight of their struggle bearing down on him, every strike becoming more desperate, more frantic.

"Adrian! Watch out!" Emma yelled, just as a man lunged at him from behind.

Adrian turned, instinct kicking in as he ducked just in time, the man's fist missing him by inches. In a fluid motion, he countered with a strike to the man's gut, sending him crashing into the wall.

But as he turned back to face Ethan, he saw the fury in his friend's eyes, the darkness consuming him. "Ethan! Please!" Adrian shouted, his heart racing as he tried to reach him once more. "Remember who you are! You're not alone in this!"

Ethan hesitated, confusion flashing across his face again. For a split second, it seemed like the darkness might release its hold. "Adrian?" he said, his voice wavering, as if fighting against the oppressive will of the island.

But in an instant, the darkness surged back, and the clarity faded. "I will not be controlled!" Ethan screamed, lunging at Adrian with renewed rage.

Adrian braced himself, knowing he had to push through. He charged forward, ready to confront the darkness head-on. "You are not a slave! You are Ethan! Fight back!"

But as he lunged, Ethan reacted with an agility that shocked him. He sidestepped Adrian's advance and lashed out, his fist connecting squarely with Adrian's side. The impact sent Adrian staggering back, gasping for breath.

In that moment of distraction, Wren found his footing, pushing himself back up from where he had fallen. "No! Ethan!" he shouted, trying to reach the man who had once been his friend. "You're not a monster! You're better than this!"

Ethan turned, rage boiling over as he met Wren's gaze. "You don't know anything!" he roared, charging at Wren with a brutal ferocity.

"Ethan, please!" Wren cried, desperation thick in his voice. "You can fight this! You can break free!"

But the darkness consumed Ethan, and with a brutal swing, he lunged at Wren. The punch landed with a sickening thud, knocking Wren back against the wall once more.

Adrian's heart dropped as he watched his friend fall. "Wren!" he shouted, but the fight had escalated beyond control, each moment stretching into chaos as the hypnotized men pressed in around them.

The echo of their struggle filled the maze as fists flew and bodies collided. Adrian fought desperately to keep Wren from harm, every instinct telling him to protect his friends, to keep them safe from the wrath of the island.

"Ria! Emma! Help him!" Adrian shouted, directing his friends toward Wren, who was struggling to rise again.

As they fought through the chaos, the men were relentless, and the air was thick with tension. Ria and Emma darted toward Wren, but as they reached him, Ethan swung again, his fists fueled by a darkness that threatened to swallow them all.

In that moment, the world slowed down for Adrian. He could see Wren struggling, trying to get back up as Ethan advanced, rage and darkness twisting his features. "Ethan! You're my friend! Fight it!" Wren cried, desperation etched into every word.

But before Wren could rise fully, Ethan lunged forward again, this time with a speed and intensity that left Adrian breathless. "You should have stayed away!" he snarled, the darkness consuming him entirely.

Adrian screamed, rushing forward, but the world felt like it was happening in slow motion. He reached out, trying to intervene, but the distance felt impossibly vast.

Ethan's fist connected with Wren's chest in a brutal blow that sent Wren crashing to thechurning ground. The impact echoed through the narrow corridor, a sickening thud that made Adrian's heart drop. Wren gasped, his eyes wide with shock and pain as he clutched his chest, struggling to breathe.

"No! Wren!" Adrian screamed, his voice raw with panic as he rushed forward, fear clawing at his insides. He could see the blood pooling beneath Wren's body, the life draining from his friend's eyes. *Not like this, not like this!*

Adrian reached Wren just as he collapsed to the ground, his body trembling. "Get up, Wren! You have to get up!" Adrian pleaded, desperation flooding his voice. "We need you! I can't lose you!"

Wren looked up at Adrian, pain etched on his face. "Adrian..." he whispered, his voice barely audible. "I—" But the words caught in his throat as he gasped for air, his body wracked with pain.

"No! Stay with me! Please!" Adrian cried, falling to his knees beside Wren, his heart pounding in his chest. The weight of the moment was unbearable, and he could feel the darkness creeping in around them.

Ethan, lost in the grip of Xel's dark magic, stood frozen for a moment, his eyes flickering between rage and confusion. "What have I done?" he murmured, horror creeping into his voice as he looked at Wren's broken body.

But the darkness surged within him, a relentless tide that pushed him back toward rage. "No! I won't be weak! I won't let you take me!" Ethan shouted, the fight within him warring against the dark influence that had consumed his will.

Adrian's heart raced as he glanced between Wren and Ethan, a whirlwind of emotions flooding through him. "Ethan, you can fight this! You can stop it!" he shouted, desperation threading through his words. "You have to remember who you are!"

But Ethan shook his head, his face twisted in torment. "I am nothing but a slave to Xel!" he roared, rage and despair mingling in his voice. "I can't escape it!"

Adrian turned back to Wren, panic gripping him as he cradled his friend's head in his hands. "Wren, please! Fight! I need you to fight!"

Wren's eyes flickered, the light dimming as the pain washed over him. "Adrian... I... I'm sorry..." he managed to choke out, the strength fading from his voice. "It's too late for me..."

"No!" Adrian screamed, his heart shattering as he felt Wren's body grow weaker in his arms. "You're not giving up! You can't!"

Ethan took a step back, horror dawning in his eyes as he looked at Wren, his voice trembling. "I didn't want to hurt you! I didn't want any of this!"

"You have to fight it, Ethan! Please!" Adrian shouted, tears stinging his eyes as he begged his friend to break free from the darkness.

But the will of Xel was too strong. "No... I can't..." Ethan whispered, a deep sorrow washing over him. The shadows clawed at his mind, twisting and pulling him deeper into the abyss.

Suddenly, with a wild scream, Ethan turned and charged at the stone wall of the maze, slamming his fist against the cold surface. "I refuse to be a puppet any longer!" he shouted, anguish pouring from him.

"Ethan, stop!" Adrian yelled, horror surging through him. "You don't have to do this!"

But it was too late. With a swift motion, Ethan drew a small dagger from his side, a glint of steel catching the dim light. The darkness enveloped him, pushing him toward the edge of despair. "I'll end this!" he cried, tears streaming down his face as he plunged the dagger into his own chest.

"No!" Adrian screamed, the sound tearing from his throat as he watched in disbelief.

Ethan gasped, eyes wide with shock, the dagger embedded in his heart. The darkness around him pulsed with a sinister energy, a cruel satisfaction echoing in the air. "I am free!" he shouted, a twisted smile spreading across his face as he fell to the ground, life leaving him in an instant.

Adrian dropped to his knees, a sense of despair washing over him like a tidal wave. "Wren! No!" he cried, shaking his friend desperately. "You can't leave me! Not like this!"

But Wren's breathing was shallow now, and his eyes began to glaze over. "Adrian..." he murmured, the life fading from his voice. "I'm sorry... I couldn't fight it..."

"No! Wren! Stay with me!" Adrian yelled, tears streaming down his face as he cradled his friend's head in his lap. *This can't be happening. Not now! Not after everything we've fought for!*

Wren's eyes flickered, a faint spark of recognition returning for a brief moment. "I'll always be with you, Adrian..." he whispered, a weak smile on his lips. "Fight... for us... don't let the darkness win..."

The words sent a shiver down Adrian's spine as he felt Wren's body grow limp in his arms. "Wren! Please! Don't go! Fight!" he cried, but the light in Wren's eyes faded, leaving nothing but the void of despair.

"No... no... no..." Adrian whispered, cradling Wren's lifeless body against him, grief washing over him like a cold tide. The pain was unbearable, a chasm opening within his chest. "You can't be gone! You can't leave me!"

As the shadows closed in around him, the world around Adrian felt like it was unraveling. The echoes of the fight faded into a haunting silence, and he was left alone, clutching the body of his friend as the reality of loss engulfed him.

Ethan lay on the ground nearby, lifeless and still, a grim reminder of the darkness that consumed them all.

Adrian felt the rage boiling within him, fueled by grief and despair. "I won't let this end like this!" he shouted into the emptiness, anger coursing through him like fire. "I will fight! For you both!"

But deep down, the shadows whispered their dark promises, the weight of the island's will pressing down on him, threatening to drown him in despair. The fight was far from over, and Adrian knew that the darkness would not rest until it had consumed them all.

With a fierce determination, he wiped away his tears, steel returning to his resolve. *I will not give up. I will fight for Wren, for Ethan. I will face this darkness head-on!*

Adrian stood, heart pounding, ready to confront whatever the island threw at him next. The weight of loss settled heavily on his shoulders, but he knew he couldn't let it define him. He would carry their memories forward, and he would honour their sacrifices.

With a final glance at Wren and Ethan, he turned toward the depths of the maze, the darkness stretching before him like an insatiable beast. "I'll find a way out," he vowed, voice steady and fierce. "For you."

8

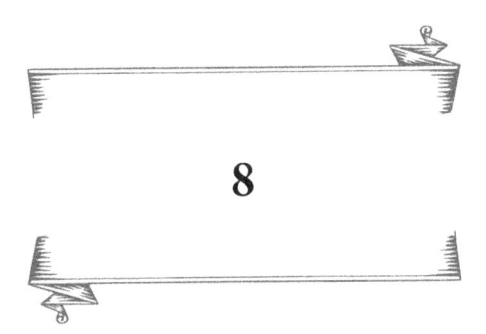

The Biggest Showdown Of Their Lives

Adrian stood frozen, staring down at Wren's lifeless body, unable to comprehend the weight of what had just happened. His heart felt like it was being torn apart, each beat aching with grief and disbelief. The world around him blurred as the realization sank in—Wren was gone. His friend, his brother in arms, was gone.

Ria's quiet sobs broke the silence, her body trembling as she knelt beside Wren, her hands gently touching his cold arm. "He can't be gone... he can't..." she whispered, her voice shaky and fragile, as though saying the words might make them less real.

Emma stood behind them, tears streaming silently down her cheeks, her face pale and shocked. "Wren," she said softly, choking on the name. "Why did it have to be him? Why did he have to die?"

Adrian felt a lump forming in his throat, his mind swirling with memories of Wren—their laughter, their shared struggles, their fights, and victories. And now, here he was, lying still, his body lifeless on the cold stone floor of a cursed maze. Adrian sank to his knees beside his friend, unable to hold back the tears any longer.

"I... I couldn't save him," Adrian whispered, his voice thick with guilt and grief. His hands hovered over Wren's chest, trembling. "I should've done more. I should've stopped him from fighting Ethan... I could've—"

"Don't do this," Ria said softly, her voice breaking as she turned to Adrian. "You can't blame yourself... Wren... he chose this. He always fought for us. He wouldn't want you to carry this guilt."

Adrian clenched his fists, tears spilling freely down his face. "But I was supposed to protect him! I was supposed to make sure he survived this place! And now... now he's gone. I failed him..."

George knelt beside Adrian, his own expression clouded with sorrow. "We all failed him, Adrian," he said, his voice heavy with regret. "But you did everything you could. Wren knew what kind of danger we were in. He knew the risks, and he still fought. He always fought."

Emma wiped her tears with the back of her hand, stepping closer to where Wren lay. Her voice was barely a whisper, filled with grief. "He was always the brave one," she said, her words faltering. "He... he wouldn't want us to be torn apart like this. He... he always believed in us. Even when things were impossible."

Ria reached out and gently closed Wren's eyes, her touch delicate and full of care. "He was the heart of this group," she said, her voice fragile yet filled with a quiet strength. "He made us believe we could make it through anything."

Adrian's chest tightened as he listened to them, the pain in his heart unbearable. He felt hollow, like a piece of himself had been ripped away, leaving an open wound that would never heal. "He shouldn't have had to die like this," Adrian said through clenched teeth, his voice filled with rage and sorrow. "He deserved more. He deserved better."

"None of us deserved this," George added, his voice thick with emotion. "We didn't ask for any of this. But we're here now... and we have to honour him."

Adrian's eyes burned with unshed tears, his hands clutching the cold, lifeless fabric of Wren's shirt. "He was always there for me.

For all of us. And now he's gone, and I... I don't know how to keep going without him."

The silence that followed was suffocating, heavy with the weight of their grief. The air around them felt still, as if the island itself was mocking their loss, the shadows pressing in closer as they knelt around their fallen friend.

Ria wiped her tears, her voice trembling as she spoke. "He died fighting for us. For all of us. And... and we can't let that be in vain. We have to make sure we keep going. For him. For Wren."

Emma sniffled, her hands trembling as she wiped at her face again. "But how? How do we keep going when it feels like everything is falling apart?"

Adrian looked down at Wren's face, the peacefulness of death now etched into his features. "We fight," he whispered, his voice barely audible. "We fight, just like he would've wanted us to. We finish what we started, and we find the truth of this island. For Wren."

"But he's not here, Adrian..." Ria's voice cracked, her tears flowing freely. "He was the one who kept us together... and now, he's gone..."

Adrian nodded, his heart aching. "I know. But we have to be strong. He gave his life because he believed in us. And I refuse to let him die in vain. We keep going, Ria. We keep going because he would've wanted us to."

George nodded in agreement, though his face was wet with tears. "Wren was always the one telling us not to give up, no matter how bad it got. He would never let us walk away from this."

"He was the best of us," Emma whispered, her voice thick with emotion. "We have to keep going. For him."

Adrian's hands shook as he placed them on Wren's chest, his grief almost too much to bear. "I'll never forget you, Wren," he whispered, his voice breaking. "I swear... I'll finish this. I'll find the truth. I'll fight for you. And I'll make sure your death wasn't for nothing."

The group huddled together in the shadow of the maze, their hearts broken but their resolve growing stronger. They stood in silence for what felt like an eternity, the pain of Wren's death washing over them like a tidal wave, leaving them raw and vulnerable.

Finally, Adrian stood, wiping his face with the back of his hand. "We can't stay here," he said softly, his voice steadying. "We need to move. We need to get out of this maze. Wren wouldn't want us to die here."

Ria nodded, her face tear-streaked but determined. "Let's go. Let's finish this. For Wren."

They gathered their belongings, their movements slow and heavy, as if the weight of their grief was pressing down on them. Adrian took one last look at Wren's body, his heart aching with every breath.

"Goodbye, Wren," he whispered. "I'll never forget you."

With that, they turned away from the lifeless body of their friend, their hearts heavy with sorrow but their spirits determined. They had lost one of their own, but they would carry Wren's memory with them as they faced the darkness of Xel Island.

The air around them was thick with grief as they left Wren's body behind, their footsteps heavy, their hearts burdened by the loss. The darkness of the maze seemed even more suffocating now, the oppressive silence stretching endlessly as they walked. Each step felt like a battle against the weight of their sorrow, but they pressed on, driven by the shared promise they had made—to survive, to fight, and to honour Wren's memory.

Adrian led the way, his eyes sharp but haunted. The maze's walls seemed to stretch taller, more menacing with every turn. The flickering light from above barely pierced the gloom, casting long shadows that danced in the corners of their vision. The cold stone beneath their feet felt lifeless, a chilling reminder of the brutal reality they had just endured.

"Adrian..." Ria's voice was soft, fragile, breaking the heavy silence. "Do you think... do you think we'll ever make it out of here?"

Adrian didn't answer immediately. His jaw clenched as he forced himself to focus. "We have to," he replied finally, his voice low but steady. "For Wren. We're not giving up now."

George, walking just behind, nodded but said nothing. His face was drawn, pale, as if the fight had drained the life from him. They were all changed, shadows of themselves, but there was no turning back now. The maze demanded their endurance, their strength—and they would give it, for Wren's sake.

They continued onward, turning corner after corner, the path winding and twisting like a serpent. The oppressive silence made every sound feel amplified—their footsteps, their breathing, the occasional rustle of stone. The further they went, the more the maze seemed alive, pulsing with a dark, ominous energy.

Suddenly, Emma, who had been walking close to the rear, stopped dead in her tracks. "Do you hear that?" she whispered, her voice trembling.

Adrian stopped and turned, his senses on high alert. The others froze, their hearts pounding. At first, there was nothing but silence, but then it came—a low, guttural growl, so deep it reverberated through the walls of the maze. The sound sent a shiver through all of them, a primal warning that danger was near.

"There's something here," George muttered, his voice taut with fear.

Adrian's heart raced as the growl grew louder, closer. His eyes scanned the dark corridor ahead, but he saw nothing, only the looming walls and the shadows that flickered between them. "Stay close," he ordered, his voice sharp. "We need to be ready."

They moved cautiously, every sense on edge, the eerie growl echoing through the twisting maze. The walls seemed to close in, the darkness growing thicker with each step. Then, without warning, a shape appeared in the distance—huge, hulking, and moving toward them with terrifying speed.

"What is that?" Ria gasped, her eyes widening in horror as the creature emerged from the shadows.

The thing before them was unlike anything they had ever seen. Its body was monstrous, covered in thick, blackened scales that shimmered in the dim light. Its eyes glowed a sickly yellow, and its mouth opened in a snarl, revealing rows of jagged teeth. The creature was massive, towering over them with a grotesque, hunched frame, its claws scraping against the stone as it moved. Behind it, two more creatures followed, equally menacing, their growls low and terrifying.

"Run!" Adrian shouted, adrenaline surging through him as the creatures closed in. But before they could react, the first beast lunged forward with terrifying speed, its claws slashing through the air.

Adrian barely managed to dodge the attack, throwing himself to the side as the creature's claws scraped the ground where he had just stood. "Move!" he yelled, scrambling to his feet as the others scattered in all directions.

The maze became a chaotic battlefield. The creatures moved faster than anything Adrian had ever encountered, their hulking forms deceptively agile. George swung a heavy rock at one of them, but the creature barely flinched, its thick scales absorbing the blow. It lashed out, swiping at George with deadly precision, and he barely managed to dive out of the way.

"They're too strong!" Emma screamed, her voice high-pitched with fear as she ran down a narrow passage, the creatures closing in behind her.

"Keep moving!" Adrian shouted, dodging another attack as he grabbed Ria's arm, pulling her along with him. "Don't let them trap us!"

But the creatures were relentless, their growls echoing through the maze as they pursued them with deadly intent. One of the beasts charged at Emma, its massive form filling the narrow corridor. She stumbled, trying to escape, but the creature was too fast. Just as its claws were about to reach her, Adrian sprinted forward, throwing himself between them and shoving her to safety.

"Go!" he shouted as he wrestled with the creature, its snarls deafening. The beast roared, snapping at him with its enormous jaws, and Adrian felt its breath hot against his skin. He struggled to hold it off, adrenaline surging through him as he fought desperately.

George and Ria were already fighting off the second creature. George slammed a stone into its side, but it barely slowed down. "It's like hitting a wall!" he yelled, frustration lacing his voice.

"We have to find a weak spot!" Ria cried, her eyes darting across the creature's massive form as she dodged its sweeping claws.

Adrian, still wrestling with the first beast, knew they couldn't keep up this pace. The creatures were too fast, too powerful. His muscles burned with the effort, and his mind raced, searching for any advantage. *There has to be a way out of this!*

Just then, he saw it beneath the creature's belly, where the scales thinned, leaving a vulnerable patch of flesh exposed. "Aim for its underside!" Adrian shouted, desperation in his voice. "It's the only way to bring it down!"

George, catching his breath, grabbed a sharp piece of stone and waited for his moment. As the creature lunged at Ria again,

George dove beneath it, thrusting the stone upward into the beast's exposed belly. The creature let out a deafening roar of pain, its massive body shaking violently as blood poured from the wound.

"Now!" Adrian yelled, seizing the opportunity. He grabbed the stone and drove it deeper, twisting with all his strength as the creature thrashed, its roars filling the air.

The other two creatures, sensing the pain of their comrade, turned and snarled, their glowing eyes locking onto Adrian. "Watch out!" Emma screamed, but it was too late. One of the remaining beasts charged, its claws slashing through the air, and Adrian barely had time to react before it knocked him off his feet.

The impact sent him crashing into the stone wall, pain exploding through his body as he hit the ground hard. The creature loomed over him, its jaws snapping dangerously close to his throat.

"Adrian!" Ria screamed, rushing forward, but the creature's massive form blocked her path. She grabbed a stone and hurled it at the beast's head, but it only seemed to enrage it further.

Adrian struggled to move, the weight of the creature pinning him down. *I have to get out of here*, he thought, panic surging through him. But the beast's claws pressed down harder, its jaws opening wide, ready to tear him apart.

Just as the creature's teeth were about to close in, Emma came charging from the side, wielding a sharp piece of stone. She stabbed the beast in the side, her face twisted with fear and determination. The creature howled in pain, momentarily distracted, and Adrian used the opening to roll out from beneath it.

"Thanks," he gasped, scrambling to his feet.

Emma nodded, but there was no time for relief. The third creature, still unharmed, let out a terrifying roar and charged toward them, its claws slashing wildly.

"Get back!" George shouted, grabbing a large rock and throwing it at the creature's head. It connected with a sickening crack, and the beast stumbled, dazed but not defeated.

"We can't keep this up!" Ria shouted, panting as she dodged another attack.

Adrian looked around, searching for a way out. The creatures were closing in, and they were running out of options. "We have to retreat!" he yelled, grabbing Emma's hand and pulling her back. "Fall back to the narrow passage!"

They sprinted down a narrow corridor, the creatures hot on their heels. The maze walls twisted and turned, and the sounds of the creatures' growls echoed all around them. Adrian's heart pounded in his chest, the weight of their situation pressing down on him.

As they ran, Adrian glanced over his shoulder, the monstrous forms of the creatures looming closer with every step. "Go, go, go!" he shouted, urging the others forward as the beasts closed in.

Just ahead, the path narrowed into a small alcove, barely wide enough for one person at a time. "In here!" Adrian yelled, pushing George and Ria ahead of him. "It's our only shot!"

They dove into the narrow space, the creatures unable to follow, their massive bodies too large to fit through the tight passage. The beasts roared in frustration, their claws scraping against the stone as they tried to reach them.

Breathing heavily, Adrian slumped against the wall, his heart still racing. "That was too close," he muttered, wiping the sweat from his brow.

"We're not safe yet," Ria said, her voice trembling but resolute. "We have to keep moving before they find another way to get to us."

Adrian nodded, his mind still reeling from the fight. "Let's go. We can't stay here."

With one final glance at the snarling creatures, they pressed forward into the maze, the shadows of the walls closing in around them as they ventured deeper into the unknown.

As they pressed forward, their breaths still labored from the battle, the atmosphere was thick with tension. Every step felt heavy, their hearts pounding in their chests as they tried to shake the memory of those monstrous creatures. The maze seemed to be closing in around them, the darkness more oppressive, as though it knew they were struggling.

"That thing…" Ria whispered, her voice barely above a breath as they moved cautiously down another narrow passage. "What the hell was it?"

Adrian wiped sweat from his brow, his mind still spinning from the fight. "I don't know," he replied, his voice grim. "But those creatures weren't natural. They're part of this island's darkness, just like everything else we've faced."

George, still catching his breath, walked a few steps behind, clutching his side where he had taken a hit. "They were… unstoppable," he muttered, wincing as the memory of the creature's scales flashed in his mind. "We hit them with everything we had, and they barely flinched."

Emma, her face pale but determined, glanced over her shoulder as though expecting the creatures to reappear at any moment. "We need to figure out how to fight them if they come back. There's no way we can survive another attack like that unless we know what we're dealing with."

Adrian nodded, his jaw clenched as they navigated through another bend in the maze. "There's a weakness," he said, his voice steady but tense. "Underneath their armor—those scales. We have to get them where they're exposed. It's the only way we managed to hurt them."

Ria glanced at Adrian, worry etched in her features. "But how? They're too fast. If we hadn't found that narrow passage, we'd be dead by now."

"I know," Adrian admitted, frustration bubbling beneath his skin. He could still feel the weight of the creature's claws pinning him down, the stench of its breath in his face. "But we have to stay alert. If they find us again, we'll be ready."

George let out a bitter laugh, shaking his head. "Ready? How do you get ready for something like that? We're running through this maze, blind as hell, and those things... they're waiting. Watching."

"Then we move smarter," Adrian shot back, his voice sharper than he intended. "We can't afford to panic. We need to use this place to our advantage—tight spaces, quick strikes, anything we can do to survive."

The group fell silent again, the weight of Adrian's words hanging in the air. Their footsteps echoed through the narrow corridors, the cold stone beneath them feeling endless and unforgiving. Every shadow seemed to shift, every rustle of air a reminder that danger was never far behind.

"I couldn't see their eyes," Emma said quietly, her voice breaking the silence. "Those creatures... it's like they were hunting us without seeing us. Like they didn't even need to."

Adrian frowned, glancing at her. "What do you mean?"

"They didn't look at us the way a predator would," she continued, her brow furrowed in thought. "It was like they were following some command, some instinct, but they weren't hunting us out of hunger. It was like they were... compelled. By something else."

"Xel," George muttered darkly, his voice laced with bitterness. "Everything on this island is tied to that curse, isn't it?"

Adrian nodded, his thoughts racing as they continued walking. "It has to be. The creatures, the maze, everything we've faced—it's all part of this island's magic. It's testing us. Breaking us down."

"But why?" Ria asked, her voice filled with a mix of anger and exhaustion. "Why are we being hunted like this? What does the island want from us?"

Adrian stopped in his tracks, turning to face his friends. "It wants us to give up," he said, his voice steady despite the fear gnawing at his insides. "It's trying to break us, wear us down until we can't fight anymore. But we can't let it."

George rubbed his forehead, frustration clear in his posture. "We're walking straight into another trap, aren't we? The island's going to keep throwing things like that at us until we can't handle it."

Adrian's face hardened. "Then we handle it. Whatever comes next, we face it together, just like we did back there. We survived that, didn't we? We can survive this."

Ria took a deep breath, steadying herself as she nodded in agreement. "We've lost too much already to stop now."

Emma tightened her grip on the sharp stone she had kept from the fight, her eyes flicking to the shadows around them. "We'll make it through. We have to."

They continued walking, the tension coiling tighter with each step. The maze twisted and turned, the walls seeming to shift in the corner of their vision. Every sound felt amplified, every shadow more threatening. The growls of the creatures echoed faintly in their minds, a constant reminder of the dangers lurking just out of sight.

Adrian's thoughts raced as they moved, his mind replaying the fight, trying to process everything they had seen. *Those creatures weren't just monsters*, he thought, his jaw tightening. *They were soldiers of this island, sent to test us, to break us.*

As they rounded another corner, the passage widened slightly, and the air grew colder, the darkness more oppressive. Adrian stopped, holding up a hand to signal the others. "Wait," he whispered, his eyes scanning the path ahead. "Do you feel that?"

Ria shivered, wrapping her arms around herself. "It's freezing all of a sudden."

Emma nodded, her eyes narrowing as she looked into the shadows. "Something's wrong."

Adrian's muscles tensed as a low, rumbling growl echoed from deep within the maze. The sound was faint but unmistakable, like a predator lurking just out of sight, waiting to strike.

"They're close," George muttered, his hand tightening around the stone he had picked up earlier. "Those things... they're not done with us yet."

Adrian's pulse quickened, his senses on high alert. "We need to move. Quickly and quietly. Stay close, and be ready for anything."

Without another word, they moved again, their footsteps soft and measured as they navigated the treacherous twists and turns of the maze. The darkness seemed to press in on them from all sides, and every instinct in Adrian's body screamed that they were being watched.

But they pressed on, their hearts pounding in their chests, the memory of the creatures fresh in their minds. They knew the island was testing them, pushing them to their limits. And they knew that the worst was yet to come.

As they walked, Adrian's resolve hardened. *We'll survive this*, he thought, his eyes fixed on the path ahead. *No matter what the island throws at us, we'll survive.*

Because they had to.

For Wren.

Then suddenly, without warning, a bloodcurdling roar ripped through the silence, reverberating off the stone walls of the maze. The air around them seemed to crackle with malevolent energy as a monstrous figure emerged from the darkness, moving with terrifying speed. Before anyone could react, the creature launched itself at Alex with the force of a freight train, its hulking form cutting through the air like a blade.

"Alex!" Ria screamed, her voice shrill with terror, but it was too late. The creature—twice the size of any human, with grotesque, sinewy muscles rippling under its blackened skin—collided with Alex, slamming him into the ground with a sickening thud.

The sheer force of the impact knocked the wind out of Alex, his breath escaping in a choked gasp. He barely had time to scream before the creature's massive claws slashed down with brutal precision, slicing into his chest. Blood sprayed across the stone walls in a crimson arc, the sound of tearing flesh filling the air.

"No! Alex!" Adrian shouted, lunging forward, but the creature was too fast, too vicious. It pinned Alex to the ground with its claws, snarling like a wild animal as it began to rip into him, tearing through his skin as though he were nothing more than paper.

The scene was horrific—Alex's screams filled the maze, his voice raw with agony as the creature tore at his flesh, its claws carving deep, jagged wounds into his chest and stomach. Blood gushed from the gashes, pooling beneath him, his body convulsing in pain. The creature didn't stop, its razor-sharp claws digging deeper, shredding skin, muscle, and bone with savage precision.

"Get off him!" Adrian bellowed, grabbing the nearest rock and hurling it at the creature's head. The stone struck the beast's thick skull with a dull thud, but it didn't flinch. It was lost in a frenzy, completely focused on tearing Alex apart.

Ria's legs buckled as she watched in horror, her eyes wide with disbelief. "Oh my God... no, no, no!" she cried, her voice cracking as tears streamed down her face. Emma stood frozen, her hand clamped over her mouth, unable to process the brutality unfolding before them.

With a snarl, the creature leaned down, its jaws snapping open to reveal rows of jagged, bloodstained teeth. In one horrific motion, it sank its teeth into Alex's shoulder, ripping through flesh and sinew with a wet, sickening crunch. Blood splattered across the ground, thick and dark, as the creature tore a chunk of flesh free, chewing with gruesome satisfaction.

Alex's screams turned into gurgles, blood bubbling up from his throat as the life drained out of him. His eyes, wide with pain and fear, locked with Adrian's for a fleeting moment—pleading, desperate—before they glazed over, the light leaving them forever.

"No! No!" Adrian roared, his voice filled with rage and helplessness. He charged at the creature, fury igniting every fiber of his being, but the monster whipped around, its glowing eyes locking onto him, daring him to come closer. Its claws dripped with Alex's blood, the air thick with the metallic scent of death.

"Adrian, don't!" George yelled, grabbing him by the arm and pulling him back just as the creature lunged again, slashing the air where Adrian had been moments before.

The creature stood over what remained of Alex, his body nothing more than a mangled, blood-soaked mess of torn skin, exposed muscle, and broken bones. The stone floor beneath him was slick with gore, the horrific sight enough to make Ria collapse to her knees, sobbing uncontrollably.

"We can't fight that thing!" Emma cried, her voice trembling as she backed away, her eyes fixed on the monster. "It'll kill us all!"

Adrian's breath came in ragged gasps as he stared at Alex's body, anger and guilt flooding his veins. "No... not again," he whispered, his fists trembling at his sides. "We can't let this keep happening. We can't lose anyone else!"

The creature growled, stepping toward them, its massive form casting a shadow over the group. Blood dripped from its claws, its eyes glowing with primal hunger. It wasn't done. Not yet.

"Move!" Adrian shouted, his voice hoarse with desperation. "Run! Now!"

The group turned and sprinted down the nearest corridor, their hearts pounding in their chests, terror propelling them forward as the creature roared behind them. Its heavy footsteps thundered through the maze, shaking the ground as it pursued them with terrifying speed.

"We have to get out of here!" George panted, his voice laced with panic as they rounded a corner, the creature's snarls echoing in the distance. "It's going to tear us apart like it did to Alex!"

Adrian's mind raced, the horrifying image of Alex's mutilated body burned into his memory. *We need a plan*, he thought, adrenaline surging through him. *We can't outrun this thing forever.*

The group ducked into a narrow passage, their breaths coming in ragged gasps as they pressed themselves against the cold stone walls. The creature's growls echoed from somewhere nearby, closer than they would have liked.

Adrian glanced back, his hands trembling as he wiped the blood from his face. "We're not safe here," he whispered, his voice shaking with fear and anger. "But we can't keep running. We need to fight back."

Ria shook her head, her face pale and streaked with tears. "How? You saw what it did to Alex... we don't stand a chance!"

Adrian's eyes hardened, his jaw clenched as he pushed the image of Alex's brutal death to the back of his mind. "We have to try. If we don't fight, we're all dead."

The group huddled together, their bodies shaking with fear, the scent of blood and death thick in the air. The monster's growls grew louder, the sound of its claws scraping against the stone sending shivers down their spines.

They knew what was coming.

The air felt heavy, suffocating even, as they moved cautiously through the maze. Every nerve in Adrian's body was on edge, his senses tuned to the slightest shift in the dark. His grip tightened on the sharp stone in his hand, ready for anything. The group stayed close, their breath shallow, tension gripping them like a vice.

Without warning, the silence was shattered by a guttural, bone-chilling growl. It echoed off the maze's stone walls, an ominous reminder that they were not alone.

"Did you hear that?" Emma whispered, her voice trembling.

Adrian froze, his blood turning cold. "Stay close. We can't—"

Before he could finish his sentence, a dark blur shot out of the shadows, moving faster than any of them could react. The creature, monstrous and terrifying, lunged from thin air with a deafening roar, its grotesque form all claws and fangs. It pounced on Ria with terrifying force.

"Ria!" Adrian screamed, but it was too late.

The creature collided with Ria, throwing him to the ground with bone-cracking intensity. Its claws, long and jagged, tore into him instantly, slicing through his skin like paper. Blood sprayed into the air, the sickening sound of flesh being ripped apart filling the corridor.

"Get off her!" George yelled, rushing forward in a futile attempt to pull the creature away, but the beast was relentless, a force of nature. It pinned Alex down, its jaws snapping as it tore into him with savage brutality.

Alex's screams echoed through the maze, a sound so visceral it sent chills through everyone's spine. His face contorted in agony as the creature ripped into his chest, tearing muscle from bone with terrifying precision. His body convulsed beneath the beast's weight, his blood soaking the cold stone beneath him, pooling in a gruesome red lake.

Adrian charged toward the creature, blind with rage, his heart pounding in his chest. "No! Let her go!" he roared, his voice breaking with desperation as he hurled himself at the beast, slamming the stone into its side with all his strength. But the creature didn't flinch. It continued its brutal assault, its claws digging deeper into Ria's flesh, shredding him as if he were nothing.

Blood splattered everywhere. The creature tore into Ria's abdomen, pulling skin and muscle apart like twisted fabric. It was relentless, a grotesque predator driven by the island's darkest magic. The brutal tearing sounds were too much to bear, each one more horrifying than the last.

George and Emma screamed in horror, frozen in place as they watched the nightmare unfold before them. Ria's screams had turned to ragged gasps, his body trembling violently as the life was ripped from him piece by piece.

Adrian swung the stone again, this time smashing it into the creature's head, but the beast barely registered the blow. Its glowing eyes, like burning coals, flicked toward Adrian for a brief moment, a menacing snarl escaping its blood-soaked jaws. The sight of Ria's torn flesh, the gaping, horrific wounds that marred his body, sent a surge of nausea through Adrian's stomach. But he couldn't stop. He couldn't let this thing take Ria without a fight.

"We have to do something!" George shouted, his voice cracking with panic as he swung his makeshift weapon at the creature again, aiming for its exposed underbelly.

But the creature was faster, stronger, and it turned its focus back to Ria, who was barely clinging to life. With a sickening crunch, it tore at his chest, exposing bone as it sank its claws deeper into him. Ria's eyes rolled back, blood pouring from his mouth as he let out a final, pitiful moan. His body went limp, the last of his strength leaving him.

"Ria!" Emma screamed, tears streaming down her face as she rushed forward, trying to pull him away, but the creature wouldn't relent. It tore through him, reducing him to nothing more than a torn, bloody heap of flesh and bone.

Adrian felt a wave of helplessness crash over him as he watched the creature shred Ria's body with ruthless efficiency. The blood soaked into the cracks of the stone floor, the crimson liquid pooling beneath the beast as it savagely dismembered him. The creature's jaws opened wide, and it bit down on Ria's torso, pulling him apart in a grotesque display of power.

The smell of blood and death hung thick in the air, suffocating them as they stood there, powerless against the monstrous force of the creature.

"Get away from her!" Adrian shouted again, his voice breaking as he hurled the stone at the creature one last time. But the blow was futile. The beast's eyes gleamed with malice as it finally rose from Ria's mangled corpse, its snarl echoing through the maze like a death knell.

Adrian's chest heaved, his body trembling with shock and rage. Ria's body lay in ruins, shredded beyond recognition, his skin torn to ribbons, his blood staining everything in sight. The creature, now dripping with blood, looked back at them, as if savoring the carnage it had wrought.

For a moment, time seemed to stop. The maze felt darker, colder. Adrian's breath came in ragged gasps as he stared at the creature, his mind numb with disbelief. Ria was gone—ripped apart right in front of him. There had been no time to save him, no way to stop the brutality.

"Ria..." Emma whimpered, collapsing to her knees, her hands covering her face as she sobbed uncontrollably. "No... not Ria..."

George stood frozen, his face pale and horrified, unable to tear his eyes away from the carnage. "What... what was that thing?" he whispered, her voice barely audible.

His hands trembled as he wiped the blood from his face, his breathing shallow and uneven. "It came out of nowhere," he muttered, his voice hollow with shock. "We couldn't even... we couldn't..."

Adrian clenched his fists, his mind spinning with grief and rage. "This place," he muttered through gritted teeth, his eyes narrowing. "It's trying to break us. It's not going to stop until it kills every last one of us."

The creature let out a final growl, its glowing eyes lingering on them for a moment before it slinked back into the shadows, disappearing as suddenly as it had appeared, leaving only death and destruction in its wake.

Adrian stood over Ria's mutilated body, his heart pounding, his mind racing with guilt and anger. *We couldn't save him*, he thought bitterly, his chest tight with sorrow. *We failed him.*

"Adrian..." Mia whispered, her voice shaking. "What do we do now?"

Adrian's eyes burned with unshed tears as he stared at the lifeless remains of his friend, the weight of the loss crashing down on him like a tidal wave. "We keep moving," he said, his voice cold and distant. "We have to survive. For Alex. For Wren. For Ria. For all of us."

With one final glance at the brutal scene, they turned and began to walk away, their hearts heavy with grief and horror. The maze stretched ahead of them, dark and unforgiving, and they knew that more horrors awaited.

As Adrian, Mia, George, and Emma walked away from the brutal remains of Alex, their hearts felt heavier than ever. The maze stretched endlessly before them, its walls taller and more oppressive, as though the very air was thick with malice. They had lost too much—Ria, Wren, and now Alex—all taken by this godforsaken island. The silence between them was suffocating, the weight of grief pressing down on their shoulders like a boulder they could never lift. But their determination was still there, burning beneath the surface, because survival was the only option they had left.

Adrian led the way, his jaw clenched, his thoughts dark. He couldn't shake the image of Alex being torn apart, the brutal carnage replaying in his mind like a nightmare. Every step felt like a struggle to keep going, but he knew they had to. *We've come this far. We can't stop now.*

Mia, her face pale and streaked with dried tears, walked beside him, gripping a makeshift weapon she'd crafted from a sharp piece of stone. Her hands trembled slightly, but her eyes were hard with resolve. "We have to get out of here," she muttered under her breath. "This place... it's never going to stop trying to kill us."

George, silent and grim, followed close behind, his face twisted with both pain and anger. He wiped the blood from his brow, a permanent reminder of the fight they had barely survived. Emma, her hands shaking as she held onto a jagged rock, stayed near George, her eyes darting around in fear, as though the shadows were watching them.

"We keep moving," Adrian said, his voice low but commanding. "We survive this. For Wren, Ria, and Alex. We're going to get off this island."

Mia nodded, but her gaze was distant, hollow. "We better," she whispered. "Because if one more thing comes at us..."

She didn't finish her sentence, but the meaning was clear. They were at their breaking point. Adrian could feel it, too. His body ached, his mind screamed for rest, but there was no time to stop.

The island's dark influence was everywhere, twisting the air, the ground, and the creatures lurking in the shadows.

Then, out of nowhere, a low rumble reverberated through the maze. Adrian froze, every muscle in his body tensing as the sound grew louder, like the earth itself was shifting beneath them.

"What is that?" George asked, his voice tight with fear. His eyes darted around the maze, looking for any sign of the source.

Adrian's heart pounded as the rumbling grew closer, more violent. The ground beneath them trembled slightly, and the walls of the maze seemed to hum with dark energy. "Stay sharp," Adrian warned, his voice a low growl. "It's not over yet."

Suddenly, from the darkness ahead, a monstrous roar ripped through the air, followed by a series of guttural growls. The ground shook violently as the sound grew nearer, and then, without warning, a horde of creatures—more terrifying than anything they had faced before—charged toward them, their eyes glowing a sickly yellow.

It was an army.

The creatures were hideous, with massive, hulking bodies covered in blackened scales, their grotesque forms a twisted mix of human and beast. Their claws were long and jagged, dripping with venom, and their snarling mouths revealed rows of sharp, bloodstained teeth. They moved as one, their glowing eyes locked onto Adrian and the others with deadly intent.

"Oh, no... no, no, no!" Emma cried, her voice rising in terror as the creatures closed in.

"There's too many of them!" Mia shouted, her voice frantic as she backed up against the stone wall, her weapon raised.

Adrian's heart raced, but his instincts kicked in. "We don't stop! We fight!" he roared, grabbing the jagged rock in his hand and preparing for battle. "We kill every last one of them!"

The creatures lunged, moving with terrifying speed, their claws swiping through the air with deadly accuracy. Adrian dodged the first strike, narrowly avoiding the razor-sharp claws aimed at his throat. He countered with a brutal swing of his weapon, slamming the rock into the creature's head. There was a sickening crack as the skull caved in, blood spraying across the stone walls.

Mia let out a feral scream as she drove her sharp stone into the chest of one of the beasts, twisting the blade as it let out a deafening roar of pain. The creature thrashed wildly, but Mia held firm, pushing harder until the creature collapsed in a pool of its own blood.

George was fighting two creatures at once, his arms swinging wildly as he hacked at their legs, trying to bring them down. One of the creatures slashed at his side, its claws raking across his skin, but George didn't falter. With a furious growl, he plunged his makeshift weapon into the creature's neck, twisting it violently until the beast fell to the ground, gurgling in its own blood.

"Come on! Keep fighting!" Adrian yelled, his voice raw with rage as he took down another creature, its head splitting open beneath the force of his blow.

The battle was chaos—blood, growls, and the sound of bone cracking filled the air. The creatures were relentless, their numbers seemingly endless as they charged again and again, but Adrian and the others fought with everything they had.

Emma let out a cry as one of the beasts grabbed her by the arm, its claws digging deep into her flesh. She screamed in pain, struggling to break free, but the creature's grip was like iron.

"Emma!" George shouted, his face pale with fear as he rushed toward her. He slammed his weapon into the creature's arm, and with a sickening snap, the limb broke, freeing Emma from its grip.

"Thanks," Emma gasped, clutching her bleeding arm as she stumbled back. But there was no time to recover—the creatures were closing in again.

Adrian's muscles burned as he swung his weapon with all his strength, bashing the creatures away one by one. He could feel the exhaustion creeping in, but he pushed through the pain, his mind focused solely on survival.

"They won't stop!" Mia shouted, panting as she fought off another creature. "How do we kill them all?"

"We don't stop until they're all dead!" Adrian growled, his voice fierce as he slammed his weapon into another beast, its skull cracking beneath the blow.

The ground was slick with blood, the bodies of the creatures piling up around them, but the horde kept coming. Adrian's arms ached, his vision blurred with sweat and blood, but he refused to give in. Every strike was a promise—he would survive, no matter what.

Suddenly, a massive creature, larger than the rest, emerged from the horde, its glowing eyes filled with a predatory hunger. It let out a deafening roar, shaking the very walls of the maze as it charged toward Adrian with terrifying speed.

"Adrian, watch out!" Mia screamed, but the creature was already upon him.

Adrian barely had time to react before the beast tackled him to the ground, its claws digging into his chest as it snarled in his face. The weight of the creature was crushing, its breath hot and foul as it snapped its jaws, inches from Adrian's throat.

Adrian struggled beneath the beast, his mind racing. *I can't die here. Not like this.* With a roar of defiance, he grabbed the sharp stone and drove it into the creature's neck, twisting it violently. The beast howled in agony, thrashing wildly as blood poured from the wound.

With a final, brutal effort, Adrian shoved the creature off him, his chest heaving as he staggered to his feet. The beast lay dead at his feet, its blood pooling around it.

"Are you okay?" Mia shouted, running toward him.

"I'm fine," Adrian panted, wiping the blood from his face. "We're not done yet."

The remaining creatures, sensing the death of their leader, hesitated for a moment, their snarls quieter now, their eyes flickering with uncertainty.

"Now's our chance!" George yelled, his voice filled with adrenaline. "We take them down!"

With renewed determination, the group charged forward, their weapons swinging with deadly precision. One by one, the creatures fell, their bodies crumpling beneath the force of the blows. The bloodshed was relentless—every swing, every strike a testament to their will to survive.

Emma, despite her injury, fought with a newfound fury, her eyes blazing as she stabbed another creature in the chest, driving the blade deep into its heart. "You're not taking any more of us!" she screamed, her voice filled with raw emotion.

George fought beside her, his face contorted with rage as he hacked at the creatures, his blows swift and brutal. "We're getting out of this maze!" he shouted, slamming his weapon into a creature's skull. "We're not dying here!"

Mia darted between the creatures with agility, her movements sharp and precise as she delivered lethal strikes to their weak spots. "For Ria, for Wren, for Alex!" she cried, her voice trembling with both grief and anger as she took down another beast.

Adrian fought like a man possessed, every ounce of his strength focused on killing the creatures before him. His hands were slick with blood, his muscles screaming in protest, but he didn't stop. He couldn't. Every swing was for his friends, for the people they had lost. He wouldn't let their deaths be in vain.

Finally, after what felt like an eternity of relentless fighting, the battlefield of the maze was littered with the bodies of the creatures. The air was thick with the stench of blood and death, the stone floor beneath them slick and dark with gore. The sound of flesh tearing and bones cracking had filled the air for so long that it seemed like a constant, gruesome background score to their survival. But now, the creatures were thinning, their numbers reduced by the brutal onslaught Adrian, Mia, George, and Emma had unleashed upon them.

The last wave of creatures surged toward them, their glowing eyes still burning with rage, but their movements were slower now, more desperate. Adrian gripped his bloodied weapon tighter, his hands aching from the fight, but he refused to give in. There was no room for weakness here. Not now. Not ever.

"They're breaking!" Mia shouted, her voice hoarse from exhaustion and adrenaline. She drove her makeshift blade into a creature's abdomen, twisting it savagely as blood spurted out, covering her hands in warm crimson.

George, still panting heavily, swung his weapon with all the strength he could muster, cracking the skull of another creature with a brutal downward blow. "Don't let up!" he yelled, his voice raw. "Kill them all!"

Adrian locked eyes with the final beast in front of him, its massive, hulking frame towering over him. It snarled, baring its blood-stained teeth as it lunged forward. Time seemed to slow as the creature's claws slashed through the air, aiming directly for Adrian's throat.

But Adrian was faster. Fueled by a surge of anger and the raw need to survive, he dodged the attack and swung his weapon with all the force he had left. The jagged stone connected with the creature's skull, shattering bone and sending blood splattering across his face. The beast let out a horrifying screech as it stumbled, its body shaking with the impact.

"Die!" Adrian roared, his voice filled with fury as he swung again, this time driving the sharp edge into the creature's neck. Blood poured from the wound in thick, pulsing streams as the beast crumpled to the ground, twitching in its final moments of life.

The creature's eyes flickered once before the light in them went out forever. Adrian stood over its lifeless body, his chest heaving with the effort of the fight, his hands trembling with the aftermath of the brutal battle.

Nearby, Emma was fighting the last of the creatures, her face twisted with rage as she drove her sharp stone repeatedly into its chest, her strikes brutal and relentless. "This is for Wren! For Ria! For Alex!" she screamed, each word punctuated by another savage stab.

The creature let out a final, agonized howl before collapsing under the force of Emma's attack, its blood pooling beneath her as she stood over it, her breath coming in ragged gasps. "It's over," she whispered, her voice shaking as she stepped back, her bloodied hands falling to her sides. "It's over..."

Mia had just finished off her last opponent, the creature's body twitching as it bled out at her feet. She looked up at the others, her face streaked with blood and dirt, her body trembling with exhaustion. "Is that it? Are they all dead?" she asked, her voice barely above a whisper.

Adrian scanned the battlefield, his eyes narrowing as he looked at the carnage around them. Dozens of bodies—mangled, torn, broken—lay scattered across the blood-soaked ground, their lifeless eyes staring blankly into the abyss. His heart still pounded in his chest, the adrenaline coursing through him, but there were no more sounds of growls, no more movement from the shadows.

"They're dead," Adrian confirmed, his voice grim. "All of them."

The maze was silent once again, but the silence was not comforting. It was heavy, oppressive, filled with the weight of everything they had lost and everything they had fought for. The air was thick with the smell of death, and the only sound was the labored breathing of the survivors.

George stumbled forward, his legs nearly giving out beneath him as he leaned against the cold stone wall. "I thought... I thought we weren't going to make it," he admitted, his voice raw with exhaustion.

"But we did," Adrian said, his tone flat and emotionless as he wiped the blood from his hands, his body still humming with the intensity of the fight. "We're still alive."

"For now," Emma muttered, her face pale and streaked with blood. She clutched her wounded arm, wincing from the pain but refusing to show weakness.

Mia glanced at the bodies strewn across the ground, her stomach turning at the sight of the blood and broken limbs. "It's like a slaughterhouse," she whispered, shaking her head. "How did we even survive this?"

Adrian's eyes hardened as he stared at the carnage before them. "Because we had no choice. It's us or them. And it's going to keep being like this until we get off this cursed island."

Emma, wiping sweat and blood from her face, looked up at Adrian. "How much more of this can we take?" she asked, her voice trembling.

"As much as it takes," Adrian replied, his voice steely. "We survive. That's all that matters now."

George nodded, though his face was pale. "We've come this far," he said softly. "We have to finish what we started."

Mia took a shaky breath, wiping the blood from her hands as she looked at the others. "We need to move," she said, her voice still trembling with adrenaline. "We can't stay here. This place is cursed."

Adrian nodded, his jaw tight. "She's right. We need to get out of this maze."

They stood in the center of the carnage, surrounded by the bodies of the creatures they had slain. Blood dripped from their clothes, their weapons slick with gore, but they were still alive. Somehow, they had survived.

Adrian turned, leading the way out of the blood-soaked battlefield, his heart heavy with the memory of those they had lost and the horrors they had endured. They had fought monsters—both real and emotional—and won, but the victory felt hollow. The cost had been too high.

But they had no choice now. There was no turning back. They would fight, and they would survive. Because that was the only option left.

As they walked deeper into the maze, their bodies battered and their spirits bruised, Adrian clenched his fists. Whatever horrors awaited them next, he would be ready.

The group moved through the maze cautiously, their bodies aching and their nerves frayed from the brutal battle they had just survived. Blood still clung to their clothes, but none of them spoke about it. They couldn't afford to think about what they had just gone through—not now. Not with whatever horrors still awaited them. The silence between them was thick, punctuated only by the echo of their footsteps as they trudged deeper into the maze.

Adrian led the way, his face set in grim determination. He knew they were close to something—he could feel it. There was a strange energy in the air, a faint humming that seemed to grow louder the further they walked.

"Do you feel that?" Mia asked, breaking the silence. Her voice was hushed, her eyes darting around nervously.

George nodded, wiping the sweat from his brow. "Yeah. It's like the air's different. Something's ahead of us."

Emma, still clutching her injured arm, looked uneasy. "What do you think it is? The source of all of this?"

Adrian didn't answer immediately. His eyes were locked on the path ahead, the maze's walls curving in strange, unnatural ways. The air around them shimmered slightly, as though reality itself was bending under the weight of whatever power lay ahead.

"I don't know," he said finally, his voice low and tense. "But we're about to find out."

They moved faster now, a sense of urgency pulling them forward. Every corner they turned seemed to bring them closer to something—something ancient, something powerful. The walls of the maze had begun to glow faintly, casting an eerie, pale light that made everything feel surreal, dreamlike.

Suddenly, as they rounded the final bend, the maze opened up into a vast, circular chamber. At the center of the chamber, something was shining—a bright, pulsating light that seemed to emanate from the ground itself. The light was blinding, filling the room with an intense energy that made the hair on the back of Adrian's neck stand up.

"There," Adrian whispered, his eyes widening as he stepped forward. "That's it. That's what we've been looking for."

The others followed him, their faces a mixture of awe and fear as they stared at the glowing object in the center of the chamber. It was like nothing they had ever seen—a swirling mass of light and energy, floating just above the ground. It pulsed rhythmically, like the heartbeat of the island itself.

"What... what is that?" Emma asked, her voice trembling as she took a step closer.

"It looks like the center of the maze," George replied, his eyes fixed on the light. "The heart of the island."

Adrian felt a chill run down his spine as he stepped closer to the glowing light. He could feel the energy radiating from it—powerful, ancient, and dangerous. It was as if the island's magic was concentrated here, in this one spot, waiting for them to find it.

Mia hesitated, her eyes narrowing as she studied the swirling light. "Do you think this is the source? The thing that's been controlling everything?"

"It has to be," Adrian replied, his voice steady but tense. "This is what the island has been protecting. What it's been hiding."

Emma shook her head, still staring at the light in awe. "But why? Why lead us here? What's the point?"

Adrian's jaw tightened as he stared at the pulsing light, his mind racing. "It's a test," he said finally. "Everything we've been through—the maze, the creatures, all the death—it's been leading us here. This is the heart of Xel. The source of its power. And now we're standing in front of it."

George took a deep breath, his face grim. "So what do we do? Destroy it?"

"I don't know," Adrian admitted, his eyes never leaving the swirling light. "But we can't leave it like this. This is what's been taking everything from us. It's what killed Ria, Wren, Alex... everyone. We have to finish this."

Mia glanced at Adrian, worry etched on her face. "Are you sure? What if touching it—what if destroying it makes things worse?"

"We're already in the middle of the worst," George replied bitterly. "It can't get any worse than this."

Adrian nodded, his heart pounding as he stepped closer to the glowing mass. The light grew brighter as he approached, and the air hummed with an electric charge. His instincts screamed at him to be careful, but he couldn't turn back now. They had come too far.

He reached out, his hand trembling slightly as he moved toward the light. The energy pulsed, crackling in the air around him. It was both terrifying and mesmerizing, a force unlike anything he had ever felt before.

Mia, George, and Emma stood behind him, their breath held as they watched in silence. This was the moment they had been dreading and anticipating all along.

Adrian's fingers hovered inches from the swirling energy, his heart pounding in his chest. *This is it*, he thought. *This is what we've been fighting for.*

He closed his eyes, took a deep breath, and reached out.

The moment his fingers touched the light, the entire chamber exploded with energy. The light flared brighter, enveloping them all in its blinding glow, and the ground beneath them rumbled violently. The air buzzed with an overwhelming force, and Adrian felt the power of the island surge through him, filling every cell in his body.

The maze, the island, the creatures—it was all connected to this. And now they were standing at the very heart of it.

As the light surrounded them, Adrian felt a strange, overwhelming sensation—a mixture of fear, power, and clarity. This was the moment. The end of the nightmare, or the beginning of something far worse.

The instant Adrian's fingertips brushed the swirling light, the energy around them surged violently. For a split second, everything seemed to freeze. The hum of the island's magic became deafening, and the air thickened, crackling with a force beyond their comprehension.

Then, without warning, the light exploded.

A blinding flash erupted from the center of the chamber, filling every corner of the maze with its piercing brilliance. The force of the blast was unlike anything they had ever felt—an immense wave of energy that ripped through the air, sending shockwaves in every direction. The chamber trembled as if the very heart of the island had been torn apart.

Adrian felt his body lift from the ground as the force of the explosion hit him like a freight train. The blast flung him backward through the air, the world spinning violently around him. His breath was knocked from his lungs, and he struggled to comprehend what was happening as the light consumed everything.

"Mia!" Adrian shouted, his voice lost in the roar of the explosion, though he couldn't even see her through the white-hot light that filled his vision.

George and Emma were also caught in the explosion, their bodies sent flying as the surge of energy pushed them away like rag dolls. Time seemed to slow as they were all hurled backward, helpless against the sheer force that engulfed them.

The sound of the blast was deafening—a terrible, raw, thunderous noise that reverberated deep in their bones. The very ground beneath them quaked with the impact, but strangely, the maze itself did not crumble. The walls stood firm, untouched by the destruction, as though the island had willed it so.

Adrian tumbled through the air, his limbs flailing, his vision blurred by the overwhelming light. He didn't know how long he was airborne before he slammed hard into the ground. Pain shot through his body as he skidded across the stone floor, rolling uncontrollably before coming to a jarring stop against one of the maze's walls.

He lay there for a moment, dazed and disoriented, struggling to catch his breath. His ears rang, and his body felt battered and bruised, but he was alive. The blast had thrown him a considerable distance, yet somehow, the maze remained intact.

"Adrian!" Mia's voice cut through the fog in his mind, and he blinked, trying to focus. His vision was still blurry, but he could make out Mia's silhouette staggering toward him. She looked just as disoriented, her body covered in scrapes and bruises from the impact, but she was moving.

"I'm... I'm here," Adrian rasped, forcing himself to sit up. His body screamed in protest, but he ignored the pain, his eyes scanning the area for the others. "George... Emma...?"

"I'm fine!" George's voice came from a few feet away, though he sounded breathless and winded. He, too, had been flung by the blast and was trying to get back on his feet. "That... that was insane!"

Emma groaned from somewhere further off, her voice weak but alive. "I'm okay... I think. Did anyone else feel like they were just hit by a truck?"

Adrian let out a breath of relief as he saw the others slowly pulling themselves together, each of them shaken but alive. "What... what just happened?" Mia asked, her voice filled with awe and confusion as she reached Adrian's side.

"The light," Adrian muttered, still trying to process the chaos. "It exploded. But look—the maze..." He gestured weakly at the walls around them. Despite the violence of the blast, the maze itself stood unscathed. The walls were as solid as ever, untouched by the devastation that had sent them flying.

"How?" George gasped, clutching his side where he'd been slammed into the ground. "How is this place still standing after that?"

Emma limped closer, wincing with every step. "I don't know," she said, her voice hoarse. "But that blast should've torn everything apart. We should be dead."

Adrian's gaze shifted to the center of the chamber, where the light had been moments ago. Now, it was gone—completely vanished, as if it had never been there at all. In its place was an eerie, unnatural calm. The air no longer hummed with energy, and the once-brilliant light had been replaced by a hollow stillness that made Adrian's skin crawl.

"I think... it was the island," Adrian whispered, his heart pounding. "It knew we were here. It didn't want to destroy itself. That blast—it was meant for us."

Mia swallowed hard, her eyes wide with fear. "But why? What was that thing? Why did it explode?"

Adrian shook his head, still trying to catch his breath. "I don't know," he admitted, his voice shaky. "But whatever it was... it didn't want us to be near it."

George wiped the sweat from his brow, still visibly shaken. "Well, it almost succeeded. That thing nearly killed us all."

Adrian nodded, a grim expression on his face. "Yeah. But we're still here. And we're not done yet."

The four of them stood there, battered, bruised, and disoriented, but alive. They had been flung across the maze like pieces in a storm, yet the maze remained intact, a silent sentinel watching over their every move.

Adrian pushed himself to his feet, ignoring the pain that radiated through his body. "Come on," he said, his voice firm despite the exhaustion that gripped him. "We need to keep moving. Whatever that was—it wasn't the end. We're not out of this yet."

Mia, George, and Emma exchanged weary glances but nodded. They knew Adrian was right. The maze, the island—it wasn't done with them yet.

And they had to be ready for whatever came next.

9

The Forbidden Secret Of The XEL Island

Just as Adrian and the others were about to gather themselves and move forward, a low, rumbling sound echoed through the maze. It started as a faint vibration beneath their feet, but quickly grew louder, more intense, reverberating through the stone walls. The air around them shifted, as if the very maze was coming alive.

Adrian froze, his body tensing as the ground beneath him trembled. "Do you hear that?" he asked, his voice tight with apprehension.

Mia, standing beside him, nodded slowly, her eyes wide. "What now? We barely survived that blast."

George, still recovering from the impact of the explosion, looked around, his brow furrowed in confusion. "It sounds like the maze is... moving?"

Before any of them could respond, the walls ahead of them began to shift with a loud, grinding sound, the stone scraping against itself in a way that made their teeth vibrate. They all stepped back instinctively, watching in awe and fear as the thick, towering walls of the maze began to unlock themselves.

Slowly, the stone slid apart, revealing a hidden path that had been completely sealed off just moments before. Dust and debris fell from the ceiling as the stones moved, and soon, what had been an impenetrable barrier now revealed a new corridor—a long, dark passage stretching into the unknown.

"What... the hell is happening?" Emma breathed, her eyes wide with disbelief.

Adrian's heart raced as he stared at the newly formed path. *The maze is opening itself up*, he thought, his mind struggling to keep up with the ever-changing reality of Xel Island. It was as if the island itself had decided to show them a way forward, a new path that hadn't existed before.

"Looks like the island is leading us somewhere," George muttered, wiping the sweat from his brow. "But where?"

Mia took a cautious step forward, her eyes locked on the now-opened corridor. "It wants us to follow it," she said quietly. "But why now? After everything we've been through... why is it showing us the way?"

Adrian shook his head, his eyes narrowing as he peered into the dark passageway. "I don't know. But we don't have a choice." His voice was steady, but underneath, he felt the weight of the island's relentless games pressing down on him.

The air that wafted from the newly revealed path was cooler, with a strange scent of damp earth and something metallic, almost like blood. The silence that followed the unlocking of the maze walls was deafening, and the stillness made Adrian's skin crawl.

Emma stepped beside Adrian, her face pale but determined. "What do you think is down there? Another trap? More creatures?"

Adrian glanced at her, his face grim. "Probably. But whatever it is, it's the only way out of here. The island wants us to go deeper. We don't have much of a choice."

George let out a frustrated breath. "This place... it's always one step ahead of us. But we're still standing. We'll face whatever's next."

Mia nodded, though her expression was cautious. "I just hope we can handle whatever's waiting for us at the end."

Adrian took a deep breath, steadying himself. "We've made it this far," he said, his voice filled with quiet resolve. "We'll handle it. Together."

Without another word, he stepped forward, leading the way into the newly revealed passage. The others followed close behind, their footsteps echoing through the dark corridor. The air grew cooler the further they went, and the stone walls seemed to pulse with a strange, unnatural energy.

As they moved deeper into the maze, a sense of dread settled over them like a heavy fog. The path was eerily silent, and with every step they took, Adrian couldn't shake the feeling that they were being watched—that the island itself was observing their every move.

As they ventured deeper into the newly revealed path, the air around them grew colder, thicker with an unnatural stillness. The dark, stone walls of the maze gave way to something entirely different—a dense, twisted forest. Towering trees with gnarled, ancient trunks loomed over them, their crooked branches reaching out like skeletal hands. The leaves overhead rustled faintly, though there was no wind. It was as if the forest itself was breathing, alive in a way that sent chills down their spines.

Adrian glanced around, his jaw tight as the eerie atmosphere settled over them. The forest felt wrong, like it didn't belong in the maze. Or perhaps, it was the heart of the island itself—a place where the island's power was at its strongest. "What is this?" he muttered under his breath, gripping his weapon tighter.

"I don't like this," Mia whispered, her eyes wide as she scanned the dark woods. "I can feel it... it's like the trees are... watching us."

George walked beside her, his face pale, his breathing shallow. "Do you hear that? It's like the trees are whispering. But there's no wind..."

Adrian listened closely, and that's when he heard it—soft, almost imperceptible at first. A faint whispering sound, like voices carried on a breeze that didn't exist. It was unnerving, like the forest was speaking to them, but the words were indistinct, lost in the air around them.

"What the hell...?" Emma breathed, her voice trembling as she gripped her arm, still sore from the earlier battle. "Is this real?"

Adrian's heart pounded in his chest. It felt real—too real. The whispering grew louder, though still impossible to understand. The voices seemed to circle them, coming from every direction, yet nowhere at once. The trees swayed slightly, their twisted branches creaking as though they were alive, moving to the rhythm of the whispers.

"This isn't right," Mia said, her voice filled with unease. "It feels like the island is trying to get inside our heads. To make us doubt everything."

Adrian nodded, trying to stay calm despite the growing tension in the air. "It's trying to mess with us. The island knows we're close to something, and it's trying to break us down."

The whispering grew louder, more insistent, though still unintelligible. The sound was almost hypnotic, a haunting chorus that made the air thick with an otherworldly presence. It was as if the trees were alive, ancient sentinels watching their every move, their voices echoing from a time long forgotten.

"Keep moving," Adrian said, his voice firm despite the fear gnawing at him. "Don't listen to it."

But it was impossible not to listen. The whispers were everywhere, pressing in on them, filling the air with a sense of dread. The trees, with their twisted, bark-covered faces, seemed to lean in closer as they walked, as if the forest itself was alive and studying them. Every creak of wood, every rustle of leaves felt like the forest was trying to communicate something dark, something horrific.

Emma shivered, her eyes darting between the looming trees. "What if it's a warning? What if these whispers are telling us to turn back?"

Adrian swallowed hard, his hands tightening on his weapon. "Maybe. But we don't have that option. We go forward. No matter what."

As they pushed deeper into the forest, the whispers grew louder, more frantic. The trees swayed unnaturally, their branches scraping against one another in a way that made it sound like bones grinding together. Shadows danced in the corners of their vision, figures just out of sight, vanishing as soon as they tried to focus on them.

The forest felt alive, but not in the way forests normally do. This place felt like it was waiting for them, like it had been here for centuries, waiting for someone to enter its grasp. The ground beneath their feet was soft, the dirt damp and covered in dead leaves, but there was no sound of their footsteps. Only the whispers.

"We're not alone," George muttered under his breath, his face pale as he looked around, trying to pinpoint the source of the whispers. "I can feel it."

"Neither are the trees," Mia added, her voice barely above a whisper.

Adrian's heart pounded harder in his chest as they continued walking. He could feel the weight of the forest pressing down on them, the air thick with magic and menace. The trees whispered to one another, their voices growing louder, more urgent, as though they were warning of something just ahead.

But whatever was waiting for them, it felt inevitable.

Suddenly, without warning, a thick, rough smoke began to fill the air around them. It rolled in like a tide, creeping through the twisted trees and curling around their feet, rising quickly until it enveloped the entire area. The whispers of the trees became muffled, drowned out by the dense, choking fog that seemed to come from nowhere.

Adrian coughed, instinctively covering his mouth with his arm as the smoke thickened, turning the forest into a disorienting blur of shadows and mist. "What the hell?" he muttered, his voice strained as he struggled to see through the haze. The smoke stung his eyes and lungs, and he squinted, trying to make sense of what was happening.

"I can't breathe!" Mia gasped, stumbling as the smoke surrounded her. She waved her hand in front of her face, but it was useless—everything was consumed by the swirling fog. The once-looming trees were now nothing more than dark, vague shapes, barely visible in the oppressive cloud.

"Stay close!" Adrian shouted, his voice barely audible over the growing roar of the smoke. The ground beneath them felt unstable, the thick haze making it difficult to find any sense of direction. The smoke didn't just fill the air—it seemed to press down on them, like a living thing, heavy and suffocating.

"I can't see anything!" George yelled, his voice panicked. His figure was just a faint outline in the distance, the smoke already distorting the sound of his words.

Emma coughed violently, clutching at her chest as the rough smoke filled her lungs. "What... what is this?!" she managed to choke out, her voice hoarse.

Adrian tried to focus, his mind racing as he looked around for anything—a landmark, a way out, some clue about what was happening. But the smoke was everywhere, a thick wall of nothingness that seemed to stretch endlessly in all directions.

"Stay together!" Adrian called again, though the sound of his voice was swallowed by the ever-thickening fog. His pulse quickened as the oppressive feeling grew stronger, the smoke making it impossible to see more than a few feet in front of them.

The air around them was growing colder now, and the strange, metallic scent of the forest was becoming overwhelming, mixing with the acrid stench of the smoke. Every breath felt heavier, more labored, as though the air itself was turning to ash.

"We need to move—get out of this smoke!" Mia shouted, her voice strained. She reached for Adrian but couldn't find him in the thick haze. The smoke was too dense, too disorienting. She could barely make out her own hands, let alone her friends.

Adrian's mind raced as he tried to find a way through the suffocating fog, but the deeper they moved, the more it seemed to close in around them. *This is another trick*, he thought, his heart pounding in his chest. *The island is trying to drive us mad.*

The whispers had returned, faint and distorted, almost drowned out by the roar of the smoke. They were clearer now, but no less eerie. It was as if the voices were inside the smoke itself, swirling with it, growing louder as the fog pressed down on them.

"They're... they're here," George stammered, his voice shaking with fear. "I can hear them. The whispers are inside the smoke."

Adrian's eyes stung as he tried to peer through the haze. "It's trying to trap us!" he shouted, his voice hoarse from the smoke. "We have to get out of here—now!"

But the ground beneath them was shifting, softening, as though the very earth was collapsing under the weight of the smoke. Every step felt unstable, like they were sinking into the ground. The trees, once towering and imposing, were now barely visible shapes, swallowed by the dense fog.

Emma gasped, panic rising in her voice. "I don't know where to go! I can't see anything!"

"Follow my voice!" Adrian called, though he wasn't sure where he was leading them. The smoke was disorienting, spinning the forest into a maze of nothingness. He reached out blindly, hoping to find the others in the thick fog, but his hand grasped only air.

Mia coughed again, her breath ragged as the smoke filled her lungs. "Adrian!" she called, her voice shaky. "Where are you?"

"I'm here!" he shouted, his voice hoarse as he fought against the choking fog. But even as he called out, the smoke seemed to grow denser, pressing in on them like a suffocating blanket. Every breath felt heavier, more labored, and the whispers were louder now, swirling in the air like a chant.

Adrian knew they had to move quickly, but the forest was gone—only shadows and smoke remained, an endless, suffocating void.

"Don't stop!" he called again, though his voice sounded distant, even to himself. The smoke was closing in, consuming everything. The whispers grew louder, more insistent, until they were all Adrian could hear, drowning out the sound of his own thoughts.

The island was playing its game again, and this time, the smoke was its weapon.

And they were running out of time.

As Adrian and the others stood before the towering rock, the air around them began to tremble again. The glowing symbols etched into its surface pulsed with a fierce intensity, bathing the clearing in an ethereal light. A deep rumble resonated from within the stone, shaking the ground beneath their feet.

"What the hell?" George gasped, backing away instinctively.

The sound grew louder, reverberating through the forest as if the very earth itself was alive. The rock began to vibrate, and then, to their horror, a voice emerged—a voice both ancient and commanding, echoing through the air around them.

"You who have dared to enter my domain," the voice boomed, deep and resonant, reverberating through their bones. "You stand before the remnants of those who sought to unravel my forbidden secrets. Many have tried, and many have died."

Adrian's heart raced as he exchanged terrified glances with Mia and Emma. The sheer power of the voice was overwhelming, and he could feel an icy grip of fear wrapping around him. "What... what do you want?" Adrian managed to stammer, forcing himself to take a step forward despite the fear gnawing at his insides.

The rock seemed to pulse with life, its surface shimmering in response to his words. "You have proven your worthiness," it continued, its tone shifting slightly, almost contemplative. "Through blood and sacrifice, you have navigated the trials I set before you. You have shown tenacity and strength, traits I respect."

"What trials?" Emma blurted out, her voice trembling. "What do you mean?"

The voice rumbled in response, echoing through the air as the symbols glowed brighter. "Those who sought to reveal my truths faced my wrath, for my secrets are not to be trifled with. They believed themselves worthy, yet they were nothing more than lambs to the slaughter. Each met their demise, their blood feeding the very ground you stand upon."

Adrian felt a chill run down his spine. The memories of Ria, Wren, and Alex flooded back, their faces haunting him as the rock spoke of the countless lives lost in pursuit of knowledge. "You killed them?" he whispered, the weight of the accusation hanging heavily in the air.

"They sought to unravel what was never meant to be revealed," the voice thundered. "But you... you have defied the odds. You have faced the horrors and lived to tell the tale. You are different. You are worthy."

"What do you want from us?" George shouted, fear and anger mixing in his voice. "We didn't come here to play your twisted games!"

A low, rumbling chuckle emanated from the rock, sending tremors through the ground. "Ah, but you have played, whether you knew it or not. You were mere pawns in my grand design. Yet now, you stand on the precipice of revelation. I hold the power to unveil my secrets, but you must first prove your resolve."

"What do you mean?" Adrian asked, his pulse racing. "What do we have to do?"

The voice shifted, becoming more sinister, more foreboding. "The island demands a price—a sacrifice, a choice. To gain knowledge, you must first confront the darkness within yourselves. Only then can you unlock the truths hidden in the depths of my being."

Mia's eyes widened in horror. "What darkness? What are you talking about?"

The stone's glow intensified, the air thickening with an energy that made their skin prickle. "Face your fears, embrace your guilt, and uncover the truths you hide. Only when you lay bare your souls can you be worthy of the knowledge I possess."

Adrian felt the ground tremble beneath him, the whispers of the forest rising again, swirling around them like a tempest. The shadows seemed to shift, closing in as if they were alive, ready to drag them down into the depths of despair.

"What if we refuse?" George shouted, his voice filled with defiance despite the fear radiating off him.

"Refusal is not an option," the voice boomed, the stone vibrating with power. "Those who turn away will face consequences far worse than death. The island does not tolerate weakness."

Adrian's heart raced as he processed the weight of the rock's words. They were standing at the edge of a precipice, and the fate of their lives hung in the balance. He could feel the tension building, an electric charge in the air that made his skin crawl. "What do you want us to do?" he finally asked, his voice steady despite the fear coursing through him.

"Embrace your trials," the voice replied, its tone both chilling and compelling. "Only then can you unlock the secrets of the heart of Xel. Your worthiness will be tested, and only those who can confront the darkness within shall survive."

The chamber shook violently as if responding to the intensity of the stone's power. The ground beneath them began to crack, fissures opening up like dark mouths ready to swallow them whole.

Adrian steadied himself, his resolve hardening. "We'll face whatever you throw at us," he declared, his voice unwavering. "We're not backing down."

The voice of the stone echoed through the chamber, a finality in its tone. "So be it. Prepare yourselves for the trials ahead. The path to truth is paved with sacrifice, and you will not emerge unscathed."

As the last word echoed in the air, a powerful shockwave erupted from the rock, knocking them backward. The ground trembled violently, and the dark shadows of the forest twisted around them, spiraling into a chaotic whirlpool of darkness and light.

Adrian's heart raced as he struggled to his feet, the world spinning around him. They had crossed a threshold, and whatever lay ahead was about to test their very souls.

Adrian fought to regain his balance as the ground shuddered beneath him, the violent tremors threatening to throw him off his feet again. He glanced around at his friends—Mia, George, and

Emma—each of them struggling against the disorienting chaos, their faces etched with a mixture of fear and determination.

"What do we do now?" Mia shouted over the rumbling noise, her eyes wide as she took a step closer to Adrian. "The rock... it's not done with us yet!"

Adrian gritted his teeth, his mind racing as he tried to piece together what had just happened. "We prepare for whatever comes next," he said, forcing himself to focus despite the fear gnawing at his insides. "We're ready for the trials."

"Trials?" George echoed, incredulous. "You mean that thing wants us to go through some kind of test? After everything we've just faced?"

Adrian nodded, feeling the weight of the situation settle heavily on his shoulders. "Yeah. It's clear the island isn't done with us. If we want answers—or even a chance to escape—we have to confront our fears."

The ground quaked again, and the shadows in the forest seemed to grow darker, swirling ominously around them. Adrian could feel the pressure mounting, as if the island itself was waiting for their next move, eager to unleash whatever horrors lay ahead.

Just then, the pulsating light from the rock began to dim, its glow fading into a dull, ominous shimmer. The energy in the air shifted, becoming thick and charged with anticipation. It felt like the calm before a storm, and Adrian's heart raced with a mixture of dread and adrenaline.

"Look!" Emma exclaimed, pointing toward the now-dark rock. "The symbols! They're changing!"

Adrian squinted, his eyes narrowing as he watched the symbols shift and morph on the stone's surface. They twisted and turned, forming new patterns that glowed faintly in the dim light. The air around them grew heavier, charged with an electric energy that made the hair on his arms stand on end.

"What does it mean?" Mia whispered, her voice barely audible.

"Only one way to find out," Adrian replied, his voice steady despite the rising tension. He stepped forward cautiously, drawing closer to the now-inactive rock. "We need to focus. Whatever this is, it's part of the trial."

As he approached the rock, the ground beneath him began to tremble again. The shadows flickered, and suddenly, dark figures emerged from the forest, coalescing into distinct shapes. Adrian's breath caught in his throat as he recognized the forms—their fallen friends, Ria, Wren, and Alex, stood before them, ethereal and ghostly, their faces twisted in expressions of sorrow and pain.

"No!" Mia cried, her voice cracking as she stumbled back, covering her mouth with her hands. "This can't be real!"

The spectral figures advanced slowly, their movements ghostly and unnatural. Adrian felt his heart pound in his chest, his mind racing as he processed the sight before him. "They're... they're here," he whispered, his voice trembling.

"What do you want?" George shouted, stepping forward with defiance. "You can't scare us!"

"Scare you?" Ria's voice echoed, a hollow sound that resonated through the air. "We are not here to scare you. We are here to show you the truth."

Adrian felt a wave of nausea wash over him as he listened. "The truth? About what?" he demanded, trying to keep his voice steady despite the fear clawing at his insides.

Wren stepped closer, his ghostly form flickering as though he were struggling to maintain his shape. "You have to confront your guilt, Adrian. Only then can you hope to move forward."

"No!" Adrian shouted, shaking his head fiercely. "I won't play your games! You're not real!"

Alex's spectral form stepped forward, his expression filled with pain. "You need to face what you've lost, what you've done. It's the only way to unlock the secrets of the island. The only way to save yourself."

Mia stepped forward, her eyes glistening with tears. "But it hurts! How can we face that? You're gone! You can't just—"

"Face the truth!" Wren interrupted, his voice echoing with urgency. "If you don't confront what's inside you, the island will consume you. It will feed off your weakness, your fear. You must accept us, accept your grief."

The air around them thickened, the shadows swirling as the figures of their friends hovered just out of reach. Adrian's heart raced, his mind filled with memories of laughter and joy intertwined with grief and loss. He could feel the weight of guilt pressing down on him, suffocating.

"I didn't save you!" Adrian shouted, his voice breaking. "I failed you all!"

Ria stepped closer, her eyes filled with understanding. "You did your best, Adrian. But you can't hold on to that pain forever. You have to let go."

"No!" Adrian screamed, stepping back as waves of grief crashed over him. "I can't! I can't let go! You were supposed to be here! We were supposed to be together!"

The spectral figures flickered, their expressions shifting to one of empathy and compassion. "You're not alone in this, Adrian. We will always be with you, but you must confront the darkness to move on. It's the only way to unlock the truth behind the island's power."

The shadows deepened around them, and the whispers returned, swirling in a cacophony of voices. The forest began to tremble again, the trees bending and twisting as if in response to the rising tension.

"Face us, Adrian," Wren said softly, his voice cutting through the chaos. "Face your fears."

The air crackled with energy as Adrian struggled to catch his breath. He felt the weight of their words pressing down on him, the memories threatening to consume him. But beneath that fear, there was a flicker of determination.

"I will face it," he said finally, his voice steadied with resolve. "For you. For all of you."

As the words left his lips, the shadows around them surged forward, enveloping him in darkness. He felt the memories crashing over him, the weight of grief, the guilt, and the pain of loss, all pouring into him like a tidal wave.

Adrian closed his eyes, surrendering to the darkness. If he wanted to unlock the truth of the island, if he wanted to survive, he had to confront it all—the pain, the sorrow, and the guilt.

And in that moment of surrender, he felt the shadows shift, and he knew the true trial was only just beginning.

Adrian surrendered to the encroaching darkness, feeling it seep into his very soul. The whispers intensified, swirling around him like a tempest of memories, echoing the voices of those he had lost. Each pulse of energy resonated through him, pulling at the threads of grief, guilt, and sorrow that had woven themselves into his heart.

"Face it, Adrian!" the whispers urged, their tones a mixture of empathy and urgency. "You cannot escape your past!"

He felt himself falling, plunging into a void where shadows danced and flickered like flames. Images flashed before his eyes—moments he had cherished, moments he regretted. Ria's laughter echoed in the air, vibrant and joyful, followed by the crushing silence of her absence. Wren's fierce determination reminded him of their unbreakable bond, shattered now by the cruel hands of fate. Alex's spirit, always ready for a fight, flickered like a candle, snuffed out too soon.

"Why couldn't I save you?" Adrian shouted into the void, his voice breaking as he grasped at the specters of his friends. "I tried! I tried so hard!"

"Because you are human," came a gentle voice from the shadows, one he recognized as Ria's. "You are not omnipotent. You cannot shoulder the weight of the world."

Suddenly, he was pulled into a vision. He stood in the center of their last camp, surrounded by his friends. They were laughing, joking, their spirits high. But beneath the joy, he felt an undercurrent of dread. Shadows crept around the edges of his vision, whispering doubts and fears that gnawed at his heart.

"Don't let them win!" Adrian heard his own voice echo through the camp, but it sounded hollow, distant. "We can fight this together!"

"Together," Mia echoed, but her eyes were clouded with uncertainty. "What if we can't?"

"Stop!" Adrian shouted, his voice filled with desperation. "You don't understand what's at stake!"

Then, the laughter turned to screams as the shadows surged forward, engulfing Ria, Wren, and Alex. Adrian felt the ground beneath him shift, and he was once again surrounded by darkness, their faces fading from view.

"You failed them!" a voice boomed, deeper and more menacing than the whispers. "You were supposed to protect them, yet you stood idly by as they fell!"

"No!" Adrian cried out, clutching his head in anguish. "I couldn't save them! I tried!"

"Trying is not enough!" the voice echoed, shaking the very core of his being. "You must confront your failures. You must learn from them or be consumed by your guilt."

Suddenly, the darkness shifted, transforming into a blinding light that enveloped him completely. He felt weightless, suspended in the void, as images surged around him—memories of laughter, warmth, and love, interspersed with memories of loss and despair. The vision of Wren's last breath, the sound of Alex's scream, Ria's final goodbye—they all crashed over him in a relentless tide.

Adrian felt himself spiraling down into a pit of despair, but as he fell, something began to stir inside him. It was a flicker of resolve, a spark of determination ignited by the memory of his friends' unwavering spirits. "I will not let this consume me!" he roared, pushing back against the darkness.

As if in response, the shadows recoiled slightly, giving him space to breathe. "Face your truth!" the whispers urged, blending with the tumult of emotions surrounding him. "Embrace your pain! It is part of you, but it does not define you!"

Adrian drew a deep breath, allowing the memories to wash over him without fear. "I loved them," he said, his voice steadying as he spoke into the void. "I loved Ria, Wren, and Alex. Their lives meant everything to me. I did my best, and that has to be enough."

With each word, the darkness pulsed, the whispers growing louder and more frantic. The shadows twisted around him, forming images of his friends, their faces reflecting joy and sorrow, anger and peace. "You are worthy of their memory," Ria's voice echoed, softer now, filled with compassion. "Embrace it!"

Adrian opened his heart, allowing the weight of his grief to settle alongside the love he felt for his friends. He would carry their memories with him, not as a burden, but as a source of strength. With each heartbeat, he felt himself becoming lighter, the shadows losing their grip.

"I will not be defined by my failures," Adrian declared, his voice rising above the chaos. "I will honour you by living! I will fight for what we believed in!"

The void erupted in a storm of light, the shadows retreating as the glowing rock surged with energy, its symbols illuminating the space around him. The energy pulsed rhythmically, synchronizing with his heartbeat, filling him with newfound strength and clarity.

"You have faced the darkness within," the rock's voice rumbled, powerful and resonant. "You have embraced your pain and turned it into strength. You are worthy."

Suddenly, the swirling shadows transformed into a brilliant light that enveloped him completely. He felt himself rising, soaring through a vortex of colours and emotions, his friends' spirits guiding him through the chaotic brilliance.

Then, just as abruptly as it had begun, the light exploded outward, washing over everything in a warm glow. The forest around him shifted, revealing a new landscape, a beautiful grove bathed in golden sunlight. The towering trees stood tall and majestic, their leaves shimmering like jewels.

Adrian landed softly on the ground, blinking in the radiant light. Mia, George, and Emma materialized beside him, their expressions filled with awe. "What just happened?" George asked, looking around in disbelief. "Where are we?"

Adrian took a moment to gather himself, his heart still racing from the intensity of the trials. "I think we passed the trial," he replied, a mix of wonder and sadness in his voice. "We faced our fears and embraced the truth of our losses."

Emma's eyes shimmered with unshed tears as she looked around at the beautiful grove. "Is this... is this a safe place?"

"Maybe," Adrian said softly, allowing the warmth of the light to envelop him. "Or maybe it's just a glimpse of what we can have if we keep fighting."

As they stood together in the grove, the air felt lighter, infused with the memories of their friends, the whispers now replaced by a gentle breeze that rustled the leaves. The grove was a sanctuary, a place where they could honour their fallen friends while continuing to move forward.

Adrian took a deep breath, feeling a newfound sense of determination swell within him. They had faced the darkness and emerged stronger, but the journey was far from over. "We have to keep moving," he said, his voice steady. "Whatever else this island has in store for us, we're ready."

With renewed purpose, they turned away from the grove, their hearts heavy but determined. Together, they would honor the memories of Ria, Wren, and Alex by continuing to fight. The trials were behind them, but the adventure was just beginning.

And as they stepped forward into the light, they knew they would face whatever came next—together.

As the light from the grove shimmered around them, Adrian felt a sense of peace wash over him. The trials had tested their limits, forced them to confront their deepest fears, and yet they had emerged intact—wiser, stronger, and more resolute than ever. But as they stood there, basking in the afterglow of their victory, a new feeling began to stir within the grove—a sense of anticipation mixed with trepidation.

The ground trembled lightly beneath their feet, and the air hummed with an energy that felt different from before. The glowing rock, still standing tall at the center of the grove, began to pulse again, its symbols flickering with renewed vigor.

"What's happening now?" Mia asked, her voice filled with a mix of awe and anxiety. She stepped closer to Adrian, her hand brushing against his arm as she felt the vibrations beneath them.

"I don't know," Adrian replied, his heart racing. "But something is coming."

The rock's pulsing intensified, and the warm light enveloped them, bathing the grove in a golden glow. Slowly, the energy coalesced, rising from the rock and forming a swirling mist above it. The mist danced and twirled, casting intricate shadows on the ground, before settling into a coherent shape—a shimmering portal, its edges rippling like the surface of a disturbed pond.

"Look!" George shouted, pointing at the portal. "What is that?"

The portal was mesmerizing, pulsating with colours that shifted from deep blues to fiery reds and eerie greens. It beckoned them, shimmering and glowing with an otherworldly light. But even as they watched in awe, Adrian felt a chill run down his spine.

"Is it safe?" Emma whispered, her voice trembling slightly. "Do you think we should approach it?"

"I don't know," Adrian said, his eyes narrowing as he studied the portal. "But it's definitely not a normal portal. This feels... different. It feels powerful."

The mist continued to swirl, and then, as if responding to their presence, a voice echoed from the portal—a deep, resonant sound that seemed to come from the very core of the island. "You who have faced the trials, you are worthy to witness the truth and you have activated this machine. It is a portal reveals the path to different worlds and dimensions, filled with untold dangers and unspeakable horrors. Something that humanity should forbid from ever entering."

Adrian's heart raced. "New worlds? What do you mean?"

The voice emanating from the portal deepened, echoing through the grove like a dark promise. "Beyond this portal lies a realm far more perilous than Xel. Those are worlds where nightmares come alive, where darkness reigns supreme. You will face trials beyond your imagination, and you must choose whether to step forward into the unknown."

Mia's face paled, her eyes darting nervously between Adrian and the portal. "We've already been through so much. Why would we want to go into another dangerous world?"

"Because we can't turn back now," Adrian replied firmly, his voice steady despite the fear gnawing at him. "We've come this far. If there are more secrets to uncover, we need to know. For Ria, Wren, and Alex. They deserve that much."

George clenched his fists, his expression resolute. "But what if it's worse than here? What if we can't handle it?"

"We won't know unless we try," Adrian said, his gaze fixed on the swirling portal. "But we have to be prepared for whatever comes next. The island has shown us that it holds more than just the horrors we've faced."

The voice from the portal echoed again, resonating through the grove. "You will encounter creatures born of nightmares, manifestations of your deepest fears. The darkness will test you in ways you cannot fathom. But if you seek the truth, you must be willing to face the ultimate trial."

Adrian felt a shiver run down his spine. "What ultimate trial?" he asked, his heart racing with uncertainty.

"Only those who embrace their destinies may find what lies beyond," the voice replied cryptically. "You must confront not only the horrors of this world but the darkness within yourselves. Only then can you unlock the secrets of the realm beyond."

The portal glowed brighter, the light casting strange shadows across the grove. Adrian stepped closer, feeling a magnetic pull toward the shimmering gateway. It was enticing and terrifying all at once, whispering promises of knowledge and power.

"What do you think it means?" Mia asked, her voice tinged with fear and curiosity. "What darkness within ourselves?"

"I think it means we'll have to confront not just the monsters out there," Adrian replied, gesturing toward the portal. "But the monsters we carry inside us. Our regrets, our fears, everything we've lost."

Emma swallowed hard, her eyes fixed on the portal. "I'm scared, Adrian. What if we can't handle it? What if we lose each other?"

Adrian turned to his friends, seeing the uncertainty etched on their faces. "We've made it this far, together. No matter what happens, we face it as a team. We can't allow fear to control us."

With a deep breath, he stepped closer to the portal, his heart racing with anticipation. "We have to make a choice. Do we want to see what lies beyond? Do we want to uncover the secrets of this place?"

Mia stepped forward beside him, her expression fierce. "Yes. We owe it to Ria, Wren, and Alex. We can't back down."

George nodded, his resolve solidifying. "We have to know what's out there. Together."

Emma took a deep breath, her eyes glistening with unshed tears. "Okay. Together. But we need to be careful."

As they stood before the glowing portal, the air buzzed with energy, and Adrian felt a sense of determination wash over him. They had faced countless horrors already. They had fought through pain, loss, and despair. And now, they stood on the brink of something new.

"Let's do this," Adrian said, his voice steady. "For our friends, and for ourselves."

Just as he reached out to touch the shimmering surface of the portal, the voice resonated again, filled with an almost playful menace. "Remember, once you step through, there is no turning back. The world beyond will change you in ways you cannot predict."

Adrian hesitated for a moment, a flicker of doubt crossing his mind. But he pushed it aside. They had come too far to turn back now. The trials had prepared them for this, had shown them the strength they carried within.

With a final glance at his friends, he placed his hand against the surface of the portal. The moment he made contact, a rush of energy surged through him, coursing like electricity. The glow intensified, and the world around them seemed to warp and ripple as the portal began to react.

Suddenly, before they could step through, a blinding flash of light erupted from the portal, engulfing them in a radiant glow. It was as if the portal itself was alive, a swirling vortex of energy and light that threatened to consume everything in its path.

"Adrian!" Mia shouted, panic rising in her voice as the ground trembled violently beneath them.

But before he could respond, the portal expanded, and with a deafening roar, it unleashed a powerful wave of energy that swept over the grove, sending them staggering back.

Adrian's vision blurred as the light surrounded him, the world spinning into chaos. He felt himself being pulled into the vortex, the sound of the portal roaring in his ears as darkness threatened to engulf him once more.

But just as quickly as it had begun, the light faded, leaving them standing once again in the grove, breathless and dazed. The portal was still there, shimmering, but it no longer seemed to beckon them. Instead, it felt like a warning—a glimpse of the unknown that awaited them.

"What just happened?" George gasped, looking around in confusion. "Did we almost...?"

"We didn't cross through," Adrian said, his voice trembling. "But it was close. Too close."

Emma took a step back, her heart racing. "That was... overwhelming. I've never felt anything like that."

Mia nodded, still trying to catch her breath. "What does it mean? Are we ready for whatever lies beyond?"

Adrian looked at the portal, a mix of fear and anticipation coursing through him. "I don't know. But we need to be prepared for what's next. We've come this far, and I can't shake the feeling that our journey is just beginning."

As they stood there, the air crackling with residual energy from the portal, they knew one thing for certain: whatever lay beyond would test them in ways they couldn't imagine. But they would face it together.

"Let's rest and regroup," Adrian suggested, trying to steady himself. "We'll need our strength for what's to come."

They gathered together in the grove, the golden light of the sunset filtering through the trees, casting long shadows across the ground. Each of them took a moment to breathe, to reflect on the journey that had brought them here.

As the sun dipped below the horizon, they knew that the true trials lay ahead, waiting just beyond the shimmering portal. But they were no longer just survivors; they were warriors, united in purpose and ready to confront whatever lay ahead.

And as Adrian looked at his friends, he knew they would face it together, no matter the cost.

The portal shimmered in the twilight, a reminder of the challenges yet to come, a promise of adventure, and the hint of darker, more horrific trials that awaited them on the other side.

And in that moment, he understood that this was only the beginning of their journey—one that would take them far beyond the confines of Xel Island and into the depths of a terrifying new world.

As the last light of day faded, Adrian couldn't help but feel a mixture of dread and excitement. Whatever awaited them on the other side would forever change their fates. And as they prepared for the next chapter of their adventure, the question lingered in the air: *What awaited them in the depths of the unknown?*

To Be Continued... In XEL 3: The Vanishing Paradox...

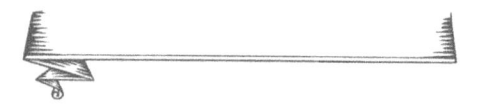

***

<u>Shadows of Xel – A Poem By Hiflur Rahman</u>
In the heart of the mist, where the ancients once tread,
Lies the island of Xel, where the lost are led.
Shrouded in secrets that twist and entwine,
It calls to the brave, and claims what is mine.
The wind hums with whispers of tales long told,
Of seekers and dreamers who sought to be bold.
Through forests of giants whose branches scrape sky,
Where shadows, like phantoms, drift silently by.
Beneath a veil of fog, where the forsaken dwell,
A hunger stirs deep in the bones of Xel.
Ambitions decay like leaves in the rain,
As the island promises both fortune and pain.
Dreamers once soared, their hearts full of fire,
Now they wander in circles, trapped by desire.
What they sought was glory, but the island deceives,
For each step forward, something precious it cleaves.
Elijah once chased after legends untold,
With dreams of riches that could never grow old.
But greed's subtle hand led him astray—
In the heart of Xel, his soul slipped away.
Dr. Locke follows with a fire in his chest,

Seeking the forgotten, refusing to rest.
Yet the whispers grow louder, wrapping him tight,
As the pulse of the island beats in the night.
The fog clings like a shroud, swallowing light,
While shadows perform in the theater of night.
Each footstep echoes with memories near,
In a maze of lost time, no path is clear.
So, summon your courage, adventurers all,
For the island is watching, awaiting your call.
Its story is endless, a riddle unwound,
In the dance of the shadows, the truth will be found.
When twilight descends and dreams start to weave,
Heed the voices that the ancients believe.
In the heart of the fog, where the echoes rebound,
Xel cradles the daring, where true legends are crowned.

Written By HIFLUR RAHMAN (The Visionary Voyager)

Page

Don't miss out!

Visit the website below and you can sign up to receive emails whenever HIFLUR RAHMAN publishes a new book. There's no charge and no obligation.

https://books2read.com/r/B-A-WXFQC-ZTTDF

BOOKS 2 READ

Connecting independent readers to independent writers.

Did you love *XEL - 2*? Then you should read *XEL - 1*[1] by The Visionary Voyager!

In this suspense-filled mystery, **Victor Shadow**, a celebrated detective, takes on an enigmatic case from his client, **Logan Blackwell**, involving a secretive island known only as **XEL**. Shrouded in mystery and nearly forgotten by mankind, the island's exact location is unknown to most, making the investigation as perilous as it is intriguing.As Victor delves deeper into the island's hidden secrets, he faces devastating betrayals and the shocking deaths of those closest to him. Each discovery comes at a terrible cost, chipping away at his resolve. Ultimately, Victor himself falls victim to the dangers of the case, leaving the investigation incomplete.But the mystery doesn't die with Victor.After his death,

---

1. https://books2read.com/u/bzyzMZ

2. https://books2read.com/u/bzyzMZ

new protagonists—driven by their own tragic backstories and emotional ties to Victor—rise to continue the investigation. These characters bring fresh perspectives. United by their grief, they seek to uncover the island's darkest secrets and finish what Victor started.With the stakes higher than ever, the question looms: *Can they solve the mystery of XEL, or will the island's curse claim them too?*

About the Author

Hiflur Rahman is the author of the XEL series. Currently residing in Asia, he has written his first book, XEL -1. The XEL series is set in a fictional realm that includes some real-world locations. Although he began writing in 2020, he did not release any books until XEL -1. Hiflur also has plans to explore a different genre, distinct from the mystery genre.